Crossing the line

THE GEG SERIES
BOOK THREE

JACQUELYN AYRES

The playlist for *Crossing the Line* can be found here:
http://spoti.fi/1QTGdcb

Dedication

To everyone I have ever loved fiercely.

Author's Note

Dear Readers,

In chapter twenty-three, you will find a crossover scene that I co-wrote with Elle Christensen. The girls you will meet are from her Fae Guard series, and you will find this particular scene with the GEGs in her third installment, as well—*Chasing Hayleigh*. Her Fae Guard series can be read as standalones, also, and I've included the first chapter to *Chasing Hayleigh* in the back of this book. If you love the GEGs, I know you will love her series, too! They're pretty damn funny, those Faes!

From the desk of Madelyn St. Claire

There is a fine line between misery and happiness. The problem is; crossing the line over to happiness can seem a lot scarier than staying on the side of misery. With misery, disappointments and figurative kicks to the gut are expected. So, it coats you with armor, never fully allowing anyone or anything, like positive thoughts, in. With happiness, you are completely vulnerable to taking life's blows. And with that, comes a higher risk of happiness being taken away completely.

Cherophobia—fear of happiness.

The trick is to embrace both sides of the line and learn how to balance them well. We need misery in our life to feel the pain, the loss, the anger . . . all that it offers. We need the happiness to remind us why we feel the blows of misery so strongly. If we didn't have that, well, then none of us would give a shit about anything. And what a terrible world we would find ourselves in.

I choose to cross the line every day. Some days, it's harder to do than others. I always find that those particular days tend to be the most rewarding.

Remember, it is always better to take a lot of "first steps" than no steps at all.

XOXO Maddie

Chapter One

Maddie

Phobias.

We all have them. However, most of us don't walk that fine line between fear and just plain crazy.

I do.

Do you?

~~Fear has existed as long as man has~~

"No shit, assmunch!" I say almost under my breath, crossing out that last statement. Ugh! Why did I agree to write this article?! The same reason why various other medical professionals do—validation. Validation amongst colleagues and students . . . mostly. The regular "Joe Schmoe's" couldn't care less about our hypothesis on anything; they're too busy reaching for *People* magazine rather than *Journal of Anxiety Disorders*. I don't blame them; I am too. "Fuck off," I mutter and slap my notebook shut.

"I'm sorry, were you talking to me?"

I look up quickly. *Shit—it's Wednesday!* It's "Viking Day." Did they have Vikings in Australia? If not, then I think there's been a mix-up; his family must've emigrated there.

His name is Declan Pierce. And it was only an hour ago that he was "piercing" the ever-loving-hell out of my love tunnel with his giant Viking cock. One look and I swore he wasn't going to fit, but he yanked my skirt up and pushed me down on my desk. His hand possessively, yet gently, grasped my neck. His fingers splayed the length of my jaw, holding me in place. He shushed me as his free hand found its way between my legs. When he tore my panties away from me, I whimpered; I was so fucking wet for him, and it put a cocky ass smile on his face. "It will fit. Let me show you how good it will fit, love," he said while stretching my entrance with his thick, long fingers. Because I'm one who likes to see proof—I submitted. Ever get fucked so hard and good, you can't keep your mouth from gaping open, or enable your throat to produce some sort of sound? That's how he fucked me. Gaping-mouth fuck. And I *loved* it.

He commanded me to come—I came.

He released my neck and pulled out with a thunderous groan. *"On your knees, Ms. St. Claire!"* I obeyed and was rewarded with his throbbing, swollen cock, filling my mouth and hitting the back of my throat until it exploded, releasing another wondrous, epic groan from him. Afterward, he sat in the plush chair most of my clients seem to prefer and helped me up onto his lap where he cradled me. His large hands caressed my body in a nonchalant manner. It didn't matter what kind of manner it was; he was touching me, and that was all I needed. Then in a deep, husky voice, he started talking in my ear, saying deliciously naughty things about my pussy. The first thing he said is a must. And I'm sure you will agree with me.

"Mmm . . . any idea how amazing it was to feel your tight, little pussy, pulsating around my cock?"

2

See that right there? That's psych 101 when it comes to sex talk. Men always want to hear about how big you think their cock is (in a positive light, of course). Well, women are no different! I don't care if her vag lips are flapping in the wind, and you can stick your hand up in there to give a "thumbs up" to your cock while you're fucking her; tell her that pussy is tight! She'll love you and your "big" cock a little more! ;)

"Ms. St. Claire? Ms. St. Claire?! Are you alright?"

"Huh?" I snap back.

"Are you ok?" He places the back of his hand to my forehead.

"Yes, why?" I ask nervously because—*he's touching me!*

"One minute I'm asking if you were talking to me, the next, your eyes glassed over, your face turned bright red, and you were breathing rapidly. Is everything okay?" He crouches down to me.

"Um . . . oh. Sorry." I shake my head. "I was lost in my thoughts . . . sorry," I say again.

"What on Earth were you thinking about?" He chuckles lightly. "I thought I was going to have to call a medic!"

I could easily tell him that I was lost in the thought of our impromptu "session" earlier, but he probably won't remember it to reminisce along with me. That's because he wasn't really here. He was only fucking me in my mind. He fucks me there every day, at some point. Always on my desk. My own little—made for my mind—porno. *Think of something here!* "I don't even know," I say and give him, what I think is, my most perplexed look.

"Are you diabetic?"

"No. Don't be silly. I'm fine." I wave his idea off.

"Have you eaten?"

"No," I answer and feel my palms start to sweat. I'm just realizing how close his face is to mine.

"That's it then!" He slaps his knee. "Here, I've brought you a coffee." Taking it out of the drink tray, he places it on my desk near me. "Please, eat my muffin."

I'd like for him to eat my muffin!

"Thanks, but you don't have to do that." I smile, eyeing it. "Maybe just half." I give in before he puts up a fight. What? It's the—limited time only—banana muffin from Dunkin's. I'm not passing up on that shit! He nods, smiling as he pulls the plush chair (the one he was just cradling me on, telling me how tight I was . . . ahem) closer to my desk and takes his coffee out of the drink tray, as well. "You don't have to bring me coffee every week."

"Oh, I'm sorry. Did you want something else?" Declan reaches for my cup.

"No!" I smack his hand away and rescue my coffee.

"A little passionate about your coffee, aye?" His smile hits his eyes.

"Just a bit," I agree and take a sip. "I meant that you don't have to do this in general."

"I rather enjoy Wednesdays now, if I'm to be honest." He shifts in his seat. "This one hour of the week seems to be the only hour I get that has any normalcy to it."

"Why do you say that?" I cross my legs, letting my right one hang over the left, and it bops . . . bops . . . bops.

"I have to tell you, that's terribly annoying," his voice is teasing and seemingly more amused than annoyed as his hand puts pressure on my leg to make me stop. I stare at his hand, secretly wishing it to travel to my lady business. *Ugh! What is wrong with me?!*

"Sorry," I almost whisper. "So, tell me why you feel that way," I continue.

"I want to hear about your week. Tell me, what's new with your friends?" He taps my knee then pulls his hand away.

"Declan—"

"—Dec"

"Dec, this is the third week you've popped in on me with coffee. All we've done is talk about me. I'd like to hear some dialogue from you." I'm calm but assertive, I think.

4

"No." He shakes his head. "I'm not here for a therapy session. I'm here to talk to a very witty, charming, and beautiful woman. If I talk about me, you will turn this into a session, and I will refrain from coming back."

"Um . . . thank you for the compliment. No thank you to the judgment."

"I'm not judging you. I just want to have coffee with you and pleasant conversation. I don't want to come in here and unload my bag."

I would so love for him to unload his bag!

Pull it together, Maddie! "Well, that's not fair."

"You listen to people all day, every day. Don't you want to take a break and be the one to talk for once?"

"I don't just listen. I coach. I talk it out with them. Don't slap a label on me." I may have come off a little pissed with that last comment.

"I didn't mean to state how you do your job. I just meant that I like to listen to you and . . . I don't know. I should just go. I'm sorry for offending you." He stands up.

I stand up with him. "Do you talk to anybody? Especially about your son?" I ask quickly.

"Have a nice night," he says quietly before heading out of my room.

"Declan! Dec!" I call after and follow him down the hall. "Stop!" I grab his arm.

He knocks on the door to Ted's office, ignoring my pull. "I'm sorry, we have to leave early today—something's come up," Declan says once he opens the door.

"Dec . . . wait." I try to get him to turn but he is of Viking quality, and I'm just, as Pa Ingalls would say, a half-pint. Finally, I give up. He and his son head down the hall.

Good job, Captain Asswhore!

"So, Jeff . . . how did it go?" I focus in on my four o'clock, trying once again to forget about what transpired here between Declan and me earlier.

"Not good." He looks down, shaking his head.

"What happened?" I uncross my legs and re-cross the other way as I bring my pad closer to me to jot notes down.

"Her parents had stairs." His hands ball into fists.

"Did you at least try?"

"Nope."

"Jeff . . . we talked about this," I say, my voice laced with disappointment.

"I know. I just couldn't." He looks up at the ceiling, teeth clenching and jaw twitching. It's not hard to see the anger boiling inside of him.

"Did you ask her if there would be stairs?"

"Why would I do that?! So she could know I'm a fucking freak?" he almost yells.

"You're not a freak," I say calmly.

"Really? Who the fuck is afraid of stairs?" He throws his hands out.

"Lots of people, Jeff, otherwise, it wouldn't have a diagnosis."

"Oh, please! Let's talk about that for a moment; why the fuck would they name it Bathmophobia? It sounds like I'm afraid of taking a bath."

"That's Ablutophobia," I correct him. Though, I don't know why—he's right; some of these names are so stupid and don't fit the fears. "Let's move on. What did you say to her?"

"I made myself vomit."

"What?!" I lean forward. "How did you do that?"

"It's a gift; I can vomit on cue."

I look down at my notepad: *Can vomit on cue. Future discussion—hx of bulimia?*

"What are you jotting down?" He leans forward as if he could see it better. He can't; I have the pad completely tilted towards me.

"What happened after you vomited?"

"She freaked out. I freaked with her as if I had no clue it was going to happen." He smiles slightly like he's proud of his accomplishment of fooling her.

"Then . . ." I lead.

"She called her parents, canceled, and we went back to my place. She took care of me all night, and I made sure to reward her in the morning." He waggles his eyebrows at me. I can't help it—I laugh.

"So, now what?" I tilt my head and narrow my eyes a bit. "You can't throw up every time you arrive at her parents' house."

"We invited them to my place." His smile broadens.

"Someday, though, you're going to have to take them up on their invitation back to their house." I raise a brow.

"Bridges . . . they can't be crossed until you get to them."

I look down to my pad, rolling the top page up to get to a clean one: *Bridges . . . they can't be crossed until you get to them.*

What?

I get all my best one-liners from my clients!

"Are you serious about Alexa?"

"Of course! She's the one!" He sits up straight.

"Are you sure?" I ask as I roll the paper back down on my pad, getting ready to end out the session.

"Yes! Why are you questioning me?!" He gets all defensive.

"Maybe because you haven't told her. I want a session with you and Alexa, Jeff. It has to happen. If you are serious about this girl, she has the right to know what you are working through. It's a step in your healing process—one you need to take," I say in my most assertive voice.

"Fuck."

"Do it."

"Ok." He runs his hands through his hair.

"Are we good for next week?" I eye my planner. Yes, I'm old school and still use a planner for my appointments. You wouldn't be laughing at me on days we lose power! I'm the only one who laughs then. Sometimes, you gotta keep certain shit old school.

"Same time, same place, Doc." He smiles and stands up, adjusting his jeans. And by that I mean, pulling them up. Jeff is twenty-five and wears his pants off his ass like it's still cool.

It's not, right?

I mean, why the hell was that ever considered cool?

Dumbasses.

"Ok, see you then." I smile and wave back as he salutes me and walks out of my office. I don't understand the whole salute thing but whatevs. . .

Thank Christ that was my last client of the day. I don't think I could sit through another one.

I don't even have his phone number.

I wish I could stop thinking about him, but I can't. I don't understand what happened today. What I do know is that there is something worth digging into that he doesn't want me even near, never mind digging.

Why would he say that about me, anyway? What have I done to get profiled like that? Think, Maddie, think.

Three weeks ago . . .

I walked out to the waiting room to put a ridiculous amount of psychology books that I kept "borrowing" from colleagues at the front desk and there he was . . . the Viking. And . . . he was sitting next to . . . a Viking. Fucking Mitch. I knew it right away. Mitch (my best friend Charley's boyfriend) was getting me back for the text and phone call where I bared my heart to him about Declan, only, I thought I was baring my heart out to Charley until CiCi informed me that it was Mitch, pretending to be her. Long story short—I got him back. He decided to return the favor. He hired somebody to sit in the waiting room, next to Declan, dressed as a Viking. I could've killed him, only . . . it was funny. I turned on my heels and ran—straight into the wall, dropping all of the books. Then . . . I fell back . . . over the stupid, small, side table I *always* say we need to move. Declan Pierce (AKA—the Viking) came to my rescue, and that's how it all started.

"Ms. St. Claire, are you alright?" He hovered over me. "Why are you carrying so many books at once?"

Fuck. He's Australian.

"My panties are wet."

"What?!"

Oh. My. God! Please, did I just say that out loud?

"I said, I'm all set." I try to think as quickly as possible.

"Right!" he says assertively and helps me on to my feet. I get a little woozy and fall into his chest.

Totally did that shit on purpose.

He holds me tightly to him.

Jealous? Watch and learn, kids.

"Are you alright?" His finger softly lifts my chin to bring my eyes up to meet his. Honest to God, it should be illegal to be this gorgeous. His hair is blond; shoulder length. He has a sexy beard of scruff—fuck. Eyes? The clearest of blues. Fuck (did I say that already?)—he's hot. And—he's holding me.

Move over, Mary.

I may be pregnant.

"Yes. I don't know what happened." No need to ramble the truth out at him. I like to hand out my dose of crazy in small increments, build a person's tolerance up. Know what I'm sayin'?

"Let me walk you back to your office; you seem a bit shaken up." He breaks our stare down. It was becoming rather awkward (If you

were in the studio audience, you would've been chanting for us to kiss.).

"Um, sure." I snap out of it. We begin walking down the hall.

"You're limping," he states.

"Yes. It seems I've left one of my shoes in the waiting room." I stop and close my eyes. God, can I be any more of dumbass? How does one walk this far without realizing they are missing a shoe—with a five-inch heel?! He squats down and slowly takes my other heel off.

"You have beautiful toes," he says, seemingly nervous. A bubble of laughter erupts out of me before I can think quick enough to stifle it. Poor guy, he was already shaking his head like he couldn't believe that was the best compliment he could come up with. Soon enough, his shoulders shake a bit, matching my amusement. Suddenly, I feel better and less nervous. Funny how one moment can do that; like someone waved a magic wand. He stands back up, causing me to feel like singing a chorus of "The Lollipop Guild." I offer a little smile and turn to continue down the hall. I feel the weight of his hand at my back. I look up and over at him. "Just to be safe," he says quickly, "I don't want you to fall."

Too late.

I nod in agreement and let him guide me the rest of the way.

Since then, we've spent my free hour on Wednesdays talking while his son has his session with Ted. I can't remember any time that I've ever pried because we really have only talked about my friends and me. Those crazy bitches take up a lot of time to talk about with all of their antics! And, it was nice sharing some of our stories with someone who doesn't already know us . . . or about us. What? We've all lived in this area most of our lives, of course we're "known" around town. Minds out of the gutter, people! Okay. . . slightly out of the gutter. Let's get back on topic, shall we?

It's just . . . the thought of waiting another week to see if he'll show up is already killing me. *Maybe* this happening was a good thing. *Maybe* I'm not supposed to be with him. *Maybe* he is bat-shit-crazy. Or maybe . . . just maybe, I'm supposed to be alone for the rest of my life.

Well, one thing is for sure—I need to pick up tampons on my way home. My overdramatic thoughts are a telltale sign of impending doom for almost five days. I slip my feet back into my heels (I like to be barefoot most of the time in my office), grab my purse, and head out the door, shutting the light off as I leave.

Chapter Two

Declan

CHECKING IN ON HUNTER, I PULL HIS COVERS UP AND KISS THE TOP of his head. It's the only time I get to kiss my son anymore, him being ten and all; he tells me he's too old. He's too young to have been through all he has been through so far. I often wonder, had the circumstances been different around his childhood, would he still welcome my affection like he did once before? If Renee wasn't his mum, would we find ourselves at a fun activity Wednesday nights instead of therapy?

I fear I will never know those answers.

I fear nothing will ever cleanse his mind of the images he has seen.

I fear that, no matter all the effort I've put in, my son will eventually be lost to me, as well.

I leave his room, taking one final glance for the night as I close his door. My immediate thought goes to her—Madelyn St. Claire. Funny, how the mind works; thoughts changing as quickly as the scenery when you walk from one room to another. I shouldn't have behaved the way that I did. I've thoroughly enjoyed getting to know her these past few weeks. If only she knew the amount of therapy it gave me to talk to someone about *them*. I'm so tired of my situation being the focus of most conversations with people. I needed a break somehow, and she gave that to me without even realizing it. I tried, in the most polite way, to steer her away from the topic of "me." She's relentless—that one! I suppose she can't help herself, given her profession. Thanks to my behavior, she probably thinks I'm the reason Hunter needs therapy. I must fix this immediately. Only . . . I'm leaving for several weeks to fill the other half of our European tour obligations.

This has been the heaviest tour season we've had since I signed up with the Boston Pops Orchestra. Though I'm sad to be without Hunter during this stretch, he will have a great time with my parents in Queensland. He loves spending his summers there with them. I have to say: I'm jealous. My parents are pretty terrific. Unlike my son, I got to experience a normal childhood, with two parents who loved and supported me. At least I get to give him a good dose of what I had.

We leave in five days. I'm not sure I'll be able to get in to see her, or even what her schedule is the other days of the week. I could send her flowers, but, from what I've noticed the past few months, she doesn't have a good track record keeping them viable. She needs something that can endure the kind of care she gives. Ah-ha! I've got just the thing!

I sit on my couch, throwing my legs up on it while I grab my laptop. Within moments, it comes to life, and I immediately search for flower places online. I query the first place; I'm not impressed. Though, what I've chosen is not particularly pretty. I wonder what she will think of this. What if she finds this inappropriate? It's not like I'm a patient of hers. Still, this could come off weird. I'll chance it, given her quirky nature. I don't allow a second thought when writing out the card to go with it; I *want* her to know I'm interested. I hit send and quickly close my laptop before I try to cancel.

I rest my head on my hands as I stare up at my ceiling. *God, she's gorgeous.* Curvy little thing. Mmm . . . I love her curves. It takes a lot of restraint on my part to not let my hands reach out and run the course of them. She looks nothing like the girls I've been attracted to in the past. First off, you would've never found me with a petite girl. I've always gone for the leggy ones. Maybe it's because of my own height. At six foot three, I'm well over a foot taller than her. She's got a "larger than life" personality though that makes her seem ten feet tall.

I'm quiet by nature, so I love nothing more but to sit back and listen to her talk. She's so animated. Very fidgety; it's part of her charm. I quite like it. I quite like her. It's been a long time since I've felt this way—having a crush on someone. I forgot what it was like, feeling excited about someone, about seeing them, talking to them. It's been twelve years since I last experienced this—ebullience.

I'm petrified.

Last time turned out to be a nightmare rather than the fairytale ending it had the promise to be. A nightmare lasting seven years and counting. It has filled mine and my son's days with a darkness I didn't know existed. I mean, I knew of it. I imagined that it would be difficult. But, you never know until those shoes you are trying to imagine being in are actually your own. Those shoes are like cement, and even if you could run, it's so dark, you can't see an exit. Might as well throw shackles on, too.

But, I do have an escape. I have my music. When I place my cello in position, with the first contact of my bow gliding across the strings, it's like a burst of light shining in. The more I play, the brighter the light becomes, the more I am lost in the warmth of the bliss I feel. The solitude. The power. There is no greater medicine. If only for that moment, I am lost in whatever piece I am playing, it heals me, helping me to hold on . . . to fight. It is my haven.

If only Hunter had something like this. It might be the one thing to keep him from letting the darkness win. He has no interest in my passion. I'm okay with that. However, he has no true interest in anything. I've done everything I can do to help him find his passion. I know he's only ten, but most ten-year-olds have a passion for something, even if temporary. Nothing. To top it off, his reticent behavior surpasses mine. If I didn't see it with my own eyes last summer, I would've never believed my parents when they said he behaves like a normal boy there. Of course, he didn't see me witness this. I'm glad because it would've surely ended.

My parents have offered to take him on a full-time basis. It looks great on paper when taking everything into consideration. Only . . . it would be like I gave up; abandoned him. Even though that certainly isn't true; his best interest always comes first. I think, in the long run, that would definitely backfire and look like what I fear it would. Besides, it's just him and me—we need to figure this out. I want my son, and the relationship we had, back.

"Dec, you need anything before I retire for the night, honey?" I hear Rosie's voice coming from the threshold.

I sit up and look over towards her, "No, Rosie, thank you." I offer her a smile.

"All right. Goodnight, then." She smiles back as she unties her apron and turns to head back to the kitchen.

I'd be lost without Rosie. She's been with us for six years now and has pretty much helped me in the raising of Hunter. Her children are all grown and off doing their own things. Her husband took off about fifteen years ago with a younger model of Rosie. He's mad; Rosie is a beautiful woman. I can hardly believe she's sixty-five. She's fit, has incredible skin, and a stylish bob that's dirty-blonde with highlights. She's very young and hip; looks about fifty. She needs to get out there; there's some poor bloke waiting and wondering when she's going to come along. I've nonchalantly tried to introduce her to the men I know who might be a good match. Apparently, I'm not a good matchmaker. I wonder if Madelyn knows of someone. I'm sure she does. *Yes, Dec—brilliant! It won't seem odd at all for you to inquire about a possible mate for your housekeeper.*

I jump off the couch and run along to my room to change. I'll never get to sleep tonight if I don't clear my head. There's only one thing that helps me in that department—kicking my arse in the gym. After throwing sweats on, I head back down the hall. My at-home gym is in the basement, far enough away from everyone so that my music doesn't wake them. I do love the setup of my townhouse; master bedroom is on the first floor, Hunter's room, as well as two guest bedrooms, are on the second, and Rosie has taken the top floor, converting it into a small studio apartment for herself. Everyone has their space, but we're all still close enough to run into each other.

"It's 10 P.M.," Rosie says as she notices me before going up the stairs.

"Yes." I nod.

"You only work out at night when something, other than the usual, is bothering you." She eyes me suspiciously over the brim of her deep-purple, plastic reading glasses. I know well enough to not try to brush off her concern. When Rosie gets her "I'm going to get to the bottom of this" look, she always does *just that.*

"You know me too well, Rosie." I shake my head before pulling my hair back into a tie.

"Step into my office." She shuffles her hand in the direction of the kitchen.

"Beauty before brawn," I say, prompting her to go first.

"Well, that could be confusing since I'm a tough cookie, and you're just plain pretty." She winks and adds a little chuckle before taking off ahead of me.

"If you were any other person, Rosie, I'd be put off about that."
I laugh.

She takes her usual place at the table, and I do the same. "Don't
make me pull teeth, Dec." She's back to business with her over the
brim stare. She *is* a tough cookie.

"Okay . . . other than the usual stuff, you say?"

"Yes."

"You know that woman I've had my eyes on for some time
now?"

"Yes."

"I made a complete arse out of myself today."

"How so?"

"She pressed. I was afraid that was going to happen, as you
know. Today was the day it happened and even though she wasn't
obnoxious in any way about it, my reaction was. Now, I'm not going
to see her for several weeks; I can't even rectify it." Folding my arms
over each other on the table, I rest my chin on top of my left one.

"How obnoxious are we talking?"

I give her the play by play. She clicks her tongue and shakes her
head when I'm done. "Declan, it doesn't sound to me as if she pried
any more than one normally would. It also sounds to me as if your
reaction caused her to poke a little harder, trying to figure you out.
I mean, that is part of her job—trying to figure people out in order
to help them. Why did you sabotage yourself like that?" She throws
her hands out.

"Sabotage?" I lift my head up, jerking it back.

"Yes! Instead of giving her a little crumb so that you could then
redirect her back to her life, you set up a trap for her and blew out
of town the moment she stepped into it as if it were her fault she
placed a single toe there in the first place. Oh, bad form, Declan,
bad form!" Her hands push at the air in front of her. I'm speechless.
"You've had yourself so worked up, preparing for a moment like this
to happen; you were fending off the eye of the storm when in reality,

it was a little gust of wind." Rosie doesn't seem to have a problem finding any words.

"Don't you think you're being a bit dramatic? I mean, it didn't go down exactly as you've just played it out." It's taking a lot from me not to have a small bit of laughter over this. Maybe she's just tired tonight; she's not one to over exaggerate.

"Maybe I am, but I'm a little disappointed in you. You *need* to take back this part of your life. Renee made terrible, terrible choices, destroying your family, your trust, and your heart. But, it's been seven years since you've closed that chapter of your life."

"*Hardly!*" I snap. "I wish I could close that bloody chapter! You know perfectly well that I will never be truly rid of her."

"And there it is," her voice glum.

"There is what?"

"Your crutch, out on display."

"Rosie, what on Earth are you talking about?"

"This woman that you are fond of, she's the first woman you've dared to allow yourself to feel anything towards since Renee. The idea of feeling that way and it leading to something petrifies you deep down inside. That's why you behaved so obnoxiously today. The question is: did you do it to protect yourself from the unknown or to protect her from the known?"

"Who'd want to carry this baggage with me?" I ask in defeat.

"Anyone with a strong backbone, and who loves the hell out of you, honey." She tilts her head and lets a small, encouraging smile hit her eyes.

"Will you marry me, Rosie? You seem to fit the bill."

"Pssh . . . you couldn't keep up with me, killer," she teases.

"You got an older sister, then?"

"Oh, go downstairs now and run on your wheel, you mamster!"

"Mamster?" I laugh.

"Yes! You're a man who runs on those damn machines like a hamster—you're a mamster." She gets up.

"Thanks for clearing that up for me, Mrs. Webster."

"It's Ms. Oxford, if you will." She winks. "Night, my gentle giant," she says with a sigh in her voice as she heads over to me, gives me a hug, and motherly kiss on my head. That's just what she is to me, another mum.

"Night, Ro." I smile up at her.

She heads off but stops just before she walks out the kitchen and turns. "So, what are you going to do about what happened and not seeing her for a while?"

"Oh, I've sent her a cactus with an apology and a promise of coffee when I get back."

"A cactus?—because *nothing* screams romance like a plant shaped like a phallus that has tiny needles all over it to prick you with? We need to work on your A-game, son; you're more than a little rusty." She closes her eyes like she's asking for strength from above, then turns on her heel and leaves. I can't help laughing at her comment; at no time did I consider the shape of the cactus. *Wow.* She'll have me diagnosed as eccentric in no time. *Good job, Dec!*

With a lighter air about me, I go downstairs to my gym. No need to kick my arse now after that talk, but a good run will clear the rest of my mind. Or . . . make me think of her cute little laugh. Or . . . how animated she gets when she talks about her friends. The way she licks her lips before looking away from my stare when a moment of awkward silence happens between us. *I'd love to be the one to lick those lips of hers.*

I run the last leg of a quick 5k. My focus clear—I want her. I need her. I haven't felt this certain in a long time.

It scares the fuck out of me.

Chapter Three

Maddie

"WHAT THE FUCK DO YOU MEAN HE GAVE YOU A CACTUS?" JULIE shouts.

"Shh, Julie! I have you guys on speaker phone," I remind her.

"Why do you have us on speaker?" Ava asks.

"Because you bitches will blow out my eardrum trying to talk over each other."

"Good move because I'm about to scream at Julie for asking that stupid fucking question," CiCi bellows. "Why do you do that? She said he gave her a cactus! How else do you want her to fucking explain that?"

"You know what I mean," Julie groans.

"No, I don't. It makes no fucking sense. I hate when people ask that stupid fucking question." CiCi is the queen of pointing out obvious things that don't really bother other people.

"Can we get back on topic here?" Charley pipes up.

"Good idea," I agree. This is what I get for holding a conference call with my four best friends, or as we refer to ourselves: The GEGs (The Green-Eyed Girls, if you're just tuning in.)

"Fine! What's with the cock tree?" CiCi, of course. Let's just pause for the laughing and verbal hi-fives.

"Clearly, he wants to prick me," I finally say when the hyenas calm down.

"Or . . . he fears for the lives of beautiful, yet fragile, flowers of any kind," Charley surmises.

"That too." I nod in agreement.

"How do you feel about not seeing him for a while?"

"I don't know, Ava. I mean, I really hate how we left off. Obviously he does too, but maybe this is a good thing, us not seeing each other. Maybe I'm reading too much into things, and it will help curve these projections of feelings and thoughts I shouldn't be having."

"Oh. . . are we going into full-fledged 'I like him, but I don't think he feels that way towards me'—code for: I need validation—bullshit right now? Because if we are, I'm gonna go ahead and put the phone down to protect my eyes from getting stuck when I roll them far into the back of my fucking head."

"Shall we talk about your Kyle issues then, Ceese?" I snap.

"I don't have issues."

Let's just give them all a minute to stop laughing at her.

.

.

.

That'll do.

"You're all a bunch of fucking assholes. Anywho—my point is, shortstack—you're a hot piece of ass that happens to come equipped with an intelligent brain and witty charm. Why wouldn't he be into you?!" CiCi stresses.

"Thanks, Ceese. Just don't start grabbing my lady balls to get my attention, alright?" I tease. That's how she got Kyle's attention. Well, his man balls.

"But they're so shiny and purty."

"Eww . . . cue the music to *Deliverance*," Ava groans.

"This coming from the lady who loves my vag," Charley laughs. That comment may have something to do with Charley agreeing to be the surrogate mother to Ava and Trent's child. Then again, it might not be. You never know with this crew!

"Do you girls ever have a normal conversation?" Jay interjects.

"Uh . . . Jay?"

"*Gess, my little jalapeno?*" He gives me his best Mexican accent. It sucks.

"Stop being a fucktard. Why are you on the phone?"

"To keep up my appearances as the token gay friend," he dead-pans. *Fucktard*—you see?

"You're the only gay token I'd put in my slot," Charley quips.

"Mmm. . . I would've turned straight for you—I'll pause for the collective gasp—if only the hot CEO didn't come along," Jay admits.

"We'll still have our inappropriate texts, baby," Charley coos.

"I will always give you good text. No one and *I mean* no one will *ever* text you hard like I do."

"Can we round the fucking wagons here, please?" I groan.

"Sorry, Maddie. Charley mentions her slot and all else flies out the window," Jay says as if he's in pain over the thought.

"Jay, the Viking is over six feet of solid muscle with shoulder-length blond hair and blue eyes. Also—he's Australian," I give the stats.

"And now back to our regularly scheduled program, kids! Before we discuss whether he has the feels, let's get to the important shit—how's he hanging?" Jay gives his best reporter impersonation.

"I, myself, would love to know the answer to that question," I say and finish up with a wishful sigh.

"Play suggestive music next time he stops by," Jay offers.

"Like what?"

"'Push it' by Salt N Pepa," Ava suggests.

"'Me So Horny' by 2Live Crew." Julie.

"'I Touch Myself' The Divinyls." CiCi

"'My Humps' by The Black Eyed Peas," Charley adds in.

"No way! You need something a little more subtle, yet awkward," Jay finally interjects. I'm glad he did because I don't have the energy. Can you imagine me playing any of those songs?

"Oh, this should be good, coming from Jay." I can hear CiCi rolling her eyes.

"I do, indeed, have the perfect song," he states. "'I Just Had Sex' by The Lonely Island."

"Oh. My. God! Please play that, Maddie!" Julie practically screeches.

"No. Not that I've ever heard it before, but just from the title—it's a firm *no!*" Why the fuck do I call these assholes? "Look, I'm gonna go; I think I've gotten all the help I could get out of you guys." Which equals—*nothing.*

"Maddie?" I can hear the concern in Charley's voice.

"I'm fine. My next client is here," I lie.

"Later, biatch," CiCi starts the round of goodbyes. Slowly the other girls follow suit. Yes, that includes Jay.

"Charley?"

"Yeah?"

"Why are you still on the phone?"

"Because I know something is wrong," she hits the nail on the head.

"I'm a little upset," I admit.

"I'm listening."

"Sometimes I just need to be serious about stuff. I need to have a serious conversation. And I need serious help. Don't fucking say it," I add quickly.

"I won't. I won't agree that you need some serious help." I can tell she's trying not to laugh. "I'm sorry."

"It's alright; I set myself up for that." I let a smile break through.

"You're right to get upset, Maddie. However, you're smart enough to know that if you need all of that, then you have to call us individually. Unless it's a huge traumatic event, we're gonna act like assholes when we're grouped together."

"You're right. I know better, but I just wanted to talk it out once and not five times. Charley?" I try to steady my voice.

"Yeah?"

"I really like him."

"I know."

"Something is making him act this way, and I just don't know if it's something I can handle. I don't like not being prepared," I lay it out.

"Like John Lennon once said, *Life happens while you're busy making other plans.*"

"He actually sang that; it's in a song."

"Smart motherfucker; it's the advice that keeps on giving," she quips. "Anywho . . . what I'm trying to say is that you can't always be prepared for everything. Sometimes you gotta reel in that Type A personality of yours. You know firsthand, Maddie—nothing in life is as perfect as you imagined it would be as a little girl. You can have everything but not without compromise, patience, and belief in yourself. Whatever his past is—that's his past. We all come with baggage, but that shit needs to stay in the trunk where it belongs. You know it's *there*. We all *know* it's there. But, none of us travel down the road with our luggage on our lap. We don't toss it out of the car either. That luggage holds everything—the good and the bad. We wouldn't be who we are without both. It's all relevant. So, whatever's in his luggage, he may need help sorting it into the right piles; making sense of it all. I can't imagine a better person than you to help him with that," she finishes.

"Oh, I don't know; I think you can give me a run for my money," I tease.

"I'm too busy sorting mine and Mitch's luggage. It's quite the load—no pun intended." She laughs.

"Thank you, Charley. You were just the right person for me to talk to." I get teary-eyed. I *really* needed that kind of heart-to-heart.

"I love you, Maddie. And, you know the girls love you. We all know you really like the Viking. We're just stupid when we're all together. It's comic relief from our stressful lives. And, you know, we need that, too."

"You're right. I love that we are that way. I guess I didn't *read* myself too well today to know that wasn't exactly what I needed at the moment. Thanks for being the intuitive bitch you are and staying on the line with me." I open my compact up to check the damage.

"It's the gift you receive for pushing life out of your vag; suddenly you become fucking Ghandi."

"You could have your own show: *Becoming Ghandi.*"

"Sold! That's brilliant! Will you be my executive producer?"

"What do they even do?" I ask. No really—what *do* they do?

"Nothing. It's a title they throw at you when they want to give you credit for breathing but are not exactly sure of what to call it," she quips.

"I may have to agree with you. I mean, why does one show need ten producers? It's sketchy."

"We're on to them."

"Let's get off the phone before *they* find out," I add then laugh.

"Ok, but eventually, we should really get to the bottom of this."

"Are you being serious?" I laugh.

"Yes! I can't leave that shit hanging!"

"Alright, then. You see what you can find out. I'm gonna try my hand at doing normal things for an hour or two." My eyes skirt over my appointment book; only two more clients.

"Ha! Good luck with that!"

"Thanks. Love you."

"Love you, too. Bye, Captain."

"Fuck you." I shake my head.

"If it didn't happen during the college years. . ."

"So many opportunities missed. . ." I trail off in a sigh, say goodbye again, and hang up.

I sit back and stare at my cactus. His note stares back in a bold font.

> *I'm sorry. I will be out of the country for several weeks. I shall bring you coffee when I come back. I hope you will accept it and my apology. I think I may have found a plant you won't manage to kill. :)*
>
> *Fondly,*
> *Dec*

Fondly? *I like that.*

I have to wait several weeks to see him again. *I don't like that.*

Tossing my keys on the entrance table to my house, I pull my heels off with a grateful groan; someday being vertically challenged will be the death of me. My answering machine is blinking rapidly. I have ten messages. This can only mean one thing—my parents are home from their cruise.

I love my parents. No, really—they are wonderful. I had a

normal childhood. If we had to put the "fun" in dysfunctional, we would've failed. Oh yes, the St. Claire's are the model family. The Cleavers, if you will. Mom and Dad are the love of each other's life, and everyone knows it. They have two children—both successful; my brother, Preston, is an OB/Gyn. I swear that's his "get out of jail free" card for still being single. I think my parents figure what with all the pussy in his face every day, one will eventually catch his interest. Their daughter (*moi*, of course) being surrounded by quacks (as they call them) all day certainly would garner more of their attention in the love department. *Lucky me...*

Deep breath.

By the power of Grayskull... I hit play.

"Oh, shoot. Honey, it's seven; you shouldn't be working so late. Maybe you're on a date?" she adds in a hopeful tone. "Part of me hopes that's true, and part of me doesn't; I have wonderful news for you!" *I can barely contain my excitement.* "As you can guess, Dad and I are back. Oh, Maddie, what a wonderful time we had. You *really* must go on a cruise. The islands were just absolutely breathtaking. You could see the water clear to the bottom . . . so I heard."

Mom suffers from Thalassophobia—fear of the sea. A lot of people have that because of the movie *Jaws.* Of course, Mom says she just doesn't like what the seawater does to her skin. God forbid she'd get labeled with anything outside of what's acceptable. I digress. . .

"The air is so much cleaner there; I didn't have to take my allergy pills once! The temperatures did wonders for Dad's circulation." *Jesus Christ, they were gone for only a week.* "The people of Barbados were so wonderful. I swear I have never come across more accommodating people in my life. Ohhh, the babies we met on that island!"

You're failing me Grayskull, you're failing me.

"The *colors*—so vibrant! It's such a simple life there; I'm envious." She sighs. My mother couldn't do simple if someone had a gun to her head. "The trip back was quite eventful—pockets of turbulence!" Because I'm a good daughter, I gasp as if she were here, telling me all of this nail-biting shit in person. She carries on talking about their meal, the comfort of their seats, the designs of the fucking clouds. My mother is one who is ultra-focused on the details nobody else gives a shit about.

Message one = seventeen minutes.

You see why I called on the power of Grayskull?

Last week, I relied on The Force.

Nothing works.

Best part? I will hear this all again in person . . . because it's "different."

I play message two . . . cuz' I'm brave like that. "All I'm going to say is that I will hire the drag dressed up like Cher for the blissful day," my brother says then hangs up. I can't help but laugh. My brother has always had a magical way of warning me of impending doom.

I wait with baited breath as the next message gets ready to play. "Oh, goodness me! I almost forgot the good news!" Mom says almost out of breath with disbelief. My mother is a true New Englander, but I can't help but swear there is a Southern lady from the 20s trapped inside of her. "I ran into the Petersons—Cory is single! I just couldn't believe it! How a young, handsome man like he hasn't been snatched up by some lucky lady yet is beyond my understanding! I mean, how is that possible?" Hmm. . . I don't know. Perhaps I should ask Jay since he was balls deep into Cory three years ago. He may have an idea or two. . .

"Anyway . . . we're having the Petersons over for dinner Saturday night. They are bringing Cory. I may have mentioned a certain daughter who is still on the market." She coughs lightly. "I told them you would be here too."

Fuck you, Grayskull!

"Ok, honey. Call me when you get home. Love you," she says

super sticky sweet.

Next message: Preston's voice fills the air with his laughter.

Next message: my brother is now belting out a Cher song.

Next message: "I love you, Sis. I'm sorry," he says wholeheart-edly . . . followed up with a burst of laughter.

Next message: "Hands down—you'd wear the hell out of those pants." My brother is an asshole.

Next message: "Your brother called me . . . I'll just put the phone down and allow the awkward silence to happen," Jay says and true to his word, I hear him place the phone down. Three minutes pass by before I give up and skip to the next message.

Next message: "I bust your chops a lot, but it's moments like this when I'm glad you're technologically stuck in the 90s; awkward silence moment wouldn't last that long on voicemail. On a serious note; Cory is a great guy. He's probably rolling his eyes as much as you are. He needs to just tell his parents already, though. They must know. However, I don't have to tell you how powerful denial can be. Remember that ten or twenty times we told your parents I was gay and your mother waved at the nonsense in the air, stating I just needed to find the right girl?"

And then he introduced Victor as Victoria to them—the woman of his dreams. Judith St. Claire had herself a good Southern giggle (it was that lady trapped inside of her), waved even more nonsense and commended Jay on his great sense of humor.

If only we were in black and white. . .

Perfection.

Last message: I suddenly feel like hanging out with you and your parents Saturday night. Crazy, right? Let me know what time I should be there; I'd like to arrive fifteen minutes early to get my seat up front and center to this shit show. Later, biatch!" Preston must've called CiCi. Nah . . . all he had to do was light up the GEG signal (Jay).

I have not an ounce of energy left in me to call any of them back. I need to get out of this; I'll use my energy on devising a plan. Plans require wine. I'm a firm believer in following the rules. Baths help too. Red wine and a hot bubble bath combined with exhaustion sounds like it would lead to a great tragic headline . . . if I were a celebrity. I'm not, so . . . *safe!* Yes, I said that like an umpire.

WINE IN HAND, I sink down into my sanctuary—my deep, claw-foot tub. I'm one who tends to save her pennies for a rainy day. However, my *en suite* is the exception to the rule. I spent many a rainy penny to have the bathroom of my dreams. It was worth it, believe me!

I am *completely* out of random men to show up with as my date. I have no idea as to what I'm going to do. I love my parents dearly, but they don't shine at all when it comes to my love life. Hell, they don't even spark a little. It's like some weird status thing with them. I'm thirty-four and unmarried; somebody might think there is something wrong with me, for Pete's sake!

My phone lights up. I pick it up off the little side table I keep next to me to hold the essentials during a bath: phone, book, and wine. Just a PM from Charley: *Cory?!!!! I'd turn Jay straight way before you'd ever turn Cory!*

She's on the money with that one!

Suddenly, the craziest idea comes to me. I click on Facebook and search for Declan. Ahh! There he is! Jesus, Mary, and Joseph— he's fucking hot. I take a big gulp of my wine . . . until my glass is fully empty, of course. I'm about to do something I would never do in a million years. I just need to give myself another few minutes to allow my lady balls to grow to precisely the right size.

Balls ready, I hit the message icon on his page:

Thanks for the cock tree (dubbed that by CiCi)! You're right; I haven't killed a cock yet!

Shit! I can't write that. I go to hit the backspace button.

No! Oh, God, No!

Fuck my life—just fuck it!

I didn't mean to send that. I may have had some wine which has affected my fingers' ability to find the backspace button.

You can't imagine the relief I feel in knowing that no cocks have been harmed in your care.

Oh my God—he's on! I sit up straighter in my tub. What do I say? What do I say?!

I'm sure I bring relief to a lot of cocks.

Wait!

My fingers are clearly on strike from my brain.

Where are you? Please tell me you are home!

In my tub. Bubble bath.

I may have fallen to my knees.

Sorry, that wasn't appropriate.

I may be biting my lip.

Are you flirting with me, Ms. St. Claire?

Shit. I'm being completely unprofessional! What is wrong with me? I shouldn't be doing this! Even if I wasn't reading him wrong, me, behaving like this is!

Because if you are . . . that'd be great. . .

I may also be drinking wine.

Did you also watch Office Space tonight, too?

Guilty.

What else did you do tonight?

I'm calling you.

How?

Suddenly, my cell rings, but it's a weird ring. I stare at it, confused as Declan's profile pic lights up my screen. "Hello?" I answer.

"Is this ok?" He seems unsure.

"How are you doing this?"

"It's a feature on *Messenger*. I thought that if we had a normal chat, fingers wouldn't be wreaking havoc." I can hear the smile in his tone. I can also hear the sound of my heartbeat threatening my eardrums as my nerves shoot through the roof. I wasn't prepared to have any sort of conversation with him for the next few weeks or so. "Madelyn?"

"Maddie," I correct him.

"Maddie," he repeats. "Is this ok? Am I overstepping a boundary?"

"I'm not sure."

"I'm not a client of yours."

"You're the president." I laugh.

"What?"

"Sorry, it was a commercial, years ago and, clearly, a bad joke." I smack my palm lightly against my forehead several times.

"To answer the earlier question: I packed. Well, Rosie packed. I grunted when a decision needed to be made." The light gulping sound of him taking a swig of wine echoes through.

"Rosie?" I clear my throat. Or . . . as you may like to call it: pushing the green monster down.

"The ruler of my universe; usually labeled as the housekeeper-slash-nanny."

"Oh."

"I'd like to answer a question you asked me yesterday," his voice, suddenly quiet, and very much serious.

"Which one? I recall I asked you a few." That may not have come out very well.

"You did, indeed. I am very sorry about my behavior, Maddie." I can hear the huge dose of sincerity he's delivering. Not sure how with all that sexy-as-fuck accent thrown in with it. "I talk to *everybody* I know, especially about my son. Nobody gives me the chance *not* to. They don't know how to talk to me about everyday things; it always comes back to what my son and I are going through. I find it very therapeutic to hear about your life every week. It's like a vacation, really."

I wait, but his pause is long, cueing me that it's my turn to say something. "So, you coming in every week to talk to me has been a form of therapy for you?" I ask hesitantly. I'm not going to lie; I'm bummed. I thought he was truly interested in me. At least, I had hoped.

"Yes."

"Oh."

"Wait!" he almost shouts. "I don't mean to say that I only spent time with you to receive some sort of therapy. I . . . you . . . um . . . I'm not sure how to explain myself correctly," he says, sounding exasperated. "I just . . . Maddie, when I'm with you . . . when we talk . . . it's like nothing I've been through or am going through has happened. I get to be *just me*, not the *me* with all of the crap that has happened. Does that make any sense to you?"

"Because I talk about my life and my friends?"

"Yes!" I can hear the cheer in his voice. "God, you have no idea how good it is to hear about someone else's life instead of going through every detail of your own as if you're a broken record."

"Well . . . not to trump you, but I sort of do." I laugh lightly.

"Yes, of course. But, you know what I mean, right?" he begs.

"I do."

"I didn't mean to be rude yesterday. I'm very fond of you, Maddie," he admits. I feel my heart begin to race. Obviously it was just a test run when he first called; this is the real deal. "I know I'm leaving for a while, but I wonder, if you're not already spoken for, if you'd be so inclined to wait for my return; I'd like to take you out on a proper date."

"You're asking me out?"

"Yes."

"When are you leaving?"

"In four days."

"I will go out with you on one condition." Yes, I'm gonna go there. Wouldn't you?

"What's that?"

"My parents are back from their cruise. They have set me up on a blind date at their house this Saturday with a friend's son. I would like to bring you as my date to get me out of this God awful mess. If you choose to accept, then I will wait for you."

"Deal," he says quickly.

"That was quick." I'm taken aback.

"The idea of another man trying to win your affection—no thank you," he says assertively . . . like the way he says things to me when he's fucking me on my desk . . . in my mind.

"Okay," I say through my nerves then give him my address to pick me up.

"I'll see you in three days, Ms. St. Claire."

"Dec?"

"Yes?"

"I'm just going to say one thing before I abruptly hang up on you," I warn.

"What's that?"

"When you call me Ms. St. Claire—it's really fucking hot." And with that, I hang up.

My phone pings, alerting me to a private message on Facebook:

See you Saturday . . . Ms. St. Claire.

Chapter Four

Declan

I'M SO NERVOUS. WHAT IS WRONG WITH ME?! IT'S NOT LIKE I'M A teenager going on his first date! But, Christ Almighty, does it feel that way!

"Dad! What's the matter with you?" Hunter calls out from behind me, obviously seeing my reflection in the mirror to know something is up.

"I'm nervous." I laugh slightly as I turn to him.

"Why?" He walks into my room.

"I really like her," I admit . . . to my ten-year-old son.

"She seems really nice, Dad." He smiles and I realize, at this moment, that we are having a very normal, non-dysfunctional conversation. It's like seeing the light at the end of the tunnel.

"Isn't she?" I don't want to lose him now.

"Why are you nervous?"

"I just am. How do I look?" I change the subject.

"You look very dapper."

"Dapper?" I laugh. He joins me, and I fight off the emotions that are flying in, trying to destroy the moment I'm having with him.

"Yes." He beams. Then, suddenly, his smile drops. "Just don't mention Mum to her. Don't tell her this stuff."

"I won't. I will only tell her about me and that I have the most amazing son any man could ever want."

"You really feel that way, Dad?" his voice falters.

"Every day, Hunter."

He nods slightly, gives me a little smile, and heads out of my room. If I were someone on the outside, looking in—that would make me sad. But, I rejoice. That was the *best* conversation I've had with my son in over a year. I'm not so nervous anymore; I could take on the world. . .

I PULL UP TO HER HOUSE and swing into the driveway. I say a little silent prayer not to screw this up. There's a lot of pressure here, though. Not only is this our first date, though unofficial, but I am also meeting her parents. I sort of want to run for the hills. *Stop procrastinating, Dec!* Right! I turn my car off and get out, making sure to grab my gift for her. As I walk up to her front door, staring at my gift, I can visualize Rosie glaring at me over the brim of her glasses. Yes, I am forming a pattern of purchasing very odd things for Maddie. I almost want to run back to my car to discard it. But, then, she opens the door. My jaw drops.

Little black dress.

Curves.

I may need to hold onto this box to cover the growing excitement in my pants.

"Hi. . ." she trails off with a smile.

"Hi."

"Do you want to come in?" She takes a step back. It takes me a minute to respond because I'm still focused on the loaded question she just asked me.

"Thanks."

"Are you okay?" She tilts her head. Another little quirk she has.

"You look absolutely gorgeous," I say almost breathlessly. Makes sense since I am feeling breathless.

"Thank you." She blushes. "You look very handsome, as well."

"Oh . . . um . . . this is for you." I hand her the rather awkward sized box.

"Thank you. Should I open it now?" She's trying to be pleasant about it, but I can tell she's confused out of her mind by the way she just jerked her head back slightly, her eyebrows knitting together.

"Whenever you want." *Please, don't open it now. On second thought. . .* "Perhaps you should open it later, as we are running low on time," I suggest.

"Are you sure?" Head tilt.

"Absolutely." I nod.

"Ok." She smiles and sets the gift on the table where her house phone sits. She gives me her full attention, an expectant smile on her lips.

"Ready?"

"I feel as if I should ask you that. I may never hear from you again after this night." She laughs nervously.

"I highly doubt that." I put my arm out for her. She takes it, and I lead her outside. She stops to lock the door, then retakes my arm and follows my lead to my car. "Anything else I should know about tonight?"

"Just what I told you." She waits as I open the passenger door to my Lexus.

"What's our story?" I ask as she climbs in. I close the door, giving her a minute to think about it as I walk over to the driver's side.

"What do you mean?" she asks as I slide into my seat.

"Maddie, we can't just show up without a story. They'll be onto you." I look over as I start up the engine. "Are we new? Have we been dating a while?" I'm dying to kiss her. It seems silly, but if we are to go as a couple who's been seeing each other for a bit, then I get to do all the things boyfriends do. . . like kiss his girl.

"Oh. Geez, I hadn't thought of that. I guess we should say we've been dating a little while. Not too long or my mother will know I'm lying." She's all wide-eyed, in serious plot mode.

"So, the beginning of a relationship then?" I verify.

"Yes. I think that would be best, right?" She looks to me with furrowed brows.

"I agree. We need to take some steps, though." I can't believe I'm doing this.

"Steps?"

"Yes. If we are newly dating, it shouldn't be awkward when I kiss you," I state matter-of-factly.

"Kiss?" she asks, and I can hear the tempo of her breathing change.

"Yes. Maddie, couples who are newly dating often steal kisses and ogle at each other." I may go straight to hell, but damn if I care. "I think we're all set in the 'ogling department;' I can't keep my eyes off of you."

"You can't?" She plays with her fingers nervously.

"Never," my voice slightly cracks at my confession. Her eyes jerk up sharply at me. "I'm going to kiss you, Maddie," I announce. My breath is picking up speed to match the sound of my heart beating loudly in my eardrums.

"Ok," her voice soft and trusting, almost curious.

I shift my body slightly so that I can better angle myself. Slowly, I descend, watching as the tempo of her chest rising increases as my proximity closes in. "You are so beautiful," I breathe only an inch from her lips.

"Dec, I—"

I slam my lips against hers urgently. Slowly, though, I pull back, sucking her bottom lip in on my way. She whimpers and the sleeping giant inside of me awakens. Eagerly, I rush in to fully connect with her again. My tongue slides out to explore the slit between her lips, beckoning it to open. She complies and I dive in, wanting to taste her, ready to explore her mouth like no other. I feel her fingers thread into my hair, then grasp at it harshly, pulling me forward. The feeling of her tongue, sliding against mine ardently, confirming that this pull has not been all one-sided sends me off to a place I know I don't want to come back from.

I pull away. "Maddie," I say breathlessly. "I have to stop, otherwise, I won't be able to in a minute. I want to touch you. I want to touch you in a way that wouldn't be deemed appropriate on a first date," I almost beg. I need her to make me stop.

"This isn't our first date, Dec, remember?—fucking touch me!" She fists my shirt and attacks my lips.

I . . . um . . . holy shit—she's hot.

I dive back in. But this time, I let my hands wander. When my left hand travels up her side and grasps her right breast, Maddie pulls at my hair harder, encouraging me with the action and the sounds escaping her throat. Then, like someone went and pulled the plug—I stop.

Is she like this with every guy she has an interest in and how often?

I can't stop my thoughts. If this isn't something she did so very often, how could she be so comfortable doing it? And, how far would she actually let me go? How far does she let the other men go?

"Declan?"

"We should go." I sit up, readying myself to drive.

"Okay but, are you all right?"

"I'm good," I answer sharply.

"You're not," she insists.

"What's the address?" I ignore her inquisition.

"I'm not telling you until you tell me what just happened." She gives her dress one last pull, straightening it back into place.

I whip my head in her direction, "Is this the norm for you?" I bite.

"I don't understand your question," she says. I watch as her eyes dance around, seemingly taking me in, possibly trying to figure me out.

"Is this how you behave on every first date?" I almost seethe. This is not going to end well; I already know this. I'm pretty sure— at least, I hope—I already know the answer. I just can't manage to push away this irrational jealous moment of rage I'm having. Five minutes into this date and I'm royally screwing it up.

Maddie closes her eyes and begins some sort of breathing regimen. Every time she purses her lips to exhale, I feel the fabric of my pants strain from the rise she gives me. Her lips are so full and as soft as I had imagined. I want to claim them again. *Doubt that would go over well.* Just as I open my mouth to plead for her forgiveness, I notice her chin quiver. Her teeth lightly clamp onto her lip, as if she were trying to stop it. A look of disappointment washes over her face, and I feel my heart sink. I'm getting the sack; it's evident.

She finally opens her eyes, and I can see my confirmation loud and clear. Clearing her throat, she takes a deep breath, faces forward, and grabs her seatbelt to latch. "Two-twenty Forest Hill Drive."

I stare at her, dumbfounded.

"My mother won't like it if we're late," she adds. I put my car in reverse and head down her driveway, pulling out onto her street. "Take this first left. Go down four blocks and then take a right."

I do as I am told. I have a million things running through my head; I can't pick one single good one to say to her. I don't want her to analyze me. It's not fair of me to think this way, but I can't help it. I also can't say that to her again; she didn't like it the first time I said it. Besides, she's probably already analyzing me, and I don't know what I could say that may change her thinking of me. *I'm just not ready for this—damn it.* I thought I could be. I was wrong.

"There will be a fork in the road soon; stay to the right. You'll want to make the first right after and it's the fifth house on the left," she instructs as she pulls out her phone and starts texting.

"Who are you texting?" I cringe just as I say it. Why am I coming off as such a possessive freak? This is not me at all!

"Last night's first date. He left a few things behind when he left this morning. I want to make sure he picks them up," she states as she throws her cell back into her purse.

"Very cute, Maddie," I say under my breath.

"Hmm," she muses.

I lighten my grip on the steering wheel to allow color back to my knuckles. "Well, I'll be sure to grab all of my stuff in the morning." I glance over and give her a wink, trying my hardest to snap out of it.

"Ha! You wish." She crosses her arms and stares out her window.

I pull into her parents' driveway, whip the car into park, and turn to her. She brings her attention back to me. "You have no idea how badly I *do* wish."

Her eyes widen at my admission. "Well, it's not going to happen," she assures me, nose in the air . . . stubbornly.

"I know." I look down. "It won't ever happen." I shake my head before looking back up at her. "I thought I was ready to try at a relationship. It's clear from the way I insulted you, five minutes into this date, that I'm not. I'm sorry, Maddie. Let's just make the best of tonight and then we'll part ways."

"That's it? That's what you have to say?"

"I have a million things I want to say; nothing will be right. It appears I'm completely committed to sabotaging myself. I'll spare the both of us," I offer.

"By being a coward?"

"I'm not being a coward," I admonish. "I think I'm being very brave . . . selfless, if you will."

"I won't," she snaps. "Sprinkle whatever the hell you want on top of it but, at the end of the day, Dec, you are still handing me a load of crap!"

"It's not a load of crap!" I raise my voice.

"Right. You know what? Thank you." She raises her hands between us. "This was a great lesson learned, one I shouldn't have had to learn. I crossed boundaries. I should've never contacted you; it was unethical." She grabs the door handle and lets herself out.

"I'm not your patient!" I bark, getting out of my side.

"Well, you should be!" she screams back. I swear on my eyes, that statement just knocked the wind right out of my sails. Her face drops. "Oh, Dec . . . I'm sorry. I shouldn't have said that." She makes her way towards me and reaches up to touch my face. I jerk back, causing her hand to freeze mid-reach.

"Goodnight, Maddie," I breathe. I turn on my heels and climb back into my car, ignoring her calling out to me as I back down the driveway and leave.

I can't go home; he'll know I messed up.

Chapter Five

Maddie

"No way! Do *not* tell me you just beat my record!" Preston practically whines behind me on our parents' walkway. I'd like to say it's an act he's putting on for me to make me feel better, but it's not. Preston St. Claire is very proud of his "shortest date ever" record.

"Boo-yah, motherfucker," I say half-heartedly and offer him a slight smile as I turn to face him. It's more than I can really offer at the moment.

"I don't believe you. How long?" He looks at his watch.

I grab a hold of his wrist, looking down at it, as well. "Fifteen minutes, hombre."

"I'd lie down on the ground in defeat, but Cory's inside, waiting on you with baited breath. *Soooo*—still winning!"

"I wish I could quit *you!*" I marry the famous quote with my sarcasm. They went together nicely, I believe.

"Yeah, but if you did, you'd be all alone with June and Ward—same time, same channel—every day." He throws his arm around my shoulder, guiding me up the walkway.

"And what would the Beaver do without her older brother?" I chime in.

"For the love of all the *Flowers in the Attic*, please do not refer to yourself as the Beaver. It's just plain wrong." He shakes his head, and I laugh. I have a habit of making statements that I think will be casual or cool. *Think* is the keyword here. I won't question my brother's knowledge of *Flowers in the Attic* since I subjected him to the film adaptation of the book years ago. I then proceeded to tell him about the brother and sister getting it on and falling in love. Needless to say, I don't discuss the books I read with him anymore; he holds them against me.

"Speaking of beavers. . ."

"Nope. But, please feel free to turn more and more into our mother by asking me every damn week." He pulls me into an almost headlock and gives me a noogie. Apparently, this is something big brothers never grow out of doing.

"Can you act your age, please?" I complain.

"I am."

"Your real age. You know, the 'I'm getting ready to approach a midlife crisis' age," I tease.

Preston opens the door to my parents' Colonial, the house we grew up in. The only house on the block that looks as if it's still sheltering teenagers in the 90s.

"Mom! Look at who I found wandering the streets!" he yells out.

I glance down the small hallway off the grand entrance (though it's not that grand) and see my mother making a beeline for me. Her eyes wild with excitement as she takes in my dress. "You look lovely, darling! Cory won't be able to keep his eyes off you in that dress."

"Yes, he'll be dying to know 'who' you are wearing?" Preston says under his breath.

"You are a certifiable asshole," I say under my own as I elbow him.

Just then, Mom envelops me in her arms. "I can't wait to tell you all about our cruise."

"Great!" See?—It'll be different in person.

"Well, I hate to cut this short, but I just got paged to the hospital," my brother pipes up. I immediately let go of my mother to turn to him with pleading eyes.

"I didn't know you were on call tonight," Mom pouts but in a playful manner.

"I wasn't, but apparently there's been a midwife crisis I need to deal with." He raises an eyebrow at me. I mouth "asshole" to him. He gives me a wink.

Judith St. Claire and Eliza Peterson were clearly separated at birth. I'm almost two hours into the evening I will forever dub "the night I met my soul mate." Of course, Mom and Eliza think we mean this in the traditional way (Cory and I made the announcement an hour ago), and they are verbally hi-fiving the hell out of each other for their mastery in match-making.

Yes, exactly one hour and two minutes ago, Cory and I fell in love with each other over a conversation about shoes. He noticed (he's the *only* one who noticed) my retro shoes from the 1940s. They are called the Ballet Dancer's Red Shoes, a replica, made by Chinese Laundry. The high platform sole, raised four inch heel, and delicate ankle strap give me the classy "pop" I love to utilize shoes for.

He demanded to know the name of the thrift shop I bought them from.

I gave it to him.

He said, "Hmm," with a nod.

He demanded to know the price I paid for them.

I gave it to him.

He gasped in excited disbelief.

He asked me if I knew the history behind the shoe.

What I knew—I gave it to him.

(They were made with cloth just like in France during that time because leather was not allowed but allocated to the war effort for soldier's boots and shoes instead.)

What he knew—he gave it to me.

(Ballet shoes were the exception. Made out of leather or canvas, women would carve an insole out of cardboard to stick in the ballet slippers and wear as a regular shoe.)

Shoe porn is underrated. Another five minutes and I would've been ordering a strap-on to match my shoes. I think we both know who the "top" would be.

"Son, why don't you tell Maddie about the promotion you're up for?" Mr. Peterson shuffles his hand our way. You can clearly tell that he is uncomfortable, what with the way he jumped into our conversation like that; his nervous energy.

Diagnosis: Veritaphopia—Fear of knowing, telling, and revealing the truth.

What?! I can't help it when people make it so easy.

Cory's smile falls. He takes in a deep, consoling breath (I think that was more for him than me) as he closes his eyes, then re-opens with a look like he's "on." My heart may be breaking a little at the moment. No one should have to put an act on for anyone, not parents, lovers, friends—no one! "I'm being considered for Managing Partner." He gives me a warm smile.

"Cory works for JBT Financing Group. He's really made a name for himself in the financial world," his dad throws in.

"I'm guilty of all names but one," he admits then pokes at the inside of his left cheek with his tongue in a suggestive manner that makes a giggle escape me.

Mr. Peterson clears his throat, "Anyhow, his already bright future has turned up several watts. With his financial security, good looks, and chivalrous attitude—"

"—But, wait—there's more!" Cory cuts his dad off, poking fun at Mr. Peterson's sales pitch.

"He'll make a great catch. Any woman should be honored to have his affections," his dad finishes off with a lot less gusto.

"You left out smartass; I'm disappointed in you," Cory says as he sits back, allowing my mother to place a cup of coffee in front of him.

"I was hoping she wouldn't notice that wonderful trait." He half smiles then grabs the creamer to put in his own coffee.

"Maddie's a smart girl; I'm sure she's noticed all the colors of my rainbow personality." He winks at me. I have, and I love each and every one. Jay may have some competition.

I look back over at his dad. He has a somber expression on his face as he watches his spoon swirl around and around in his coffee. I certainly wouldn't audition to be one of Dionne Warwick's psychic network friends, but it looks to me like Mr. Peterson is ending his last cycle of denial; it's finally hitting home.

What I am witnessing is one of the many symptoms of the human condition: expectation. The Petersons brought to this world a very intelligent, handsome, and courageous boy. They poured what was left of their hopes and dreams into him. Of course they expected—what they considered—a perfect outcome: wife, kids, career . . . a house with a white-picket fence, even. I think I have a good enough read on them to know that they aren't the "let's find you Jesus, so he can taketh the gayeth away" type of parents. They are the "I'm afraid for him" parents. Afraid for his safety, afraid he won't be able to achieve the goals he has set forth in life, and afraid he'll never have that family they dreamed of him having someday.

Fear is so powerful. To me, it's the most fascinating symptom of the human condition, and that's why I've made it the one I specialize in. The good thing about Cory having this type of parental unit, compared to the other, is that there, most likely, won't be any feelings of abandonment on either side. Oh sure, they might hurt each other here and there, but these are the type of parents you want in this situation (besides the ones that automatically don't care who you love). Eventually, they will fully accept his sexual orientation, and soon after, they will realize that being gay doesn't hinder him from anything. He can have it all. Safety? It doesn't matter if your kid is gay, straight, bi, black, white, Hispanic, yada yada—you will always worry about their safety.

"Mr. Peterson?" I call out softly. He looks up from his coffee, giving me his attention just as my mother and Cory's mother walk back into the dining room. "He's going to be just fine." I keep my eyes steady on him. "The only thing that can hold any of us back from our dreams is ourselves," I add.

"Owen? What is she talking about?" Mrs. Peterson asks as she heads over to the seat next to him, her voice cracking.

"You know, Eliza dear." He grabs her hand as she sits.

"Wait—you guys know?!" Cory asks in disbelief.

"Yeah, son. We were hoping it was just a phase." Mr. Peterson shrugs.

"The Backstreet Boys are still my favorite boyband," Cory states in a matter-of-fact tone as he shoots them a sarcastic look.

"Valid point, son." His dad chuckles.

"I don't understand what's going on here," my mother interrupts.

"I'm gay, Mrs. St. Claire," Cory informs her.

"But you're so good looking; you just need to find the right girl."

"I think I'll stick with the left ones; they understand me the best." He winks.

48

"I don't get it," my mother says.

"That's because it's all happening in Technicolor," I chide.

"What?" she asks just as confused.

"Don't worry about it, Judith." His mom gives mine a smile. "However, if you don't mind, I think we'll be heading home now. It seems my family has a few things we need to discuss."

"Oh. Well, please, take a pie home with you; I've made two," Mom offers as she stands up. "Maddie, can you please go let your father know that our guests are leaving?" She turns to me.

"Don't worry about it, Judith. Just let him know that I'll call him about the game," Mr. Peterson assures her. My mother gives a nod and a smile, but I know she is embarrassed beyond belief. My dad sticks to his schedule come rain or shine. It doesn't matter if the Queen of England is here; an hour after dinner means an hour in the crapper, working on a royal flush—for the Queen, of course.

"Would you guys mind dropping me off at my house? I don't live too far from here." I bite my lip and wince a little unsure if they would mind.

"Where's your car, Maddie?" Mom asks.

"A friend dropped me off. I thought he would stay, but he had to leave." Now I'm the one who's embarrassed.

"We can do that; no problem." Cory smiles and gets up as well.

We all say our goodbyes (several were awkward. I'll let you guess who made it that way) and head out. Just as I climb into the backseat of their car, I grab my phone out of my purse. I had the volume turned off and I just want to make sure I didn't get any emergency calls. I put my pin in to unlock my screen, and Declan's face is in a Facebook messenger bubble with the number three next to it, indicating he left that many messages. I click on it.

I shouldn't have left you like that.

Please let me know when you're ready to leave.

I have no problem picking you up.

Fuck off.

"Damn. Who is that and what the hell happened?" Cory whispers, leaning over to me so his parents can't hear us.

"The guy I had hoped would turn into 'thee guy.'" Just as I say it, I feel my heart clenching. I just can't get over what he said to me. Should I have acted aggressively like that? Probably not. But, we're adults, for Christ's sake. We both, I think, have been crushing on each other for a little while. Why was my behavior such a big deal? Besides . . . I'm horny as hell! Everybody in the *entire* world—but me—is getting laid.

"Okay, but what happened?"

"I don't know. I honestly don't know. We were fine one minute, and the next, he was insulting me. He wasn't setting out to do that; I know that much. But, it still hurt just the same. Why can't I just meet someone normal?" I groan under my breath.

"There is no such thing as 'normal.' There is only 'normal enough for you.'" He pats my leg.

Just then, my phone pings again with another message. I look down.

Do you have a ride home?

Yes. Cory (blind date) is bringing me home.

We actually hit it off pretty well.

"Don't do that." Cory taps my phone. "I know you're pissed, but playing games isn't going to get you anywhere."

"I know." I sigh. "This is not me. I don't behave this way. I just want him to leave me alone so I can think," I ramble.

"How is a response like that going to help you think? It's just going to trigger an argument that will snowball out of control, and you won't even remember what you needed to think about it in the first place because you'll be so pissed about the other nonsensical things you two said." He looks away.

"Getting a flashback?"

"Yes."

"I'm sorry." I grab his hand and squeeze it. "Do you want to talk about it?"

"We broke up a year ago and not a day goes by that I don't miss him." He takes in a deep breath as if he's trying to ward off the emotions that are boiling to the top.

"Can you reach out to him?" I ask. I glance up toward his parents. I have to say; I'm impressed. They may not be able to hear what we are talking about, but they must be able to hear the sound of us whispering and yet, they don't question us. I call out the next turn to them before I give Cory my focus again.

"I have. He won't talk to me, though."

Suddenly, alarms start ringing off in my head. Oh no! Oh please don't let this mystery guy be Jay! It can't be! It would ruin my universe. I want to keep Cory around, but I'd never choose him over Jay. "Cory?"

"Yeah?"

"Please tell me it's not Jay." I cringe.

"Uhh . . . no." He laughs.

"Oh, thank God! I thought my day had really gone to shit: losing a prospective boyfriend *and* a gusband." I let out a big sigh of relief.

"Jay and I are cool. Although, he may not be happy with me taking away one of his sister wives." He winks.

"He'll get over it. Besides, I'm only wife number two; Charley's the queen bee of his heart." I smile at him before turning my head to focus at my house coming into view. The very house with a Viking statue in front of it.

"Well, looks like it'll take more than a cyber flip off to make this guy quit," Cory says as he leans near my ear. "You shouldn't quit that either; you should climb it, girl, like your name is Xena: Warrior Princess."

I smack his chest and go into a fit of giggles. "Give me a hug, smartass." I throw my arms around him.

"Adding more fuel?" he inquires.

I hush him. "Thank you for the ride, Mr. and Mrs. Peterson." I let go of Cory and give both of their shoulders a little squeeze before grabbing the door handle.

"Our pleasure, sweetie." Mrs. Peterson smiles back at me.

"I want a full report, ASAP," Cory warns, shaking a finger at me.

"Yes, sir." I kiss his cheek and then climb out. I close the door and head up my walkway, watching Declan fidget.

Put his luggage in my trunk—no—put his luggage in the trunk!

I really need to get laid.

Chapter Six

Declan

My heartbeat races. I can feel the sweat pooling into my palms as she heads up the walkway towards me. She seems very relaxed. Maybe it was that guy Cory that put her in this state. Of course, this idea doesn't help me with *my* state. *Stop, Dec!*

"You have a license to stalk here?" she asks calmly as she retrieves her keys from her purse.

"I wasn't aware they were handing those out these days," I play along.

"Oh, they give out a license for everything now." She looks up at me then jiggles her keys and nods towards her door. "Can I . . .?"

"Yes! Yes, of course; I'm sorry." I move out of the way once I get my fumbling mouth all sorted.

She walks by me and proceeds to unlock the door. "You want to come in?" she asks over her shoulder.

"If you don't mind the company of an unlicensed stalker, I'd love to." I give her a slight smile.

"I'll take my chances." She holds the door open for me. I give her a curt nod and walk in, battling to keep my nerves calm. I'm not quite sure why she's even allowing me to enter her house after tonight's debacle. "Have a seat." She holds her hand out, directing me to the living room. "I'm going to get a glass of wine, would you like some?"

"Sounds lovely, thanks," I answer as I find a seat on her olive-green couch.

While she's in the kitchen, I take the time to really study my surroundings. I can't help but smile about the similarities between Maddie and her bungalow. When looking from the outside, her house seems quaint and cute, like Maddie. Being inside, however, totally blows my socks off; it's massive compared to the quaintness of outside—much like Maddie (her personality, I mean).

"Your fireplace is gorgeous," I say as she walks back in with two glasses of red.

"Oh, thank you! The house is a new build, but I really wanted it to look like an older house." She takes a seat next to me. "I love the sophistication and warmth of an older home as opposed to most, nowadays, who are all for the contemporary look."

"I think you pulled it off. I love all the dark wood." I look up at the large beams going across the room.

"Can you guess my favorite part of this room?" She taps my lap excitedly. I can't help but chuckle at her childlike behavior.

"Hmm. . ." I trail off as I look around. It wouldn't be the fireplace since we already discussed it. The archway to the dining room has entablatures with built-in, glass-encased bookshelves. "The archway?" I point.

"Yes! I love to go to antique shops or flea markets and find older versions of the classics to put on the shelves." She looks over her shoulder at them.

"What kind of classics . . . which ones?" I inquire. I could listen to her talk about herself—her life—all night.

"Oh, any I can get my hands on really. I have Jane Austen, Mark Twain, Harper Lee, Emerson, Thoreau, just to name a few." She takes a sip of her wine. "I love the bindings of the old books; goes with the feel of the house."

"So, have you read them all?" I entice my palette, as well.

"Heck no! I like my trashy novels." She nods her glass before having some more.

"Trashy novels?" The corner of my mouth slowly lifts as if it's reacting to a magnetic pull.

"The dirtier—the better. It has to have a good storyline, though," she adds quickly.

"Yes, of course; it's essential," I quip.

"Are you making fun of me?" She tilts her head.

"Never." I reach out to graze my knuckles down her cheek, but she jerks her head away from my gesture. I let my hand fall slowly. "Sorry," I murmur.

She looks down rather than at my face. Her left hand finds the cross on her chain and she slides it back and forth, seemingly in deep thought. "Ooh!" Her head pops up. "I have a great idea." She jumps up and walks to the hallway on the right side of the fireplace. Not a moment later, and she's walking back in with index cards and two pens in her hand. "Here's three index cards." She hands them to me. "We're both going to write one thing to discuss on each card." She smiles and sits back down, busying herself. I let out a frustrated sigh. Is she really going to turn this into a therapy session? She *did* say I should be her patient. Just as I am about to tell her that I'm leaving, she looks over and nudges into me. "It could be anything, Declan, favorite music, most influential person in history. The girls and I do this every once in a while; it's fun. Of course, we always find a way to make our topics turn inappropriate." She laughs.

"You do this with your friends?" Shit, is she trying to put me in the friend zone? *Not happening.*

"Yup. We've known each other forever so it's a fun way to see how much we really do or don't know about one another," she says as she finishes one card and flips it over onto the coffee table.

"Maddie?"

"Yes?"

"Don't you want to discuss what happened earlier?" I find it very odd that she hasn't even attempted.

"Nope. It's in the past. I'm going to stay hopeful that your moment of douchebaggery was out of character for you and probably won't happen again," she states as she continues to write. "Now, hurry up; I'm almost done." She whacks my leg.

I look down at the index cards and begin to scribble.

1. Music.

2. Favorite place to be kissed.

3. Smells—love and hate.

There! I'm very pleased with my quick thinking and even more pleased with my boldness for number two.

"I'm done." She straightens up.

"Ladies first." I gesture to her cards.

"Ok. Number one: favorite time of the day?"

"Four a.m.," I answer.

"What?!" She looks at me as if I'm crazy.

"I work out at that time; it gets my head on straight for the rest of the day."

"Wow. I'm probably just finishing up my first full REM cycle at that hour."

"Maddie, that's not good. You need your sleep." I grab her hand and squeeze.

"Ha! Tell that to my brain."

"Have you tried Yoga?" Just as I ask, I remember her talking about Yoga with her friends all of the time. "Never mind; I forgot for a moment about Ava's studio." I bring her hand up to my lips. "So tell me, when is yours?" I ask before planting a kiss on the back of her hand.

"Late at night. I run a hot bath, get a glass of wine and a book. It helps so much to quiet my mind after a long day filled with weaving through the problems my clients face." Her cheeks flush.

"Do you ever talk to a colleague about your clients or whatever you're going through?" I could only imagine the kind of weight that burden must carry.

"Yes, I do. I talk to Lana every few months or so. She comes to me, too. It's very helpful as we bounce ideas off each other very well." She leans towards the coffee table and swipes her wine back up. "Your turn," she states with a nod before she takes a sip. The fact that she's allowed her hand to stay in mine is very encouraging.

"Oh . . . um. . ." I look down. "My first category is music. What are you partial to?" I ask, fully focused on her lips that are lingering at the rim of her glass, her eyes squinting. I can tell she's in deep thought about my question, and she's absolutely adorable.

Suddenly, she jerks her head back. "Why are you smirking at me like that?"

"Sorry. I was just sitting here, watching you in deep thought and I couldn't help but think how adorable you are. I hope that doesn't offend you, being called adorable," I add quickly.

"I've been called worse, believe you—me!" She widens her eyes, then relaxes again, the corners of her mouth curve up. "Adorable's not so bad; it's sweet."

I reach up for another attempt to brush her cheek.

Success.

So soft. . .

"There's definitely a lot of sweetness here," I surmise.

"Wow . . . that was cheesy." She laughs. I can't help but join her; that was cheesy.

"Alright, that's enough, young lady. You haven't answered." I tap her nose lightly with my finger.

"Oh right! I love all different types, but lately, I've been on an Indie kick. You?"

"Classical, which is a given. But I do love the old stuff." I reach for my glass as well.

"Do you mean Big Band music?" She curls her legs under her and rubs at her left ankle.

"Why do you wear such high heels, Maddie? Come, give them here!" I place my wine back down after a sip, release her hand, and motion her to give me her feet.

"No, you don't have to." She pushes my hand away.

"I want to. Give," I demand.

"No. They've been in shoes all night." She shakes her head.

"Now," I get more stern.

Maddie studies me for a moment before rolling her eyes. "Fine," she says in a frustrated groan then uncurls her legs and places her feet in my lap. I start with her right foot; it's so little.

"I think these are the cutest feet I've ever had the pleasure to rub."

"I rather like them myself. My best feature." She smiles.

"Hardly!" I bark.

"Oh? What do you think my best feature is?" She tilts her head.

"Well, I haven't seen all of your features . . . yet." I waggle my eyebrows, making her laugh. "However, from what I have seen, you are perfectly beautiful from head to toe; how can I choose?"

She laughs but it sounds a bit sarcastic. "You've got quite the balance going."

"What do you mean?"

"You know all the right and *wrong* things to say, and you manage to say them both well."

"Wrong?" I furrow my brow.

"Ahem," she drinks more of her wine, "what you said earlier," she adds quickly.

"Maddie, I—"

"—No. I don't want to talk about it."

"We should, though. It's unhealthy not to do so."

"What's the point, Declan? I'm giving you an opportunity to not have to waste your time back-peddling."

"Why?" I ask sharply. "Why are you giving me a chance at all?"

"There are a lot of reasons," she states calmly before hitting her wine again.

"What are they?"

She leans into the couch as she cradles her glass close to her chest. "For one, we all come with some sort of past. But, we are all affected by them differently. I know that your behavior today was most likely due to your past. I also know that you are not ready to discuss it, so I won't push anymore. Finally, I know that it is human nature to lash out at people we feel safe around. *There!* I analyzed you. I can't help it; I've been analyzing people way before I ever threw a degree up on my wall," she finishes in a very defensive stance, waving her hand around.

"I do feel safe around you," I offer before I can even think about stopping myself. "But, I felt that way about another. Let's just say, I'm not the intuitive type." I focus down on her feet, switching to the other one.

"She probably gave you good reason to—until she didn't anymore. How old was she when she changed?"

"Early twenties."

"Well, I'm thirty-four. Pretty stuck in my ways, unlike an easily impressionable twenty-year-old girl."

I look up at her. "No way!"

"No way, what?"

"No way you're thirty-four!" Honestly, I didn't peg her to be older than twenty-eight.

"I am. Why, how old are you?" A hint of insecurity flashes across her face.

"Thirty-two, Gramma." I wink.

"That's not nice." She pouts.

"Don't do that."

"What?"

"Stick your bottom lip out like that," I warn as I hone in on that delicious lip.

"My age doesn't bother you?"

"Not at all." I reach up again, cupping her cheek. "How is it that no one has snagged you up yet?" I lean in.

"I'm picky." She shrugs.

"Number two," I breathe.

"Huh?" She leans close to me.

"My question. Number two is: where is your favorite place to be kissed?" I line up our mouths.

"I like kisses on my neck. Most importantly, though, I love Australian kisses."

I lean back away from her; curiosity is killing the cat. "This seems like an odd question, me being from Australia and all, but what's an Australian kiss?"

"Oh, it's the same as a French kiss, only, it's down under," she states straight-faced. I, however, burst into laughter.

"You are a bold one, my little minx." I pull her to me so that she's just about on my lap. I can't remember the last time I smiled this big. I can only imagine that her smile matches what mine must look like. I grasp her neck with my right hand, holding her still as I slam my lips against her own. At first, her body tenses but within seconds, she sighs a sigh of contentment, and she practically melts against me. I lick across the slit of her lips, willing them to part. They comply, and I waste no time deepening the kiss. Her left leg slides over my lap so she can straddle me. The material of my pants stretches to accommodate the change in my adrenaline. My hands find residence on her hips and grasp tightly, holding her in place as my hips rise to grind into her. A moan escapes her throat.

Maybe it's the last copious sips I took of my wine affecting me, but any sort of gentleman that existed inside of me has gone missing. Mindlessly, I go for it. My hands slide down her thighs only to return, gliding the hem of her dress up with them.

I feel so raw—so bloody turned on; I want to tear her in two and gently make love to her all at once. Her fingers thread through my hair.

She pulls.

I groan, knead her ass, and suck in her bottom lip, releasing it only to catch it quickly with my teeth.

I bite.

She yelps, tugs my hair harder, grinds against me harshly, and attacks my lips.

Check, please!

Any reserve I had has followed the gentleman into the abyss. I toss her down on the couch and climb on top quickly. "Open!" I command. Instantly, her legs part fully and wrap around my waist. Cupping her cheek, I run my thumb across her bottom lip, taking the sight of her in; her beautiful, bright green eyes are now several shades darker. Her nostrils flare with each rapid breath she takes as if that action would keep her under control. Her lips are slightly red and puffy, giving solid proof of my attack on them. I soak in her beauty.

"Declan. . ." she trails off in a whisper. My eyes dart back to hers. "Are you . . . are you thinking badly of me again?" her voice is quiet still and the shake in it gives way to her nerves.

It takes me a moment to register what she just asked me and I jerk up immediately. "No, Maddie! God, no!" I tap and pull her legs off of me so that I may sit up proper. I run my hand through my hair in frustration as I try to think of what to say—the *right* thing to say. Maddie slowly slides back and up to a seated position, pulling her dress down.

She clears her throat, nervously. "I . . . um . . . I haven't been

with anyone in two years," she softly informs me. "This isn't . . . um
. . . my usual behavior."

She's definitely nervous; that's the only time she "ums." Boy,
have I made a mess of things. "We've both had too much wine," I
say. Clearly, I'm not capable of saying the right thing. "What I mean
to say," I add quickly as her mouth opens to speak, "is that we're
both, possibly, behaving out of character." Well, that's no better. *I'm
complete shit at this!*

"Possibly?" She tilts her head to the side. "So, that means that
there's a chance you believe this is my norm?"

"No!"

"You insinuated that earlier, why the change of heart?" her tone
much sharper now.

"I find only the wrong words," I say in defeat. I don't want to
argue with her. I've made a terrible impression on her that I don't
know how to change.

"Keep digging; you're bound to come across some right ones."

"I don't believe I know how to ride a bike anymore."

"I haven't gone ice skating in twenty years. I'd probably suck at
it more now than ever. What does any of that have to do with right
now?"

I chuckle lightly. She raises an unamused brow at me. I decide
it's best to explain what I mean, Lord help me. "Everyone has been
telling me for a long time to get back out there; it's like riding a bike.
Maddie, you're the first woman, in eight years, who has inspired
me enough to climb up on that bike. Today, despite very sweet moments, has been a complete disaster. It's like I fall just as I get my
feet set on the pedals. I don't know what I'm doing." I take in a deep
breath. "I was a jerk earlier, said stupid stuff. Just now, when I hesitated, staring at you? I was admiring your beauty. But, I studied
you too long maybe because instead of seeing my admiration, you
saw me questioning your virtue. First day and I'm doing everything
wrong. I sent you a *cock tree* for *Christ's sake!*" I groan and bury my

face into my hands.

Within moments, I feel Maddie's hand below the back of my neck. I lift my face up. Apparently, this is a cue for her to sit on my lap. I'm not complaining; don't get me wrong—whole bike metaphor issue (I'm bound to miss a pedal). I've never felt so clueless in my life. *Well, that's not true.*

"Declan, three things," she says as she places her other arm around my neck. I stare at her, unwilling to trust any words that I may let out. "First: I was right. I knew if you kept digging, you'd find the right words. You did." She plants a soft, quick kiss on my lips, leaving me hungry for more. "Second: every new relationship—no matter what kind—comes with training wheels. How else would we learn about the other person? You don't walk into any type of relationship as if you know that person already. That's just unrealistic. Everything in life has a learning curve." Another kiss. "Third: I love the cock tree. And not just because I love cock, but because you took the time to put thought behind the person I am. The person who loves flowers and plants but can't keep one alive even if there were a gun held to her head. It's hard to kill a cactus." She gives me yet another kiss though this one is difficult as I am still laughing about the calm and cool way she just said she loved cock.

"I got a lot of flak for sending that to you. It made me second guess the gift I brought you tonight," I admit.

"Oh! I didn't open it yet! Should I open it now?!" she asks, her child-like excitement returning.

"Please do. I feel more confident about it now." I smile. She squees and gives me another kiss before letting go to get up and grab it off the foyer table. How does she bounce back so quickly? I mean, I've been quite the case today. Before I can put any more thought into it, she's back and takes a seat next to me. "It's for work," I state as she slides her fingers under the tape. She tears into it quickly, making me laugh again. She does that a lot . . . make me laugh. When she reveals the Feet Warmer and Massager by Sharper Image she shoots me an inquisitive look. "You always wear such high heels; I know some of them make your feet ache. I also know that you constantly take them off when you're with a client. It can be cold in the office at times. Half the time, when you're rubbing your feet, I'm not sure if it's because you're feet hurt, or they're cold, or both. So, I want you to bring this to work and plug it in. As soon as your client takes a seat, you can take your shoes off and have a nice massage while your feet are kept warm," I explain. Her eyes fill up. "Did I say something wrong again?" I panic.

"Not only are you pedaling, there's no one holding onto the back of your seat." She throws her arms around my neck again and attacks my lips, box in between us.

"Christ," I pull away, "I'm glad I didn't give you jewelry; I don't think it would've warranted this reception."

"Shh. . . keep pedaling." She pushes the box out from between us and straddles my lap again.

"Maddie. . ." I move my head back from her advances.

"What?"

"I think I should leave now."

"I'm sorry—*what?!*"

"I want you; do not misunderstand this. I want to leave on a good note with lots of promise." I cup her face, letting my thumbs caress her cheeks.

"Declan, I'm really into you. I'm on your lap, grinding into you with panties whose dam is about to break because the hot number underneath it hasn't had a lead role in two years, if you know what I mean. I'd say you're doing pretty good in the 'lots of promise' department."

"I'm not trying to upset you."

"Then stop. I'm a grown ass woman—we both are. Well, you're a guy. . . but you know what I mean. There's no goddamn schedule of when things are supposed to happen. They happen when they feel right," she preaches.

"It doesn't feel right. I don't think we should have sex when I'm getting on a flight tomorrow, not seeing you for weeks. No, Maddie. I am very interested in kissing the breath out of you before I leave, but that is all I will be doing tonight." Ah! The gentleman returns!

Maddie abruptly climbs off my lap and heads out of the room to the foyer. I get up to follow her, curious. She opens the door and waves her hand suggestively. Maybe dismissively is a better word. "Goodnight, Declan."

"May I kiss you?" I ask unsure.

"I would just like you to leave." She looks everywhere but at me.

"Maddie?"

"Bye."

"May I see you when I come back?"

She refuses to look at me but manages to nod her head slowly in agreement.

"I have to say that I'm very confused."

"Better than being embarrassed," she mutters.

"You have no reason to be embarrassed," I say in disbelief.

"Please go."

"Maddie?"

"Go!" she finds her voice.

"I'll see you in a few weeks, then." I reach to touch her face, but she jerks her head away. I fall, skinning my knees.

You do know that was metaphorical, right? I didn't actually just fall before her, skinning my knees. That would've been awkward, don't you agree? All right, carry on, then.

I take in a deep breath and let it escape through my pursed lips quickly before I finally give up. I'm no sooner out the door and she's slamming it behind me.

Complete shit at this.

Chapter Seven

Maddie

"I. Am. *Never*. Drinking. *Again!*" I state before I give the porcelain god another hug and heave-ho. "What. The. Fuck. Did. I. Drink?" Why do I always sound like Captain Kirk when I'm drunk?

I deserve this. It's what I get for clearing out my cabinets last night. Everything just tasted wonderful and like there was purpose behind it. *Oh God, look away!*

"Uggggghhhhh!"

I wipe my mouth with the back of my hand and flush "purpose" down the toilet. "Please . . . make it stop. I promise I'll never do it again," I plead with The Almighty.

An hour goes by. . .

I'm drunk, so it's probably really like only two minutes, spanning an hour.

Right?

What the fuck was I saying?

I'm grateful. Yes, that's it! I'm grateful. I am now past the porcelain god stage and smack dab in the middle of the uncoordinated sex stage . . . with myself. You know what I'm talking about, right? Odd poking about, over enthusiastic grunts (even though you're not sure if you're feeling anything at the moment), and the reenactment of Viking dialogue. Oh. You don't have the reenactment during your self-expeditions? It's just as well; he started sounding like Sean Connery in the end. Not sure how that happened, but that's a guy who could slap his wrinkled balls against most any woman still. Am I right?

CiCi's right; vibrators are so fucking loud. I think they do it on purpose to make a woman feel guilty about pleasing herself. Not me. That shit could sound like a Boeing 787, and I'd have my landing strip ready for it. Speaking of landings. . .

Yes! Yes! Yes!

Wait.

No!

No, c'mon!

C'mon, c'mon, c'mon!

Damn it!

Elvis has left the building.

Fuck my life.

"Blake, I need a Jack and Coke." I slam my fist down on the bar like I'm in some type of old western movie.

"Jack and Coke?" He raises both eyebrows.

"Yes, damn it—*now!*"

"On the house, shortstack." He gives me a slow smile. Blake

knows that when I turn to Jack, my day has been all shades of shit. He gestures "hello" with a nod of his head to whomever it is that has walked through the door. "You girls want your usual?" he asks.

Thank God my friends are here! I turn to watch them parade over. They all have smiles on their faces. Why wouldn't they?— they're all getting fucking laid! *Bitches!* Here I am, "captain" of the Asswhores, and I'm not even getting so much as a slip of a pinky in my ass!

"Captain, my captain!" They greet me in unison . . . while kissing a bird off to me. It's their new ritual.

"Whoa! What the fuck is this?" CiCi booms, looking at my drink. "You haven't had a Jack and Coke in months."

"Let's sit." I gesture to our table. *Our* table, that is always miraculously unoccupied by anybody else, at any given time, like the couch at Central Perk on *Friends*. Yes, I'm totally singing the theme song in my head. *God, Rachel had great hair.*

"Maddie! Hello?" Julie waves her hand in front of my face.

"Sorry, I was jammin' to the theme song to *Friends*." I focus back. Not a minute goes by, and Charley is tapping the beat on the table, CiCi and Julie are singing the lyrics, and Ava is doing the guitar sounds. I, of course, throw in the clap (not that kind of clap!) and do the awkward dancing around since I'm the only one not seated.

"Should I even bother to ask?" Blake laughs as he places our drinks down.

"We need a fucking couch, dude!" CiCi informs him.

"One that we can randomly move outside, in front of the water fountain," Julie adds.

"What water fountain?" he asks.

"The one you should've erected for us a long time ago," Charley states.

"There's only one GEG that I will erect anything for, and that's this gorgeous thing, right here." He gets around to Julie and kisses the top of her head.

"Ok. . .stop." She nudges him away. Blake has been Julie's main course for a while but doesn't think we all know it, including him. **Gamophobia**—the fear of commitment. But, that's a story for another time.

"Bye, girls!" He rolls his eyes but takes off. I'm sure it's mostly due to the place getting packed.

"What's up, buttercup?" Ava smacks my hand.

"Oh . . . I think we should start from the beginning!" I take a seat and get ready to vent.

"Which was?" Charley leans in for a chip.

"I made a trip to the vibratory last night."

"I'm always in the vibratory." Julie passes it off.

"Yeah, well, it's been a while since I've gone so I may have had a marathon. I mean, I went at her like I owned her!" It was well over an hour; I know that much.

"Objection!" CiCi shouts.

"To what?" we all say.

"On the grounds that you do own her, so don't say stupid shit like that."

"Fuck you. Anyways . . ." I lean in. "This morning, I wake up to this buzzing noise. I wasn't ready to open my eyes yet, but I couldn't take it another minute. I went to move, and before I knew it, I had my answer." They all sit and stare at me. "I fucking left it in! I fell asleep!" I say in a low voice through my teeth.

"What kind of batteries do you use?" Ava manages after coughing a bit; her drink must've gone down wrong.

"Energizer."

"And that bunny just kept going and going. . ." four smartasses say as if they were the only ones who would come up with the irony.

"Are you all done now?" I say as soon as the last laugh ends.

"I don't know; we may *buzz* around here for a while, keeping our whistles wet." CiCi laughs.

"I can't stand you." I throw a peanut at her.

"Yeah, I love you too. Now, what's the story behind the story?" she asks before she brings her beer up . . . for the chugging contest?

"Whoa. . . what the hell is up with you?" Julie asks her mid-chug.

CiCi slams her beer down, belches ("burp" is too ladylike of a word to describe the Saskatchewan mating call that just bellowed from her), and wipes her mouth with the back of her hand. "I'm having a rough day, too," she offers. "Go first, though. I'm hoping your shit is worse than mine."

"That's so nice of you; thanks." I widen my eyes slightly and roll them.

"Let's go, or you'll lose your turn," Ava states impatiently. What the hell is that about? Are we all having a bad night tonight?

"Make sure to sit on an angle, Ava . . . you know—so I can hear when the timer, you've got up your ass, goes off. I wouldn't want to cut into anybody else's bitch session," I snide.

"Can everybody get off their rag so Maddie can get on the soapbox already?—Geez!" Charley groans.

"Sorry," Ava says, her chin quivering. We all stare at her. "Stop." She shakes her head dismissively, pats the corners of her eyes with her fingertips then fans at them. "Please go, Maddie," she begs. "I don't know what's wrong with me, so there's nothing to talk about. It's just fucking hormones from the fucking hormones I have to in-ject into my ass every week." The more she explains, the more irri-tated she gets.

"Maybe you should just tell Trent you don't want injections in your ass anymore." Julie smiles.

"I love my cape, though." Ava's mouth cheers up in the corners. We all giggle. Well, I snort. I can't wait for Christmas this year. I know that sounds like a random thought to you, but it will make sense once I tell you why.

Every Christmas, we all buy each other something like normal friends would do. But then, we decided—oh . . . about a decade ago—that while we still wanted to exchange like usual, we needed to add a new tradition to our ritual. To make it un-normal. . . you know . . . more like *us*. So, every year we each pick a name for the "special" gift. This gift has to represent one of the many inside jokes from that particular year. We do it on a special night, the first weekend in December, where we have a sleepover because Lord knows there will be a lot of drinking to coincide with the laughing. It's a great night and a great way to get our holiday season off to a start. It charges us up, and then we go out the next day, charging our cards up. Honestly, we've all secretly agreed that we look more forward to that weekend than Christmas at all. Luckily, with Charley being the only one with kids, the tradition has stayed pretty solid over the years. Hopefully, it always will.

The point of me telling you all of this (besides bringing forth fantastic ideas for other groups of women to partake in. . . yeah, I know you just looked at your calendar and thought of texting your bff. Do it after this paragraph, please) is because I am willing to bet all of my shoes (my pride and joy) that it won't matter whom picks who this year; we are all getting capes. In case this is your first rodeo with us, a couple of months ago we had a heated debate in Ava's yoga studio over calling each other asswhores . . . in public. Charley said that we sounded as if we should have capes with AW stitched on them like superheroes. And *that's* when we all announced the color of our capes. I said, "Red, white, and blue because I'm the captain, bitches!" Yeah . . . as you can see from the greeting they gave me, I haven't, nor will I ever, live that one down.

Once everyone calms down from our collective laughing fit, the girls encourage me to talk. Okay, they're pelting peanuts at me; no need for me to make us look like the cast of *Little Women*.

"Alriiiight—*stop!*" I guard my face with my arms. They finally finish their ambush. I relax my arms only to get one more to my forehead. I give CiCi a look that would translate into "really?" or "grow up!"

"It wasn't me!" she screeches in defense. Charley's doing a poor job of letting her sister take the blame by laughing so hard you can tell it's coming from her belly. I groan with frustration then give in a little to my own laugh.

There's no point in being frustrated; we've been this way forever. I wouldn't trade them. They are the sisters I never got to have biologically. Much to my parents' relief, I haven't mourned the absence of those biological sisters since the beginning of the sixth grade, when we moved here from Natick, Massachusetts.

Kids are assholes.

I know; another random thought. I was just thinking back to my first day at Hampstead Central. They called me "Velma," saying I looked like the character from *Scooby Doo*. I did, but that's beside the point. It hurt my feelings because they said it like it was a bad thing. Ruined that show for me for life. When it carried on to the playground at recess, it was Charley and Ava who came to my defense. And when *they* were ganged up on, it was CiCi and Julie who came to *our* defense. The other kids backed off not just because CiCi and Julie were eighth graders but because they were scarier than hell back then, too. They took me on as their fifth wheel that day, and we've been inseparable ever since.

Shit. Ava's hormones must be seeping over to me; she's the one who always brings up our memories and gets all emotional. I push away at the tears in the corner of my eyes. "I love you guys," I announce.

"Seriously, what is going on with you two? You're both starting to freak me out." Julie's focus goes from me to Ava and back to me. I look over at Ava, and she's in full-blown tears, not an "I just had a flashback and am feeling sentimental about our friendship" tears.

"Ava?" I ask, so concerned with my friend, I forget my worries for a moment. I hand her some napkins and rub her back. "What's the matter?"

"Trent," she sobs in a hiccup. "I think he's tired of me. Sex has become a chore for us. I can almost feel him cringing when I tell him it's time," she cries and leans my way to place her head on my shoulder.

Ava and Trent have been married for ten years. They've been trying to have a baby for nine. They look great on paper, but for some reason, it just hasn't happened for them, even *with* IVF. Charley, God bless her and her uterus, has stepped in to help them out by being a surrogate. While they wait for the doctors and Charley's body to get ready for that, they decided to go for one more round of IVF as a last ditch effort, just in case it doesn't work using Charley, either. They are so desperate; it breaks my heart. I have tried to guide them as much as I can during this process but A: I'm too close to the situation and them and B: I have absolutely no experience in this, whatsoever, to be guiding them well. They have seen Lana from time to time because of these reasons (read: I forced them to) but mostly, they come to me. It's what's most comfortable to them.

"I call bullshit!" CiCi yells because the band is starting to play. "I love you, Ava, but that is complete bullshit!"

Ava lifts her head off my shoulder like she's gonna fling the first thing she grabs at Ceese. "It's true!" She slaps the table instead.

"Last night you wore your leather pants. You know, the one that makes us all hot for your ass?" CiCi asks. We all groan. We joke around a lot, but there's not one of us around this table who's remotely into chicks. Yet, none of us are afraid to admit that Ava in her leather pants may actually persuade all of us to bat for the other team.

"If I could have a bronze statue of your ass in those pants, I would have one just so I could molest it as I walk by without anything ever becoming awkward between us," Julie admits.

"You've put a lot of thought into that, Julie. That, in itself, may be deemed "awkward." Ava laughs as she does the air quotations.

"Well, since we've reached that pinnacle, may I have your leather-pants-ass bronzed?" Julie bats her eyes. I glance at Charley and laugh at the look she gives me. She's always asking me to find medication for these girls—mostly CiCi.

"Can I get to my point, please?!" CiCi yells over everything and everybody now (It's *really* crowded in here now).

"What?!" we all yell back.

"Trent was eye fucking you all night! He watches you like a hawk. More like a lion, ready to pounce. There. Is. No. Way that dude is not into you anymore! Your brain is whacked from all of those hormones!"

"Really?" Ava sniffs.

"Yes!" we all scream in unison.

Ava stares at all of us; a slow smile crosses her lips like she's up to something. She pulls her phone out and begins to text. I lean over to be nosy. She's texting Trent, telling him she's thinking about the leather pants she wore last night and that it may be time to get rid of them. *We girls are clever, aren't we?* Except me; I'm not so clever. I finally find a guy I like, and I scare him off by throwing my vagina at him like a cavewoman. Ugh. I digress. . .

Trent immediately responds with a very commanding, "DON'T YOU FUCKING DARE!"

All is right in Ava's world, my friends.

Mine?

Ooga, ooga, ooogggahhhh!

I suck.

"Calling all GEGs, calling all GEGs! Get your sweet arses up here and make this band sound good!" Blake calls us out over the microphone. This is what happens when you are regulars at the local pub (Mick & Marley's), you're friends with the owner (with benefits, if your name is Julie. . . ahem), and you and your best friends have been singing together like you're waiting for your big break for over twenty years: you headline without warning or payment. They like us though and feed our egos—payment in full!

We're thrilled, of course, but we walk up there like we're doing *them* a favor. We act as if we're not sure what song to perform.

"Hit it!" CiCi commands into the microphone. The band starts up, and we perform "And We Danced" by Macklemore. We kill it, too. That may or may not be because we rehearsed it this weekend at Charley's.

What?!

Blake pulls this shit all of the time; you think we'd come unprepared? No way! We only make asses out of ourselves in our personal lives. There's no room for that shit on stage; you never know who's watching.

The dream is still alive . . . sadly.

Chapter Eight

Declan

I TAKE MY SEAT, CENTER STAGE, WITH OSCAR (VIOLA), DAVE (cello), Penelope (1st violin), and Shuang (2nd violin). Placing my cello between my legs, I take a deep, cleansing breath to put all my focus and energy into the piece we are about to play. It's Shubert's String Quintet in C Major, and it is pure magic; one of my most favorites.

Sliding my bow across, we begin, enticing the audience into a flirtation of notes that dance around them, pulling them onto the stage with us, where we can keep their attention hostage for the next twenty minutes.

I imagine Madelyn; the flirtation of the notes—foreplay. I imagine us laughing as I tickle her with notes, my hands dancing across her body, slowly focusing more on their expedition rather than the flirtation. The way her body arches, coinciding with the slow symphony. My hands determined on my instrument; my lips tasting her skin. Crescendo; my lips pull at her nipple, encouraged by the sounds that escape her throat.

My tongue glides across her chest, peeking out; playful notes . . . teasing. I climb; my hands search aggressively. Her body receptive to mine . . . to the music. It's like a drug. A healthy, wonderful drug. I'm lost in it. In the music. In her.

Danger.

I fight it. She pulls me back. We wrestle. She holds my face. I breathe in her calm.

She scares me.

My feelings scare me.

Her hands cup my face. Her eyes shine brightly in the moonlight.

She's mine. I am hers.

Her legs wrap around me fiercely.

My bow skirts across the strings softly, assuring me that I am safe. She nudges her nose against mine gently, her hands slide into my hair. "Please," she sings in a whisper so desperate, so vulnerable. I slide into her harshly and relish in her gasp. Releasing my hair, she wraps her arms around me, holding tightly as I move slowly . . . deeply inside of her.

Our eyes are locked onto each other.

My cello vibrates between my legs.

Maddie arches her neck.

Final Crescendo.

We fall.

It's been two weeks. Two weeks of performances; a different city every other night. Two weeks of messages on bloody Facebook because I was a right idiot, never asking for her personal number. Oh, I've called her office. Yes, I've had several long-winded chats with her voicemail. I've begged her not to be embarrassed. I even mentioned my fantasy every night on stage while I play Shubert, just to even the playing field. Nothing.

I know she reads the messages because it indicates she does so. I'm starting to feel like an idiot. Told her as much, too. I've only got one more thing to tell her. I click onto the message icon and am shocked when I see a message from her. I never heard the alert.

Madelyn St. Claire: Charley, what's the name of the vibrator you recommended? The Viking and I were lost in the throes of passion last night and mine broke. Perhaps I should buy two. FML. #NoShame #BecauseYouAlreadyKnowTooMuch I have to get back to work, just leave the name here. Thanks! Love ya!

I'm seeing red.

Possibly hyperventilating.

The Viking? *The VIKING?* Who. The. Fuck. Is. The. Viking?! That's it—I'm done! Message *finally* received, loud and clear! I don't need this kind of shit in my life again.

Declan Pierce: The Viking, huh? Two years?—my arse! Next time, pay attention to who the hell you are messaging. You could've had the decency to respond just once to tell me you were not waiting and that you've already moved on! Instead, you let me carry on every day. You signed for my gifts, never once refusing or returning them. Was this a fun little game for you to play—you're that bored? Goodbye, Maddie. Hope you and the Viking are happy.

I hit send. Then . . . I block her. I slam my laptop shut and throw it across the room.

"Dude, what the fuck?" Oscar gasps. It was a rather sudden movement, and Oscar is terribly afraid of his own shadow. Not really, but he comes off that way; very jumpy.

"If I hear one more person tell me to get back on the bike or make myself available, or anything else that comes *remotely* close to those bloody, pathetic words of encouragement, I may be arrested for bodily harm!" I get up to pick up the shattered pieces of my laptop.

"She finally answered you?" He sits up in his bed and puts his glasses on. We were supposed to be getting to sleep early as we have a flight to Venice at 6 a.m. He'll probably request a different roommate tomorrow night. I know I would, if I were him.

"Oh, she answered all right!" I say through my gritted teeth.

"Can I ask what she said?"

"She messaged me by accident. It was addressed to her friend and she talked about the guy she is having a relationship with." My breaths come fast and hard as I pace.

"And you're sure she wasn't talking about you?" He scratches his head.

"No. He's Norwegian." I drop to a seated position on my bed and bury my head in my hands. *I was so sure she was different.*

"Maybe you're mistaken?" he asks, not even trying cover up the doubt in his voice.

"No. Look, I really don't want to talk about it. I'm sorry I startled you. Try to go back to sleep. I'm going to go hit the gym." I get up.

"Dec, it's midnight, man. We have a flight and two performances tomorrow!" He throws his hands out.

"Best I get a move on then, so I can clear my head and get some sleep." I slap his shoulder and grab the hotel key on my way out. I'm already in sweats and a tank. I usually don't wear workout clothes to bed but it was all that was clean. The elevator opens just as I approach it. A couple exit, laughing and kissing. Oh . . . the damn irony! I thought this kind of shit only happens in a bloody movie. I push past them and hit the button for the first floor.

I use my key and walk into the gym, jumping on the first treadmill I see. I spend a lot of time on weights and various cardio regimens but running? That's my escape besides music. If only for a moment, I can run away from my life without actually running away.

I start off at a slow pace, gradually increasing speed and incline. A mini movie plays in my mind of various moments we shared the month we were finally getting to know each other. Her infectious laughter plays loudly in my ears, the animated expressions she gives me during her many stories—they blind me. The way she jumped into my lap like she was meant to be there, coating my lips with her kisses.

This is stupid. I'm being stupid! I've known her for a damn month. Yes, I may have taken notice of her months earlier. I may have made sure that Hunter and I always arrived early so I could catch a glimpse of her, hear her talk, watch her walk down the hall with that sweet little arse swaying the way it does.

I growl at my thoughts and turn the speed and incline up even more. It doesn't help. I can't shut her out. This is ridiculous. I am ridiculous! When you get to the point where you start to look and act like the Russian in *Rocky IV*, during his intense training, it's time to stop. I slow the speed and hit decline down to a walk and flat surface as I'm gasping for breath.

I'm going to become a monk.

That is all.

My cell rings as I wait for my luggage to come down the belt. Our flight to Venice was unremarkable. I have been awake for thirty hours now and have the two performances Oscar warned me about. If I survive this day—*that* will be *re*markable. Looking down at my cell, I see that it's Rosie. I answer quickly as it is odd, given she knows I'm most likely at the airport and Hunter is in Queensland.

"Dec?"

"Yeah, Rosie, what's going on?" I walk away from the crowd

that has formed in baggage claim.

"Renee's been admitted again," her voice is hesitant.

"What?! Now what happened?" Isn't this just the stick to place my shit on?

"She went to Dodgekins & Haus, demanding all of her money. She called them thieves, cursed them out, and warned the other clients. She then called the police down there. Long story short, the police arrived and were not in her favor, and she went ballistic. I guess it was pretty bad. She was screaming at things that weren't there. Well . . . I don't have to paint the picture for you; you've seen it enough." She sighs.

"Has Natasha been reached?" I pinch the bridge of my nose. I don't need this right now. I have *never* needed this.

"Yes. That's all taken care of. It's Keith. He wants you to find a new firm."

"*Fuck!*" I yell. I'm so bloody sick of this shit. This is the fifth goddamn firm I've gone through. I should say that Renee's gone through. I can't do this anymore. I just can't. "I will call them in the next few days. Thanks, Rosie." I turn my head as a bunch of my colleagues yell to me that the luggage is coming. Fucking *luggage*; don't I have plenty of it?

"Should I still expect you in three weeks?" she asks.

"Yes."

"You don't sound good, Dec. I mean, besides the obvious. Are you all right?"

"No. And yes, it's besides this stuff. I have to go, Rosie. I will call you tomorrow. I have a double-header today." That's what she always calls it. She's a huge baseball fan; the Red Sox are her passion. Several years back, I got her season tickets. It was like she won the lottery. Her Christmas is when those tickets arrive every year, and she gets to plan out her season.

"Okay. Make sure to eat and sleep!" she barks a final motherly order. I just agree. If I told her, she'd hand me my arse on a platter. I hang up and slip my phone into my pocket, as I walk to Oscar, who was nice enough to grab my luggage for me.

"I'm almost afraid to ask, man," Oscar says as he passes the handle of my bag to me.

"Then don't," I snap, grabbing it and my cello case. I turn on my heels for the exit to the bus waiting for us.

After giving the driver my belongings to pack underneath, I climb onto the bus and make my way to the very back, hopefully keeping as far away as I can from everyone. It's better for them to not be near me at the moment. Christ, if I could get the hell away from myself right now, I'd jump at the chance.

I sit with a huff and release some testosterone on the seat in front of me, jabbing at it a few times with my fist. I am really so sick of this aspect of my life. Not the performing—the Renee aspect. Amazing woman; she can destroy or make my life difficult from almost four thousand miles away at the drop of a dime.

I hate her.

Do I? Do I really hate her? I have never let my anger and disappointment reach this level of emotion. But, yes, I do. I hate her. It sounds awful. At the same time, it's liberating to acknowledge that I feel this way, like a burden has been released.

Patience takes a lot of work; it's utterly exhausting at times. There should be an acceptable cap for the amount of patience you give someone on certain matters. This way, when you've finally had it and tell them to fuck off, people don't look at you as if you're some sort of monster. I'm at that point. I want to cut ties completely with her. I've done everything I can to help her, to keep a door open for her to get her life together so that she may be a part of our son's. Eight years is a long time to be patient with somebody when you keep handing them all the tools they need to succeed only for them to act like you are doing the opposite.

It's so easy for people to tell me that "it's her disease." "It's her addiction." "She can't help it." "You're doing the right thing."

The fuck I am!

I'm enabling her. I have been for the past eight years. Maybe she needs to hit a real rock bottom before she can finally climb. I don't know what the answer is. I don't know what to do. We are no longer married, but I still take my vows seriously. *In sickness and in health.* Her sickness ended our marriage, but I still feel that she is my responsibility, her well-being. No, Renee doesn't have a choice to not have a mental illness. She does, however, have a choice to stay on the medication that will help keep it in check. She has a choice to stay clean after each visit to rehab. She has a choice to stay well for her son, who desperately needs the affection of a loving mum. She only chooses the things that destroy her and everyone who has ever cared about her. So, why should I choose to let her continue to hurt us? Why should I choose to consistently show up for her? All she does is scream at me for it, when I do.

I need to make some real changes in my life. I'm tired of playing the role of idiot in it. I'm done. Done with it all. I've got three weeks left of this tour to devise a plan to make the changes. That's what I'm going to keep my focus on. Not Renee. And certainly not Madelyn St. Claire.

One month later. . .

The racing of my heart pulses loudly in my ears as I walk down the long carpeted corridor. I feel butterflies in the pit of my stomach. Not the good kind of butterflies; the kind that make you feel as if you will be sick. It's the feeling of doom that I get every time I know I'm going to see Renee. I never know what I'm going to walk in on, what state she'll be in. I just pray I don't get a glimpse of the girl I fell in love with so many years ago. That's the girl I'm loyal to. The one that I bend over backwards to take care of. The one that still breaks my heart every time she disappears. I will *always* love *that* girl. The other versions of her make it much easier for me to keep my wall up.

I stop before reaching to open the door to the family room and take a deep breath. No matter how she receives me when I walk in, I know she will be a force to reckon with as I leave. Today is the day that I tell her I've cut her off.

Another slow inhale.

I open the door and walk in. She immediately uncurls herself on the couch and stands up. My heart plummets. The pain of the drop makes me die a little more inside. Compared to the girl I fell in love with when I was just twenty, she's unrecognizable. God . . . she looks like she's fifty years old. I don't even know any fifty-year-olds who look as aged as she does. She's all bones. Her face is covered in scars from picking at her skin during hallucinations. And it's sunken in so bad; there are no words.

"Hi," she says quietly, fidgeting with her fingers before tucking a loose strand of dirty-blonde hair behind her ear.

"Hi." My feet are stuck like they're in cement.

Her chin quivers and her pale-blue eyes fill up. "Dec, I want to come home, baby," she manages through the burst of a small sob.

"You're being discharged in two days," I remind her. I know what she is saying, but I am choosing to ignore it to spare us both. I am a little shocked, though; she hasn't said this to me in six years. That was the last time I ever took her back. I will never do that again. I wish I hadn't then, but that time helped me to move on emotionally for me and for Hunter.

"I know, but I think you missed what I said." She takes a few steps forward and reaches her hand up towards my face.

I step back and jerk my face away. "I didn't miss what you said."

"So, I can come home, then?" A hopeful look comes across her face.

"Eventually, you can go home . . . to your own place." I walk

84

past her to gain some distance. "Please, have a seat." I hold my hand out, motioning her to the couch she had just gotten up from. I take a seat on the one across from it and wait for her.

"This is the best I've been in years, Dec," she starts her appeal as she sits. "I know this time I'm gonna come out of this on top. I've never felt such clarity before."

"What number is this, do you even remember?" I say through my teeth. "Actually, I'm glad you feel this way." I calm down. I need to keep my anger at bay if I am to get her to cooperate one last time.

"Really?" She smiles enough for me to see her teeth, or what's left of them. *Christ.* How many times have I pre-paid a dentist to take care of this for her only to have a check sent back to me at the end of the year because she never showed up for treatment?

"Yes." I nod, trying to stay focused. "I've arranged for long term care for you at a rehab center in Colorado. It's a one-year program, so long as you do well." I stop for a moment as I watch her shake her head back and forth as if in disbelief. "Renee, this has been a battle that has lasted almost a decade now. These one-month programs are not working for you. You need a real chance, and I'm afraid this is the only way that may happen. After you graduate from the program, I will take care of your rent and utilities for one year to help you get back on your feet, but then, that's it. I'm done. There's nothing more I can do for you." I sit back and wait, hoping she doesn't fight me on this.

"Can I come home after . . . I mean . . . instead of you paying rent somewhere? Can I just come home to my family . . . have my life back?" she chokes through her tears.

Stay strong, Dec. Stay strong.

"You've always had the ability to gain your life back, Renee. I just can't be a part of it. Too much time has passed. Too much damage has been done." I fight the urge to wince as my heart drops some more.

"I'm your wife, Dec! The mother of your child. Doesn't that

mean *anything* to you?!" she raises her voice slightly.

"For God's sake, Renee, do you even have to ask that?! I have done *everything* in my power to help you through this—*everything!* I'm drained. You've depleted everything from me: trust, patience, and compassion. I have nothing left to give you." The hatred comes back in full vengeance, and I stand up to pace the room, anything to calm it down.

"What's her name?" she demands from behind me.

I turn around quickly. "Let me get this straight," my tone sharp and condescending. "Instead of taking into consideration the past eight years, where you chose to self-medicate with crystal meth, cheated on and lied to me, abused and neglected our son, stole, whored yourself out, *refused* to stay on your meds, *refused* to stay on course for sobriety, the only conclusion that you can come to over my rejection is that there is another woman involved?!" I roar. "Start being accountable for *your* actions, Renee!" I get in her face.

"What are you going to do, Dec?—throw me across the room again like you did that time you broke my ribs?" She pushes at my shoulders.

"Oh! You mean the time I yanked you off our son when you were choking him close to death because the voices told you the demons got into him?!" my rage spews freely.

"I didn't do that. I wouldn't!" she cries. "I would never hurt my baby."

"You did. He was only four years old. He still suffers from nightmares." I feel my lungs struggle to keep up with the pace of my anger as I try to fight the swarm of emotions running rampant through my body.

"It wasn't me. I would never hurt him." She shakes her head wildly.

"For Christ's sake, Renee, they only played the security video a hundred times in court," I say in defeat. They say you can't argue with crazy. No truer words have ever been spoken. I watch her as she continues to cry and shake her head incredulously. "There have been many things in my life that I have disliked, but I have never felt pure detestation towards anyone or anything. I've realized recently that you've changed that about me." I grab the handle to the door before I finish. "I. Hate. You," I finally say it out loud. "I would never allow my thoughts to go there until this last stunt with you, and you know what?" I pause, but she doesn't even acknowledge me. "Admitting this feeling to myself actually gave me to the push to finally let you go. I don't wish you any ill will. In fact, I hope to one day run across the girl I fell in love with. See, I don't *hate* her. Though it was only for a short time, she filled my life with love and joy. I hate this Godawful person who took her place." I open the door. "You have two days to decide whether you're going to the place in Colorado. If you don't, you're on your own. Goodbye, Renee." I walk out as she crumbles to the floor crying. Even if I wanted to, I couldn't give her any solace. The image of her choking Hunter is on loop in my head. I just need to get out of here. I need to get far away from her.

Chapter Nine

Maddie

One month earlier...

I JUMP UP ON MY KITCHEN COUNTER TO SNACK ON A PLATE OF cheese and Pink Lady apples. Hannaford's supermarket says these apples go well with wine, so I poured myself a generous amount because I trust that store immensely. It's not the greatest dinner, but if I eat one more fucking salad, I may cut a bitch.

I look around at my kitchen, taking in the rustic look I went with. It's been two years, and I'm still in love. My cabinets are a sage green and distressed. The island I'm sitting on is cream and distressed with reclaimed rock elm for the countertop. The tiled backsplash is a combination of the green and cream, tying everything in together while my octagon tiled floors have a slight hue of red in them to compliment the stools that sit beneath the island. I accented with various copper pots and décor on the wall. My favorite? The rustic, iron, rectangular chandelier above the island. Yes, it's like I ripped it out of a magazine. I'm not ashamed to admit that I'm a DIY junkie. Well, I don't actually do it myself. I watch the channel (it's my crack), tape it, tell Jay, and then he works *his* magic.

This is where I put my focus. I don't have a family to fill my house yet, but it's ready for when I do. For now, I just take it in. And no matter how much the silence swallows me whole, I am hopeful that there will come a time when I can't remember the quiet. Being thirty-four, I'm not going to lie; I'm nervous it will never happen.

Declan is the first guy I've been interested in, in a long time. There's something to be said for a guy who sits back and listens to you ramble on all the while his eyes smile at you. Up until recent events, I found him to be a very calm and reserved sort of person. I found it soothing, almost like the yin to my yang. I'm not quite sure why I imagine him to be a beast in the sack, but I do. Maybe it's the whole "it's always the quiet ones" theory.

I'm being a jerk. I should answer him. He's been so sweet, sending me gifts every day and messages to let me know he's thinking of me. I'm just so embarrassed by my behavior. I mean—desperate for cock much? I used to hate that word. Now it's one of my favorite words in existence. I don't know when or why my attitude about it changed, but I used to hate olives, too. Now, I eat them on everything I can.

I've had time to think, though. I needed to distance myself to do so. I think I'm so desperate to have what all of my friends seem to have that I'm rushing the most important part . . . the "falling" part. How stupid of me, really? I mean, not only do I do this, but I do this to a guy who clearly has massive trust issues because of his ex. I don't know what she did, but I can tell from his behavior that she messed him up pretty good. I need to slow it down, keep my hormones in check. This isn't just about me and my needs. Which also means that I need to reply to him, apologize for the dead air.

Good talk, Maddie!

Just as I grab my glass of wine and take a good congratulatory gulp for squaring my shit out, my phone pings, indicating a pm on facebook. This must be Charley replying to me about the death of my vibrator. I swipe it off the counter, already laughing before I read her response. Only, it isn't her that is responding. My glass of wine slips out of my hand and crashes to the floor, shattering dramatically as if the script about my life called for it.

"No! No! No!" I yell in a hushed tone. Oh no! He thinks I'm seeing somebody else. I'm such a fucking idiot! Why didn't I pay attention to who the hell I was sending this to?! He must've popped up just as I was about to message Charley. Before I can think another thought, my finger is flying across the virtual keyboard on my phone.

Madelyn St. Claire: Declan, I'm sorry I sent that to you by mistake, but it isn't what you think. It's an inside joke! God, this is so embarrassing! YOU ARE THE VIKING! I broke my vibrator fantasizing about you. Jesus, I need to go hide under a rock now. Please don't think badly of me. I've distanced myself because I needed to get over the embarrassment I felt with the way I behaved. Clearly, I need to accept the fact that I habitually embarrass myself and no matter how much time I take, there is no cure for it. Please call me. There is no one else. Please believe me.

I hit send, then look up to see if he reads it. But . . . not one word showed up. He blocked me. He must've done it while I was typing because it now says that I cannot reply to this conversation. I quickly search his name to see if my suspicion is correct.

Son-of-a-bitch.

Here it comes. I can feel it rising from my toes. My face twitches trying to fight it off, but I am too weak and it consumes me—ugly-motherfucking-cry. "What the fuck? He didn't even give me a chance to defend myself," I blubber through my sobs. I know; this seems all very dramatic. But, in my defense, I was just sitting here, feeling unsure about whether I'll ever have a family and, not that I am adamant that Declan would be in that picture, but I was also thinking about how sweet he is and how much I like him. So, excuse me if I'm a little (okay, a lot) upset about coming to another dead end. When shit like this happens to you again and again, how can you help but *not* wonder what the fuck is wrong with you?

I'm going to become a nun.

A flying, non-fucking nun.

That is all. . .

I should win an Academy Award because that was one hell of a performance I just gave. It was so good, I can barely see through my tears on my short drive home. Today is Sunday. Not just any old Sunday in the month but the one selected for dinner at the O'Brien's, Charley and CiCi's parents. We've done this for years. Shannon and Happy have been like parents to all of us GEGs not just their own kids. And they see us as their daughters. Today, I noticed something I hadn't quite paid attention to before—the number at the table is growing. Everyone now has a significant other . . . that is . . . except for me. I mean, Blake wasn't there, but that's because Julie isn't ready to acknowledge what we all know about those two. He'll be there soon enough, though.

I felt myself get choked up and did the only thing I could do to get out of that "place"—I lied. I *never* lie, but I just couldn't tell them all what happened. I never even managed to tell them what happened before this last time. I was going to at the pub that night but as usual, conversations got shifted away from me. And that is *my* fault, not the girls. They steer a little, and I go full throttle ahead in that different direction. It's just easier for me to talk to everyone about *their* problems.

So, I told them that Declan brought me coffee again. I acted a little too excited about it. Shannon (I actually call her "Ma") told me not to mention him again until he was putting cream in more than just my coffee. It was pretty funny. Had she known what was going on, I know she wouldn't have said that.

I feel even worse for lying, though. Like I was making up a boy-friend just to fit in. *Wow.* I guess I was, huh? *I'm so pathetic.*

You know what's even more pathetic? I looked up the schedule for the Boston Pops to see when he might be coming home. It's not for another few weeks. What if he changes therapists for his son, or the time? My only hope to get to him, so that I can explain, is when he takes his son for his appointment. And yes, I've already thought of creating a new Facebook page so that I could pm him through there, but I squashed that thought. I don't need to look psychotic.

That's another reason why I won't tell the girls; they would slam him with messages, promising castration. They're hardcore, what can I say?

All I can do is sit and wait . . . and try not to turn into Jabba the Hut. I'm an emotional eater so that last one's really gonna give me a run for my money.

One month later. . .

I take several deep breaths. I've been anxious for this Wednesday to finally come and now that it's here, I'd much rather hide in my office. I can't do that, though. I need to face him. I grab some refer-rals I had written out over the past day or two to put in the boxes of the colleagues they are going to. This is my reason to head down to the waiting room. One more deep breath and I leave my office, in pursuit of a Viking.

The hall seems longer than usual, at the moment. My heart is beating fast; I'm so nervous.

I turn the corner.

He's not here. There's only the usual parents and clients for this time slot and day. There is one new woman I've never seen before. Oh well. Maybe he's not back yet. I put the referrals where they need to go and head back to my office. I stop at Ted's door and knock before opening it, knowing he's kept this hour open for when Hunter gets back. "Ted, I . . . oh, I'm sorry!" I say quickly as I notice Hunter sitting across from him.

"Did you need something, Maddie?" Ted asks.

"It can wait." I smile. "I apologize. I didn't realize you were back to your usual schedule." I glance at Hunter.

"It's ok."

"Alright well, I'll leave you two to yourselves." I nod and close the door.

"I need to see you in your office—right now," a voice startles me from behind. I turn and find it's the woman I noticed in the waiting area.

"I'm sorry, do I know you?" *Please don't let this lady be psychotic.*

"Not personally but I would hope Dec has mentioned me." She tightens her grasp on the strap of her purse.

I think for a quick minute. "Rosie?" I almost whisper.

"Yes. Please," she waves her hand out, "can we talk in your office."

"Yes. Yes, of course," I agree and turn to lead the way. As soon as I let her into my office, she begins to pace. I shut the door. "Would you like to take a seat?"

She looks over at the chair (you know which one . . . ahem). "I'll stand. I won't take up much of your time. I don't even know what to say to you; I'm so angry."

"Okay, well—"

"—How dare you hurt my boy like that?" she cuts me off. "And no, I didn't give birth to him, but he is still *my* boy! How could you do that to him? Why did you feel the need to lead him on? You should be ashamed of yourself." She points an angry finger at me.

"Rosie, the only thing I'm guilty of is not responding to his messages." I lean my ass against the front of my desk. "Did he tell you the whole story, what I said?" I fight the urge to cross my arms and grasp the edge of my desk instead. I don't want to send out the wrong message with my body language.

"Not word for word, only that you've been seeing a Norwegian all the while stringing him along," she states, crossing *her* arms across her chest.

A Norwegian?!

"Why are you laughing?—this is not funny!" she practically yells at me.

"Oh, Rosie," I calm down, "please . . . have a seat." I hold my hand out to the chair again as I grab my phone and sit in the one across from it. "Please," I reiterate. "I want to show you something. This has all been a misunderstanding, which I tried to explain to him but he blocked me before I could." I wait for her to finally sit down. She holds her purse close to her chest as she takes a seat. Geez . . . I'm not going to snatch your purse, lady! I know, I know; it's her keeping her guard up, but it still looks ridiculous. "Okay?"

"Yes. Go ahead." She nods and tries to act impassive. I know she wants to rip me to shreds, though. That earns a lot of respect from me because I know that it comes from a place of love for Declan. I'm glad he has somebody good in his corner.

"What I am about to tell you is going to embarrass the hell out of me, but I don't care anymore. I just want him to know the truth," I start. "You see, I like Declan very much. I don't know what his ex did to him, but I know she's the reason why we've had so many bumps in the road once we acknowledged our growing feelings. I mean . . . *ridiculously large* bumps in the first twenty-four hours," I emphasize.

"Can you get to your point, please?"

"Yes. Sorry." I shake my head to get back to it. "When Declan started bringing Hunter here a few months ago, I noticed him when I went out to the waiting room for any reason. And, I noticed that he was noticing me. For a couple of months, all he would do was stare at me. It was intimidating. At the same time, it was exciting; I found him to be very attractive. He never spoke a word. I didn't know his name. All I kept thinking was that he looked like a Viking." I laugh a little. "Long story short, that's how I began referring him as when I would talk to my friends. It stuck. We still call him *The Viking* even though I've gotten to know him personally. I just never got around to telling him this. About a month ago, I went to message one of my best friends. Just as I was about to click on her avatar, he must've popped up because I clicked on him instead." I look down to my phone, pulling up Facebook. "I sent him this message instead of her. And what was supposed to make her laugh made him very angry with me, thinking the worst." I hand her my phone to read the message. "I can show you other examples of me calling him the Viking, if need be," I say as she looks down. I can feel my cheeks heat up from the embarrassment. You'd think I'd be used to this by now, right?

Rosie's shoulders shake. I'm hopeful that this is a good sign that she believes me. "Did you ever get the name of the vibrator?" She looks up.

I crack a smile. "No, damn it. Besides, I haven't even been in the mood for myself. You have to understand how much this has upset me. He didn't even give me a chance to explain." I take the phone from her as she hands it to me. "Do you need me to show you other examples?" I shake it before putting it on my desk.

"No. I believe you." She visibly relaxes, purse strap slides off her shoulder, and she places it on the floor before crossing her legs.

"You were right."

"About?" I tilt my head.

"His ex has done a real number on him. It's why he has trust issues. I don't know how much he's told you."

"Not too much."

"It's not my place to tell you what happened, or what he's been going through for the past eight years."

"No, it's not. That's up to him and when he's ready," I agree.

Rosie's eyes fill up, and she looks up to the ceiling while she slowly wipes underneath them to stop the tears. "Do me a favor?"

"Yes?"

"Don't give up on him." She looks back at me. "Give him time. Understand that he's got a lot to work through and that while he's trying his hardest to do so, he can come off as a complete shit at times. He'll be so worth it, though. That man has a heart of gold. He's so good, Maddie. He's just been beaten to the core." She grabs my box of tissues.

"I know. And, I had an idea that it wasn't *him* that was difficult, just what he went through. I'd like to think I have a pretty good read on most people. Besides, I didn't help with the way I behaved. I was very impulsive with him. That's not how I normally act. I'm sure it didn't help." I take in a deep breath and blow my bangs out of the way. "Trouble is, I don't know how to get him to talk to me, give me a chance to explain."

"You leave that up to me." She glances at her watch. "I have to go; Hunter's appointment is almost over." She stands up.

"Wait! Can you give Declan something for me? I bought it before all of this happened." I get up and go around my desk to open the file drawer on the right. I pull out the wrapped box and nervously hand it to her. "I put the gift receipt inside the card. The date on the receipt should help him realize that he's the only one I think about." I hope my voice doesn't sound as unsure as I feel.

Growing up, I collected Precious Moments. My collection got

so big; I had to ask everybody to stop buying them for me. I only buy them for myself now, and they have to be really significant and special. I was in Hallmark one day and came across this one. I couldn't imagine a more significant piece. It's a boy and girl riding a bicycle for two. I'm more nervous about the title of the piece: "All For The Love of You On a Bicycle Built For Two." It says a little more in that title that I feel comfortable with at the moment, so I wrote him out a card telling him that we can pedal together. Something like that. I wrote it over a month ago; I can't remember my exact wording.

"I will." She glances down at it with a smile on her face. "I'm really glad that I'm overbearing. Sometimes it does come in handy. And, I'm so glad I got to meet you, Maddie."

"Me too, Rosie. I know Declan thinks the world of you." I go in for a hug. I can't help it; I'm a hugger.

"The feeling is mutual." She squeezes me back tightly. "I have a feeling you're going to be good for him."

I swallow nervously. This sounds so very official. It's slightly weird since it involves him and he's not *officially* back in my life. Time will tell. "I hope so."

We break from our embrace, and I walk over to my door to open it for her. One last smile and she walks out. I close the door and walk behind my desk where I plop into my chair like a ton of bricks. Part of me is hoping that my client, Jeff (fear of stairs, remember him?), calls me at the last minute to cancel. I took tomorrow off because I wasn't sure what was going to happen today and I knew I wouldn't get any sleep the night before, which I didn't. But now my mind is already in "off" mode. I could call him and cancel, but I hate to do that because it's always the ones you don't think you have to worry about that you get the calls on. I mean, don't get me wrong, we definitely get the calls on the people we do worry about.

I could just sit here and wonder if Rosie will have a talk with Declan. Will he listen? Will he call me? Come see me? Apologize?

Oh God. I'm behaving like all those other women I roll my eyes about. It sort of pisses me off. I haven't done anything wrong out-side of being a little aggressive. Why am I bending over backwards to accommodate his behavior? *Because you want to accommodate other aspects of him.* Shut up, inner Maddie . . . whore. *Whore would indicate you're actually fucking something or somethings that aren't battery operated.* Whatever!

Chapter Ten

Declan

I DECIDED TO COOK TONIGHT. ACTUALLY, ROSIE DECIDED I SHOULD cook tonight since she was taking Hunter to his appointment. Go ahead; call me a coward. Rosie did. I don't care; I don't want to see her. But, I'm not going to affect my son with this by changing out his therapist, a guy he seems to be doing well with.

I glance at the clock again. They should be home any minute. Perfect timing since I've just finished up here. I've also folded all of the laundry. Cleaned the bathrooms. Vacuumed . . . all levels. Did a few or fifty push-ups.

So?—I have nervous energy.

Hearing them come in through the front door, I practically dive into a seat at the kitchen table and grab the paper to read. No need to get them suspicious with all my running about, doing Rosie's job.

"You in the kitchen, Dec?" Rosie calls out.

"I am," I announce and look up at them as they walk in.

"Here." She hands me a present.

"What's this?" I shoot her a look of confusion.

"It's for you but don't open it yet. Did you make lemon-pepper chicken?" She smiles and heads over to the oven, opening the door.

"That's what you requested." I pick up the gift and rotate it in my hands.

"Hey, Dad." Hunter clears his throat.

"Hey, chief, how was your session tonight?" I look up at him.

"It was alright." He shrugs. I give him a curious look. "She seemed sad that you weren't there," he adds quietly.

"Oh . . . well, I had to handle a few things; you know that." I try my hardest to keep an impassive expression on my face.

"But you'll be there next week, right? I don't want her to worry."

"Uhhh. . ." I trail off.

"He'll be there," Rosie answers for me. I turn my head sharply to glare at her. She glares back but it's more like she smacking me upside my head. Same kind of treatment my own mother gives me. Where do these ladies learn how to do this?

"You will?" He grabs my attention again. "Because I feel a lot better when you're there with me, Dad," he says. I can hardly believe my ears. I never knew that it meant anything to him that I was there.

"Yes, of course," I agree and dare to pull him in for a hug as I stand up. He reciprocates and my heart explodes in celebration. Have we really turned a corner here? "Alright, go and get your hands washed for dinner," I say as soon as we break. He smiles up at me before taking off to the bathroom. I turn to Rosie. "Did you see that?" I nonchalantly point in the direction my son has gone, half shocked still.

"I did." Her smile is the widest I've seen it in a long time. It drops a little as she takes on a stern look. "I need to tell you a few things, and I don't want any lip from you until I'm done."

"How about some tongue? Can I sneak that in?" I give her, what I'm sure is, a Cheshire grin. She throws a wooden spoon at me in response. "Oh, hey—stop it now!" I complain but with amusement in my voice.

"Your son is *very* fond of Maddie."

This stops me in my tracks. "He doesn't really know her," I try to argue.

"No. But he knows that you spend that hour with her. He told me, he likes how happy she makes you. That you're so much different now. He likes seeing you happy; it makes him feel safe and sure. His words—not mine—remember that. He's afraid that if you don't bring her coffee, that you'll stop seeing her all together and then you'll be sad again." She looks past my shoulder as if she's making sure he doesn't come back into the kitchen.

"I can't go every week and pretend that things are ok!" I bite quietly. "She's seeing another man, for Christ's sake! A one track mind—that girl." My blood pumps wildly through my veins and my adrenaline charges up the charts. It all plays loudly in my eardrums.

"I hope you're really hungry tonight because you're going to be eating your words." She shakes her head in disbelief and fans her hand out at me dismissively as Hunter walks back in.

"So, have you put much thought into what you'd like to be for Halloween?" I ask as I head over to the fridge for our drinks.

"I don't know. I just know I don't want to do the same thing as everyone else."

"You're running out of time, bud." I walk over to the table with flavored water in hand.

"I know." He shrugs. He does that a lot lately. Rosie puts his plate in front of him, and he digs in right away. I don't hesitate, either.

"Is he all settled?" Rosie asks as I come into the living room.

"Yes. What are you reading?" I sit down next to her on the couch and push at the cover a little to see the title.

"Something that will make you blush. Quit it." She smacks my hand away.

"Is that a trashy novel?" I inquire teasingly. My heart sinks instantly as I think of Maddie and her claim to love that type of reading.

"Yes. Don't make fun of me, either. Not for nothing, but if men would quit complaining that they don't know what women want and pick up one of our, so-called, trashy novels, they may learn a thing or two. It's all here in black and white." She shakes the book at me.

"Rosie, you really must try to not throw yourself at me like this. I will not read a novel to woo you. I don't pay you to take care of all of my needs, just some of them," I admonish.

"If you don't get your act together, I'm going to be the only one who hangs around for your sorry ass."

"You know I'm teasing you, right?"

"Yes, I do. But I'm not teasing you. You've made several big, messy mistakes lately." She puts the book down on the side table and resituates herself on the couch as if she's getting ready for a marathon discussion. Suddenly, I feel worn out from the day. . .

You don't buy it?

She won't, either. Grrr

"Go on, then. I know you still have something to tell me." I act bored.

"You. Were. Wrong!" She pokes her finger into my shoulder with each word.

"You'll have to elaborate as, like you say, I don't know my head from my elbow."

"The Viking?" she questions in a sarcastic tone. "He's you!" she states matter-of-factly.

"Come off it," I dismiss her.

"She tried to explain it to you." She shakes her head. "But you blocked her before she could. So now, you're going to listen to me!"

I stare at her in silence. Slowly, she relays to me what Maddie said to her. I have to admit; I am *extremely* pissed off at Rosie for going to her. I told her to avoid Maddie at all cost! "I'm *not* the Viking! I'm Australian!" I argue.

"She didn't know that when she first noticed you!" she defends her tooth and nail.

"I don't believe her."

"She showed me the text. She *tried* to show me other personal conversations where she and her friends called you "The Viking."

"Why is she even talking about me to her friends?" I snap. I can't help it; the idea that I've screwed up again with her is beyond frustrating.

"For the same reason you talk to me and any of your friends about *her*. Stop being such an asshole about this."

"Rosie!" I yell. It's not the first time she's called me this or has gotten angry with me over something but the fact that she seems to be on Maddie's side is not sitting well with me.

"Don't *Rosie* me! You were wrong, and you need to apologize." She points an accusatory finger at me.

"I can't," I barely say. "All I've done is mess things up with her. I had a good solid few weeks in me and then it went all downhill from there. I think it's best I just leave her alone. I'm obviously not ready for a relationship." I pick her gift up off the coffee table. I had placed it there and stared at it since I walked in.

"Dec, if ever there were a more patient and understanding woman to come along, I wouldn't believe it. That girl is gold. She put her own feelings of embarrassment aside to reach out to you. Her face was almost purple when she explained everything. I felt terrible for her and tried to make light of it, but I'm a stranger to her, and that was a very personal thing to share. She cares about you; it's all over her face. If only you could've seen her look of disappointment when she came out to the waiting room and realized you weren't there. It about broke my heart." Rosie sniffles.

"Rosie, I've never known you to get worked up like this." I grab her hand and squeeze it, feeling worse with every passing moment. I don't think I've ever once seen Rosie muster up a tear, have her voice shake—nothing. She's a "keep pushing onward" sort. Very strong. Maybe too strong for her own good.

"Everyone has a past, Dec. We're more alike than you may realize." Her dam cracks and she wipes her tears away just as quickly as they come.

"Your husband?"

"No."

"A lover before him?"

"No."

"May I buy a vowel?"

She whacks me, then laughs. "It was my sister. I pushed her away. God," her breath gushes out, "it's all so silly now, but the damage is done."

"What happened?"

"I've never told a soul." She shakes her head.

"I would hope that you can come to the conclusion on your own that I would never judge you. Even if you did something terrible years ago, you are not that Rosie now . . . the Rosie I've come to love and trust . . . even though you've turned down every single one of my proposals," I tease.

"I'm a young girl; I don't want to rush into anything," she jokes back. "And yes, I know that you are probably one of the only people I could tell and know that I wouldn't be judged." She gives me a warm smile before taking in a deep breath. "When I was just out of high school, I found myself falling into the wrong crowd. It was gradual at first. I met a couple of them, including Keith, through my friend Tori. Keith and I had an instacrush that we quickly believed to be love. I met the rest of the gang through him. When I met them, I thought of them as just a gang of friends. And they were . . . friends, that is. But, they were also a real gang. Nothing like the big ones you hear about; just a group of kids who began forming ideas about life and society that weren't exactly backed up by media or community. I think they started out as something that had the possibility of being a positive thing, but it only takes one bad seed sometimes to turn the others. Instead of inflicting good change on the community, they lashed out because of the chip on their shoulder. They started getting a Robin Hood complex, except they didn't give to the poor; they kept it for themselves. Pretty noble, huh?" She gives a quick chuckle. "By the time I realized what was actually going on, I was already very much involved with Keith, and being young and stupid, I wouldn't leave him. Instead, I tried to get him to leave them. I wasn't very successful. Before long, my father found out about Keith's involvement with the PYC—"

"—PYC?" I interrupt her.

"Prideful Youth Core," she answers with a roll of her eyes. "Sounded more like an after school program than a 'gang.'"

"How did your father find out about Keith's involvement?"

"He was the lead detective on the case. There had been a string of robberies. There was never enough evidence to pin the crime on them, just circumstantial."

"What does all of this have to do with your sister?" I'm very curious. I didn't even know Rosie had a sister.

"I'm getting to that. Sorry, I'm trying to shorten this as much as I can." She gives me a half smile.

"No rush. I'm just really curious."

"Let me try to speed things up a little." She taps my hand. "Word got around that I was trying to get Keith to walk away from them. They handled this by robbing my house, knowing my father's position. By this time, my parents thought so poorly of me; they thought I had helped them mastermind the burglary—my way of getting back at them for trying to get me to leave Keith. I, of course, defended myself, but my father wanted proof of my innocence; he wanted me to give him names and a confession. Had I actually known any information that would've helped, I would have. But, I didn't know a single ounce of it. It was all to get back at *me*! Needless to say, they gave me a final ultimatum: give them the information or leave and never come back."

"Surely they didn't mean it," I challenge.

"They sure did. My parents were strict to a fault," she states adamantly. "I had no info and therefore I no longer had a home. Pamela was younger than me; she couldn't understand why I was leaving. I knew I was becoming an example so that she would keep herself in check," her voice falters. "Back then, we didn't have the abilities we do now to stay in touch without anyone knowing. I tried at first, but every time they found out that she talked to me, they made life hell for her. So, eventually . . . I stopped all communication." She starts to silently cry. "When I was twenty-two, she walked past me and quickly turned, calling out my name. I tried to ignore her until she grabbed my arm to gain my attention. She threw her arms around me, crying that she was so happy to see me . . . how much she had missed me."

"What did you do?" I ask as soon as she stops and cries some more.

"I . . . I told her I didn't know who she was and that I'd appreciate it if she'd let me go."

"Why would you do that?!" I ask in shock.

"Because, I wanted her to have all the things in life she deserved. I didn't want her to end up out on her butt too, struggling, going from one bad relationship to the next." She slides the back of her hand up against her nose to wipe the snot away.

"Let me get you some tissues." I get up and go into the bathroom to get some. This story is crazy. That's only because Rosie's been in our lives for so long; it's hard to believe that I never knew any of this. I head back in. "She must've been devastated, Rosie."

"Yes, I'm sure. But mostly, she was angry; I could see it all over her face. That was the last time I ever saw her." She lets out another whimper before blowing her nose. "I loved my sister more than anything or anyone in the world. I let the behavior of others get in the way of that. They were *my* crutch to not let anyone truly in. In return, I've punished myself, and those I've loved, much more than they ever could have. That's why I'm getting so upset with you. I don't want you to go down the same path as me." She looks me straight in the eyes and the power behind this soul searching look has my protective wall cracking.

"How would I even begin to fix this?" I groan.

"Slowly. Just go very slow," she advises. I laugh. "What's so funny?"

"God bless her, but I think if I go any slower, Maddie will pull out her hair." I stop and think about the way she winds up taking control. She's so sexy. So very hard to refuse. I don't know how I've managed to do so.

"Well, get back to the basics; start with coffee again." She stands up. "Make sure you open your gift." She points. "I'm going to bed. I'll see you in the morning. Thanks for listening, Dec." She smiles and leans down to kiss me on my forehead.

"Night, Rosie. Thank you for entrusting me with your story." I grasp her arm and squeeze it for emphasis.

She gives me a little nod. And with that, she's off to bed.

I turn my focus on to the gift Maddie gave me. I lean forward and pick it up again. Slowly, I unwrap it. Opening the box, I pull out a figurine of two kids riding a bicycle built for two.

Complete shit at this.

My heart is pounding all over my chest like it's trying to finally escape solitary confinement. I leave the figurine out and go to put the Styrofoam it was packed in back into the box only to find a note. I open it.

> Declan,
>
> I saw this and couldn't help but get it for you. I just wanted to remind you that you don't have to pedal through everything alone. I'd like very much to do some of the pedaling together.
>
> Love, Maddie

I think this confirms things—I'm an arsehole.

It's been two weeks since Hunter's had an appointment with Ted. This was not by my choice; I was ready to bite the bullet last week and beg her forgiveness. But, since Ted had a family emergency, it couldn't be helped.

It's probably best as it's given me more time to get myself in order. Renee has gone off to the rehab in Colorado. I am grateful for this and truly wish for her to find her way again—for her and Hunter's sake. Truth be told, though, I'm not sure how receptive Hunter will be once and *if* she ever cleans up her act and wants to resume her role as "Mum." I guess we'll cross that bridge if we ever get to it.

I slowly move up in the carpool lane at Hunter's school. This process is not for the faint at heart. Carpool at school could easily be the root to any parent's possible road-rage later on in the day. It never seems to end.

Finally, my son comes into view, and he waves happily at me. God, this last trip to my parents' must've really done something for him. "Hallo, Da!" he boasts as he opens the door to get in.

"Da?" I laugh a little. His smile is huge as he looks down to find two coffees in a tray and a bag.

"Did you remember how she likes it?" he asks.

"Yes."

"And did you get her a pumpkin muffin, like I told you?"

"Yes." I laugh.

"Good, Dad. That's real good!" he states in a prideful voice as he pulls the seatbelt over his shoulder and buckles in. Within moments, we are out of carpool-lane-hell and on our way to his appointment in Londonderry.

WE GET OUT of the car and make our way into the building. "Are you nervous?" he asks on the elevator.

"Always." I exhale aggressively.

"It's because you like her so much. I get that way around Abigail. And then, I always manage to say something stupid that makes her cry," he informs me.

"*Who* is Abigail?" I swear this cannot be *my* son; he never shares with me!

"The girl I like. She's really pretty. Very fancy; she always wears dresses with lacy socks." He kicks at an imaginary something on the floor.

"Why do you make her cry?"

"Because I tell her her freckles are freakish instead of cute." His shoulders slump.

"Why do you do that?!" I widen my eyes in shock.

"Because I'm scared she won't like me as much as I like her, so I'm protecting myself," he says just as the doors open.

Like father, like son.

"Have you put any thought into why this makes her cry?" I ask as we head down the hall.

"No, not really besides that it's mean."

"Yes, it's mean, but it probably hurts her more because, just maybe, she likes you, too." I smirk at him.

"Oh no!" he groans in disbelief.

"Tell her you're sorry and that you actually like her freckles very much," I offer as we get into the office waiting room and sit.

"Then what?" He throws his hands out.

"Damned if I know; I'm in the same boat over here." I chuckle lightly at the irony. Just then, I hear her voice and my palms get sweaty as my heart races. She and her client come around the corner into the waiting room and our eyes lock for a moment before a look of disappointment comes over her face. She returns her attention to the client, wishing him a good week before he leaves.

"Hi, Maddie!" Hunter calls out just as she turns to head back to her office.

"Hi, Hunter." She turns back, offering him a meek smile.

"My dad's brought you coffee and a pumpkin muffin, see?" He points it out.

"Oh . . . that was nice of him, but I'm on a diet. Have a good session, Hunter." She smiles again and continues onward to her office.

So much for all that "pedaling together" business!

"Wow," Hunter says under his breath. I look over at him. "You must've really screwed up for her to turn down a muffin; girls love cake."

"Watch your language, Hunter!" I snap lightly. "And the pot shouldn't call the kettle black, Mr. *Your Freckles Are Freaky.*"

"Why didn't you say anything to her, Dad?" I can hear the frustration in his voice. I widen my eyes and shrug angrily.

We sit in silence for a few moments until the movie, *Like Father, Like Son,* with Dudley Moore and Kirk Cameron, pops into my head and I start laughing. This really could be a scene from that movie.

"Hunter?" Ted calls out to my son, cutting off my laughter.

"Coming." He gets up and looks over at me. "Go and apologize," he says sternly. I salute him on his way.

And then,

I sit here,

Being complete shit at this.

The door swings open, and a guy walks through on the phone. "I'm here, Babydoll, get that sweet ass of yours out here." He hangs up and gives me a curt nod. He's a big bloke . . . a bit too stylish, if you ask me. He turns in the direction of the hall leading to the offices. Suddenly, he whistles and lets out a *whoot*. I watch to see whom he's giving the cat call too.

Of course.

"You are *fucking* hot!" he carries on.

Me?

Imagine a bull just before he's about to charge the red cape.

"Shut up, Jay!" She brings her finger up to her lips for emphasis. "There are sessions going on."

"Oh . . . there's about to be another session going on in a minute." He pulls her into his arms.

Jay? Jay? Oh—*Jay!* That's her best friend. He's completely harmless as he is very into men. Though, from what Maddie's told me— he's a pot stirrer.

I take in a few deep breaths, finally calming down. My eyes dart up as Maddie approaches me. "This one mine?" She goes to lift it out of the tray.

I clear my throat, "Yes."

She takes it and leans down till her mouth is at my ear. "Thank you. I already made plans this hour since you've been staying away. Regardless, though, I can't do this with you *here*," she whispers.

"Don't let anyone fill my slot," I say back to her quietly.

"Nobody has been near *your* slot." She leans back and arches an eyebrow at me.

111

"Good."

"Have a good night, Declan. Thanks for the coffee," she says again before leaning back to kiss my cheek.

"Night, Ms. St. Claire," I say in my deepest octave. She closes her eyes, takes in a deep breath, and gives into a shiver. When she opens her eyes again, they are a dark olive.

"C'mon, before our hour is up," Jay complains.

Not another word is spoken between us as she backs up and finally turns to leave with him. I am left here with a terrible need to adjust myself.

Chapter Eleven

Maddie

SOMETIMES I JUST WANT TO SAY "FUCK IT" AND BE FAT. IT'S NOT bad enough that I have to be vertically challenged, but I have to fight the call to be an Oompa Loompa. It's 9:30 pm and I'm just fixing myself dinner. I have half the mind to skip it and go right to my wine. Now those calories are ones I can easily justify.

Just as I'm about to bring the spoon, filled with soup, up to my mouth, my doorbell rings. "Ugh . . . c'mon!" I groan. I bet that's one or more of the girls. Jay got to see the Viking today before any of them. *His lips are looser than a high-priced whore's vag.* I make my way to the foyer. The bell rings again with a loud pounding on the door for a follow up. "I'm coming!" I yell before yanking the door open.

Holy Fuck.

Declan rushes in, making me back up as he charges me. He kicks the door shut before grasping the back of my neck, pulling me toward him and attacking my lips. I give in because, let's face it—he's a Viking, and I am an "Oompa doompa, doopity-doo."

I thread my fingers through his hair and pull. He growls and releases my neck to reach down under my ass. He grabs my thighs and lifts me up. My legs instinctively wrap around his waist as his tongue probes harder into my mouth. "Fuck!" he groans. "You're naked under your robe!" he accuses . . . rightfully so. I don't say a word, too consumed with the rhythm of our panting as we stare into each other's eyes. I contemplate mentioning his shirt pushing against my wet pussy like a restrictive form of panties. "Where's your bedroom, Maddie?" His hands knead my ass as he begins to walk into the living room. "Down this hall?" he asks as he heads down the right one. I nod.

"Shouldn't we talk?" I finally push through the hormones.

"Only if it's dirty." He leans forward and collects my lips again. This time, he is gentle.

"Declan?"

"I will tell you everything after, I promise." He leans his forehead against mine as he enters my room.

Oh my God—this is really happening. This is really happening? I should stop him, right? I mean, he has a lot of explaining to do. We haven't had a very good start. We need to communicate. I need to know that he won't think badly of me after this. I need to know that he is actually ok to do this.

He places me on my bed and slowly works at the knot of my sash. Goosebumps run rampant across my skin as my starts to slip open. His big, strong, warm hands slide it completely open. I whimper, feeling them caressing my breasts, his thumbs slowly circling my nipples. "Jesus, Maddie, you're so fucking beautiful. Your body is amazing." He leans down and takes my left nipple into his mouth. I arch into his touch, needing more and cry out when his teeth clamp down. "Feel good?" he asks as he blows on it.

I only have one reply. . .

Oogah, oooogah. Ooooogahhhhh!

But, I'll keep that to myself.

He erects himself and yanks his coat off. He then pulls his shirt over his head. Let's just say, I really appreciate his 4 am workouts. He tugs on my robe, "Let's get this off of you, shall we?" I nod and lean up to take it off, trying not to think of the muffin top that forms when I do so. You're giving me the knowing nod right now, aren't you? It can really suck being a woman, at times. I'd like to just enjoy this without any thoughts of what's rolling where. I digress. . .

"Are you ready for your favorite kiss?" he asks as the fingers from his right hand slide down my torso slowly until they come to my clef. He licks his lips as he stares at my lady business.

"What do you think?" I ask as I unwrap my legs from his waist and spread them wide.

He looks down, letting his fingers slide down my center. "God . . . you're so wet," he says under his breath as if he's in shock. He circles my opening.

"Please," I beg and try to help his finger push in by moving toward him.

"What, sweetness? What do you need? Tell me," he baits me.

"You—everywhere. I need you," I admit.

"This? Do you need this?" He slowly pushes his finger in. I clench down, holding it hostage. "Hmm . . . you like that?" he coos. I whimper. "Do you want this?" He pushes a second finger into me, and I'm wild, riding them as if I'm looking to win gold for my country. I squeeze my eyes shut, soaking in the sensation of his two thick fingers stretching me.

Suddenly. . .

Oh. Dear. Sweet. Jesus!

Cunning linguistics.

Know what I'm sayin'?

I fuck his face and his fingers hard. The bomb shelter scene in *Grease2* may be playing out in my head, cuz', like I said before, I'm doing it for my country. "Stop! Stop! Don't you fucking stop!" I scream as I reach the "Stairway to Heaven."

I buck.

His tongue flicks.

My hips circle dramatically.

He sucks.

Duck . . . duck . . . duck. . .

Goose!

"Declan!" I scream, jerking my body toward him, my legs shaking uncontrollably. He rips away from me and works at his jeans. *Oh my God. Oh my God.* He yanks them down, and I fear for my life. I mean . . . I imagined (as we all do) for him to have the sort of cock size that will have you petrified.

I may have imagined too hard.

Pray for her.

Pray really, really hard.

No pun intended.

"I imagined this moment a million times," he announces as he strokes himself. "I had it all wrong—you look more beautiful than I imagined, waiting for me; your pussy so needy."

Did you hear him say that too?

Holy. Fuck.

"Please," I beg some more.

"You want this?" He pumps his cock a little more.

"I need it." I look him straight in the eyes.

"Me too . . . so bad, Maddie . . . so fucking bad." He climbs over me. I reach up to brush his lips with mine. His tongue darts out, enticing me to part my lips. My tongue glides against his slowly, eliciting a growl from him. He slides his cock up and down my center.

"Fuck me, Declan. Fuck me so hard, I forget my name," I whisper against his ear.

Slowly, he slides into me until I am full to the core with him. My body arches as I try to accommodate him—no easy feat, mind you. "God!" he groans. "So. Fucking. Tight!"

Sex Talk 101: PASS!

Can I get an amen?

I lock my legs around him in a vice grip and thank God he's taking the time to acclimate himself. It's been so long, and he's so . . . well, you know. It hurts . . . but a good hurt.

He cups my face softly. "Are you okay?"

"Yes," I breathe.

"Are you ready?" he murmurs as he plants kisses as soft as a whisper all over my face.

"Mm hmm. . ."

He pulls back to the point where he's almost out of me, but then slowly begins to fill me again, this time, reaching deeper. I hope he's only warming up because if he stays at this pace, I'm going to lose my mind. His hand grasps my left hip, pulling me against him tightly. He rubs his nose against mine lightly, his breath shaky and hot. "I want you to feel every inch of me invading you . . . claiming you. Your pleasure is my main focus because it will bring me much joy to watch you come undone," his voice, so sexy.

This must be the "Pleasure Principle" Janet Jackson was sing-ing about.

Right now, I'd like to be a part of "The Rhythm Nation." *Miss Jackson (cuz' I'm trying to do the nasty), kindly get the fuck out of my head.* "Declan," I turn my focus back to him, "please, I can't wait any longer," I beg and grind my hips into him for encouragement. His face dips back down, and his teeth clamp gently onto my bottom lip, pulling at it till it breaks free.

Pant.

Pant.

Pant.

He shifts, slipping his hands underneath my knees and pushing them back toward me. His arms then slide down the sides of my thighs and up underneath my back, till his hands curve over my shoulders, grasping hold of me. With the exception of my hands to hold on to him, I am trapped. And completely vulnerable. *Ohhh . . . . fuuuuccck!*

Declan pulls his hips back, then slams into me fiercely, soliciting a groan from my mouth. He does it again several times; long, deep, and harsh thrusts. All of the sudden, he tightens his grasp on my shoulders and unleashes a beast of a deep pounding session on me. I can't move. All I can do is lie here and take it while I scream out his name mixed with a bunch of nonsense. "Is this what you've been wanting, sweetness?" he growls.

"Oh God, yes!" I cry. He picks up his pace. *Dear God, he's picked up his pace!* "Oh . . . God, he's pounding my pussy so good!"

Declan laughs in the middle of his grunts.

I stare at him.

"Shall I narrate along with you?" he pants with a grin on his face. His pace slows back down to the long, deep thrusts.

"Did I say that out loud?" I try to catch my breath, glad for the slight reprieve.

"Mm hmm," he hums before his mouth claims mine.

"I only speak the truth, sir," I murmur against his lips.

"The Viking is having trouble taming the feral beast inside of him, for Ms. St. Claire's pussy is not only warm and inviting but tighter than he's ever had before. It. Must. Be. Conquered, so that no man or beast will ever come near the Viking's lair."

"Lair?" I giggle.

"Yes." He kisses me. His hold on my shoulders tightens, and I know what's coming next. I take in a deep breath like I'm going under water. But, as soon as he unleashes the beast, the breath gets knocked right out of me. His pounding is even fiercer this time, causing me to claw at his back and making me plea with him. My legs start shaking; it's too intense. It's too much. I can't take it. I

118

pound at his back, telling him so. "Let go, Maddie! Let it happen!" he demands.

"I can't! I can't!" I cry.

"You can and you will! Give it to me now, Maddie!"

My toes curl.

I fist his hair.

My mouth opens wide.

I cry out.

(Thankfully, it sounded nothing like "ooogaaaahhh")

"Bloody. Fucking. Hell, Maddie!" he groans before spilling himself inside of me. I'm too busy holding the death grip on his cock to think about that. A few more pumps, fully equipped with panting grunts and he collapses on me, my pussy still pulsating around him. She's needy, what can I say?

Soon enough, he releases my shoulders and unearths his arms, allowing my legs to slide down his sides. He turns, taking me with him so that we are facing each other. My eyes stay focused on his as his fingers ghost over my face.

"What are you thinking?" I break the silence.

"How lucky I am to be here with you." His fingers play with my lips gently.

"I'm surprised you're here with me. I'm surprised at myself." I reach up and hold his wrist.

"What do you mean by that? Do you regret being with me . . . like this?" I can hear the vulnerability in his voice.

"No. I just," I struggle to find the right words. "Maybe the timing, rather than the action. I have to admit, I'm a little nervous about what you are thinking of me."

"I am sorry," he states clearly. "My behavior before had nothing to do with you, but my own insecurities from my past relationship. If there is anything I can do that I haven't or don't think of, please tell me." He stares clear into my soul with those piercing blue eyes.

"All that I ask is that you communicate with me. That you don't form conclusions until you go over your concerns with me first. I am a very patient woman, Declan, but I also have my limits." I squeeze his wrist.

"I promise. And just to emphasize that I'm ready to communicate, I will tell you everything about my past—what I've been going through." He plants a prolonged kiss on my forehead.

"Right now?"

"Yes."

"Can we make our way to the kitchen? I haven't had my dinner yet." I look up at him.

"What?! Maddie, why didn't you tell me? Come now—let's get you fed." He pulls away to climb out of bed.

"When was I supposed to say something, when you were impaling me with your tongue or when you were impaling me with your dick?" I ask incredulously. Declan barks out a laugh, and it makes my heart happy to see him in such a cheerful state.

He licks his index finger and marks at the air, "We'll put that point on your side of the board."

"I hope you've imagined my side being bigger than yours," I sass.

"Let's go before I find something else to do with that mouth of yours instead of shoving food in it," he teases as he grabs my hands to pull me out, as well. My face only an inch away from his glorious chest, I toe up and plant a kiss where his heart is. His arms encircle me, holding me close as he kisses the top of my head.

We stand here, it seems, for eons. Suddenly, music blares from my cell that I had put on my charging dock when I first got home. It's completely different from any of my ringtones that I have programmed in. Then, I hear the lyrics.

Oh.

My.

God!

"Did he say 'I just had sex?'" Declan asks through a chuckle.

"Yes. Apparently, a woman let him put his penis inside of her," I answer. I'm going to kill Jay, just so you know. Grrr.

"I can relate to that guy," he says thoughtfully as I pull out of his embrace to answer my phone. "I'm just not sure why it's your ringtone."

"Because this asshole programmed it in there before he left." I wave the phone at him before answering. "I fucking hate you, right now," is how I greet him.

"Why on earth would you say something so harsh to me?" He acts hurt.

"Because Declan is here and you fucked with my phone!"

"The Viking showed up?! I want all the deets!"

"Not now. What did you need?" I ask as I watch Declan slide his boxer-briefs on. Me? Oh, I'm just standing here, naked as a Jay bird!

"All I need is love. . ."

"And?" I'm getting a little impatient. I mean, I've got blue eyes trained on me. Lips are being licked as he watches. A slow prowl is beginning to take place. And my heart rate has just doubled.

"We need a girls' night . . . at your house—all of us."

"Why my house?" I gasp lightly as Declan's hands slide onto my hips. He dips his head down to the crook of my neck and peppers my skin with ever-so-soft kisses that make my eyes roll.

"Because there are no distractions at your house, and it's big enough for everyone to fit comfortably."

"Umm . . . yeah. Ok. Um . . . I have to go. Plan the night and let me know." I thread the fingers of my free hand through his hair and pull as his kisses become aggressive.

"Can't you just pick a date with me now?" he practically whines.

"No, I can't. There's a Viking here who's ninety-five percent na-ked. There are teeth involved, for Christ's sake, Jay!" At this urgent statement, Declan's shoulders shake. He really gets a kick out of me, huh?

"Ok. I will let you go and praise the vag gods for letting yours finally get some," he says before I end the conversation and drop the phone to fill that hand with his hair, as well. I yank harder, bringing his face to mine and attack his lips.

I can feel him working at his briefs, yanking them down. He steps out of them, our mouths still connected. Before I know it, he's got me up in the air, and my legs encircle his waist. I grunt as he slams my back up against the wall. And . . .

He nails me to it.

God, does he fucking nail me. . .

"Jesus, Maddie! Say it!" he groans through his relentless thrust-ing.

"Jesus, Maddie!" I repeat.

He laughs. "No. Say. You. Are. Mine," he corrects me. I would except I'm too busy climbing already. No will power over here. "Say it!" he barks.

"I . . . oh, God." I start shaking my head back and forth, willing the intensity away. His right hand comes off the wall and snakes in between us, under my left thigh. His left hand follows suit. My legs now hang over his arms as his hands grasp my hips, bringing me down on him harshly to meet his thrusts. It's so full this way. I want to escape—it's so intense. I push at his shoulders, trying to climb away. He only tightens his grasp and thrusts harder. I clench down on him, no longer able to push my orgasm off.

"Yes, Maddie. That's it, give it to me," he urges me as I begin to crumble. I hold tightly to him and cry through the pleasure. "Fuck!" he groans. "Your sweet, little pussy feels so good."

Please hold while I come a little harder from his words.

You too, huh?

Well . . . let's not make this awkward.

Just as I come down, I remember what he asked me to tell him. "I'm yours," I say through my rapid breathing. His eyes lock onto mine as we ride through the last few waves. They are soft and affectionate towards me. With one last thrust and slight shiver from him, he rests his forehead against mine. Our breaths—so loud as we try to even them out. His hand squeezes down between us, breaking our connection and allowing me to slide down till my feet touch the ground. I hold onto him for a moment to get my bearings. "Thanks for the ride, big guy." I pat his chest as I look up at him and wink.

"What am I going to do with you?" He bites back his smile.

"Seems to me; you have that under control." I beam.

"C'mon . . . put a robe on or something; you need to eat." His hands cup my face, and he plants a chaste kiss on my lips. I follow his orders, and we head out, hand-in-hand, to the kitchen.

"Wow . . . your taste is impeccable, Maddie," he says in awe as he looks around at my kitchen.

"Don't I know it?" I drink the sight of him in. A smile bursts through his lips when he realizes that I'm talking about him and not my kitchen. I mean, I think I made it pretty obvious. All I have to say is that I'm really channeling a whole lot of CiCi with this relationship. Not extreme-CiCi of course (let's all raise a figurative glass to Kyle, right?) but like, training wheels-CiCi. I'm proud of myself, actually. I set a goal a long time ago to be completely (mostly) myself in relationships from now on. This includes voicing what *I* like, whether in the bedroom or not; open and honest. I don't know why I had such difficulty with that before. To be honest, I can only blame my insecurity with my body. I'd like to say that the work I've put in to get over those insecurities are finally paying off.

"Can I ask you a personal question?" Declan interrupts my thoughts.

"Yes?"

"Why do you fear your orgasms?"

Fear of orgasms?!

What?!—No way!

Doctor . . . heal thyself.

"What are you talking about?" I avoid his eyes and head over to the fridge.

"You practically beat me to a pulp, wanting me to stop when you're about to come. Have you always been this way?" I feel his fingertips run up and down my arm lovingly.

I turn to him. "No."

He furrows his brows slightly and his hands grasp my biceps gently. "Am I hurting you?"

"No."

"Are you sure? I'm going to be gentle next time, just to be sure." He nods as if in agreement with himself.

Open and honest, remember?

"It's intense," I admit quietly.

"Well, I gathered that."

"No. It's *really* intense. It's just . . . you're so massive. It's just so full; I can't escape. The build from that is like nothing I've ever experienced before. It feels like it's just too much for me to handle. I *can't* handle it," I admit.

"You do, though, and it's so beautiful to watch," his voice, encouraging me.

"You like the way I come for you?" I give him a coy smile.

He groans. "Are you trying to skip dinner, altogether?"

"No, no. I need to eat before midnight, or we might have a whole *Gremlins* scenario on our hands." I pat his chest.

"We definitely don't want that." He smiles and leans down for a kiss. "Go sit down; I'm going to cook for you," he announces.

"You're gonna cook for *me*?" I get all wide-eyed, so the hearts can fly out of them easily.

"Yes, go and sit so I can wow you." He lets go of my arms and moves out of my way. I saunter over to the table and yelp as he smacks my butt. Ahem . . . well, now. . .

"I already made myself some soup. You can just pop it in the microwave." I point out the bowl sitting on the counter. He looks at the bowl then scoffs with arched eyebrows, like my bowl of *Progres-*

so soup was below his culinary standards. "Well, what are you gonna make me; it's late." Panicking about calories is part of my DNA, and I'm almost maxed out for the day. Though, I did just have some rigorous exercise.

Declan doesn't answer me as he rummages through my fridge, then looks for my pantry. I point to it. "I was under the impression that Rosie did all of the cooking for you," I say as he walks back in. He's completely in the zone; it's mesmerizing to watch.

"She does . . . mostly," he pulls his hair back into his tie, "but sometimes she lets me takeover or asks me to make a few of my specialties." A few strands of blond hair fall back down, breezing past his broad, muscular shoulders. His scruffy beard just a touch darker than his full head of shoulder-length hair. If you could have before you, the sight that is before me, you wouldn't need any butter for your muffin, either. Then, there's the Australian accent. Yes, I'll wait while you climax . . . try to keep it down, though.

"Maddie, I'm very concerned about your lack of fresh food."

"It's just me."

"And so you don't deserve fresh fish and vegetables?" he's short. "That's no excuse."

"I just bought fresh salmon!" I jerk up straighter in my seat.

"Five days ago, sweetness," he states calmly as he looks up from the peppers he's chopping.

"I like that you call me that," I change the subject and offer him a shy smile.

"It suits you." He winks at me then gets back to the veggies.

"What are you making me?"

"Shh. . ."

I roll my eyes and grab the *People* magazine I left on the table, to finish the crossword puzzle. Just as I finish the last clue and do an inner victory dance at getting them all this time, Declan sets a plate in front of me. It's a gorgeous spinach salad with feta cheese and a scoop of Tuna fish—plain. "This looks lovely," I say as I look up at him. "Am I out of mayo?" I ask because *plain tuna!* I know I'm not out of bacon, though that's absent.

"No mayo. I've put avocado in, though." He points the pieces out.

"So, I'm out of mayo?" Funny, I thought I had some for the sandwich I made yesterday.

"You have mayo. I just didn't add it in. It's much healthier to eat the tuna this way."

I stare at him.

"Try it." He pushes it toward me.

"I'm just gonna grab the mayo first." I go to get up.

"It's better for you this way; try it." He places his hand on my shoulder to stop me.

I look down, and fight the tears I feel slowly building. You see, according to the fucking asshole who came out with the charts, dictating to you what your weight should be, I'm on the line where whistles are blowing, warning of impending doom. It doesn't matter that I'm a healthy and an athletic twenty pounds over the going rate or that I could run circles around those chicks that are spot on—I'm overweight. And . . . he's seen me naked. See where I am going with this?

"I *have* tried it—I *don't* like it. I want to get some mayo," I say clearly and sternly. I'm not doing this. I'm not going to allow one moment to unravel all of the hard work I've done over the past two years to accept and love my body (pay no attention to my Oompa Loompa comments earlier; that's nothing compared to how I used to feel).

"Are you upset with me?" His fingers push my chin up so that I can look into his eyes. "Why are you crying?"

"I'm not crying."

"You're visibly upset." His thumbs wipe under my eyes slowly.

"I like mayo in my tuna fish."

"So much that it brings you to tears?" he does a little airy sort

126

of laugh.

"I'm a very passionate person." I hold my head high.

"Maddie. . ."

"Look, I'm overweight, yes, but I do everything I can to stay healthy and keep my weight steady. I refuse to give up certain things, like mayo and cream in my coffee! If you have a problem with the way I look, well . . . you know where the damn door is!" I let him have it.

"Are you kidding me right now?" His eyes are wild in disbelief. I stare at him silently, my heart beating loudly in my ears. "Apparently," he gets up abruptly, sliding his chair back aggressively, "I haven't done a very good job," he announces as he heads to my fridge, retrieving the mayo from it.

"A good job at what?" I speak up, though I suddenly sound very mousy.

He finds a bowl from a cabinet on the first try; *I'm impressed.* He grabs his chair and slides it back to the table before sitting. Grabbing my fork, he takes the pile of tuna back, tossing it into the bowl. He opens the mayo and scoops it out. "That's enough!" I panic at the amount. He growls, tossing some back into the jar. He begins mixing it all together and adds salt and pepper before re-mixing and plopping it back onto my salad. He sits back in a huff and points to my dish for me to eat. Nervously, I dig in.

"You wanted me to fuck you," he says out of nowhere, still angry. "I wanted to take my time, enjoy every inch of that gorgeous body of yours. Instead, I gave you what *you* wanted. Maybe if I had done things the way I had intended, you wouldn't be questioning my thoughts about the curves of your body—same ones that often bring me to my knees—or that sweet arse of yours that drives me wild." He reapplies his hair tie, angrily. "I'll be rectifying this situation once you're done eating; I don't care how much you beg me to get a move on." He grabs the magazine like he hates that specific publication.

Me?

Oh, just shutting the fuck up and feeding my face.

Vikings are extra hot when they're angry.

Just thought I'd put that out there, in case you were wondering.

"So. . ." Because the silence is killing me. "Are you going to make angry-gentle love to me? Isn't that an oxymoron?" I push the salad around, looking for a big chunk of feta to pop into my mouth.

He darts an eyebrow up at me, then looks back down to the magazine without a word. "Look, I'm sorry," I give in.

"I just don't understand where that came from. You have never complained or made comments to me about your weight. I don't like it. I don't like when women put themselves down." He shoves the magazine away.

"I wasn't putting myself down," I remind him. "I was defending myself. You made me feel like you were suggesting that I watch what I eat. It pissed me off."

"I was suggesting that you try the tuna without mayo because I like it that way. Most people that pass on it dry do it because they haven't tried it that way. It had nothing to do with your weight! And *who* even told you that you were overweight in the first place, because they are a bloody idiot?!" he seethes.

"Oh." Whoops. "Well, the weight chart doctors go by. I'm five-foot-one when I remember to stretch my neck. Ten extra pounds on me is like fifty on another person. And, you're right; I don't normally say anything about it because I know I'm healthy. But, that doesn't mean I don't think it, especially at times like tonight when I'm hungry *and* hormonal. When a woman is hungry and hormonal, the negative little bitch that lives inside her mind rears her ugly head."

"We should name her then, so you can warn me when you feel her wicked ways coming over you." A slight smile breaks through his lips.

"Hmm . . . but what, though?"

"Sunny," he says quickly, "because of her disposition."

"Yes! She'll never know we've named her something cheerful! Brilliant idea!" I finally find the hunk of feta I was hoping for and throw it in my mouth triumphantly. Declan sits back, watching me, his shoulders shaking as he bites his smile back.

"I'm releasing my brand of crazy on you too quick, aren't I?"

"I rather enjoy your brand of crazy, so please . . . don't ever hold back." He reaches forward and tucks my almost-grown-out bangs behind my ear.

"I promise." I grab his wrist and turn my head to place a kiss in his palm.

"Do you want a drink? I forgot to grab you one," he asks.

"No, I'm good. I do think we should start with one of the two topics we need to discuss." I let go of his wrist and resume consumption of the salad.

"Two?"

"Your past and the fact that we didn't use protection twice." I don't want to make it sound like I blame him because we are both at fault.

"I honestly didn't think about it. It's probably because I know that neither of us have had another partner in a long time, and I can't get you pregnant."

Wait—what?!

"How do you control that? Do you tell your swimmers to sit this one out on the bench?" I laugh. I'm not laughing inside, though.

"I'm not that powerful." He laughs with me. "No, I had a vasectomy six years ago."

Cue the crickets.

Can somebody put the hormones away, please?

I'm gonna call on Chaka Khan this time. . .

Because she feels for me. . .

"Let me get this straight." *Breathe in through your nostrils . . . out through your mouth.* "You've . . . you knew. . ." *Stop breathing so much . . . you're hyperventilating!*

129

"Maddie, what's wrong?" He reaches for my hand, but I pull away.

"No—don't!" I snap. "Why would you do this?!"

"Do what?"

"Pursue a relationship with me, knowing you would be unable to have children with me? Not that I'm certain we'd make it that far, but there's always a possibility. Why wouldn't you be upfront with me? Why would you waste my time? I want children, Declan, and I'm not getting any younger!" I stand up and start pacing around, my heart trying to beat right out of my chest. "I'd rather invest my time in a man I know there could be a future with." I run over to the drawer that holds my Ziploc and brown lunch bags, pull the lunch bag out, and circle it around my mouth, breathing in and out.

"Why are you breathing into that paper bag?" He watches me with a bemused look on his face.

"Because," I talk into the bag before inhaling again, then decide to pull it away, "I already have fucking feelings for you, you big ogre!" I yell then put the bag back in place.

"Ogre?" He gets up and begins a prowl over to me. "What happened to the sexy Viking? I was becoming rather fond of that persona." He gives me a crooked smile and palms my face.

"You find this amusing? Sure, you come here and take what you want—no concern as to how it will affect me!" I lay into him . . . through the paper bag.

He grabs the bag and tosses it onto the counter, then re-palms my cheek. "I did take what I wanted, didn't I? And, from the sounds you were making, I took it real good." He nips at my lips.

I'm gonna need a wet floor sign.

His mouth travels up my jaw and down my neck aggressively. "It's reversible," he breathes against my earlobe. The same one he's now sucking on. "I emphasized to the doctor that I needed to be able to reverse it easily. And just in case it doesn't work, I froze my sperm." He pulls back and stares into my eyes. "I've always wanted more children, Maddie. I just didn't want to have them with Renee. I couldn't chance it. I hope this knowledge puts me back in the running." He nudges my nose, then kisses me ever-so-softly.

"Your polls may be going back up . . . modestly," I say then chew on my bottom lip.

"My poll has *definitely* gone back up, and there's nothing modest about it." He smirks, and we both look down at the pitched tent in his boxer briefs.

"So that's what's been poking about." I attempt his accent. Obviously, the moment wasn't awkward enough.

"That's awful." He laughs lightly at me.

"Crikey! Looks like you've got another shrimp on the barbie, mate!" Because I don't actually know when to stop.

"I'm impressed you've lasted this long. Most jump right into that utter nonsense."

"You don't say that stuff?" I giggle.

"Have you ever heard me say 'crikey' before? No one says that where I come from. You've watched too much *Crocodile Hunter*." He kisses my forehead. "Come now, let's take a shower and then get this talk over about my past. I want to turn the next page with you; I already like our story much better than the other one I was in." He plants another prolonged kiss before sliding his hands down to mine and tugging me to start walking forward.

Chapter Twelve

Declan

Hitting the lock button on my car key till it beeps twice to satisfy me, I head back into Maddie's house with my overnight bag. I'd almost forgotten about it till I found myself disturbed to put back on my underwear again after our shower. I have issues with that—clean body, clean clothes. Rosie, God love her, always makes sure I have an overnight bag in my trunk because I've found myself, more often than not, staying with a colleague in Boston after a late night rehearsal. More thrilled was I that Maddie wished for me to stay tonight. I, of course, had to explain the reason behind the overnight bag and not that it was because I had bet on her. A bet that, had I placed, wouldn't have mattered either way—I didn't give her much of a chance to cause me to lose.

I'm rather shocked at myself, really. I think I just realized, though, that my "walking on eggshells" around her was not working. She clearly wants a more aggressive man, what with the things she's said to me and her calling me a Viking. I won't argue that speaking to her the way I did in the bedroom didn't turn me on because it *absolutely* did. I have never been one to talk like that. Of course, my thoughts have wandered there, but I never felt comfortable voicing those thoughts . . . until Maddie.

"Hey, I thought I'd open a bottle of wine, you game?" she asks as she walks into the living room, wearing the same robe I assaulted her in earlier.

"Please." I smile then pull in my bottom lip, trying to imagine what she has on underneath that robe . . . maybe praying for the same nonexistent pajamas from earlier.

"I have something on underneath, this time." Her lips pout out in a playful manner.

"How did you know I was wondering about that?" I walk over to her and reach for the knot of her sash.

"Because you're a guy and if you didn't wonder, your man-card might be taken away." She looks down. "What are you doing?" She tries to push my hand away.

"I want to see what *is* going on under here." I re-grasp it.

"No, sir!" She smacks my hand. "Go get ready for bed. I'm going to grab the wine and then, we are going to *talk*!"

"So aggressive, Ms. St. Claire," I tease. "I like it." I pull her to me by the knot in her sash and smack my lips against hers before releasing to go and get dressed for bed.

I look around her bedroom as I change. Maddie definitely has a way with interior design. I, myself, have an eye for it but only because handcrafted furniture (Dad) and interior design (Mum) is my family's business. The walls are a deep but calming gray with a gray-toned purple accent wall behind her bed. All the trims are pure white as well as her built in book cases. Her bedding is white with purple pillow accents. There is a deep purple tufted chaise lounge in front of her white-bricked fireplace. I can just picture her there, reading her trashy novels. It's a spacious bedroom; clean and crisp. I wander over to her bookshelves; they are full of books, photos, and Precious Moment figurines.

"Hey . . . I was beginning to think you got lost," her soft voice calls from behind me.

"No. I'm just very busy falling in love with your house." I turn to her and offer her a small smile as I take more in. "I love that you hung various frames on the wall; no pictures or glass, just the frames. I would never have thought to do that, and yet, it looks brilliant."

"Did you see this wall over here? I have some vintage silhouette pictures. I have more than this, but the rest are in my study." She strolls over and points to the wall that opens to her *en suite*. I follow her and stare at them.

"Is there a story behind why you collect these?" I wrap my arms around her shoulders from behind and kiss the top of her head. It feels so natural to be standing here like this with her, that it seems unnatural.

"My mom had silhouettes made of my brother and me when we were little. Growing up, I would stare at them, it seemed, for hours. That was my first introduction. I wasn't aware, though, that it was an actual form of art and that other people had them made, collected them, and whatnot. Then, when Jay was in school for Interior Design, he started dragging me to antique shops and flea markets—any place you can find a hidden treasure. One day, I happened upon this one, right here." She taps at the glass. It wasn't until then that I realized this was an actual art form. I was ecstatic; it was like finding a lost love. I bought it straight away and began hunting for others, as well as doing research. There's a deep, simple history behind them." She turns her neck to look up at me.

"Oh?"

"Yeah, the art form, itself, was supposedly named after a French economist, Etienne de Silhouette, as a derogatory reference to the brevity of his tenure as Controller-General of France in 1759. Some say it was because he was an avid amateur of l'art de l'ombre, his chateau full of his work and well-known.

"Others feel that it was named after him because his name became synonymous with the word 'cheap' in France. Just like *Habits a la Silhoutte*: men's waistcoats with no pockets. Cheaper because they required less fabric and labor. They also suggested that you had no money to put in the pockets; another slap in the face to de Silhouette for his failed policies. So, like the coats, the portraits were sleeker, cheaper, and made quicker than normal portraits; the name stuck.

"The actual art form was building popularity the century before, though, and continued through the 19th century. They were mostly created by women, trying to capture the likeness of their loved ones, especially significant others going off to war. Being a hopeless romantic, that's the history I focus on. I love when I find ones with names and dates on them. Others that don't, I simply name them myself and create a little story in my head about them. They were real people once, and everyone has a story, right?" She squeezes my arms to her.

"Yes, they do." I lean down and kiss her forehead as her face is still turned up to me. "It amazes me."

"What does?"

"How fascinated I become every time these beautiful lips move. I could listen to you talk about anything all night long." I lean further and grasp her lips softly with mine.

"I was afraid I was boring you. When I talk about things I'm passionate about, it's hard for me to shut up." She unravels my arms and turns into them, hugging me.

If someone came along and froze us like this forever. . .

I'd be ok with that.

"Don't ever feel like you have to shut up with me. You captivate me. I've told you this before; your stories, whether about your life or your passions, bring me great escape from mine. Conversations with you are a like a breath of fresh air."

"Declan. . ."

"I know. Let's go and sit in the living room and have that wine while I tell you everything," I concede, knowing from the tone of her voice where her train of thought was heading.

"You sure?"

"I owe you that much, so, yes." I kiss her again before leading her out of her bedroom.

We settle onto her couch after I start up a fire. I pat my lap and am rewarded with her cute little feet to rub. I think for a moment, then let out of big gush of air. "I don't know where to begin." I look at her, feeling a bit overwhelmed.

"You married young?" she leads in.

"Yes."

"And, you both were happy?"

"Immensely," I say and random moments fly through my head, like a film, of happy times. They sadden me . . . because we *were* so happy. The guilt creeps in. It's the same guilt that has crippled me all of these years, thinking I didn't do enough to prevent all of this.

"When did things change?"

"After Hunter was born. Actually, she was fine at first. Then, after a few months with a newborn and me gaining a seat with the Pops, she became completely overwhelmed. But, it was something more. I could tell she wasn't mentally well. We got her help, thinking it was postpartum depression."

"It wasn't?" she interrupts.

"Part of it, yes. It wasn't until a few years in that she was diagnosed with Schizoaffective Disorder."

"Ah . . . the combination of Schizophrenia and depression." She nods slightly.

"Yes." I look back down to her foot and run my thumbs up her sole, getting back to the massage. "Some time after we celebrated Hunter's first birthday, she began self-medicating. Prescription drugs were her vice, at first. She got away with it for a while. Then, the harder stuff came till she found her gold." I feel the anger boiling up in me.

"Which was?" Maddie prods by wiggling her toes.

"Meth," I simply state.

"Jesus. . ." she sighs.

"Yeah." I look over at her.

"That shit enhances the disorder. God, Dec, I can't even begin to imagine." She shakes her head.

"Oh . . . did it ever." I take in a deep breath. "It was gradual at first, you know, the evidence that something was not even close to being right with her. She was spending a lot more, but there was never anything shown to justify it. I had to open a separate account, allotting only a certain amount for our joint one. This waged a constant war between us. She called me a control freak. And, I was. I had to be, otherwise, we would've been bankrupt. Sure, I made a great salary back then, but I was also paying off our student loans on top of a mortgage, car payments, and every other bill. There wasn't much left over at the end of the month. Soon enough, her appearance started to change. Her behavior got even worse. She started blaming me for making her do things she would've never done in a million years. When I pressed her, she wouldn't answer as to what she was doing that was forced by me.

"I came home one day to find Hunter in hysterics. I picked him up and began to look all over the house for her, backyard, too. She was nowhere to be found. She left our son. I didn't know how long she had been gone for, but she didn't arrive back until three hours later. Hunter had just turned two. She was high and looked as if she hadn't showered in days. I was angry and began yelling at her, of course. She went nuts. Nothing she said made sense. She was throwing things all over the house. I had to call 911. That was the first time she was hospitalized. After that—rehab." I start on her other foot, finding comfort in putting some of my energy into that as I work through all the negativity of my past.

"Do you need to take a break?" I feel the back of her finger slide up and down my arm.

"No. I need to get all of this out in one shot."

"That's what he said." She snorts. "God," she slaps her head, "sorry."

I chuckle lightly and look over at her. "It's ok." I lean over to her and steal a quick kiss before I continue. "That was the first of many over the next two years," I start off. "I discovered that she had been doing anything to pay for her habit. That included whoring herself out."

"I can understand now why you were quick to think of me in a bad way, especially with my aggressive behavior," her voice quiet.

"I was wrong to behave that way, Maddie. There's no proper excuse," I snap. Not because I'm mad at her but, rather, myself.

"We all have reasons behind our behavior, Declan, whether we agree with them or not. The good news is that you are aware of the behavior. It makes it so much easier to correct, obviously." She removes her feet from my lap and curls them under her as she resituates herself at my side by taking my arm and putting it around her. Mmm . . . I could never tire of this type of intimacy. Let's be honest; I'm sure I will never tire of the other type she offers, either.

"Where did you come from, sweetness?" I close my eyes and rest my head up against hers. She's like a dream that only Shakespeare could conjure up.

"It's getting late; let's stay focused," she almost whispers.

"Okay," I sigh. "Like I said before, I got my vasectomy six years ago. This was right before Renee came home for the last time. I had really thought she'd made it to the other side, that it finally stuck—all the rehab stints. So much so that I was willing to work through, with her, what her addiction and poor management of her disorder had done to our marriage. The first several months were slow going; I had major trust issues, rightfully so. But, it did seem that we were headed in the right direction. I was beginning to let my guard down a little more each day. However, there was still a lot of skepticism left in me and worry. I installed cameras everywhere. This was strictly for my son's safety. Thank God I did that, Maddie." I look up to the ceiling.

"Why? What happened?" She sits up a bit, like she's at the edge of her seat.

"I came home from rehearsal and heard her yelling. I thought maybe Hunter had done something, and she was just reprimanding him, but I went into the room set up with monitors and I saw her." I stop, needing to take in several deep breaths and fight away the fear. Six years later and I feel every bit of the panic I felt that day whenever I think about it.

"What? What did you see?" Her hands palm my face, and she turns it to stare into her eyes. If this was anyone else, I'd yank away. Not with her, though; I feel calmer.

"She was choking him," I say then quickly gasp in air.

"No! Oh God, Declan!" Maddie's eyes form tears as the panic rises in her voice.

"I ran as fast as I could. I pulled her off of him and threw her across the room like she was a rag doll. I can still hear Hunter's first gasp of breath so loudly." I can feel my chin quiver, and my eyes burn to fight off the impending tears. Maddie throws her arms around my neck and pulls me into her, as she sobs. Her voice is muffled in my neck but I can still hear her say "I'm so sorry" over and over again. "Her reasoning was that her 'guides' warned her that he was possessed with a demon. She needed to get the demon out to save him. That was the day that I knew I was fully done. I got her out of there. When she was able to come home again, I got her, her own place. I started divorce proceedings. I searched out therapists for Hunter. He still has nightmares about it. She tried to claim that I abused her in our marriage. We went to court. I had to play the video of that day over and over again. She was in her own reality, as if she was seeing a completely different video from the rest of us. She screamed out in court to rewind the video and show everyone again how I threw her. To her, that was the only thing of importance, the only thing she saw." I try to shake the whole image from my head. "Even though I divorced her, I've tried to help her take care of herself. I want her to get better so that Hunter can have some sort of mum. I saw her just a few weeks ago."

"She never got healthy?" She raises her eyes up to me.

"No. I've had her in and out of hospitals and rehabs all these years. I've gone through several lawyers to handle her trust—"

"—Trust? From what?" she cuts me off.

"I've maintained financial responsibility for her."

"Why?" she almost yells.

"I've told you why," I answer calmly. "But, this last time, I've realized that I've had enough. I don't want to deal with this the rest of my life. It was affecting everything—still! I was messing up with you . . . a lot," I lower my voice and brush her cheek with the back of my hand. "I want my life back. I want the chance to be happy. I want *you!*" I attack her lips in a gentle but powerful way. My heart leaps all over my chest whenever I'm around this woman, and I love it. I love that I'm feeling again . . . no matter how scary it is. I pull away just as aggressively as I dove into the kiss. I want her so bad; I'm aching for her with every beat of my pulse. I waste no time, telling her what transpired recently: Renee begging to come home, my ultimatum, her final decision.

"So, she's there?" she asks.

"Yes."

"What if she comes out as the woman you fell in love with?" I can hear her self-confidence wavering.

"I'm not twenty anymore, Maddie."

"What does that mean?" She furrows her brows.

"It means that twenty-year-old me might be thrilled, but I am no longer him. She is no longer what I want in a woman. You are *everything* that I want," I emphasize before attacking her lips again.

"Hunter?" She breaks away. "Does he know what's transpired? What are his feelings on the matter?"

"I haven't told him. He doesn't like to talk about her. Honestly, after a while, what is there left to say? It would be like putting salt on a wound, constantly telling him his mother is getting help and that she'll be all better. I'd rather him stay focused on the things in his life that he *can* control. I'll tell you one thing, though—he's just as crazy about you as I am." I attack her again.

"Wait!" She pushes at my shoulders to gain some distance. "What do you mean?"

"He likes you a lot, Maddie. He sees how happy you make me." I smile.

"Is that why you are here . . . because of Hunter?" She seems guarded somehow.

"What do you mean by that?"

"You are trying to right the world for your son. You say he's fond of me?" She closes her eyes.

"Yes."

"Are you here for *you* . . . or for *him*? I know this may seem like a bizarre question, but he's been through a lot. I know that you want to give him a happy and normal life. Is that why you came today . . . tonight? Are you only pursuing me because of him? Don't feel bad . . . it would be completely normal for you to do so. At the same time, I need to protect myself, Declan. I can't be your answer . . . *the* answer to all of your problems. I come with my own set of crazy. I mean, not in an 'I have a diagnosed issue', but in a regular way . . .

I guess." She gets exasperated with herself. "What I mean is, I can't be that missing puzzle piece because I look like I'll fit there. I can only be the piece that is meant to come with the box. Fuck . . . am I making any sense?"

"You make so much sense, it's scary." I laugh and grasp her face in my palms. "This is about me. For the first time, in a long time, this is about *me*! Yes, it's quite the bonus that my son adores you. He adores you because he sees that you make me happy. And, you do, Maddie. You make me very happy. Yet . . . we've only begun. Please have me," I plead. "Please have me, knowing that my intentions are very real and focused on all of the right things, not just my son and his needs. I *need* you, Maddie, because you make me feel all of those cheesy lines in movies that are quoted over and over," I say with so much joy, I want to laugh . . . in a good way, though.

"I love all those sappy fucking lines." She laughs through her tears.

"Why are you crying?"

"Because, I'm scared and excited all at once." She wipes them away.

"Me too, sweetness. Me too." I kiss her.

Chapter Thirteen

Maddie

"So . . ." Ava leads.

"So . . . ?" I trail into a question as I fork through my salad before glancing up at her.

"How are things with Declan?" her tone is anxiously impatient.

"They are *really* good, actually. I'm almost afraid to say it out loud." I refocus on my salad.

"Why is that?"

"Well, we had a bumpy start." I quickly glance at her again to gauge her reaction. I haven't told her anything that has transpired over the last few months. I haven't told any of the girls, actually. "When are we doing the baby registry?" I quickly change the subject.

"Oh no! I'm not gonna have you girls do to me what you've

done to Charley in the past." She waves her hand before grabbing her drink.

"What?" I try to be serious, but I'm already ruining it by laughing. Let's just say most of us girls got out of hand with the gun. Charley spent a few hours, in tears, deleting our damage. She still somehow managed to get a lot of the stuff we had put on there. She was embarrassed as hell getting five different types of breast pumps and whatnot.

"Secondly! You are not getting out of talking about your life," she says as she picks up her fork again.

"If CiCi were here, she'd yell at you for saying secondly without ever saying firstly." I chuckle.

"Don't I know it?! I can't believe none of them could make it to yoga tonight."

"It's just been a crazy week for everyone. Though, I don't know what Julie's up to this week that she couldn't come." I stop, trying to remember the last time I spoke to her. I know that she's going through another bad cycle with her mom. Ha—Cynthia—that lady is a piece of work. I feel sorry for Julie. It must be hard sometimes; we all have great moms. Well, Ava did have a great mom. Ivy was the type of person who befriended everyone she met. She was a lot of fun, full of energy; everyone adored her. She's the only reason why I was on the cheerleading squad at all in high school; she was the coach. She encouraged me so much. God . . . I miss her.

She stayed on as cheerleading coach long after we graduated. One night, we dragged all of our moms out to a movie night. Even Cynthia came, and she behaved herself. The next morning, Ivy was gone. Kurt, Ava's dad, said that she got up and did her exercises like any other morning. Then, she went downstairs to have breakfast with him. She poured herself a cup of coffee, turned to walk toward the kitchen table where Kurt was and dropped dead. She had a brain aneurysm. She was forty-six.

"What's the matter?" Ava reaches for my hand. I shake my head trying to pass it off. "No! Tell me! What's wrong?" She hands me a napkin.

"I don't know why but, suddenly, I just thought about your mom. I miss her." I give her a frowny smile because I'm trying not to cry.

"I really wish she was here to see me become a mom." Her chin quivers and her eyes fill up instantaneously.

"Shit, Ava! I didn't mean to upset you."

"Oh please! I cry about her—for her—all the time. I found a way that helps me, though." She smiles through her tears.

"What's that?"

"When that happens, a random memory or thought of her, I like to think it's because she's right next to me. Maybe she's put her hand on my shoulder, causing me to think of her." She dabs her eyes then blows her nose.

"That's beautiful, Ava. I think I agree with you one hundred percent. Do you mind if I share that with my clients?"

"Only if you promise to tell me what's going on with the Viking!"

"Okay, okay," I concede. She claps her hands in excitement. Just like her mother. I can't help but laugh at her antics. Slowly, I begin to tell her about everything that has transpired. As she listens, she goes through every emotion I went through at the time, like it happened to her. And I stop for a moment to really take in how blessed I am to have such awesome friends. "So, since that night that we worked everything out," I laugh as she waggles her brows, "it's been fantastic. We've even begun to incorporate Hunter into one or two of our date nights, sort of like a family date night. It seems quick to do something like that, but Hunter and I have already known each other for a bit."

"How does he feel about all of this?" she asks before waving the waiter down. "I need to order that disgustingly delicious dessert." She points it out on the menu. He asks her if we'd like two spoons.

She doesn't hesitate to say no and tell me to get my own. I stare at her, trying to figure her out. Ava never indulges like this without a partner in crime. Hmm. . .

"He's thrilled. We get along great. Declan says he's like a completely different boy . . . in a good way, of course. That makes me happy. It's scary going into a relationship where there is a kid involved; I'm lucky. I'm having fun with him. As a matter of fact, he came to me, begging me for ideas for a unique costume."

"What did you come up with?" she asks, but all her focus is on the waiter bringing her monstrosity of a dessert over.

"Tomorrow, we will be putting the finishing touches on his claw machine game. His head will be inside a plexi-glass box with some stuffed animals and a big claw. We've put a joystick on the outside and buttons that actually light up. It's been a blast making this with him."

"Maddie?"

"Yeah?"

"Do you have any idea how much your face lights up talking about him?" She's in tears again.

"It does?" I tilt my head.

"Totally. I'd say you're just as much in love with Hunter as you are with his dad."

"Whoa! I didn't say anything about love. Don't rush us, please!"

"It's good to see you so happy." She ignores my comment, or at least pretends she didn't hear it.

"It's good to be this happy. I mean, I'm generally a happy person, just not this kind of happy." I swirl my spoon around in the fresh cup of coffee the waiter poured me.

"It's about time." She scoops a big bite of brownie and ice cream into her mouth. "So, are you brinnin' him to Than-iven?" she asks with her mouth full.

"I've brought it up. He's thinking about it. I don't think either one of us knows if he's ready for all the crazy that will bring. But, he has encouraged Rosie to see her boys, so I think he's coming around to the idea." I pour the cream, swirl once more, and blow on it before sipping.

"Rosie?" She wipes her mouth then goes back in.

"Jesus, Ava! This is so unlike you. Are you experiencing your monthly, dear?" I imitate my mother, making us both laugh. Oh, don't worry, I tease her (my mother) to her face, too.

"No. I'm probably getting it, though." She shoves another bite in.

"How's Trent doing?" I ask, hoping she'll come up for air.

She sighs dreamily. "I love him. . ." she trails off in the same way.

"I know." I laugh. I admire their relationship. They have the kind of love that will stand the test of time. All these years later and they behave as if they just started dating.

"He's just so excited. You'd think you'd have to worry about me going crazy, buying things. I have to rein him in!" She widens her eyes and laughs.

"Awe, that's awesome. You guys are going to be wonderful parents."

"You will be, too, Maddie." She shares in my smile and happy thoughts. Ava looks back down to her plate, scraping up the last bit of her dessert. "Jesus, I think I'm gonna vomit," she says before bringing the last bite up to her mouth.

"Why are you finishing it, then?"

"Because . . . it's the last bite; I can't leave it all by itself. It needs to be with the rest of itself," she defends her decision as if I'm the crazy one.

"I'm sure there's a phobia for not finishing dessert, but I can't think of it right now." I shake my head at her.

"Good. I don't need a diagnosis. I do, however, need to get home to that handsome hubby of mine." She grabs her purse. I grab the check. "What do I owe?" She gets her wallet out.

"Nothing; I've got it." I wink.

"No you don't, Maddie! You got the check last time!" she scoffs.

"So what? You have a baby coming. It's not like you're breaking my bank." I push her hand, with a twenty in it, away.

"I know there's no point in arguing with you, so I'll just say *thank you*." She puts the money away, and we both get up to leave. She starts futzing with my hair. "Stop by this week for a haircut."

"Yes, Mom." I hug her. We head out to our cars and give one final wave before getting in them and taking off.

Halfway home, I get an idea. "Call Declan," I command after pressing the phone option on the screen in my car. It rings a few times.

"Hey, sweetness," he answers out of breath.

"Why are you out of breath?"

"I was thinking about you and decided to have a go at myself," he says before gulping something down—loudly. I laugh. Over the last few weeks, he's become more and more playful with me and less shy.

"I hope it all worked out for you," I play along. "So, I have a question for you."

"Go on."

"Remember that I told you I may be covering a shift or two at the shelter for CiCi until she gets staff and figures everything out?" I make a left turn onto my street.

"Yes, that's right; her friend, who ran it, passed away."

"Yes. Well, she asked me to cover the day shift this Saturday."

"If you're asking me if it's ok, of course it is. Besides, I have a concert then."

"I know. What I wanted to know is, do you think Hunter would be interested in coming with me? I mean, if it's ok with you," I ask nervously. Even though we have been incorporating him in our plans, it all is still very new, and I don't want to overstep my bounds.

"I should like to think he would love to. But, I don't want to assume, either. Why don't you ask him?"

"No!" I panic.

"No? Why not?"

"I don't want him to feel obligated, which he might if I ask him. Why don't you just run it by him and see whether he'd be interested or not. Make it sound like your idea. This way, he'll feel more comfortable telling you that he wouldn't be interested. I don't think he would say that to me," I explain.

"I will do that if you promise me one thing."

"Just one?" I chuckle. "It better be a good one, then."

"Mind out of the gutter, St. Claire!" he barks in a teasing manner. "Promise me I won't come home to a new best friend for Hunter."

"Dogs are very therapeutic."

"*Maddie*?!" he drawls out my name with that delicious accent of his.

"I can't promise he won't fall in love with one. I can promise you won't come home to one, though, because you would need to be there to sign all of the paperwork."

"Promise me I won't be dragged down there the next day to fill out this paperwork, because you know I won't be able to refuse him."

"I can only promise I won't refuse you."

"That's the only part of this idea that I like." I can hear his smile. "Speaking of, I'm looking forward to seeing you tomorrow."

Instantly, the aching between my legs grows to an unbearable level. Thank God I've just pulled into my driveway. A week ago, I told Declan about my office fantasy that I had had for months. Last Wednesday, he made it happen—gaping-mouth fuck, people. And it was choir-of-angels-singing amazing. Tomorrow is Wednesday. "Will there be a repeat performance?" I ask after clearing my throat and stepping out of my car.

"All I will say to that is, wear a skirt and panties you don't care much for," he informs me.

"So, the granny ones that I can pull up to my tits?"

He laughs. "Only if they are *Hanes Her Way*."

"I love a man who knows his women's underwear," I joke.

"Sometimes, our conversations concern me."

"Please! Wait until you're around my friends, you won't be concerned about any of our conversations." I chide as I open my door. "Speaking of, have you put any more thought into Thanksgiving?" Shit. Why did I ask that? I don't want to become the nagging girlfriend already.

"Can we get through Halloween first, sweetness?" I can hear the apprehension in his voice.

"I'm sorry," I sigh as I close the door behind me, lock it, and throw my keys on the table. My answering machine is blinking.

"No need to apologize, Maddie," he says as I press play. I shouldn't have; it's habit.

"Oh dear, Maddie, you're out late again? I worry about you working all of these late night hours. How are you ever supposed to meet anyone? Please, give me a call when you get home. I think I may have a prospect for you! Love you!" she finishes. Thankfully, that's the only message.

"Well, that was telling!" Declan snaps in my ear.

"What was?"

"She doesn't have the faintest idea about us," he says through his teeth. Believe me; I can tell it was through his teeth.

"No, she doesn't," I agree. "I can honestly say it has nothing to do with you and everything to do with her. I have to break her in slowly, especially where Hunter's involved."

"Meanwhile, you go on the dates she sets up?"

"When? When would I have time to do that, if I were to do that?" Well, I spoke a little too soon tonight. I hold the bridge of my nose and try to take some deep, calming breaths, reminding myself of where this is coming from with him.

"We're not together every night," he starts to lose his steam.

"Right. Ok, I'm going to say goodnight now, Declan," I announce.

"Wait! I'm . . . Maddie, I . . . shit!"

"Goodnight." I hang up as I head into my kitchen. I pull out a bottle of wine and quickly work at getting it open and a good amount poured into a glass. Satisfied, I pad to my bedroom. It's time for a nice piping-hot bath, a good book, and my friend, red. I am allowing myself to be pissed, because I have the right to be, but I'm not going to get worked up over it. In a sense, he is right to be upset with me about not telling my parents. I love my mom, but with her being so obsessed over me finding someone, I need to make sure this relationship is solid. It's only been three weeks. That's not a long time to build a solid foundation in a relationship that started with *no* hiccups, never mind what we've dealt with already. I submerge into my tub. Ahh. . .

Suddenly, I remember Jay's request. He never got back to me with a date for our slumber party. I grab my phone and start a group text.

Me: Our mascot has requested a slumber party. Are you all available this Saturday night?

CiCi: Can I bring Pearl?

Me: It's like I don't even know you anymore!

CiCi: I know; that was so inappropriate for me. Can I bring my new bitch with me?

Me: That's much better, and yes!

Ava: Who's Pearl?

Me: Addie's dog that she left to CiCi.

Ava: Oh, that's right! Sorry!

Charley: Can't chat, but I'll bring the ice cream!

Julie: I'll snatch some liquor from Blake.

Jay: Thank God! I have 5 damn movies I've been holding off on!

CiCi: Jay! You are NOT allowed to pick the movies out anymore!

Jay: Hush, now. I'll bring the porn, too.

CiCi: Privileges have been resumed. ;)

Me: It's settled! See you guys when you get here.

Wait!

Charley! You need to make hor d'oeuvres!

CiCi: Not unless you want barfalot dip. I'll make them.

Julie: You don't cook!

CiCi: If Yan can cook . . . so can you!

Jay: Vic is catering our soirée.

Me: Vic's not coming?

Jay: Every night . . . like a freight train, honey.

Ava: T.M.I!!!

Jay: Anytime, Ava! But no, he won't be there.

CiCi: Ok, but I was going to bring my specialty!

Julie: What's that—air sandwiches and wind soup?

Ava: Charley! Bring ice cream cake!!! Extra crunchies!

Jay: I'll tell her. She's at a movie with the kids.

Me: I'm turning into a prune! I've gotta go! TTYL!

CiCi: Captain

Ava: My

Julie: Captain!

Jay: I've got nothing. ☹ I feel so left out of this synchronized text.

Me: You've got a freight train. THEY have too much time on their hands.

And with that, I shut off my phone. *Assholes.* Ok, I'm slightly giggling.

Chapter Fourteen

Declan

ONE OF THE GOOD THINGS ABOUT AUSTRALIA IS THAT IT'S fourteen hours ahead of us, so calling my parents late at night here is not a problem. Only problem is, I'm not sure who I want to have a heart to heart with about Maddie. My parents are both equally good at helping me work through things. They just use different methods. Perhaps I shall have them put me on speaker. Yes, a conference call for my sanity.

"Ah! There's the boy!" is how my dad greets me.

"Hi, Dad." I try to sound cheerful but I'm sure I've failed. "Is Mum there with you?" I ask right away.

"She is. Passing me off already?" he jokes.

"No, no. Can you put me on speaker? I'd like to speak to the both of you unless you have company." I fall back onto my bed. I decided it would be best to call them in my room so no little ears (or big ones, for that matter) could overhear.

"Sure, Dec. Everything all right?"

"It's nothing life or death, Dad; I'm just in need of some good solid advice, or a good verbal swift kick in the arse." I grab my pillow and shove it under my neck.

"Is this about the new lady in your life?" my mother says with a little too much excitement.

"How did you know about Maddie?" I inquire. "Also, I'm calling with a problem, Mum, try not to be so chirpy, will you?"

"Hunter told us! I'm quite mad at you, though," she states with a cross undertone.

"Why are you mad at me?!"

"How many times have we talked to you, and not *one* mention?"

"Oh," I sigh.

"Yeah . . . oh."

"I've been nervous, Mum. She's the first woman I've cared to take notice of, never mind develop feelings for. I've messed up with her several times as it is. God, she has the patience of a saint." I almost groan in anger. That anger, of course, would be directed at myself. I've just realized that I got angry with her for doing the same thing I've done. *What a bloody hypocrite I am!*

"Ok, you two, let's get a move on with the situation you're calling us about, son," Dad interjects.

"Right. Like I said a moment ago, I keep messing up. We seem to get on well for about three weeks until I have a bloody tantrum or react irrationally, and I ruin it." I run my free hand into my hair and pull at it.

"Is this because of Renee?" Mum asks.

"Of course. Thankfully, Maddie knows this as well, but everyone has their limit."

"What happened recently?" Dad asks.

"I got mad at her tonight, gave her quite the mouthful about the very same thing I've done."

"Which was . . .?" Mum leads.

"Not telling her parents about me. Gah! I'm such an arsehole! In my defense, though," I say quickly as I sit up. "Her mother is on a constant search for Mr. Right for Maddie. The woman turns matchmaking into an art! It's her life's mission to marry her daughter off, and well." I lay back down. *Her mother is going to despise me.*

"Declan, I'm sure that will change once her mum knows about you. You are a wonderful man and father. You have a good head on your shoulders. I know, without a doubt, that you treat Maddie very well, with the exception of your little outbursts."

"I do, Mum. I care very deeply for her." My heart twinges at the thought of losing her.

"Then, you must do whatever you can to rectify this. What else is there to say?" Dad chimes in.

"Right. She's asked Hunter and me to Thanksgiving dinner with her friends. I think it will please her if I said yes." I cringe and pull at my hair again. From what Maddie's said about her friends, they can be quite aggressive and obtuse. But, they sound like a blast, and I know they all have good hearts.

"What's the problem, then?" Mum asks.

"I'm not sure what I'm going to get hit with on our first meeting," I admit. "I'm actually nervous. They are like family to her. What if they don't approve?"

"If they've known Maddie long and well, they'll approve just because she does. That aside, how can anyone not approve of you? That's rubbish!" Mum detests.

"I'm shy, Mum; they're not."

"You never used to be."

"Yeah . . . well . . ." I sigh.

"It will be fine, son. And if it's not, we'll be there to pick up the pieces at Christmas," Dad announces.

155

"What's this, now?" I jump up again.

"Jonathan!" Mum yells. "That was supposed to be a surprise!"

"Well, Daisy, when were we gonna tell the boy, when we turned up on his doorstep?" Dad asks exacerbated.

"I just wanted to be the one to tell him." She laughs.

"You're always spoiling her fun, Dad," I tease.

"Sure, sure. That'd be true, if I had a clue half the time as to what the plans were," he argues laughingly.

"Right then, I guess I just needed to hear your voices. I know what I have to do—grovel. I will keep your Christmas surprise such for Hunter, though." I smile because I'm just as excited as I know he will be. "I love you both very much," I add.

"We love you too, Declan!" Mom shouts.

"Let us know what's happened, son."

"Will do, Dad! Talk to you later!" With that and our final good-byes, I hang up.

Damn! I was so wrapped up in myself I forgot to ask them how things were going. Last time we talked, Dad mentioned that business all but came to a standstill. My parents own their own furniture store. Everything is hand-crafted; most are custom designs. My mother runs the show from the financial and sales aspect, but my dad is the muscle and the artist; he has one apprentice.

While I appreciate the work that he does, it's never been a big enough interest for me to fully follow in his footsteps. Of course, I keep my eye out for trends and unique pieces I come across. Sometimes he'll make a variation of it. I have many of his pieces in my house; I'm proud of them. I bet Maddie will love his work.

Maddie. . .

I don't even know where to start. I need to stop and think before I react, otherwise, she will tire of me way too soon. I don't want her to *ever* tire of me. I'm falling so fast and hard for her. How could I not? She's the most amazing . . . giving person I've ever met. And— it's genuine.

With a deep breath, I hit her name under my favorites and listen as it rings. Voicemail. As soon as I hear the beep I say, "I called my parents tonight. You know what I realized? I hadn't told them yet, either. Hunter did when he was visiting them, but I never did. I only pray that your patience runs long and strong with me. I'm sorry. It's not good enough, but it's all I've got at the moment. I'll see you tomorrow, sweetness." I hang up quickly. Not because I was all done, but because I almost said "I love you." It felt natural and right to say it. It's too quick, though . . . right? I've done enough to scare her away; I don't need to add any more.

I'm not one to suffer from nervous energy but, here I am, doing all the things that drives me crazy about other people: legs shaking, anxiously looking around, sounding like Darth Vader as I try to calm myself down. Maddie should be finishing up with the client before our usual hour. I'm not sure as to what I should expect; she hasn't returned any of my calls. I'm in purgatory.

Just then, her client walks down the hall. Maddie is *not* following her. I jump up and head down the long hall to her room. I knock lightly. No answer. I let out a big gush of an exhale. Yes, I'm a little impatient. I'm over my behavior from last night, but, I suppose she's not. I open the door and charge in. She jerks her head up quickly from whatever she was working on.

"I'm sorry! I need this to stop just as much as you do—believe me!" I'm on the defense. She says nothing. "Maddie, I'm all kinds of fucked up when it comes to relationships. You know why. I only ask that you please search deep for some extra patience with me. I *am* trying to change," I plead.

"Hello to you, too." She smiles and gets up from her desk. She walks around it till she's right in front of me.

"Maddie?"

"Shh. . ." she trails off then toes up and kisses my lips ever so sweetly.

"Where do you get all of this patience from?" I say in disbelief.

"It's not always about patience, Declan; it's about understanding." She palms my face. "I'm not going to say that I wasn't pissed off because I was. I just know where it's coming from. I'm lucky that way; it gives me a lot of power over my own emotions." She lets me go and goes back behind her desk. "Is Hunter ready to finish his costume tonight?"

"Yes, I think so," I answer. "Maddie?"

"Yes?"

"That's it then? No screaming at me?" I'm in shock.

"Nope."

"What am I supposed to do with all of this extra adrenaline pumping through my veins? I was ready for a fight." I sit down feeling bewildered.

"I'd help you out with that," she starts as she takes the notebook she was writing in and tosses it in her drawer, then locks it, "but, I have to run to the craft store to get a couple more things for his costume." She grabs her purse and stands up.

"Can I come with you?" I stand up as well.

"Is Ted comfortable with you leaving?" she asks pointedly.

"I don't know. I've never left before. Do you not want me to come with you?"

"It's only going to take me a few minutes. You can wait in my office," she offers as she goes for the door.

"I guess you're still mad, then?"

She turns. "No. I just don't think you should interrupt Ted."

I tilt my head, trying to get a good read on her. "I'll stay here." I sit back down. I'm not going to argue with her. If she's still mad at me but trying not to be, well, I have to be glad that she's trying. I don't need to rock the boat any more than I have.

"I'm not mad . . . as much anymore." She opens the door wide. "Look, I'll tell our receptionist to have him call me if there is an issue. Let's go." She jerks her head toward the exit. I get up again and follow her lead. It's best.

"Ok, now connect that wire here." Maddie points to the area.

"Are you sure?" Hunter questions. This is their third time at trying to get the buttons to light up.

"Yes. That's what it says. And, honestly, what other choice is left." She laughs. He shrugs, giving in and attaching the wire to its new home. "Hit the button, professor," she orders. Everything lights up.

"It's *alive!*" my son yells out like he's created Frankenstein. Maddie is shrieking and doing "Woot woos" with a fist pump like she's channeling Arsenio Hall. She gets up quickly and helps him put the costume on. "Make sure the claw works, Maddie!" he yells through the plexiglass.

"Oh yes! Let's check it out!" She calms down and grabs a hold of the joystick. The claw moves without a hitch. Maddie cheers excitedly, bouncing up and down. I'm rather enjoying the show.

"We did it, Maddie! I can't believe we did it! Coolest. Costume. Ever!" He jumps with her. Round and round they go like a bouncing version of "Ring Around the Rosie."

"Alright, you two, before you damage what you've worked so hard on." I laugh at them.

"Your dad's right." She stops. "Let's get this off of you so it doesn't get ruined."

"You guys really blew this out of the park," I say with great pride. "And, I truly hope that you found the way I just sat back and watched very helpful."

"We wouldn't have been able to do it without you, Dad," Hunter teases me.

Eutopia.

That's what this moment is making me feel: my own place perfected. These two have been forming quite the bond. Pleased does not fully describe how that makes me feel.

"What's that look for?" Maddie asks me. I pull out of my zone of staring at them.

"I don't know what look I'm making, but I hope it is reflecting the happiness in my heart at the moment."

"I feel the same way." Warmth emanates from her smile as she looks from Hunter back to me.

"Dad, can we just stay here tonight instead of going home. I finished my homework. I'll get up a little earlier so I'm not late for school." He turns to Maddie. "You have a room for me. I won't make a mess and will make my bed in the morning."

Before I can answer, Maddie does, "Soon, Hunter; I promise. I have a lot of homework tonight. I haven't written any of my session notes this week, and where I'm going in late tomorrow, I had planned on getting it done tonight." She pushes some of his bangs back off his forehead. My heart sinks; I was going to say yes. Maddie hugs him to her and looks up at me, "Too fast" she mouths slowly. Oh. "Alright, Dad?" she asks.

"Yes, besides, you'd be going to bed at the same time. It's a school night, buddy; it's not like we can do something extra special tonight. Let's save it for a night when we can, ok?"

"All right," he sighs with disappointment. "But when we do, you and I are going to have a marathon on your PlayStation!" he warns her. I still can't believe she has her own PlayStation; I don't even know how to play half of these games. She says it's for work; it helps her to relate to the teenagers she sees and encourages them to open up more. While I believe there is some truth in that, I can also see her being a closet gamer.

"Get your stuff, Hunter; it's time to head home. I'll carry your costume," I say as I lean over and pick it up.

"Ah! Be careful!" Maddie screeches when I almost drop it.

"I got it." I straighten out. "Can you get the door for me?" I ask her.

"Yep!" she says then heads in that direction. I follow her, and she walks me down to my SUV. "Declan," she says in a hushed voice as she opens the trunk up.

"Yeah?" I put it in.

"Me saying no tonight had nothing to do with you and me and what happened last night. Hunter and I have been bonding a lot over the past few weeks, and I absolutely adore him; you know that I do. I'm just concerned where he's never had a real mother figure in his life, besides Rosie and your mom, that he may be latching onto me too quickly."

"Why is that a bad thing, exactly?"

"It's not that it's a bad thing, per se, but I'd rather he not jump in feet first without taking the time to let our respect and relationship grow. Kids are wired differently than adults. When you have a child who's missing a parent or both, they can latch on quickly, desperately trying to fill that void they have. If, for some reason, we don't work out and you begin dating again, he may do that with the next woman. Then, the next and the next. Soon enough, he'll be an adult with a void that only got filled with disappointments. He may develop a complex, thinking there is something wrong with him that nobody wanted to be his mother. There's an endless list of possibilities for how this may affect him. I'd like to help him slow down, understand his worth. It's different . . . the kind of love, growth, and validation you get from someone outside of family and close friends. You're a wonderful dad, Declan. But, there will always be things he needs that you can't be the one to provide." She palms my face.

"I really appreciate the way your brain works, sweetness." I lean down and sweep her lips. "I don't appreciate when you mention that we might not last. This is the second time you've done that. It worries me. It makes me feel like I may be running out of time with you," I admit as I lean my forehead against hers.

"Oh no! Try not to feel that way, please." She kisses me again. "I'm just trying to be a realist. It doesn't mean I think we are a ticking time bomb."

"All set, Dad!" Hunter announces from behind us. I give Maddie another swift kiss and break away from her. "Goodnight, Maddie." He goes right in for a hug.

"I. Had. So. Much. Fun," she says as she rocks him dramatically in her hug, making him laugh. She lets him go, and he climbs into the car. "Call me later after he goes to sleep." She grabs at my jacket and tugs on it.

I lean in near her ear. "How about I come back over here after he goes to sleep so I can rock *you* dramatically?" My hands slip onto her hips, and I grasp them tightly.

"You can't. If he wakes up and realizes you came back here, he will be very upset. Also, I wasn't lying about needing to get my notes done." She places her hands on my shoulders and pushes slightly to give us some distance.

"But we missed our usual meeting today." I pout. Since we've been a solid couple, our Wednesday hour office chat has now become whatever indecent thing we can think of. Maddie has a thing for desk sex. Actually, having sex in her office, in general, is her thing. I definitely don't mind obliging.

"I wasn't up for it. I'm sorry. I'm due for my, you know. I'm no good around that time as my body starts cramping ahead of time, warning me of impending doom." She rubs her belly slightly.

"Do you need me to run to the store to get you ice cream?" I place my hand on top of hers.

"That is the sexiest thing you have said to me all night. I think you just got me pregnant," she says with such a straight face, I can't help but laugh. "I have all the provisions I need, though. Thank you." She smiles and leans up on her toes. "Night, baby." She smacks her lips up against mine. I slide my hands around her waist and lift her up so that she's now leaning down into the kiss. God, I'm crazy about her. I hate whenever I have to leave her. I just want to always be with her. And that feeling gets stronger with each day that passes.

"Night, sweetness." I guide her back down onto her feet and give her one more kiss before heading around to the driver's side and climbing in.

Chapter Fifteen

Maddie

My head is completely spinning, and it's not even Christmas yet. I'd like to say the past eight weeks have been full of just holiday craziness, but it hasn't. I've had six admissions to Hampstead Hospital, alone, since Thanksgiving.

Speaking of Thanksgiving, Declan and Hunter went to CiCi and Kyle's with me. Not only had they survived, but it seems they have been welcomed with open arms.

Yes, Thanksgiving had been quite interesting what with Julie's mom, Cynthia, taking a pie to the face. Honestly—she deserved it. While that was happening, Julie was outside pleading with Blake. She had finally given into her feelings for him. She was almost too late—*almost*.

And then, the announcement came that knocked everybody's

socks off: Ava's pregnant—with twins! I had a hunch, but geez, they had been trying for so long, it was easy to push that hunch down. Mitch was less than thrilled. I know the fact that Charley agreed to be Ava and Trent's surrogate mom was not exactly at the top of his hit parade.

But, I think the best part about the holiday was seeing CiCi so happy . . . so content. It's funny how you can know somebody most of your life and think that you know *everything* about them, then suddenly, you get knocked on your ass with something you not only didn't know, but never expected.

Drew had done more damage to her than I could've ever imagined. In the grand scheme of things, it makes sense now, some of her odd issues in general, her pushing most men away. Except for the gem she has now. I couldn't have handpicked a better person for her. Kyle has been so helpful to her and so open to all of my suggestions to help her work through her past.

Spinning, I tell ya! I'm so glad that tonight is the night that starts our girls' holiday weekend. We've had to cancel our last several attempts for the slumber party Jay was dying for. Feeling bad, we decided to include him in for our tradition. You would've thought he won the lottery.

The guys are all getting together, as well, and we've sent Hunter to spend the night with the O'Briens. He and Brogan have become instant friends since Thanksgiving. I love that kid. More and more, I'm beginning to look at him as my own son—against my own advice. But as I say to a lot of my clients: advice is much easier to give than to follow.

And Declan? Oh man have we evolved since Halloween. My parents have finally met him. I'll never forget the look on my mother's face; I practically had to lift her jaw off the floor for her. "I know, right?" is all I said to her. Needless to say, I was wrong about how my mother would react to Declan having a son. I'd like to believe it's because she sees how happy I am. Preston, of course, says it's because she's run out of friends with single sons. And, her asking random new people she's just met, if they had one, was beginning to get awkward.

"She'll never have to do that again, rest assure," Declan interrupted. That was a sore subject with him, as we know.

My dad took the quickest to Hunter, fascinating the ten-year-old with his train collection. Yes, my dad is one of those guys who have a special section of the basement dedicated to his hobby. Yes, he wears the engineer's hat when he's running his trains. Hunter was on cloud nine.

My mother all but sent out "Save the date" cards when Declan invited us all to the Holiday Pops concert. She shouted out, "That's my son-in-law!" when he finished his solo performance.

If I were a cat, I'd be on my last life.

"Mom!" I practically screamed at her.

"What? I'm so proud of him, honey!" She was still clapping—spasmastically (Jay's favorite made-up word; it was fitting for that moment). I prayed he didn't actually hear her. Because—we're not married, for one. And two, we're not even engaged! She's got her mind made up, though. And here I was, worried about Hunter latching on too quickly.

My nerves are all shot to shit about Christmas. Why? Because his parents are coming in from Australia. My mother has insisted that we bring them for Christmas dinner. I may need Xanax for this. I've had several conversations with my mother about trying to control herself a bit when they get here. I don't want them to get the wrong impression. You know, the one where the girl's mom is desperate to get her married off because she's in her thirties and that biological clock won't tick forever. Sound familiar?

And. . .

What if they don't like me?! Listen, I'm not about to get cocky over here, thinking I have this in the bag. That's when gorillas start flinging their shit at you. Know what I mean?

Just as I pull into my driveway, I see Declan's SUV. *What's he doing here?* He knows I'm expecting everybody in an hour. I park next to him and cut the engine. As I grab my purse and the few bags in the passenger seat, I hear my trunk door open. I look over my shoulder and see him starting to grab the bags I have back there. "Hey," I greet him as I get out and close my door, "What are you doing here? Aren't you going out with the menfolk?" I walk up to him and welcome his kiss.

"Yes, but not for another hour or so. I figured you'd have a lot of bags and prep work you'd want to get done, so I thought I'd pop over to help you before everyone gets here." He follows me up the pathway.

"That was nice of you." I smile over my shoulder at him. "You know that Vic is catering though, right? I really don't have much to do besides wrap the last few gifts," I say as I open the door.

"Cut me some slack, sweetness. I haven't seen you in two days, and I won't be seeing you all weekend. I thought I'd sneak in a little visit with my beautiful girl."

"A conjugal visit?" I spin around and raise an eyebrow at him.

"If that's what you desire, I certainly wouldn't deprive you." He smirks playfully. I laugh lightly and continue on into the kitchen. "Do you want me to put these on the table?" he asks.

"Yes please." I bring what I am carrying to the island and start pulling stuff out of the bags.

Within a few moments, I feel his hands slide onto my hips. "Simple everyday things, like this, make me feel so content and happy," he breathes against my hair.

"Putting away groceries?" I ask in a teasing tone.

"Yes. Putting away groceries. Being here when you get home. Watching you with my son." He takes in a deep breath. "I'm so happy, Maddie. *You* make me so happy." He kisses the top of my head. I turn to him and try to push down the butterflies as his face descends. His lips peck softly at mine, his tongue playfully flicking, encouraging me to open. I willingly do so. The kiss is as smooth as velvet and elicits a small groan from both of us. His hands slide down to the back of my thighs, and he lifts me; my legs instinctively wrapping around his waist. He goes to place me on the island.

I break from the kiss. "Bedroom," I command before reconnecting with him.

"No," he says sternly. "Lie back." His chest heaving through his own commands.

"But—"

"—Now!" he cuts me off.

"So bossy," I tease before lying back. He unbuttons my dress pants and shimmies them off of me. I hear him chuckle, and I look down. "Are you laughing at my trouser socks?"

"I mean, have you ever seen anything so sexy?" He bites back his smile as he rolls each one off of my calves.

"Just be glad I shaved this morning, otherwise, you wouldn't have been able to handle all of the sexiness thrown your way." I lie back down.

"Did you shave here?" he asks, and I feel the pressure of his thumb sliding on top of my panties, up my center.

"No. I did something else there," I admit nervously.

"What?!" he asks in what seems like a mixture of disbelief and excitement. I feel him all but rip my panties off. "Jesus!" He walks away then back to me. "Jesus!" he says again before grabbing under my knees, making them bend and pushing them back to my chest. "Fucking gorgeous," he groans. I guess he likes it, then. I'm glad because Brazilian waxes hurt like a bitch.

He bends down, and I feel his lips fluttering soft kisses mixed with nips and slight sucking at the skin of my heat. My hips fly off the island several times. Each time, his hold on me strengthens. He lets go of my right leg and soon enough, I can feel his fingers teasing my entrance. "You like that sweetness?" he coos. I respond with rapid breathing. "So soft . . . so perfect." He licks then blows. "Such a delicious feast before me."

"Please," I beg. His tongue flattens against me and slides, at a snail's pace, up my center. I wiggle in protest of his teasing.

"The more you move around, the slower I will go." He raises an eyebrow to me and softly blows on my wetness, again.

"I'm going to die of impatience, just so you know," I try to complain but with him flicking softly at my clit, I don't think it hit home the way I wanted it to. Speaking of hitting home. . . "My friends will be here soon. Can we take this to the bedroom, so nobody walks in? Also, can we make it fast because I don't have much time."

He releases me, then comes over to my side and, without saying a word, he abruptly lifts me off the counter like a damsel in distress. "I'm going to take my time with you, sweetness. You'll have no choice but to relax."

"I'm already wound up for two different reasons, how am I supposed to relax?" I ask as I bury my face into his neck. I inhale the mixture of his natural scent and cologne. I swear there isn't a better smell in the world.

He walks toward my bedroom, making me feel as light as a feather in his arms. Gently, he places me on my bed, and I drop my hands to it to push further back. Declan erects himself (he's not the only thing that is now erect . . . ahem.) and grasps the hem of his shirt, pulling it up and over his head. I lick my lips before biting my bottom one, taking in the sight of this Zeus-like man with his broad chest and defined muscles. He looks like one of those men on the covers of Regency romance books. Thank God his face looks nothing like Fabio (just not my cup of tea, people). I let my eyes travel up to his face and see the curious, yet playful smirk that has taken up residence. "I'm admiring the results from your 4 a.m. workouts." I beam.

"I'm admiring tonight's 5 p.m. workout," he quips. "Take your blouse off, sweetness," he instructs. I take my time unbuttoning it, teasing him. "I thought you were in a rush?" He pops the button on his jeans and slowly unzips the zipper. He whips his jeans and underwear down in one swoop, stepping out them when he's done. My eyes immediately fall to the prize in his hand (give this man his blue ribbon!). "Maddie," he states. I look back up to his eyes. "Take it off. Now," he's stern, and I may feel a little turned on about that. I all but rip my blouse off. He leans forward, reaching around my back to unhook my bra as he plants kisses on my right shoulder. "We'll be here forever if I let you handle that." He straightens up, sliding my bra straps down my arms until it is completely off of me. He leans even further down to pull my right nipple into his mouth, sucking it hard before placing a gentle kiss. He does the same to my left, and I fist his hair. "Open, sweetness." He nudges my legs. I comply and feel the mattress shift as he climbs on top of it, his knees between my legs. "Lie back," he orders softly after a lingering kiss on my lips. I close my eyes as I do so, taking in deep breaths, listening to the sound of them. His hands coast over my body like he's never touched me before. My body is reacting to his touch in the same manner. "You don't want to watch me love on you, Maddie?" his voice so light, like a distant dream.

"No," I barely utter.

"Are you okay?" he asks before he nips lightly at my left hip bone, causing me to lift my hips off the bed.

"Mmm hmm," I purr.

"You like not knowing what I'm going to do next?" his voice raspy and sexy as hell.

"Yes," I gasp as he nips at the other side.

"So. Fucking. Beautiful," he groans between slightly stronger bites at my skin, random in the pattern he is creating. His hands grasp my tits, pushing them up aggressively as his mouth covers my left one. He pulls at my nipple then bites it hard, making me yelp. My hands dive into his hair, and I pull as he does it again.

"God, Dec—yes!" I scream as he sucks and bites even harder. I don't how he knew I needed this (pleasure/pain) when I didn't even know it. It's absolutely mind-blowing, and I can't get enough of it. Switching lanes to my left tit, he pushes my legs even further apart as he spreads his knees out a little more, becoming more prone on top of me. His cock slides up my slick heat with his every movement. My heels dig into the mattress as I lift my pussy (greedy bitch, isn't she?) to rub feverishly against him. Declan releases the girls and slides his right hand behind my neck, lifting it as his other hand palms my face possessively. My lips part just as his mouth comes crashing down, his tongue darting inside, commanding attention. I pull his hair tighter, pushing him deeper into the kiss. He releases my face and grabs my hip, adjusting me, so I feel him knocking at my door. Except . . . he doesn't really knock. "Oh God!" I scream, tearing away from our kiss. He just barged right in . . . like he owns the place. *Barbarian.* Yeah . . . I like that shit. Dec re-grasps my face and quiets me with his mouth again as he begins a sequence of slamming into me hard and deep, then pulling out extremely slow before doing it again. If I wasn't already about to fall out of my mind, the deep tingling begins, and my core tightens. His grip on me becomes tighter. He must know I'm ready to fall over the edge. I'm trying to work through it without letting it overwhelm me. *I can do this.*

Declan grunts against my mouth. His lips travel down my cheek till he reaches my earlobe. He pulls it into his mouth and sucks tightly at it before it falls out. The intensity builds up even more, and I'm on the verge of crying—it's too much. "Mmm . . . you're almost there, sweetness. I can tell by the way your pussy is milking my cock." His words causing me to tighten even more and, at the same time, I let go of his hair and push at his shoulders to get off of me. He chuckles. "You're not going anywhere, baby. You're going to take it like a good girl. C'mon, Maddie, let yourself go," he coaches, getting rougher with his thrusts, panting heavily.

"I can't. I can't. I can't," I chant almost in tears. But, it's no use, my legs are shaking, and I'm punching the hell out of his back, until finally, I erupt, crying lightly through the waves.

"That's it, sweetness," he soothes me just as he stills, then pumps . . . stills and pumps, groaning my name and some explicit stuff about my pussy. One last thrust and he collapses on top of me.

"I'm sorry," I apologize for my behavior as I always do after. I don't know why I fight it so much. Seriously—I have issues.

"I don't want to hear that anymore," he says . . . like he always does. "Besides, it kind of turns me on that you try to fight me off at the end. Is that weird?"

"No. It turns me on, too . . . you not letting me have my way." I kiss his hair. He lets out a long gust of breath. "Exactly, we better get out of this bed," I agree like I read his mind. He lifts his head off my chest and flashes a huge grin at me, confirming that I did do just that.

My doorbell starts ringing obnoxiously, and I scamper around, trying to get dressed a little quicker. "Hurry!" I whip my towel at him in a panic as he is taking his sweet damn time.

"What's got you all wound up, sweetness?" He eyes me and waggles his brows.

"I didn't even wrap the last few gifts!" I grab my head in disbelief. I hate this. I *hate* being late. I *hate* not having shit done in time. I *hate* the panic that occurs. I *hate* that CiCi has *not* stopped with my fucking doorbell, yet! "I'm gonna fucking strangle her!"

"Maddie, calm down." He grabs my shoulders gently. "I'll get the door; you finish in here." He kisses my forehead. "I'll see you in two days—I—" he stops mid-thought.

"You what?"

"Nothing." He shakes his head quickly, looking slightly freaked out.

"Whoa! What's that look about?" I try to stay focused. *I'm going to fucking strangle her.*

"I miss you already; that's all." He gives me a quick kiss and grabs his shirt before practically running out my bedroom door, closing it behind him. I stare at it for a few moments before snapping into action. I don't know what that was about, but I don't have time to figure it out right now. I throw my pajama pants on to complete my fancy ensemble for the night and grab the gifts I still need to wrap.

"He's a keeper!" CiCi announces as she walks into my bedroom.

"Wow—knock much?" Yes, I'm still irritated.

"Nah. Besides, I've seen all that you have to offer, shortstack." She winks. "Last minute wrapping?"

"Yes, damn it!" Did I mention I hate not having shit done in time?

"Stop flippin' out! Try to think of the reason why you're not done." She nudges me.

"Why's that?" I toss the roll of wrapping paper on the bed and zip my scissors up it frantically like there's a gun to my head or a timer that's about to buzz.

"You were busy getting some lovin' for you muffin."

I take in a deep breath. She's right; that is a good reason. "What is it with guys, though? When you want them to take their time, they're in a race. And, when you want them to go off like a jackhammer, that's the time they decide they are going to make *epic* love to you?"

"Make *epic* love?" she questions like she's trying it out. "I think you should have that stenciled above your bed."

"Or . . . 'Make Love Epic,'" I add to her thoughts.

"Now, that's the type of saying that will make you feel like belting out an Italian love song, like that pasta commercial." She lies on my bed, hand to head, hoisted up by her elbow.

"You mean that song by Andrea Bocelli?"

"How would I know; I'm Irish?"

"What?" I laugh.

"I don't know the Italians that sing the Italian love songs."

"I don't think it's a rule that you have to be Italian to know who they are." I fit the paper to the shirt box.

"Or to eat the pasta they sell."

"Bocelli doesn't sell the pasta." I roll my eyes at her.

"Doesn't he, though?" she pushes. "You know what would be as funny as shit?"

"Not many things. I mean, what's funnier than shit?" I tease.

"Not much. *Except*! What if he wasn't really singing about some romantic shit?"

"What?"

"All that music sounds so damn romantic, but what if he was really singing, *'Peeeeople, don't eat this pasta; it's really fucking nasty. You won't get the girl just because you bring her this name brand pasta, you diiiiickhead. Just goo-ah and pay for a whore-ah; she won't require dinnah.'*" She stops singing . . . because I wacked her in the head with a pillow, laughing my ass off.

"It's seems like you've put a lot of thought into the exact wording because you sang it perfectly; not a note off." I work at taping the box up. "Here," I toss her another, "wrap this one."

"This one isn't mine, is it? Because that would really suck . . . wrapping my own damn gift," she mutters as she gets up to help.

Soon enough, we hear everyone else parade into my house. "Be out there in a minute!" I yell.

With the last gift wrapped, we grab all of them and head out to my living room. "Those bitches started eating without us!" CiCi says in disbelief. "Let's get out there before the pregnant ones eat everything." She practically throws everything under my tree.

"Careful!" I snap, catching an ornament as it falls off its branch. I rehang it and follow her out to the kitchen. "Jesus! Did Victor think we'd be here for a damn month?" My eyes widen at all of the food.

Vic is Jay's boyfriend of two years. He's the owner and head chef at Alexandros (named after his grandfather, also a chef, from Greece). Vic had hired Jay to renovate the restaurant as it was still stuck in 80s décor from the previous owner. They immediately drove each other nuts; not in a good way. Vic was terribly rude to Jay all of the time. And every time Jay was almost done with the renovation, glad to be moving on, Vic would request a design change that would require Jay to stay on longer. It was becoming rather obnoxious. One night, Jay had enough and was going over there to give Vic a piece of his mind. Instead, he gave him a piece of ass. Turns out, it was all built up sexual tension between the two. At the time, Vic had only just accepted that he was in the closet. So, he hadn't come out of it yet. He was confused, trying to fight off the feelings he had. They had always been there, but I guess when Jay came along, they weren't so easy to push down anymore. They've been going strong since then, and we all benefit in the food-baby department.

"Where's my moo-sakkah?!"

"Ceese, why do you say it like that? It makes it sound Japanese," Charley complains.

"I'm your sister; I've got a quota to meet," she says as serious as a heart attack.

"Don't do it, Charley," Ava warns her.

"What quota?" Charley asks anyway.

"She never listens," Julie says with a mouthful of something or another.

"I have to annoy you so many times a month. Otherwise, you won't know that I love you."

We all wait for it.

Ahem . . . is this thing on?

"That's it?" I ask incredulously.

"What?" CiCi asks as she grabs her plate and heads over to the table.

"She's gone soft on us." Julie sighs.

"Nah. She's preggers and irritable. Even I'm not stupid enough to fuck with her right now." Ceese shoves a mouthful in.

We all finish grabbing our food and take a seat. There's quiet amongst the GEGs as there should be when we're stuffing our faces. Honestly, it's not a pretty sight; you should look away.

"Vic is cheating on me," Jay announces. Three out of the five of us are choking on either food or drink.

"Don't fucking play with us, Jay!" Julie smacks his arm.

"I'm not." He goes tight-lipped like he's trying to control his emotions.

"Why do you say that?" Charley rubs his back, being the more nurturing friend.

"I saw him."

"Shut the front-fucking-door!" Ceese bellows.

"His name is David. He's Vic's new personal assistant. Seems he is assisting him with a lot of things." His eyes fill up. "I caught them hugging and laughing today. Vic looked so happy." He gasps in a hiccuppy sort of breath. "I can't remember the last time he looked that happy . . . with me."

"He's not cheating on you, Jay," Charley states as if she knows and goes back to eating.

"How can you say that?!"

"Yes, how can you say that?" Ava chimes in.

"Because I *know* he is not cheating. I'm not going to tell you how I know, well, except for the fact that David has a girlfriend and Vic told me that he was getting ready to propose. Hey!" She smacks him. Boy did he pick out crappy seating arrangements for himself. "I bet that's what you saw. Maybe David proposed, and Vic was just congratulating him."

"You think?"

"Dude, are you fucking kidding me right now?" CiCi throws a roll at him.

"What?!"

"That's all you saw? There was no tongue action? No peen action? No 'how ya doin'?'" She holds her hand out, cupping it like she's fondling balls.

"Is that how you grabbed Kyle's, Ceese?" I laugh, which turns into a snort.

"I grabbed them like I knew I would own them." She jerks her head with a nod of confidence.

"No. Ok, I'm being stupid. I don't know what's wrong with me. He's just been so secretive lately. And, I swear he's been looking more forward to this weekend than I have."

"You are being stupid; Vic is crazy about you," Julie states as she pours more wine.

"I'm so fucking jealous of you guys right now," Charley groans, eyeing the wine.

"See what happens when you let your best friend and her husband knock you up?" CiCi grabs the bottle and pours more in her glass. "Don't worry, you two, we'll drink enough to cover your allotted amounts."

"Oh man! You guys get to drunk text." Ava looks really put off about this.

"We'll do a group one!" I clap my hands like a little kid.

"To each other? But we're all right here." Jay looks at me strangely.

"First of all, why would that stop us?" CiCi asks. "Secondly, I'm pretty sure she meant all of us—as in—the guys, as well."

"Let's take this party to the living room and get comfy before anything else." Julie stands up, grabbing her glass. We all agree and grab any provisions from the kitchen that we will need before heading in.

"What kind of movies did you bring, Jay? Ava asks.

"The classics: *Pretty Woman, Pretty In Pink, The Breakfast Club.*"

"Ok, but we have to watch *Eight Crazy Nights*; it's tradition," CiCi reminds us. "I'll just get it out of my purse," she says in the character Whitey's voice. She does it so perfectly, it's kind of scary. Some of the girls groan about this but, truth be told, we all laugh our asses off watching it. Adam Sandler would fit right in with us girls; he's also permanently twelve.

"First things first; it's time to solve world peace." Ava snatches a corner seat on the sofa I had Declan bring in here from my study. He also helped me rearrange the living room so that we could all talk without anyone having to turn their head awkwardly. The two sofas are facing each other but far enough apart so that I could get two armchairs at the end, facing the fireplace, between them. I brought ottomans in for whoever sits there.

"Which one of you girl scouts is gonna get this fire going?" Jay asks as he lands his ass in an armchair.

"You should have Declan chop your wood . . . shirtless. You should also invite me for that."

"Ceese, aren't you head-over-heels for Kyle?" I raise a brow.

"Dude, I'm not dead. I'm not pining for him or anything; he's just so pretty . . . and massive. Tell us the truth; you get a running start to climb that mountain, don't you?"

"He *is* massive." I smile and waggle my eyebrows.

"Alright, that's enough of that!" Charley waves her hand as if to say "move along." She sits on the same end as Ava but across from her. "How are things with Hunter?" she asks. "I tell ya what; he and Brogan are becoming fast bffs."

"I'm so glad," I say without hiding my relief. "He's such a great kid. I really love him. I'm happy that he feels comfortable with me, and around everyone. I think he only gets to experience normal everyday things like this with his grandparents in Australia." I grab a few logs of wood off the rack I have next to the fireplace and place them on the grate. "Since Declan and I became a couple, Hunter's been acting like the boy his grandparents talk about. It's nice to see them interact with each other. It makes Declan so happy. I just worry." I turn toward them after getting the fire lit.

"About?" Charley asks as she rubs her growing belly.

"What will happen with him if Declan and I should break up."

"Are you thinking about breaking up with him?" Julie looks up from her chips.

"No! Not at all. But, you never know what can happen." I stand up and head over to the opposite end of the sofa that Charley is on. Julie is across from me, and CiCi has planted herself in the chair next to Jay.

"I know *exactly* what you mean. I'm on the opposite end of that. I mean, Mitch and I are solid, but we're not married or anything . . . not that it stopped Josh from walking out," she adds, rolling her eyes.

"Best thing that douchebag ever did was walk out on you!" CiCi pipes up.

"Preach it, girl!" Jay lifts his one hand up to the sky like he's in church, feeling the word of the Almighty.

"Any*who*!" Charley grabs our attention back. "I worry a lot that one day Mitch will decide he doesn't want all of this. So much so that when Brogan asked me last month if he could start calling him Dad, I said no. Well, Mitch overheard us."

"Oh man. . ." Ava and I both trail off.

"Yeah. . . It wasn't good. I tried to explain that it was too soon. I tried to explain that we weren't even married. None of it went well." She takes in a deep breath. "You all know that when Mitch is upset, the biggest thing he does is shut down. He can scream his flippin' head off at me all he likes when he's mad about something; I'd rather that. When we argue, and he's really upset with me and not just mad, he distances himself, not touching me at all. I hate that. It's the worst torture. It doesn't happen often—thank God—but it did that night, and the next."

"Well, how the hell is that supposed to help you get over your fear of him leaving when he pulls that crap?" Julie rolls up the chip bag, growling at it as if it was making her eat the chips. Not that she has to worry; she never gains weight and eats whatever the hell she wants. Yes, she's one of *those* people. Me? I probably gained a pound just by watching her eat them.

"That's what I said to him!" Charley throws out her hands.

"What did he say?" we all ask at the same time. That happens with us a lot. We're like those freakish twins who do that, except, there's five of us . . . well, six with Jay.

"He said I was right. He apologized and got right back to being normal." Any one of us could easily tell that this pissed her off due to the huffing and shaking of her head in disbelief.

"I *hate* when Trent does that to me!" Ava points like she's putting the dot onto her verbal exclamation point. She rolls up her sleeves. "You go in there, all prepared for battle; your adrenaline is pumping, your lines are rehearsed well. You. Are. Going. To. Nail. It!" She pokes at the air again with each syllable. "And he's all 'yes, dear.' Makes me want to throat punch him. It's almost worse than when you are flipping out, and they tell you to 'calm down.'" She does the quotation marks.

"Holy hell, Mama!" CiCi jerks her head back like she's nervous. "You are one passionately pissed off pregnant lady. Ooh! We should play *Scattegories*; that was a three-pointer!"

"Under which list?" Julie asks.

"How the hell would I know? You think I go through life acting like *Rain Man*, remembering fucking category lists to games?"

"Of course, Kmart sells *Scattegories*," I chime in like I'm *Rain Man*. They all stare at me in silence, then burst into laughter.

"Have you patched things up with your mother?" Ava asks Julie just as we stop laughing.

"No." She shakes her head. "I haven't talked to her. I really don't want to. I'm really tired of her behavior. I know I can't change her; I just don't know why she is the way she is. If I had some idea, it might make this all a little easier on me. Besides, I'm really focusing on Blake right now." She tucks her long legs under her butt.

"That's good, Julie. Focus on the things you can control. You may never figure out your mom, but you can't lose yourself while trying to do so. You've been doing that for too long. I'm really glad you're allowing yourself to finally control your happiness, and allow it. Blake is a great guy." I lean forward and grab my glass of wine.

"I think it's safe to say that we all have great taste in men."

"Here, here, Jay!" CiCi raises her glass.

"Speaking of!" Ava starts laughing. "Trent added to our blooper reel the other night." And now, she's in hysterics. And when one of us is in hysterics . . . well, you know the drill.

"What made you guys even start this?" Jay asks.

"Well, I started it in college when we first met. I didn't want to forget anything, especially really funny or awkward moments, so I started writing them down. We have a few journals filled and like to review them every once in a while, especially if we're a little off with each other; it reconnects us through laughter," she explains.

"The first meeting was *the best!* Did you ever hear about the first thing Trent said to her, Jay?" Charley chokes through her laughter.

"No. What did he say?"

"We were in college. We had a few classes together. We noticed each other and would smile but never said anything. Then one day, I was in line for lunch. Trent came up from behind me and said, 'I don't know what smells better—you or lunch.' I turned to him and said, 'Well, I hope it's me, since they are serving fish.'" She laughs.

"He didn't even look?" Jay joins in on our laughter.

"Nope."

"What did he say?"

"He looked over at what they were offering, rolling his eyes and chuckling. Then, he said, 'Our grandchildren will get a kick out of this story someday.' He held out his hand for mine and added, 'I'm Trent Carter, future CEO of your heart. I don't like long walks on the beach or picnics in the park because that shit is boring. I'd rather amusement parks and road trips to where ever we feel like driving to. I'll be in charge of the music, though. I DJ at The Shack on the weekends, so I'm qualified. I'm the most liberal Republican you'll ever meet. I'm into geeky shit like numbers and science. But I'm also into you, maybe not so geeky, then, huh? I work out. Eventually, I'd like to work you out. Oh, and in case you were wondering—not a shy bone in my body. What time can I pick you up tonight?' I just stared at him—dumbfounded—wondering what the grandchildren he had mentioned would look like."

"I love this story." I sigh and take a sip of my wine.

"He didn't lack in the confidence department back then, either, I take it?" Jay pours himself another glass.

"It didn't seem like it, but he did tell me a few years later that he was so nervous, he had to change his shirt after because he completely sweated out the pits."

"I gather he picked you up that night," Jay assumes.

"Nope. I made him chase after me for a good month or so," she states with pride.

"Well, what did the dipshit do to add to the reel?" CiCi inquires.

"Oh!" She slaps the couch cushion between her and Julie. "I was horny as hell the other day and managed to talk him into coming home early. Things that would shock you were promised by me—"

"—I doubt it!" we all cut her off, then laugh. If you are from the New England area, then you would remember the Dean's Furniture commercials. He's no longer in business, but his slogan, and the way he said it, lives on through us.

"Shut up!" She joins in. "Anyhow, I had just waxed our floors that morning."

"Wait—what?! You wax your floors? People still fucking do that?" CiCi looks all kinds of confused.

"Um . . . yes," Ava answers. Charley, Jay, and I support her with eager nods of our heads. Julie looks at CiCi like she's on the same page as her. CiCi pulls out her phone. "Who are you calling?"

"Mr. Belvedere. Shh!" She holds a finger up. "Do you wax our floors? You *do?!* No, I don't need you to come over and wax my floor. Go back to playing helicopter dick with the boys. I'll call you back if I feel the need to know about any other old lady activities you get up to. Love you!" And with that, she hangs up. "It's like we're the only ones who made it out of the time warp, Jules."

"Word." She shakes her head as if in disbelief.

"Back to my story!" Ava practically yells with excitement.

"Oh yeah!" CiCi waves her on.

"He started stripping the moment he walked in the door and ran into the living room in his socks." She laughs.

"And?!" we all chime.

"He didn't stop! He . . . he went . . . fly—flying right . . . by me." Tears are now pouring out of her eyes from laughing so hard. "Went right into the bookcase, smacking his head real good, and passed out."

"Did you call an ambulance?" I ask through a laugh that could possibly cast me in the next *Revenge of The Nerds* movie.

"No. I was able to get him awake." She winks.

"You're a fucking whore!" CiCi yells.

"I can neither deny nor confirm that statement." She looks away, teasingly, like she's up to something.

"I'm sure slamming your pussy down on his cock worked better than a smelling salt would've any day." Julie hi-fives her.

"You're fucking vulgar, Julie—I love it!" Jay says with a gleam in his eye.

"Let's get the movies started; I don't know how long I'm going to last," Charley suggests.

It takes us forty-five minutes to then decide which one is going first (*The Breakfast Club*), filled in with off topic convos and lots of wine, and pretend wine for the preggos.

Incidentally, you might never want to watch a cult classic with us. We pretty much say every line out loud. We've annoyed several people over the years.

An hour and a half or so later. . .

"*You see us as you want to see us—in the simplest terms, in the most convenient definitions. But what we found out is that each one of us is a brain . . . and an athlete . . . and a basket case . . . a princess . . . and a criminal. Does that answer your question?*" we all recite. Best. Ending. To. A. Movie. Ever!! It was like it was written for us. Only, we're still fighting over who the criminal is. . .

Chapter Sixteen

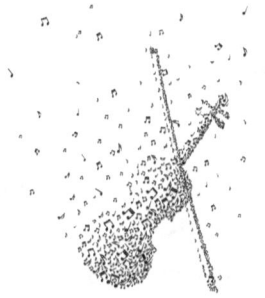

Declan

WITH THE EXCEPTION OF MADDIE, I HAVEN'T LAUGHED THIS HARD in a long time. The shots of whiskey have probably helped me along in that department, but the company I have is top notch. What has made me most comfortable is the fact that we are all sort of in the same boat. Trent is the only one who's been around a long time. The rest of us are first-year rookies. So far, Blake, Kyle and I have bonded over music. Mitch and I have discovered that we share in our impulsive dysfunction when it comes to our relationships with our women. Different reasons from the past, but the same result. Not that I want to see someone else suffer the same fate, but it is nice to know I'm not the only one going through something like this. Trent? Well, he just seems to get along with everybody. He hasn't hesitated to join in on one single topic of conversation.

Yes, I like this lot. Everything in my life seems to *finally* seem right. That feeling of looking over my shoulder is dissipating. Having Maddie in my life these past several months has really turned it around. I feel like I'm slowly climbing out of the bowels of Hell. I honestly thought I'd be stuck there forever, that Hunter would be stuck with me. Speaking of, Hunter has taken leaps and bounds in the right direction. He's coming out of his shell. *We* are reconnecting.

"Dude, you look deep in thought," Mitch pulls me out of my head.

"I was." I chuckle lightly before joining them in the next round of whiskey shots.

"Don't ponder it; share it with the group!" Kyle demands. "We're all we've got . . . when it comes to the girls. If that's what you're thinking about," he adds.

"I was partly. I was thinking about how much better my life has been since Maddie's been a part of it."

"You thinking about the next step, mate?" Blake asks with a huge grin.

"No. It's too soon." I wave my hand in disagreement.

"That's bullshit, right there." Mitch points at me.

"Dec, there is no time chart, man. I don't know why people get so fucking hung up on that shit," Kyle informs me, throwing his hands up in the air. "When you know—you know! It really is that simple." He closes his eyes then stretches his face, blinking them open slowly. "Shit, the last shot really hit me hard," he announces and tries to shake it off.

"Who's our designated driver?" Trent looks around and laughs at the lot before him.

"It was the singing ninja, here," Mitch shuffles his hand toward Kyle, "but now it looks like it's going to be Uber."

"When did you all know?" I get back on topic.

"Shit, man, I fell in love with Charlotte the first weekend I met her. It was insane. I fought it tooth and nail." Mitch sits back like he's angry about this.

"When CiCi grabbed me by the balls. . ." Kyle trails off like it was the best moment of his life. I've heard this story from Maddie and can't help but give in to a good hearty laugh.

"Ava and I went to College together. She was in a few of my classes. I chased after her like my life depended on it. I had never chased anyone before, being the pretty boy that I am." Trent laughs.

"About a month ago for me," Blake throws in. "You all saw what happened." He looks down like he's lost in the memory. "I really was going to walk away for good, and it about killed me to do so. I realized then that I loved her. Certainly it wouldn't hurt so much to walk away from somebody you didn't love," he adds. We all nod our head in agreement.

Just then, Kyle starts laughing obnoxiously. After a few awkward starts at joining him, we all give in and laugh. "What the fuck is so funny?" Mitch finally asks.

Kyle wipes his eyes with his hands. "I was just thinking that we'll all end up with whiskey dicks tonight. And then I realized that none of us are going home to our women. And *then* I remembered what CiCi told me to do earlier, which was going back to playing helicopter dick with you guys. I don't know why, but an image of that just popped in my head."

"As much as I'd love to humor your scene from *Jackass 5*, I really don't fancy you guys enough to watch you all whip your dicks around like a helicopter." Blake chuckles and pours us all some more shots.

"I love how he says he doesn't want to see all of our dicks in the same sentence he uses fancy," Mitch teases.

"Bugger off!" Blake bites back.

"I don't fancy looking at your dicks, boys," Mitch continues.

"It's only polite as I don't want to embarrass you, whipping out my beast!"

"This can only get worse and end up being the thing we all know about but never speak of," Trent warns.

"The Voldemort incident," I name it.

"Yes!" they all cheer.

"Welcome, our new brother." Kyle holds his shot glass up to me.

"You're not going to make me do something stupid to fully initiate me into the club, are you?" I'm half serious.

"I think we all drunk enough to cover the stupid department," Kyle answers.

"I may have to catch up. Cheers!" I clink my glass with his.

"Dude, why do you let CiCi get away with carving her name on your table?" Mitch asks Blake.

"This is *their* table, mate. They do what they want with it. Also . . . I like getting laid." He shrugs. We all hoot and howl, clinking glasses at this statement.

"So, do you think you can brave Christmas?" Kyle asks. I've noticed that Kyle initiates a lot of the conversation. He's a very thorough bloke.

"My parents are flying in from Australia. We're having dinner with Maddie's family. I think it will be fine. Maddie, of course, is freaking out."

"Why?"

"Have you met her mum?"

"No, not yet."

"She's lovely. We get along fantastically."

"But?"

"But . . . she tends to embarrass Maddie a lot. It's all harmless, of course. But the boundaries. . .ehh. . .?" I cringe.

"Did you warn your parents? I have to warn everyone about my Gram; I completely understand," Mitch chimes in.

"Just a bit. It's really not as big of a deal as she makes it into."

"Don't tell her that, whatever you do!" Trent warns.

"Oh no." I tap my temple.

"How's Charley feeling?" Trent turns his attention to Mitch.

"She's feeling good." Anyone could easily see how uncomfortable Mitch has become.

"This means a lot to us, Mitch. I know it's not easy. I mean, I *don't know*; I can only imagine."

"Yep. Look, I'm not going to pretend that I'm really happy about this. Don't get me wrong," Mitch holds up his hand, "I am happy for the both of you. *And* . . . I'm proud of Charlotte. To do something so selfless, like this, is amazing. I just . . . damn it . . . I want her to be having *my* baby. I'm sorry, dude." You can see the guilt creep in all over Mitch's face.

"I get it, man. I really do. I appreciate this; it's a lot, man." Trent pats Mitch's shoulder aggressively. "I don't know that I'd feel any different, if the tables were turned."

"Shit. I didn't mean to say all of that." Mitch groans, holding the bridge of his nose.

"It's fine, man. I get it; I really do!"

"No. It's selfish. I'm sorry. I am happy for you both. I'm so proud of her. God, she's awesome."

"CiCi is awesome," Kyle rings in.

"My little minx." I sigh.

"Red," Blake throws in.

"We are all fucking lucky that those crazy bitches love us so much." Trent lounges back in his chair.

"To the GEGs!" Mitch yells, holding up an empty glass. Blake immediately fills it and ours as well. We all clink and drink.

And then. . .

Ping!

But the pings go off like the fourth of July. We all grab our phones. "Is this a group text?" I ask, looking up at them. They are all staring at their cells.

"Yup," they all say collectively. I'm assuming that this is a normal occurrence. I look back down.

CiCi: Bonjour, assberets!

Kyle: Have you been reading *Fancy Nancy* to Brooklynn again, beautiful?

Charley: You better not have taught her to say that!

CiCi: What? It's French! Besides, I taught her to say La Toosh Beret. It's fancier. Nancy would dig that. She likes fancy shit.

Maddie: Declan?

Me: Yeah, sweetness?

Maddie: You're a hot Viking, and you should cut my wood shirtless. CiCi said so.

Me: You should watch me from the porch . . . in my shirt, sans panties.

Kyle: CiCi, why are you talking about other men being shirtless?

I look up at Kyle, and the dude actually seems pissed. I'm not sure why he's been given the nickname of Ninja, but I don't really want to know. I'm a big guy, but that doesn't mean I'm stupid or egotistical enough to ever underestimate any possible opponent. Besides, not to sound like a pussy, but I can't have anything happen to my hands. Our phones ping and I look back down.

CiCi: Why? Is that your job?

Kyle: No Wheaties for the rest of the week, Ceese!

Kyle throws down his phone. Well . . . this is awkward.

Me: I'm really hideous without a shirt, CiCi. You shouldn't encourage Maddie.

Julie: Where's my British Bulldong?

Blake: You mean Bulldog, love?

Julie: I did, but then the typo was so good, I couldn't correct it. Blasphemy and all.

Blake: What? Never mind, you're crazy. . . I love you.

Julie: I love you. But when I'm slightly tipsy, like right now, I love you more.

Blake: How is it that you don't know how to use commas unless you're drunk?

CiCi: Kyle's the same way!!!

Jay: Vic . . . you make me so h—never mind. I forgot. Why isn't he on here?

Mitch: Add him.

Jay: Where are you?

Mitch: Having a private chat with Charlotte.

Maddie: No cheating, you two!!

Maddie: Declan, I don't think you're the only one who got laid tonight.

Me: Damn it! We were just going to the scoreboard, and I was certain I had won!

Blake: I really like this bloke! Good job, Maddie!

Maddie: Really? You guys do? I'm so glad! Isn't he great? God, I love him. . .

I'm the one who drops my phone this time. I look up and find everyone's eyes on me. Well, except for Mitch, who seems to be enthralled with his side texting to Charley.

She loves me?

She loves me!!!

And . . . she said it on text. A group-fucking-text.

Also, she's clearly drunk.

I grab my phone again and shut it down. I don't know what I'm feeling. I'd rather not engage in this convo anymore.

"I don't know what you're griping about; your woman says she loves you and mine wants to see you shirtless. Sounds to me like you're having a banner night," a disgruntled Kyle says.

"Well, mate, that's the first time she's ever said that and it was on group text while she was drunk." I grab another shot of whiskey.

"Eh, c'mon, now. There's no reason to get bent out of shape over that," Blake tries to console me. "The point is, mate, she's so drunk, she couldn't guard herself from saying it. Focus on that! She loves you! She's happy that you get along with your new playmates!" He leans forward and slaps my shoulder.

"Just remember, *playmate*, he doesn't fancy your dick," Mitch quips. We all stare at him. "Old already?" He looks around at all of us.

"Deader than a doorknob, dude," Kyle hits him with the truth.

"She's asking where you went, man," Trent announces.

I groan and turn my phone back on. Sometimes I have no words. This is certainly most true as I stare at the texts. I quickly go into my Spotify account and copy the link for Josh Groban's "When you say you love me" and text it to her in a private text with the message, "I'd do anything to hear those words escape your lips." I hit send. And . . . I wait. My phone pings.

Ava: Trent?

Trent: There you are!

Ava: I had to pee.

Trent: See what you all have to look forward to after ten years of marriage?

Ava: What? Are you making fun of me?

Trent: Never, sugar lips.

Ava: I had to pee!

CiCi: Unless he's into you urinating on him, that doesn't classify as a "hot" text.

I almost just fell out of my chair, laughing. We all are, actually.

CiCi certainly lives up to her reputation.

Ava: Oh, are we "hot" texting?

CiCi: Welcome to the show, we've got a seat up front, here, just for you.

Kyle: Nice commas, beautiful.

CiCi: Is that what you're calling them now?

Charley: Viking, why is Maddie crying?

My blood pressure shoots up to levels I'm sure would be deemed unnatural. Oh, God! Should I have not sent that text? I instantly shoot her a text on the private pm.

Me: I'm sorry. I'm a little drunk. Please forgive me. I didn't mean to send that.

I hit send.

Wait!

No!

Maddie: You didn't? You don't feel this way?

Me: No. I mean yes, but no. Just disregard. Please.

I hit send.

I read it again.

I'm an assberet.

I look up in a panic. The guys all slowly look up at me. "What happened?" Kyle asks.

"I don't know. I'm so drunk . . . I think I've messed up terribly. She's supposed to be having fun this weekend, not dealing with my shit. It's not the same shit, but it's a pile, and it's big, and it smells. It's shit. It smells like shit. I shit on it. I shit on the love." I look around wildly, trying to find an answer to what the fuck I'm talking about. Whiskey is *not* my friend, that's for sure.

"Dude?" Trent asks.

"I haven't a bloody clue; don't ask me." I shake my head and plant it into my palms. Abruptly, I lift my head. I grab my cell to call her. It seems like a legit idea as it always does when you're drunk. Straight to voicemail—*crap!*

"Maddie! I'm sorry. I'm so drunk; I don't know what the hell I'm saying or doing. I heard you were crying and I worried that I had said too much, that I made you nervous. But Christ almighty, I'm so in love you. I meant that. I meant every word . . . or lyric, whatever the fuck. I love you. I love the way you tilt your head when you're thinking of something or asking me something. I love the way you laugh. I love that you say the most outlandish things like it's nothing. I love the way your eyes light up when you see me. I love the way you hug my son like you mean it. I love how passionate you get about the things that interest you. I love how you make me laugh. How you don't put up with my crap. How you help me through it anyway. I love how you smell. The way your skin feels; the way it reacts to my touch. The way you taste. The sounds you make when I'm making love to you. The way you bite your bottom lip while you're coming. Fuck, you're beautiful. I love you, sweetness. I could go on and on, and, if you want me to, in person, I will. I love you. Maddie, you are my heart. You are the dream I didn't think was possible. You are the drink of water after years of wandering in the desert. You are everything. *Everything!* I love you." I hang up. Noticing the awkward silence at our table, I look up.

"You do realize that you will have pussy plastered to your face for *at least* a week now, right?" Blake asks.

"Maybe two," Trent agrees.

"Can you tell Maddie to keep that message so I can take notes? I was too mesmerized to write that down here," Mitch asks.

"Fuck, guys, I love her so much. I'm such a fuck-up in this relationship; I feel like our days are numbered," I admit, looking for encouragement.

"Been there. . ." Mitch.

"Done that. . ." Trent.

"Own your feelings, man, and don't let her avoid them. That's what I've learned," Kyle shares. Actually, that is helpful.

"Fuck! I just told her, for the first time, that I love her—on voicemail! Bloody hell!" I groan.

"Dude . . . she said it on text," Mitch reminds me.

"Right! Clearly, I'm at an advantage here, right?" I plead.

"I think it's time to call Uber," Mitch says then punches things on his cell.

"What the fuck does that mean?" I ask incredulously.

"It means we're drunk, dude, and we will not be solving world peace tonight," he answers.

"Right." I sigh. I had to agree. I'm too drunk to do otherwise . . . except have another shot because—what the hell?

Complete shit at this!

Chapter Seventeen

Maddie

"Shortstack?" I hear CiCi. I'm too mesmerized, though. Declan just spilled his heart out to me on voicemail. Holy fuck—we're there. We've reached that hump and just flew over it. *The Academy would like to thank alcohol for delivering bravery to those lacking.* We did this on text and voicemail...

Thanks, technology.

You had us at "Ping."

What now? Business as usual, when we see each other? Or... do we re-admit what we've divulged? I know I can't go back. I love him. I don't fucking care how much alcohol is in my system; I fucking love him. And, I love Hunter.

"Maddie?" they all call out to me.

"Yeah?" I look up.

"What happened?" Charley asks.

I put my voicemail on speaker and let them all listen to his message. What? Don't fucking judge me! They're my best friends! You don't have *at least* one bff you tell everything to?

"Madelyn St. Claire," Jay talks into his wine glass like it's a microphone. "You are the last GEG down. The possible end of an era in sight; how does that make *you* feel?" he teases, using the cliché question asked by those in my profession.

I lift my wine glass up like it's a mic, as well. "I have to say, Jay, it's a real honor to be bringing it up the rear." I meant to say "bringing up the rear" but my buzzed performance was better received, I believe, as Jay is in hysterics. I notice Charley is in the same state as Jay, and they look like they are acknowledging something between them . . . an inside joke, maybe?

"No offense, Captain, because that was funny, but what the fuck is wrong with you two?" CiCi looks from me back to Jay and Charley.

"I've . . . I've," Jay hiccup laughs. "I've said that same *exact* line to the last few guys I've been with . . . you know . . . after the first time we shook hello." He pretends to do a reach around and waggles his brows. "It's become my signature line or, at least, it had."

"You seriously fucking say that?" Julie's eyes are full of mirth.

"It's quite the ice breaker afterwards," he informs.

"Definitely much better than, 'Well, that took a load off!'" Ava quips. We all die a gut-busting death of laughter. It was painful. Also, I think both preggos may have lost the race against their bladders, trying to make it to the bathroom. We shan't snicker, though. Yes, I just thought that in a British accent. No, I don't know why.

"Shit!" I gasp-yell.

"What?" CiCi looks up from her phone. It's just her and me in the living room at the moment. Jay and Julie went to grab more wine and food.

"I need to say something back to him!" I panic.

CiCi gets up and comes over, plopping onto the cushion next to me. "Here, switch." She gives me her phone and takes mine. It pings and I look down. "Just answer him for me." She nods towards it and busies herself typing on my phone. I can honestly say, if I weren't a bottle in (maybe two; shh), I wouldn't dare let CiCi take the wheel like she's playing the role of Jesus in a Carrie Underwood song. But, I'm about ten sheet cakes past a gym right now, so I'll let her baste the batter . . . stir the pot . . . search for the gold? Yes, I'm going for gold! Wait—what? Ugh crap, I'm in that stage of drinking that I like to compare to Star Trek. Yes, I'm gonna essplain. If you've ever watched Star Trek anything, there's always a moment where Scotty or whoever the fuck is in charge, is having trouble beaming the crew because of some massive battle the causes the same problem in every episode or movie with the damn transporter. *That's drinking!* You going along just fine, knowing what the fuck you're talking about, then—*bam*—you're fading in and out, silently screaming at Scotty to make it all work, except, there's no Scotty. So, you say fuck it and have more wine. Well, that's what I do . . . on occasions, such as this. Shit! Kyle! I look down at his message.

Kyle: You're not going to last the night without my cock in you, beautiful.

Uhh. . .

I close my eyes and chanel number 5 Ceese. That didn't make sense to me, eeber . . . either.

CiCi: I brought Purp and my nipple twisters. I'm good.

Kyle: What? Why would you do that? And what nipple twisters?

CiCi: The ones the good Lord gave me. #TuneInTokyo

Kyle: I'm spanking you when you get home!

CiCi: For being so hot?

Kyle: Yes.

CiCi: Do you like spanking me?

Kyle: Hell yes!

CiCi: I'll tell her.

Kyle: Tell who? Who is this?

CiCi: It's me.

Kyle: Me, who?

CiCi: You is Kyle.

Kyle: Who "is" you?

CiCi: I am.

Kyle: What's your name?!

CiCi: Why—d'you forget it?

Kyle: d'you is not a word!

CiCi: #Word

"Here," I pass her the phone, "I'm not drunk enough to be you sober."

"I'm not sober, though."

"Well, I'm . . . I can't sext Kyle anymore; it's weird." I grab my phone to see the damage. I look back up at her. "Clearly, you had no problem sexting my guy!"

"He'll never be the same again." She laughs and gets a look at her screen. A laugh bursts out from her. "You did good, shortstack!"

"Well, I have been psychoanalyzing you for years," I offer.

"I know. You must be exhausted."

"It's soul-sucking work, but somebody's gotta map out the crazy." I chuckle and get back to my Viking, reading *exactly* what she wrote (I only glanced before, seeing something about dry pussy. I'm sure you can only imagine with CiCi in the driver's seat. Pray for me).

Me: Sorry. You've made me speechless.

Declan: In a bad way?

Me: No, Declan Downer. In a good way!

Declan: Really? I was nervous that I overshot.

Me: You're a massive man who handles a massive instrument; overshooting is probable.

Declan: Maddie?????

Me: I hope you don't mind, but I played your message to everyone.

Declan: I suppose I can't get mad about that since I said it in front of everyone here.

Me: There wasn't a dry pussy in the house once you were finished.

Declan: You've just made whiskey shoot through my nose. Not comfortable.

Me: Even Jay's mangina quivered.

Declan: Mangina?

Me: Yes. Stay with me, here. I need to tell you something.

Declan: What, sweetness? Although, I'm not so sure at the moment. . .

Me: I have Ineedyourdickiephobia.

Declan: That sounds quite serious.

Me: You have no idea.

Declan: That's fear of. . .?

Me: Fear of going a day without a mock turtleneck.

Declan: Oh how you must suffer, CiCi.

Me: Dude?!

Declan: Whiskey makes men smarter. Also, Kyle's reading over my shoulder.

Me: It's good to know that you guys can decipher us by our brand of crazy.

Declan: Sure . . . we'll call it that. Lol.

Me: It's me. The real me.

Declan: Prove it.

Me: You have a beauty mark on your left hip.

Declan: I do???

Me: Mm-hmm. I study you, Mr. Viking.

Declan: You have no idea how turned on I am, right now.

I look up, distracted by the rest of the gang coming back in. I'm also distracted by the crazy ass sundae concoction that Julie has made. Fucking bitch. I just gained two pounds for looking; I can feel it on my ass. I look back down to my cell.

Me: Re-cap for me in a few days. I have to go. I love you.

Declan: I LOVE YOU!!!

Aww . . . he shouty-capped it at me.

Let's all sigh together.

"I need to go to bed. Can we do gifts tomorrow after we shop?" Charley asks looking as exhausted as she could be.

"Yeah, sounds like a plan. I have some extra pillows for you to put under your feet," I offer, noticing that her ankles are pretty swollen.

"Thanks. I think I need to cut down on my salt some more."

Slowly, we all make our way to our bedrooms. Ava is doubling up with me. Charley is in with Jay, and CiCi and Julie are in Hunter's room. Ahh . . . Hunter's room. . .

I love that kid.

I have never been so grateful that I keep Mondays off, for administration reasons, as I am today. I am laughed out, wined out, shopped out, and am suffering dramatically from sleep deprivation. Also, I should mention that sleeping with my cape (Julie did a great job on mine; I'm one red, white, and blue bedazzled, caped, Asswhore Crusader) on last night was a poor judgment call; the red line on my neck is proof of that. "Caroline called me yesterday," Preston pulls me out of the chant I had going on in my head: *I'm so fucking tired. I'm so fucking tired.* However, this revelation wakes me up a bit. I didn't know these two still kept in contact. Caroline is CiCi's twin. She and Preston were quite the item in high school and into college. I'm not sure why they broke up, other than they just grew apart.

"Really?" I'm intrigued; she doesn't even call her twin. CiCi doesn't say too much about it, but I know it bothers her; she's slipped up enough for me to be confident in that.

"Yes. She needed a recommendation for a good GYN, other

than myself, of course."

"Did she at least catch up with you . . . ask how you were doing?" I pour some sugar in my coffee, then aggressively rip the lids off the little creamers. We're in Derry, having brunch at our favorite place: Maryann's Diner. It's a cute 50s styled diner on Broadway, and the food can't be beat. Our families have been coming here for years. Their sausage gravy is the bomb dot com. *Stop thinking about food, Maddie!*

"She had to get off quick." Preston looks down like he's reading the different ads designed on the table. Caroline is the only woman who has ever been able to both put the sunshine in my brother's sky and rip it out the next moment. This may be the reason why I feel so much disdain toward her when it comes to him.

"I bet she did," I condescend.

"She'll be here for Christmas." His face lights up.

"She's married," I remind him.

"Yeah. . ." he trails off. I'm about to say something, but our food arrives. And, well . . . we'll just leave it at that.

Hashtag . . . happy dance.

During the process of trying not to look like a savaged beast (I put my fork down; stick with me, Ladies and Gentlemen, also . . . Alpha men in training), it occurs to me that it's kind of odd for Caroline to ask about a GYN here. She lives in Texas. Why wouldn't she just go to a doctor by her? *Crap on a cracker!* I wonder if she's moving back here! "You gonna eat that?" My brother does the slow reach. I immediately grab my fork and stab his hand. "Ow! Shit, Maddie!" he complains.

"Don't fuck with my food, dude!" This may seem like an overreaction, but then, you didn't grow up with Preston, did you? Guy's got a rap sheet ten miles long for food thievery. You have to keep a sharp eye on him; trust me. "Back to the matter at hand; is Caroline moving back here?"

He furrows his brows. "I don't know. Come to think of it,

though, it is odd for her to ask about a doctor here."

"So quick, Sherlock," I tease.

"Oh, me wonders if Seamus has left her for another lucky charm," Preston says . . . in the *Lucky Charms* leprechaun voice. I snort. Okay, okay—I'm snorting and also doing that laugh where you make no sound (except for a random snort) while a goofy ass smile is plastered to your face and oxygen doesn't seem to be an option. Seamus Higgins is straight-off-the-boat Irish, and I swear on my eyes, he looks like the human version of the *Lucky Charms* dude. Then, you know . . . you throw in the accent, his been extremely thick. . . Let's just leave it at that; I don't have to tell you what happens when any of us are around him. I will mention one time, though, when Seamus was looking for something and wouldn't tell us what because we wouldn't know what it looked like. CiCi asked him (out of earshot, of course) if it was a horseshoe . . . a heart . . . a rainbow, basically every marshmallow shape she could think of. Caroline came in behind her, heard her, and needless to say, the claws came out.

"For the love of God, woman—breathe!" Preston fans me with his hands. "Are you still drunk from this weekend?" He chuckles.

I gasp some oxygen. "Could be," I answer as I try to regulate my breathing. "That and it's been a while."

"TMI!"

"Not that, you asshole!" I laugh. "It's been a while since anyone has imitated Seamus."

"It's terrible that we derive great pleasure from it when someone does."

"We're a walking *After School Special*, for sure," I agree.

"I am curious, though."

"Are you friends on Facebook?" I ask as I dive back into my food.

"She never accepted my friendship," he says solemnly.

"I bet it's because of Seamus; he's always been suspicious of her feelings for you."

"Really?" He jerks his head back, giving me a perplexed look.

"You keep making that face, and you're gonna need Botox." I point at him with my fork.

"Already started," he states.

"What?"

"I'm offering some cosmetic procedures now, like Botox."

"You shooting that shit in the cooch?"

"Yes. It helps with Vaginismus."

"Christmas for vaginas?"

"I'm sure it feels that way after the injections." He laughs. "Also, you've spent too much time with CiCi."

"She rubs off on ya," I concede.

"Vaginismus is when the entrance to your vagina spasms, causing penetration to be very painful or unable to even happen. Botox helps those muscles to calm down," he educates me.

"Why do women have to suffer so much? I mean, it's just wrong."

"Eve should've never eaten that apple." He shrugs.

"Adam should've never whined about wanting an apple pie. Fucking prick; he set her up."

"I'm sure he meant cherry; she just didn't get the reference; it was ahead of their time. Also, who's to say it really went down that way."

"What do you mean?" I humor him.

"What if God's plan was to see who would be the strongest of the two genders to handle giving birth, raising children, and every other amazing thing women do. Guys are babies; I'll be the first to admit that . . . when it comes to being sick and in pain. Clearly, the stronger gender won. It's all worth it, Maddie; I see it every day. There is no greater joy than to hold that baby in your arms. I've delivered a few thousand babies now; it never gets old or less amazing."

"You're awesome, bro." I smile. "Too many guys would be afraid of losing their man-card for saying any of that. Someday, some lucky girl will catch your eye. I just hope she realizes what a wonderful person you are and just *how* lucky she is."

"Hmm . . . we'll see; I'm in no rush."

"Speaking of being in a rush—you *need* to help me!" I give him my most wide-eyed panicked look. Or, at least, I try.

"Defcon 2 eyes; it must be serious," he chortles.

"Christmas. Declan's parents are coming to *our* family Christmas. You know what happened when we went to see him in the Holiday Pops! You have to help me maintain the beast," I plead.

"I can't do that, sis; she's so excited about showing them the seating chart for the wedding."

"Fuck you."

He laughs. I don't find him to be very funny. This is serious. As a matter of fact. . .

"What's that?"

"Tums. I eat them like candy now. My nerves are shot over meeting his parents and Mom . . . she's not helping." I pop three in my mouth.

"That serious, huh?" The corners of his mouth lift.

"I'm in love with him," I admit.

"I know. I'm really happy for you. I like him a lot. Also, I'm revoking your shortest date ever record." He's still sour about this.

"You cannot; it was legit."

"Grr!" he growls, though . . . that was self-explanatory, wasn't it?

"Settle down, killer." I roll my eyes. "Go pay the bill while I eat these last few bites; I need to get going." I shoo him.

"Why am I paying the bill?"

"Because you're a good big brother." I wink and take my last bite

I wish I took Tuesdays off, too.

This morning's first client is a young woman who'd just started with me two weeks ago. So far, I'm still trying to rule out history of childhood trauma versus multiple personality disorder. She's having, what she thinks are, memories from her childhood. Only, she's remembering different parents and can't put her finger on it. She's been concerned for the past year that she isn't who she's been raised to think she is. So, while I'm trying to guide her, I'm also keeping one foot out of the water, sort of speak. This could all be a part of some grand delusion. It's really too early to tell.

Mentally pushing my exhaustion down, I slip my heels on before walking down to the waiting area; Alison is always punctual. As soon as I round the corner, I notice her practically bounce right out of her seat, collecting her things. Seemingly having everything she needs, she smiles and walks back down to my office with me.

"How was your week?" I ask, holding out my hand for her to go in first.

"Good, I think," she says, excitement lacing her voice.

"What happened?" I close the door and immediately get re-acquainted with my chair.

Notepad open.

Heels back off.

"I had another memory. Well, it was more like a dream. I was meditating. My name was Josie," the words all flying out of her mouth so fast.

"Josie?" I verify as I write it down. "Anything else come to you? Something about your surroundings? More details about these other parents? Any other names said that might give you more of a lead?" I can't help my interest one bit. I mean, who hasn't seen a *Lifetime* movie or two about abducted children going through life not knowing they were abducted until strange things start to happen, like memories or phony birth certificates. "Your birth certificate!" I practically shout at her. "Have you ever seen it?"

"Yes."

"Does it have a seal?"

"What do you mean?" She scrunches up her nose, giving me a perplexed look.

"Legal documents, like birth certificates, have a state seal on them to prove authentication." I uncross my legs and slide my feet into the foot warmer Declan got me. *Ahh. . .*

"I don't remember," she answers.

"Don't you have possession of it?" That's odd.

"No. My mom has it."

"Haven't you had to use it for anything?" Now I'm the one who is perplexed.

"No. Anything I had to use it for, my mom handled it: sports, college, driver's license."

"Okay, well, let's start there. Ask your mom to see your birth certificate. See if there's a seal. Make sure all the information is legit." I look over at my buzzing phone; it's Declan. I swipe to ignore.

"What if everything is as it should be?" she almost pleads, her fear seemingly reaching above the surface.

It's a fine line to walk; the difference between believing what she feels is true or chocking it up to a possible delusion. I always like to give the benefit of the doubt first in cases like these. Not that I've come across anything *exactly* like this before, but the proof is in the pudding. This means that by the time we've exhausted all outlets and come up empty-handed, I'll have a file full of reasons her mind is obviously playing tricks on her. She's so young; I'd rather it be true that she is remembering some repressed memories. The ulterior would be even more difficult for her to deal with and for me to help her through. Can you imagine believing something to be very true, yet, everyone else tells you it never happened? What a nightmare that would be.

I lean back in my chair and tap my pen to my chin. "I have an-other idea, as well," I finally say. She gives me a slight nod, encour-aging me. "I would ask your parents if they know a 'Josie.' See what kind of reaction they give you. If they ask you why, just tell them you had a dream about a little girl named Josie and you felt like the dream took place in the 90s rather than now. Don't prod them for any other information, or force the issue. This is just to see if A. they tell you and B. how they react to this sort of question. Be sure to keep an eye on their body language." I really hope my encourage-ment doesn't bite me in the ass later.

Thankfully, after she agrees, we move on to another important subject for a twenty-one-year-old girl—boys. We breeze through the rest of her appointment without a hitch on her end. My end? I've had to ignore Declan's call seven more times. As soon as Alison leaves, I grab my phone and frantically call him. When he does call me during the day, he always does it in the last ten minutes of any hour, knowing that's my in-between-client time. It was odd for him to call me after the hour. I thought that maybe he just didn't realize. But, for him to call seven more times? I'm not going to lie; my pant-ies are in a knot; something's wrong.

"Sweetness!" he practically yells into the phone.

"What's the matter?!"

"You have to get to Parkland Medical!" his voice is urgent and full of panic.

"Who's there? What's happened?!" I ask as I search under my desk for my shoes. I was in such a rush to get Alison out of here; I walked her to the door barefoot and didn't even realize it.

"Rosie's about to get prepped for surgery. She was hit by a car, mangling her leg. Hunter was with her. He called me, frantic. They went by ambulance. He's all alone. And, I'm fighting this bloody Boston traffic! Up your arse, you bloody moron!" he yells.

"Gee, no need for name calling." I try to lighten up his mood.

"I'm sorry; that was directed toward the jerk in front of me. I'm anxious. I don't want Hunter to be alone. I don't want him to be stuck in the room with social workers. I know I'm probably blowing things out of proportion; I can't help it," he admits.

"I'm on my way. I will call over to the hospital and see which social worker is on and explain who Hunter is. I know everyone who works there, Dec; he'll be in good hands until I arrive. I need you to calm down so that I don't have two of you in the ER. Do you understand me?" I ask as I grab my purse. I leave my office and lock it behind me.

"Yes. I'm slowing down and calming down; you have that effect on me." I hear him breathe a sigh of relief.

"Okay, let me go. I have to make a phone call or hundred," I mention as I walk up to our receptionist's desk. "Jill, I need you to cancel the rest of my appointments today; I've had a family emergency. Please tell my clients I will call them to reschedule as soon as I can. If any of them have appointments next week, this will not affect those," I ramble on, holding the receiver away from my mouth.

"I hope everything will be ok," she offers as she rummages through the paperwork on her desk, finding my schedule. I'm old school, remember? She gets a weekly print out of my schedule, just in case there's an emergency, as such.

"It will be. Thanks." I smile before turning and getting back to Declan as I make my way out of the office. "Okay, that's handled."

"I love you." I can hear his smile.

Shut-up—you can *too* hear a smile!

"I love you, too. I'm climbing into my car now. I'll see you when you get there, baby. Everything will be fine," I assure him.

"The moment I heard your voice, I knew it would be. See you there, sweetness." He gives me a smooch over the phone and hangs up. Okay . . . I may have just sighed like a hopeless romantic. I am, so what of it?

Chapter Eighteen

Declan

I'VE LEARNED A LONG TIME AGO THAT IT DOESN'T MATTER WHAT day of the week it is; I-93 is a parking lot going in and out of Boston. The Big Dig? Anyone who tells you that it alleviated traffic is a half-wit. All they did was take the traffic from above ground and put it underneath. Instead of having the distraction of looking at the city whilst stuck in traffic, you now get to look at ugly tunnel walls, praying a bloody panel doesn't fall on your head, or that your air conditioning doesn't stop working out of the blue while you're stuck in there with all of the other irate drivers. That aside, I do love this city. But, I love New Hampshire just as much and am glad to get away from the hustle and bustle of Boston.

I pull into the parking lot of Parkland Medical Center. It's a small, local hospital in Derry, the next town over from us. As soon as I find a space, I park and get out, locking my car behind me as I dial Maddie's cell. "You here?" she asks.

"Yes. Where should I go?"

"Surgical waiting room. They'll direct you when you come in. Come in through Outpatient, though."

"Oh, ok. I'll be there in a few." I hang up as I walk through the door. The volunteer at the desk looks up at me expectantly. As soon as I tell her where I need to be, she gives me the directions, and I'm on my way. I have three concerns at the moment.

1. How Rosie is doing.
2. If Hunter handled all of this unscathed.
3. Can I get rid of this semi I've worked up, knowing I'm about to see, hold, and kiss my woman?

Honestly, this is just not the time to react like a horny teenage boy. Besides, I don't have a book of any sort to hide my growing appendage. Just as I turn the corner, my eyes gain sight of her, and I hasten my steps.

"Dad!" Hunter cheers. Maddie looks up from her phone and our eyes lock. If my cock came equipped with a siren, it would sound like an elephant trumpeting, and it would be going off fiercely right now. I bite my laugh back at the visual I just gave myself. Surely other people get odd random thoughts like this, right?

"Hey, buddy!" I open my arms for him and ruffle his hair while we hug. "You all right?" I glance down at him.

"I'm great, Dad. Rosie's not so hot, though. I'm sorry she's in so much pain, but her leg looked awesome! I can't wait to tell Brogan how her bone ripped right through her skin." His eyes widen as he relays the God-awful circumstances of her broken leg. I can't imagine the excruciating pain she is going through. "I was so worried. That car hit her so hard, Dad. She pushed me out of the way; I scraped my knee. I didn't know why she pushed me like that. Rosie's never done anything to hurt me. I didn't realize what was going on because I had my earbuds in." He starts crying. I'm always amazed how quickly kids fall through different phases of emotions when something scary or exciting happens. "She's been in surgery for an hour now; I've been watching the clock," he informs me as he wipes his tears away.

"It shouldn't be much longer," Maddie says as she touches my arm and slides her hand up it. I release my son in exchange for her arms to be wrapped around me. "Oh!" she gasps. "Oh . . . wow," she says again under her breath.

I lean down near her ear, "I'm not impressed with my lack of control at all. Of all the times for this to happen," I complain about the unauthorized expansion going on in my pants.

"The timing does suck, but I'm still *very* impressed," she whispers then giggles lightly. Let's sit and get you a magazine." She pulls back and winks.

"Good idea." I follow her lead and quickly cover up the situation as soon as I take a seat.

TWO MORE HOURS go by before the doctor finally comes out to us. Rosie did great, but she's going to be recovering for a while. Her tibia, fibula, and ankle were broken so badly, they had to place pins and a plate in. It's her driving foot, as well. Boy, if I know Rosie, she's going to be even more pissed after the anesthesia lifts, finding out how severe the break was, than before the surgery. She's not one to stay put and have others wait on her.

I'm surprised, but they are actually admitting her. I guess she's pretty banged up; a few cracked ribs which punctured her right lung, contusions, and several lacerations. I didn't realize it was *this* bad. I look over at Maddie; her eyes are wide and full of concern. Apparently, she didn't know the severity, either.

We thank the doctor after she tells us that a nurse will come out to get us when we can see Rosie. She leaves and I turn to Hunter. "Buddy, you have one heck of a guardian angel on foot here." If Rosie didn't push him out of the way, I can't imagine he would've survived the impact.

"She saved my life, didn't she?"

"Most likely, son." I pull him in to hug him again. I think it's more to comfort myself than him.

"You should probably give her a raise." He looks up at me.

I laugh. "I think you're right. A bonus, as well, yeah?" I hug him even tighter. God, I love this kid.

She's like a dream I never want to wake up from.

I've pulled away the covers, revealing Maddie in all her naked glory. My eyes drink in the sight of her from her head down to her toes. I love to listen to and watch her sleep, her breaths so soft, her lips slightly parted, her eyes dancing beneath her lids, hopefully dreaming about me.

This amazing woman has turned her life upside down for me. We've all moved in with her since Rosie was discharged two weeks ago. It's just for now. She insisted, where the stairs would be difficult at my place. Also, she's the one mainly taking care of Rosie and Hunter. Christmas, like for a lot of professions, is my busiest time. Most days we have two performances. I've barely been home. On top of that, my parents fly in later today. They are staying here, of course.

Judith, Maddie's mom, has been gracious, as well, inviting Rosie for Christmas since she can't travel to be with her sons. She could've taken a train rather than a flight, but she's too nervous after what happened, and I can't say that I really blame her. Besides, she's family to us, and we are always happy to have her.

Rosie's not the only additional last minute guest; Ava, Trent, and Ava's dad, Kurt, will also been joining us. It seems Ava's morning sickness has only gotten worse into her second trimester, and she's not up to delivering her usual holiday spread.

A year ago, I would've never thought my life would change so soon and so drastically. I have never been so happy for it. It's like I've spent the past ten years taking all the wrong turns until one day, I just stumbled upon the right one.

Maddie takes in a deep breath and rolls onto her back, stretching her arms above her head. My gaze falls to her breasts. I lick my lips, fighting the urge to take one of her pebbled nipples into my mouth. Sliding my hand across her belly, my heart aches with the need to see it swell with my child. I lean down and slowly plant kisses where part of my future will grow. *Leave my man-card alone; she makes me feel poetic.* She gets self-conscious about her curves sometimes, but I love every single one of them.

I love to grab at them.

I love to bite at them.

I love to smack them.

Suddenly, Maddie's sweet, slumbering breaths quicken. Her hips slowly begin to gyrate, obviously reacting to the aggressive way I am now licking and biting at her skin. My mouth travels up her torso while my hand slides between her thighs, slipping through the folds of her wet pussy. She lets out a soft gasp, and her hips fly off the bed, grinding against my hand. "Mmm . . . you like that, sweetness?" I ask before I pull her right nipple into my mouth, sucking it hard, then biting it till she whimpers.

"Baby . . . please," she pleads and threads her fingers through my hair, pulling it.

I growl and move my hand to her hip, grasping it and flipping us over so she's on top of me. "C'mere," I command, parting her legs so that she's straddling me. "Higher." I encourage her to slide up more. She stops. I raise an eyebrow. "Higher, sweetness."

"But. . ." she trails off with a look of confusion.

"I want some Aussie kisses." I bite my smile back.

"You want me to sit on your face?" She tilts her head slightly.

I lick my lips and let my eyes fall to the prize then back up to her face. I squeeze her hips. Slowly, her right hand reaches up to push her hair behind her ear before she moves up the rest of the way. Just as she gets close enough, I lean up and glide my tongue out to taste her. She gasps and rises away from me quickly. I pull her back down. "Wait! Dec, wait!" she says in a whispered panic. "What if I can't control myself and I smother you?"

"Then I shall die a death that even the gods would be jealous of." I laugh. Honestly, I could pick her up and put her in my pocket; does she really think she could smother me?

"The Kamasutra gods?"

"The very ones," I answer and wait for her to get over her concern. Just to be sure I don't wait long, I lift my head off the bed again and entice her with a quick, soft lick at her clit followed by a prolonged kiss to her cleft, sucking at the skin. She lets out a sigh that could be deemed content or defeat. Maybe it was both. Either way, I now have a feast before me, and I fight to take my time rather than giving into the need to devour her. My eyes stay focused on watching her as I coat my tongue with her essence. Maddie's hands travel seductively up her stomach to her breasts. Her eyes are closed, and she's constantly nibbling on that lower lip of hers. I gasp in a deep breath as I watch her pinch and pull her nipples aggressively. I lift her hips slightly, giving myself enough space to blow on her clit.

"Jesus sandals!" she yelps quietly. I can't help but chuckle before I go back in. I've discovered, and am rather fond of, this new quirk of hers. She says odd things in bed sometimes when she likes something or is climaxing. Only when she's calling on God or Jesus, though. Last night when she came, she said *God bless Norway!* I later reminded her that I wasn't from Norway no matter how much she claims me to be a Viking. She hadn't a clue as to what I was talking about. Apparently, she doesn't realize she's been doing this. I actually like the Jesus ones better: *Jesus and the Carpenters, Jesus fucking loves you, Jesus on a cracker.* You get the picture.

Refocusing, I tease her entrance, flicking my tongue playfully around the edges. My left thumb working at her clit. I thrust my tongue inside as far as I can then retrieve it slowly and slide it up her center. I take my time, sucking softly at her skin, letting my tongue peek out for a taste every few seconds or so. My eyes glance back up to her when I hear her whimper. She has her arms up by her head, bent at the elbows, her hands working at the back of her hair, matching the rhythm of her hip gyrations. *She's almost there.* I work more aggressively at her. I feel a timid little jerk in her body.

"Oh no. No . . . I can't," she almost cries, now pulling at her hair. Her face scrunches up, and she bites down on that delicious lip of hers.

"C'mon, Maddie!" I bark.

"No. No. No," she whimpers and tries to pull away. I hold fast to her and make her stay put. Her legs start shaking, and she fights me more. This time she reaches down, trying to pull my hands away. I tighten my grip and my intensity until she caves, letting the orgasm wash over her. She cries out. Finally, I release her once her last wave dissipates.

She unstraddles me and slides down my right side, into my embrace.

Here, she stays.

Here, she cries.

Here, I wait for her to be okay.

This is happening less than it used to but it's still a part of our routine. Maddie says I'm the only person she's ever reacted like this with. When she first told me that, I felt awful. I thought I did something wrong. It turns out, I'm the only one she's ever had an orgasm with; it overwhelms her. She's had them on her own, but I guess it's different. I don't know. I'm just glad I'm not doing anything wrong. I just try to be as supportive as I can be; hold her as long as she needs me to. *Give myself a high-five. . .* What?! Don't judge me. You'd high-five yourself, too; don't lie.

"I'm sorry," she says through her tears and places several kisses on my chest before snuggling back into me.

"Shh, sweetness," I hush her and kiss her hair. Before long, she settles down, and I feel her lips dance across my chest, down my stomach. I close my eyes, feeling soothed. At the same time, my adrenaline picks up, anticipating her beautiful lips wrapped around my cock. God, what she does to me. I fist her hair with first contact and let out a soft, approving moan. I'd rather be balls deep inside of her, but this is her way of telling me that she can't handle that right now. And, it's okay. I find compromise to be so easy with her. So much that I wonder why it's been so difficult with others. Just another sign that she is the one, right?

"Maddie—stop! It's fine! Everything looks wonderful. Really, you're fussing too much." I grab her hand and lead her out of the guest bedroom for my parents. "We have to leave, sweetness," I remind her.

"Go without me."

"No." I give her my most stern face. I'm assuming this, of course, as I can't see what kind of face I'm actually giving her.

"I'm not ready. Besides, it'll be nice for you to catch up on the way home."

"My parents are not going to eat you alive!" I argue. I don't know what the hell the matter is. She is wonderful; everybody loves her. Why is she so worked up over my parents? It's becoming rather annoying. They are the most easy going, laid back people I've ever known, and—I know *a lot* of people!

"I just . . . I love you so much." Her chin quivers. "I'm so afraid they won't think I'm good enough."

"Fuck a monkey's arse, Maddie—that's ridiculous!" I yell.

"Fuck a monkey's arse?" she questions then starts laughing to a point where she's in tears.

"Stop," I sigh.

"Where does that even come from? Is that an Australian expression?"

"No."

"Straight-up Declan Pierce original?"

"Straight-up," I answer. "Can we go now?" I ask . . . unamused.

"Yes." She walks closer to me and leans up on her toes, smiling at me before she puckers up for a kiss. I lean down and oblige.

I lace my fingers with hers and lead her out to the living room where my impatient son jumps up off the couch. "Finally!" he sighs.

"Sorry, Hunter." Maddie offers him a smile then turns her attention to Rosie. "Are you sure you're going to be all right?" she asks for about the hundredth time. Rosie, obviously tired of being asked, just glares over the brim of her glasses at her. Maddie puts her hands up. "Ok, ok," she concedes.

Before she can think of another reason to prolong the inevitable, Hunter and I drag her out of the house and into the car. *Honestly! I wish she wouldn't make such a big deal about all of this.*

I RESCUE MADDIE'S fingers from her gnawing teeth. "Stop!" I command. My parents' plane landed about ten minutes ago, and we've been waiting by baggage claim for them.

"Gam! Gamps!" Hunter yells and starts to frantically wave. I look over and can't help but laugh. Jonathan and Daisy Pierce (God, love them) are waving just as frantically back at Hunter from the escalator. They are both donned in t-shirts that say G-FORCE 1 (my mother) and G-FORCE 2 (my father). These are, of course, accessorized with giant, green clown sunglasses and straw hats. Never afraid to make arses out of themselves, my parents love to do simple little things that cause a good amount of laughter from others. They've always been this way. I can't say I've always been happy about it, but I definitely appreciate that about them now. Hunter, of course, feels the same way. I give that another three years before he's decided he's embarrassed and complains about it. That's just the same age it affected me like that.

"I love them already," Maddie murmurs next to me.

"I told you so." I look down at her with a smirk as we begin walking to meet them.

"Oh! Look at my boys!" Mum cheers, clapping her hands excitedly as they get closer to us. Hunter runs into her arms. "My, my—you've grown, Hunter!" She pulls back. "Now, let me take a better look at you." She pulls off her huge clown glasses only to reveal another pair of glasses that have crazy eyes. Hunter goes into hysterics.

"Dad, you really mustn't pick up strange women, like her, anymore." I shuffle my hand out towards my mother.

"I'd be blind without her," he says as he pulls off his glasses only to reveal another pair underneath with eyes shut. Maddie snorts beside me.

"You must be Hunter's girlfriend." Mum turns her attention to Maddie.

"Gammm!" Hunter says with exasperation.

"What?"

"That's Maddie! She's Dad's girlfriend!" He shakes his head at her.

"Hi, Mrs. Pierce, it's nice to meet you." Maddie smiles and holds out her hand.

"Oh no, love—I hug." Mum pulls her in. "And you can call me Daisy. Just don't call me Ms. Daisy . . . especially if you're driving me anywhere. People drive me mad with that. But, you won't, right, Maddie?" She pulls back, grasping the sides of Maddie's shoulders, looking her straight in the eyes with her crazy-eyes glasses.

"Of course not. As long as you promise to always wear those glasses, when you are having a serious conversation with me. It really drives the point home." She laughs.

Mum starts laughing as well and pulls the glasses off. "I forgot I still had them on." She hugs Maddie again. She finally lets go so that

Dad can greet her.

"She's so cute, hun," Mum whispers in my ear.

"Right?"

"So tiny," she says as if she's in disbelief.

"There's a giant heart inside of her, though, Mum," I say as I glance over at Maddie talking to my dad.

"I already knew that, son." She smiles and hugs me again.

"Well, should we grab your bags and head back to the house? I'm sure you guys are wiped out from the flight," Maddie suggests.

"You're not kidding. I don't think my arms have ever been this tired," Dad complains, wincing as he pulls at his arms to stretch them.

"Oh boy." Hunter shakes his head and rolls his eyes.

"What?" Dad questions him.

"Let's go," Hunter groans playfully and heads towards the belt for their luggage.

We all follow his lead and soon enough, everyone has a bag they are in charge of . . . because my mother always packs as if she's staying for a month.

"Knock, knock," Rosie says quietly.

I look over my shoulder at her as I place another shirt into my suitcase. I have to go back down to Boston tomorrow. I'm staying all week till Christmas Eve. It's such a tiring schedule; I'm looking forward to my vacation after. "Come on in." I smile.

"Does it feel strange packing for yourself?" she asks as she hobbles in on crutches. She shouldn't be walking this much, but she is getting better—rib wise—and, she's not one to sit still anyhow.

"A little bit. I just want to get it out of the way while my parents are sleeping. What are you up to?" I turn around and sit.

"Nothing . . . and it's driving me crazy. Too much time to think about things," she groans and hops a little to turn around and sit on the lounge chair, keeping her leg out straight.

"I know this is doing a number on you, but you'll be back to *no good* soon."

At this, she sticks her tongue out at me before chuckling. "Well, until then, I sit and ponder things."

"What kind of things?" I inquire.

"Is Renee going to call him for Christmas? If so, how will she reach him? She doesn't have your cell, and she usually calls the house." She lays her crutches next to her.

"Hmm . . . I've been so busy with everything else; I hadn't put much thought into that. I will talk to Maddie about it. For me, I feel like Hunter is really in a good place, finally. I don't want a phone call from her to set him back. However, I do think he is old enough and mature enough to make that decision for himself; he may not want to talk to her. On the other hand, she may not even call. It's such a fine line to try and make a decision off of." Suddenly, I feel a headache coming on. I close my eyes and begin to rub at my temples.

"I'm sorry. I didn't mean to stress you out about this."

I open my eyes back up. "It's not your fault, really. I just haven't thought about her or any of the issues that come along with her for the past few months; it's been nice. But, it is something I need to think about and prepare Hunter for. I don't even know how her treatment is going. I know nothing." I throw my hands out.

"You know nothing about what?" Maddie asks, causing me to look away from Rosie.

"Hey, you got back from Charley's quick." I smile and stand up. She had run over there to pick up tonight's dinner. Charley offered to cook for us so she could try out some recipes she's considering for her restaurant she'll be opening next year.

"What were you guys talking about?"

"Renee," I sigh.

"Why?" she asks a little too sharply. I then begin to catch her up on our discussion.

"I agree. But first, you should mention this to Ted to see what he thinks. He may be the one to better broach this subject with Hunter," she offers.

"Honestly? I think you would be the best person."

"Why?" She walks further into the room.

"Because . . . you've become the mum he's never really had. He'll value your opinions and feelings, knowing they come from the heart, not just a textbook." I grab her hand and bring it up to my lips to plant a kiss.

"Don't wave that title around like that; I've barely been in his life; we've discussed this before." She pulls away, spitting this all out as if it put her in a panic. My heart sinks. "What's that look?"

"Disappointment, honey. . ." Rosie chimes in.

"But, Dec—"

"—Don't," I cut her off. "Please, just give me a few minutes. I want to finish packing and . . . I just need a few minutes."

"But, Dec—"

"—No! Just, please!"

"I love him," she tries to reassure me.

"I know." I give her a slight smile.

"And, I love you," she continues.

"That, I also know."

"We don't have to rush *everything*. Just . . . slow down."

"I can't. I know what I want. But, maybe the problem is not me knowing; maybe it's you *not* knowing."

"You are fucking kidding me right now, right? You're going to do this shit to me, *right now*? The first day your parents are here?— you're going to pull this *bullshit*?" she yells as quietly as she can, pointing her finger at me. "God damn it, Declan—GOD-FUCK-ING-DAMN IT!" And with that, she storms out of her bedroom.

"Dec, what are you doing?" Rosie asks, her voice laced in disbelief.

I grab my duffle bag and rifle through it, finding what I want to show her. I toss it to her. "This is what I want to do. I'm scared as hell, Rosie. Not because I'm unsure; I'm the surest I've ever been in my life. I'm scared that she doesn't feel as sure as me, and when she says stuff like that, it only confirms my fears." I shut up and wait for her reaction.

"This is a big step, Dec." She looks up from the box at me.

"I know. But it's the one I want to take, and I want to take it with her." I walk over to Rosie and take the box back so I can hide it again.

"She's under a lot of stress; cut her some slack. She's stepped up to the plate here, going above and beyond. She's done it because she loves you; don't doubt that." She holds her hand out for me to help her get up.

Just then, I hear the engine to Maddie's car rev up again. I run over to the window in time to catch her speeding down the street. *I made her run.* Maddie never runs. She's a firm believer in facing your problems head on. My heart sinks even deeper.

Complete shit at this.

(If I had an autobiography, that would be the perfect title.)

Chapter Nineteen

Maddie

I CAN'T BELIEVE HE'S DOING THIS TO ME ON CHRISTMAS! I CAN'T believe him! The first day his parents are here—he pulls *this* bullshit?! I don't have the energy for this. I just can't. I can't handle one more thing.

I pull into the driveway of the only person I know I can talk to in a personal crisis situation. I'm not the one who usually has many of those, but when I do, it's Shannon O'Brien that pulls me through.

I know this would bother my own mother terribly if she knew, but can you imagine me going to Judith with any of this? Christ, she already has Declan and me married off in her mind. All she would do is give me a "There, there now" pat on the back as she sends me back in the direction of my house. Her biggest concern would be me possibly never getting married.

Holy shit!

I think I just figured out the root of my problem. *Damn it!* Why can't somebody else figure out my shit? This just pisses me off even more, and I slam my car door shut after getting out, just to prove it.

"Maddie, honey, everything all right?" Happy asks as he opens the storm door for me.

"No." I pout. "Is Ma home?" I ask as I approach him and plant a kiss on his cheek.

"Yeah, c'mon in, honey." He steps back for me. "Do I gotta go fish out my favorite bat?"

I laugh at this. Not because he was joking but because I know he is as serious as a heart attack. If you've had the same friends as long as I have, then you would know that they come with a pack-aged deal—their parents. There are three different types of these parents: the ones you get along with just fine and never have any issues with, the ones you can't stand and the feeling is mutual, and, finally, the ones, like the O'Briens, where the lines are completely blurred as to who you actually are to them; they see you as their own and vice versa.

So, when Happy wants to know if he needs his bat, he's in com-plete protective dad mode, and I love him for it. I throw my arms around his neck for a big hug. "I love you, Happy. You can keep your bat at bay . . . for now." I smile as I let go.

"I don't like seeing any of my girls upset. C'mon now, let's go to the advisor," he teases and leads the way. "Shannon, I'm gonna put on a pot of tea for you two," he announces as we make it into the kitchen.

"What's the matter?" She looks up from her game of solitaire.

I try to tell her, but it bursts out of me so quickly, I sound like a hysterical five-year-old who just scraped her knee.

She looks over at Happy.

"We're gonna need those cookies you just hid in your secret stash."

"What secret stash?"

"The secret stash you don't think I know about. Cough 'em up, Jack!"

He stares at her blankly.

She gives him a more pointed look.

He lets out a big huff then turns and starts mumbling under his breath that nothing is sacred anymore, as he retrieves the cookies. My sniffles turn into giggles. These two really should have their own reality show.

"Now, let's try this, again," she says as she swirls all of the cards into a pile. "Sit across from me. We'll play double Solitaire." She waves her finger toward the opposite seat and pulls the other deck of cards, next to her, out of its box.

"I don't really feel like playing," I say.

She gives me a more pointed look.

I huff and mumble under my breath that I don't see how playing cards is going to help me. Seeing how I'm not going to win, I grab the spare deck from her and set up. Happy makes us some tea and without prompting, I spill the beans.

"I'm having a hard time understanding what your problem is. I mean, I know that this was poor timing on his part to act this way, but it seems, from what you've told me, that he's gotten over his trepidations and is ready to move forward in his life—*with you*. Was it just the timing?" she asks as she adds her cards to some of my piles.

"I've surmised that it's a few things. One—I've been waiting for him to do something to push me away again; we've been doing so good, it seemed inevitable. Two—I realized, on the way over here, that some of my reactions have to do with my mother."

"Oh, for Christ's sake, Maddie! Don't hand me the *it's-all-my-parents-fault* bullshit! You're better than that!" she raises her voice, something she's never done to me . . . because I, along with Ava, are the good ones that never get into trouble. It's a little scary on this

225

side of the fence.

"I'm not saying it's all of her fault. And, you're not being very fair; anyone's reactions to anything can stem from something someone else has said to them or done to them. More often than not, parents tend to fall into this category because they are the ones molding you into the person you become. Unfortunately, for parents, most tend to hear about the negative shit, or, at least, that's what they navigate to. You could have ten adults in the room, divided into two groups of five. One group of adults can be successful—pillars of the community. The other group can be completely opposite. *Yet,* only the parents of the effed up group get recognition—ripped to shreds whether they deserve it or not. You rarely ever hear of people blaming the parents for their kids being awesome. It's society, Ma—not my profession!" I slam my two of clubs down.

"Alright, I'll concede a little. *But,* only a little! I want to hear why you blame your mother for tonight's reaction before I concede fully." She grabs her cup of tea and settles back against her chair.

"On my way here, I was thinking about how it might bother my mother to know that I come to you with problems like these." I put my cards down and grab my cup as well, taking a sip before I continue. "The thing is, she's already got us married off. She'd try to put a little Band-Aid on my feelings and ship me right back to him as to not disturb her order of things. Due to my age, how strongly Declan and I feel for each other, and the fact that he already has a son, I feel like my mother has felt confident enough to check me off of her 'to-do' list. *I'm a box!* On *her* list of things to accomplish: successful, married daughter—check!" I do a check mark in the air.

"Keep going," she says, looking over the brim of her mug.

"Oh . . . well. . ." Gee, I thought I'd made my point.

"Maddie, I'm gonna give you a major news flash—all of us moms have a god damn list. It's called: wanting to see your kids living to their full potential and happy before you die. You'll have it, too, when you become a mom. That aside, I am the mother of five girls—all grown, as you know—you're gonna have to hit me with something a little more concrete than that mediocre shit." She puts her tea down and starts eyeing our cards once again.

"No, wait! There is a point to my point! I just got sidetracked," I explain. "The reason I said any of this is because my mother suffocates me with it. You know she did before Declan came along." I don't have to wait long before she nods in agreement. "I think now that Declan seems magically okay with everything and is now pushing to move us along quickly, it feels overwhelming. It's like the same pressure I feel with my mother's behavior. But, now, there's two of them. I feel like my right to decide my future is being slowly taken away. Also, I'm afraid that once I throw all hands on the deck, he's going to suddenly decide he doesn't actually want this." I take in a deep breath. "I'm scared," I admit. "I just need to go slower . . . to make sure."

"To make sure the other shoe isn't going to drop?" she asks.

"Yes!" I say with relief; she *finally* sees where I'm coming from.

"The other shoe will drop, honey. You know why?"

"Why?"

"Because you're gonna wait so long to *be sure* that's it's just gonna fall off that old, ugly, gnarly-assed, bunioned foot. Meaning: you wait too long, you'll outgrow the shoe you're afraid is going to drop, causing it to eventually do so." She points her stack of cards at me for emphasis. "Do you think I didn't have any trepidation about my Jackie? He is the silliest son-of-a-bitch—may she rest in peace—that I've ever met. Now, if I had waited around for him to be a different person, I wouldn't have spent the past forty years of my life making wonderful memories and laughing my ass off with him." She leans in toward me and guards her mouth with her hand. "Mostly—at him," she says in a hushed whisper.

"I heard that, Shannon!" Happy announces from the den off the kitchen.

"Of course you did, what with those bionic ears and all." She rolls her eyes, and I can't help but laugh.

"I want what you guys have . . . so badly." I feel myself tear up.

"It's not going to happen." She shrugs.

"Why?" I snap slightly.

"Because you want all the glory without the work."

"That's not true!"

"Then why are you here? You're being silly, Maddie." I try to interject, but she holds up her hand. "I'm not saying your feelings aren't valid because they are. I'm saying that you can't have what we have until you get in the ring him without the gloves, honey. Life is gonna come at you hard sometimes, but boy the blows are a lot easier to take when you look over your shoulder and see your best friend—his back to yours—fighting with you. You won't have that until you realize he, and your feelings for him, are not your opponents. Do you love him, Maddie?" She reaches for my hand.

"Yes," my voice squeaks as I try to control the quivering of my chin.

"Eleanor Roosevelt once said, 'It is not fair to ask of others what you are not willing to do yourself.' Do you think you are being very fair to him, Maddie?"

"No," I sniffle. I get up and make my way over to her, throwing my arms around her neck, I hug her tightly. "Thank you, Ma. I have to go."

"Yes, you do." She laughs. "And I won't tell your mother that you like me better than her."

"Stop it!" I giggle and give her a kiss on the cheek.

"I hear giggling in here," Happy says, grabbing our attention. "The advisor advised well, I take it?" His eyes dart to hers, and I can not only see the warmth in them, I can feel it. I want Declan to look at me like that in forty years. Of course, now that I've thought of that, I'm a blubbering mess—but—in a good way.

"Doesn't she always?" I smile.

"Aye, she does." He winks.

"Ok, I've gotta go, guys! Thank you both! You're the best non-biological parents a girl could have. I love you!" I give Shannon another kiss on the cheek and squeeze before I run over to Happy and do the same.

With that, I head out the door and back to my man, ready to toss the gloves and get in the ring. *Wait—why do we have to take off the gloves to fight life?* I wonder if I should even bother to ask Shannon later. She's CiCi's mom, and *that apple* did not fall far from the tree.

I stopped for milk.

It's an alibi to soften the blow of my over-displaced-reaction. I've only been gone a little under an hour and, given my love of perusing stores, it's a completely legit timespan for the purchase of milk.

Slowly, I follow the sound of voices in the kitchen. I didn't realize I was holding my breath until I almost reach the threshold where I can clearly hear them talking about Hunter's school. I was worried that they may have been discussing me and what happened. Who knows; maybe they already did that and moved on from it. I take one last deep breath and then saunter into the kitchen as if nothing happened. "Hey, everyone," I greet with a smile.

"Maddie, what on Earth took you so long?" Daisy asks in excited disbelief.

"I needed to buy milk and then, you know—squirrel!" I laugh, praying it sounds genuine.

"Squirrel? You bought squirrel?" Jonathan asks. "I think you've been watching a little too much *Crocodile Dundee*, love. We may be from Australia, but that doesn't mean we live off the land."

"Gampa! It's a phrase! It means she got distracted," Hunter in-

229

forms him between his chuckles.

"No . . . I meant an actual squirrel," I say. "But they were fresh out of ones with nuts." I shrug and go to put the milk away. I turn around to the awkward silence and see all of the faces staring at me blankly. Except for Declan; he's not looking at me at all. "I'm kidding! Geez . . . tough crowd," I complain. Finally, they begin to laugh a little. "A little too late, guys," I tease and grab a plate to fill with Charley's food, seeing as how they started without me. *Yeah . . . let's not go there.*

I sit next to Declan and dig into the baked potato mash casserole. God, this is just what I needed, because—*bacon!* I love when she makes this. "Sorry we started without you," Declan finally speaks up. "Everyone was hungry, and we didn't know when you would be back. I tried to text and call you. . ." he trails off at the mention.

"I left my phone here by accident."

He nods then continues to eat.

Because the sudden awkward silence that has loomed over our table is making me feel uncomfortable, I decide to engage his parents in conversation about what they'd like to do this week. They will be pretty much on their own with Hunter and Rosie during the day since I, too, will be working. "A little bit of this . . . a little bit of that, depending mostly on what Hunter would like to do. I am, however, really looking forward to spending the entire day in Boston on Wednesday with your parents," Daisy informs me. This is the first I'm hearing of this plan, so naturally I'm choking on the chunk of pot roast I just threw in my mouth. "Are you all right, dear?" she asks. I shake my head yes, giving one final cough that sounds as if I suffer terribly from Emphysema. Declan rubs and pats my back gently to try and help me.

"Sorry about that," I say as I finally gain control over myself. "I wasn't aware that you and my parents had set up a playdate," I tease, trying to sound as if I am not actually horrified.

"A while ago. Judith and I are friends on Facebook."

"You are?" *Don't widen your eyes . . . don't widen your eyes. Keep the panic at bay. . .*

"Yes! She friended and messaged me, on there, two months ago, telling me who she was."

Of course she did!

"I was so excited that she was reaching out. We've talked daily since then. I feel as if I've known her forever. Although, I am feeling a little funny about the fact that she didn't mention that to you." A crease forms across her brow as she gives me a perplexed look.

"Oh, Mum, I don't think you should fret about that." Declan stops rubbing my back and leans back into his chair, giving his attention to Daisy. "It can be nerve wracking when the parents of a couple meet the first time, never mind throwing in the usual stresses of the holiday season. Judith probably wanted to surprise Maddie with the fact that she took the initiative to make sure our holiday, all together, runs as smooth as it can be. I think it was quite brilliant of her, actually." Declan smiles and gives me a slight encouraging grin. You know what that slight grin tells me? *He knew this* entire *time!* He and my mom have become as thick as thieves. I should be pissed, but I'm not. This makes me happy. *He* makes me happy. And my mom, God bless her, tries her best to make me happy, even though I'd rather she not. I am realizing that I'm too hard on her sometimes . . . when it comes to my happiness. I mean, she's *just* being a mom, right? I think I'll send her flowers tomorrow—just because. This, of course, means that I will have to suffer through—*at least*—twenty minutes on the phone, listening to her details about each flower, how it's arranged, the vase it came in, where she's placing the flowers, why she's placing the flowers there (so people will see them, and she can go on about it to them), so on and so forth. That's the *real* gift, people—listening.

"I think you're right, babe," I say to him before looking back over to Daisy. "That really is one less thing to worry about. I'm glad you all have become friends already and are going to spend the day together. It's pretty awesome. But, if she starts asking you about seating charts and cake flavors, *run*—don't walk!" I laugh.

"Oh, I gave that to her two weeks ago." Daisy pushes at the air in front of her.

Wide eyes commence.

I couldn't help it.

"Relax, Maddie; I'm just kidding!" She winks, then gives into a little giggle. "You're mom and I have been planning on teasing you this week. I think she may get upset with me, knowing I started in on you without her."

Before I can answer her, "Let's go outside for some fresh air, son," Jonathan says to Declan. I look over to find him closed-mouth and jawline twitching away.

"What's the matter?" I place my hand on his arm. He glares at me.

"*Son,*" Jonathan is more stern now.

"Dad? What's wrong?" Hunter takes notice of Declan, as well.

"Nothing." He pushes his plate away and stands up. "Excuse me, I'm gonna go and finish packing," he states before turning around and abruptly leaving.

"Rosie?" I look to her for some guidance.

"Go. Go and talk to him."

I nod. "Please excuse me, everyone. Sorry about this." I'm not going to lie; I'm a little embarrassed at the moment.

"Go ahead, love." Daisy gives me an encouraging smile.

I get up and begin a slow chase after my Viking. Yes, I said slow. Two reasons for this: one—he needs a moment to cool off, and two—I need a moment to try and figure out why the hell he's pissed again.

"Declan?" Ugh! Mousy voice! I hate when that happens to me. I clear my throat as I walk into the bedroom. "Baby?" I try again to grab his attention.

He keeps his back to me as he folds more clothes aggressively and throws them in the suitcase on our bed. "Go and finish eating, Maddie," he commands.

"I think we need to talk," I say as I finally reach him and allow my hands to slide up his back before planting a kiss in the middle.

"I think you've said enough. I believe I've gained a clear enough picture as to how far you see us going."

"I believe you're full of shit and need to stop making things about *you*!" I snap and walk over to the section of the bed closer to the pillows, where I can sit.

"Well, we're all entitled to our opinions." He folds an undershirt like he's mad at it. "I'm leaving tonight."

"You can't."

"My parents will be fine."

"It's not that."

"What is it, Maddie?!"

"You promised me Aussie kisses tonight and I've been looking forward to them all day." I try to get a smile to crack through his stoic disposition.

"I don't think I'll be giving you those kind of kisses anymore."

Did you hear that *thump*?

That was my heart, dropping to the floor.

"Are. . ." I clear my throat to get rid of the mouse again. "Are you breaking up with me?"

"I don't know what the bloody hell I'm doing! All I know is that I love you like mad, and I can't picture a future without you. But! You have been making it very clear that you are not feeling the exact same way as me. So, I don't know what to do! Do I cut things off with you now, trying to salvage what's left of my heart? Or, do I let it all play out until you are done with me and I have nothing left?" he yells.

"You. Are. Overreacting!" I kneel up on my bed so that I'm eye to eye with him.

"Am I?" He laughs. Not like *ha-ha, that's so funny*; more like a condescending one.

"Yes!"

"Alright, let's see then." He reaches for his duffle bag on the far side of the bed and digs his hand in. After retrieving a black square gift box, he hands it to me. "This is your big Christmas present from me. I was going to give it to you in private on Christmas Eve, but I want to give it to you now and settle this for once and all. Open it." He taps on it.

"I'd rather you gave it to me on Christmas."

"Open it!" he barks. I shimmy the lid off to find an appointment card and a pamphlet. I glance over the title of the pamphlet (it's about reversing a vasectomy) then quickly bring my eyes up to look at him.

"I'm set to go in January to reverse everything because I want nothing more in my life than to be the father of your children, which also means I want the seating charts . . . the cake flavors . . . your mother proudly announcing to the world that I'm her son-in-law at my concerts. I want you to be the woman that Hunter calls Mum. *This* is what I want. I've been a nervous wreck about approaching you with this. And today, you've done nothing but prove me right for feeling that way. I don't believe you want the same things I want. At least, not with me." He takes in a deep breath, and I can see from the way his body quivers, it's to try to control his emotions.

"Yes," I say without hesitation. Quite shocking, if you ask me.

"Yes to what—that I was right?"

"No," I say quickly. "Yes to all of this, whatever step you meant it to be as long as it leads to all of the other steps, as well. Also, you should probably just start getting used to not being right, even when you are; it's just bad form not to," I ramble. My heart is racing. I feel as if it may burst.

"Maddie, think clearly on what you are telling me." His breathing is all over the place. I almost feel as if he's like a caged tiger, waiting to escape.

"I said yes without a single thought or hesitation; you can't get any clearer than that." I smile and palm his face.

"Really?" He stares into my eyes. "Yes?"

"Yes." I sniffle. And just like that, the tiger is unleashed as he grabs the back of my head and attacks my lips. After a beat, he tears his lips from mine and leans down a little, swiping everything off the bed with his forearm. "You're going to have to refold and repack all of that now," I present him with the obvious.

"I couldn't give two fucks about that right now," he says urgently as his hands run down my backside to the back of my knees where he lifts to throw me onto the bed.

"But, you could give one fuck, right?" I flirt.

"Only one fuck shall be given, and that fuck is for you." He yanks my pants off my hips and down my legs, tossing them behind him before he quickly works at his belt. There is just something about the way his jeans always hang off his hips. *Sexy motherfuck-er. . .*

I should come to my senses—we both should. His parents are here. We just made a slight scene in the kitchen. We should be heading out there to let them know that everything is ok. We should wait until everyone goes to bed! He *shouldn't* be sliding his cock up my center, making me squirm. And he *definitely* shouldn't be telling me how pretty he thinks my pussy is, how good it feels when it sheaths his cock, or that it's his favorite sweet because that shit will just drive me wild. And we just . . . we shouldn't. . .

Oh, fuck it!

If you happen to see Will Power, tell him Maddie said,

"Thanks for leaving me, asshole."

"Hold your legs, sweetness. Ready?" Before I can even answer him, he slams deep inside of me, causing me to arch my back to a degree I didn't think was possible. "Fuck, Maddie," he groans.

"Shh!" My arms flail trying to reach his mouth to cover it.

"Don't worry about them hearing me, love; you're the one who's going to be screaming in a minute." He smirks. "Now, hold your legs," he commands. I pull them to me more. "No—like this!" He pushes them all the way onto my chest. "Hold tight," he says again and grabs my hips, pulling me closer to the edge of the bed, grinding himself deeper into me. "Don't let go," one more order before he unleashes the beast in him. He was right—I'm screaming like a wanton hussy. I don't know what's louder, at the moment—me or the slapping of our bodies.

And then, it happens.

The tightening of my core.

I can't take it.

The weight of Declan's body crashes down on top of me as he continues to thrust his hips rapidly. "You have nowhere to go, Maddie," he pants in my ear. "You're going to take it. You're going to let your pussy explode. You can't stop it; don't even try."

"Please, I need you to stop," I practically cry as I try to wiggle away, which means a whole lot of effort to not even move an inch.

"C'mon, sweetness, just let go." He nibbles on my earlobe. And then, he shifts his hips slightly, and my toes curl. I won't mention the guttural scream that comes from me. My legs are shaking as best as they can under the circumstances. Declan switches to long, deep strides, causing my pussy to milk him every time he pulls almost completely out of me. "God, Maddie—yes!" he groans then sinks deep inside of me again. After several more times, he finally unloads his weapon. Yes, I said that. That thing is lethal!

"Declan, can you get off of me?" I ask soon after he completely crashes. He lifts his head and stares into my eyes, seemingly confused. "I'm really uncomfortable; I feel like my legs are going to come out of my hip sockets," I inform him.

"Oh! Yes! Sorry!" He slowly pulls out then rolls onto his back. I begin the slow process of letting my legs straighten out. I do a few knee bends just to get the circulation really going. "One of these days, I'm afraid I will break you in two," he says with a little laughter in his voice as he tries to give my right hip a rubdown. "Are you okay?" He kisses my shoulder as I turn onto my side.

"Yes," I murmur.

"You're not crying this time. Usually, when it's extremely intense, like that, you cry."

"I did while it was happening."

"Maybe you're getting better with it now. You're body's getting used to it." He squeezes my hip.

"I wouldn't say that. I don't feel like it is." I look over my shoulder at him and give into his silent request for a kiss.

"We'll eventually work through it, love. Right now, we better get back out to the family."

"Ah, yes—the walk of shame." I laugh.

"No shame, sweetness; only happiness." He kisses my nose before giving my lips another soft peck.

Chapter Twenty

Declan

THE LONGER WE ARE TOGETHER, THE MORE I HATE THESE overnights away from her, especially now that we've been staying with her since Rosie's accident. Oscar says it's because it's new; he and his wife were the same way. I'd take a lot of comfort in that, knowing that eventually we'll settle into a routine, but he and his wife are now divorced. I don't remind him of this, of course, because that would just be rude.

On the bright side, all of the guys work in Boston except for Blake. Apparently, Mitch and Kyle just recently hired Trent as one of their computer research scientists. I had asked him what that entails. Thank God I did that while we were in front of Hunter because Hunter inundated him with all kinds of questions, completely fascinated. I, on the other hand, felt like they were speaking Japanese.

While they were at it, I turned to Mitch and let him know that it would be good for business to have a Cellist in the lobby. He didn't seem to think I was on to something. Regardless, we've all been meeting up for lunch or drinks when we can. It's been fantastic. I truly feel like I am beginning to live my life again, not just muddling through it.

I haven't figured out what I'm going to do about Christmas and Hunter talking to Renee. I know it's selfish (I believe I have the right to be, though), but I don't want to do anything that will burst this little happy bubble we are in. It almost burst on its own this week. Or, at least it seemed as if it would.

Just when I didn't think it could be possible, Maddie went and made me even happier than she had already made me. I really truly was worried that she didn't want all of the things I do. We had a long talk about it that night after everyone went off to bed. She told me about the conversation she had with Charley and CiCi's mum. I am beyond grateful to that woman! I do understand where Maddie's reservations were coming from; I come with a lot of baggage. But, I did everything in my power to reassure her that she is *everything* I have ever been afraid of wanting. Yes—afraid. It is petrifying to get back out there after what I dealt with. But, you know what? I'm not the only person who has gone through something like that or even something far different, yet, just as traumatizing. I'm not the first person to get through it and find love again. And, I'm certainly not the first person to reacquaint themselves with the person they used to be. I had forgotten how much I liked this guy. He's so much better this time around . . . so much better with the likes of Madelyn St. Claire in his life.

She mentioned being worried about rushing. I reminded her that we've been at this dance for over six months; it's time we stop circling around like teenagers and get some salsa moves in there. She laughed lightly at this. The kind of laugh that lets you know she is content in the moment.

We discussed my surgery more in detail. I reminded her that it may not be successful but that we do have my frozen pops. She cringed at this and smacked my shoulder. This led to the conversation about everything Trent and Ava have been going through for the past nine years and why these dual pregnancies really are a blessing. My heart does break for them. Of course, Maddie crying a little, conveying all of the pain Ava has gone through, may have had something to do with it. It was at that moment that I truly realized something about Maddie. I mean, I knew it, but I didn't really understand the depths of it. Maddie, in the grand scheme of things, is the center wheel. Everyone comes to her about everything, and she guides them, as best as she can, without a second thought about it. I honestly believe that if she didn't have a title at the end of her name, it would still be this way. Maddie is a nurturer. She is insightful, and she is compassionate. You never see it go to her head, either. She's everyone's glue. I really don't know what I have done in my life to deserve the love of such a beautiful soul. That's just what she is: a beautiful soul. There are no words. That's why, this week, I have started composing a piece for her. I've never composed a symphony in my life. I have never felt enough passion to want to compose one. She gives me that. That . . . and so much more.

"There he is!" I hear a familiar voice call out from behind me. Ah . . . they've arrived. I turn to the sound of my mum's voice, calling out my name.

"Hi, Mum." I open my arms for her. "Dad." I give him a nod. "Judith. Ken." I acknowledge Maddie's parents, as well. I give Judith a hug as soon as Mum lets me go.

"I'm so glad we got to see you before your performance! What a real treat to see all of the behind the scenes stuff," Judith says.

"Oh yes, it's quite interesting. You must tell Maddie all about it as she hasn't been able to come backstage yet." I am laughing on the inside for encouraging Judith. My mum shakes her head at me. Clearly, she is well aware of Judith's fantastic ability of going over every detail about anything and everything. Not quite sure how she feels about it but, quite often, Maddie pretends to bang her head into a wall several times while listening on the phone. This always makes Hunter go into hysterics.

"All right, well, I have to go and finish getting ready; set up and all," I inform them.

"You look so handsome in your tux, doesn't he, Daisy?" Judith looks back to my mum.

"Best looking guy in the whole orchestra." My mum beams.

"All right, you two, stop fawning over him and let's find our seats," Ken says and places a hand on Judith's shoulder, letting my dad handle his own woman.

"Ok, but we're still meeting for dinner afterwards, right?" Judith asks.

"Yes. Now get!" I shoo them.

I have a hangover.

No, it wasn't from too much drink. Judith, God love her. I'll say no more.

I pop a few more ibuprofen and pray it will kick in soon. I have a very important date today, and she's due to arrive any moment. Just as I look at my watch, a horn blows obnoxiously. I look up and find Charley waving. I give her a broad smile and make haste to her Highlander.

"Geez, I'm not that late!" she says as soon as I open the door and get in.

"I didn't say anything!" I laugh.

"You were looking at your watch like I was already late."

"Ok. I'm going to go the safe route and not argue with you," I announce. "Are you ready to have some fun?"

"Oh, it's going to be epic, especially when you hear the prices. I'm glad I have a front row seat." She nudges me with her arm.

"I really am so grateful that you're taking the time to do this with me. You're a great friend, Charley." I smile. Maddie is very blessed to have such wonderful friends. And now, they are all my friends. I feel like I'm cheating on a test, really. It's great to be a part of an incredible group, no matter how fucking crazy they are. And . . . *they are!*

"I'd do anything for Maddie. And now, of course, for you." She looks over at me and tears up. "She really is the best, Dec. I'd be lost without her—we'd all be. She's just . . . she's who you want to be when you grow up. You know what I mean?"

"I do. But, I have a secret to tell you."

"What's that?"

"She feels the same way about you—about all of you!"

"You better make sure you always make her happy. Like real happy. Like she can't be happy about everything. But, like just the stuff that means stuff."

"Charley?"

"What?"

"Please do me a favor."

"What's that?"

"Cut back on the Kardashians."

"Oh fuck! I'm doing it again, aren't I?" She slaps her steering wheel.

"Um . . . like, yeah." I laugh.

"Ugh! I can't help it. It's my secret addiction."

"Charley?"

"What?"

"It's not a secret, love," I inform her.

"Shut up!" She slaps my arm. "Where are we going first?"

"You tell me. I am but a pawn with a wallet. You show me what will make her happy; I will show you the money."

"Declan?"

"What?"

"Stop reciting movie lines like they're your fucking originals."

"I do that?"

"Yup."

"It's my secret addiction."

"Now . . . you're stealing my shit. Get your own shit."

"I'll work on it." I laugh.

Just then, Charley points to the first jewelry store and miraculously finds a parking space two doors down from it. We park and go in. Making a bee-line for the engagement rings, we start looking. A stocky woman, with short brown hair, wearing a business suit walks up to us behind the counter. "May I help you?"

"Just looking at the moment, thank you." I smile up at her.

"Ok, well, if you spot something, let me know," she says as she eyes Charley up and down, like she's judging her.

"Seriously, lady? It's been the new millennium for over a decade now—you wanna get over it?!" Charley snaps.

"Thank you," I say. "You don't have what I'm looking for," I add quickly before grabbing Charley's hand and leading her out.

"Sorry," she sighs when we get outside. "I fucking hate judgmental people, even more so when I'm preggers."

"It's alright. I didn't see anything that screamed Maddie's name anyways."

We hit five more shops before it dawns on me—we're looking in all the wrong places. "Charley! Is there a shop that handles antique jewelry around here?" I ask with a bit too much excitement.

"Yeah. Shit! Why didn't I think of that? You're good, Dec!" She smacks my knee like she's proud of me. I think she is, actually.

Within moments, we're on Newbury St., pulling up to Brodney Antiques. Oddly, I have a fantastic feeling about this. I say oddly because I'm not usually one who believes in stuff like this . . . like what I'm feeling. But, I embrace it anyhow because it just feels good, like a kid on Christmas morning good, and I'll just leave it at that.

We race in. Well, I race . . . Charley may be waddling a bit, but I won't say that because I am actually a very intelligent man with a good dose of common sense. Yes, rare breed, am I.

Shh . . . stop laughing. I'm looking.

Ahhh!!!! Yes!! I've found it!

It's screaming her name!

It's from the 1930s, European cut diamond (a little over one and half carats) with twenty-eight accent diamonds, and it's perfect. Absolutely perfect for my sweetness. Charley screams with excitement and starts crying. I may also be crying. Don't judge me; I'm in love.

I'm so happy.

Bloody *fucking* hell—I'm so happy!

The clerk takes it away to give it one good final cleaning before boxing it up. Charley and I hug like we've won the lottery and all of our dreams have come true. We may also be hopping around, but I'm sure it looks embarrassing so let's not focus on that. We're just both bloody happy.

And I realize something. "Charley. . ." I trail off, a little out of breath.

"What? What's the matter?" She holds onto my forearms.

"I wasn't even close to being this happy the first time around," I say sort of astonished.

"I wasn't, either, Dec. There's a lot to be said about finding love when you're older. When you're in your twenties, you're still a kid, trying to figure out who you are and who you want to be. It's a different ball game in your thirties and older. You've grown a lot more, experienced a lot more—know more about who you are and what you want out of life. Much better this time, isn't it?" She smiles through her tears. Yes, she would know. All I can do is hug her and dance around with her, laughing like a kid. Feeling the same kind of freedom you have as one. It really is so much better the second time around. I'm not knocking the people who figured it out the first time around—I think they are bloody geniuses. Kudos to you! But, man . . . when you got it all wrong the first time . . . and then this wonderful person walks into your life—no words, mate.

Charley and I finish up with lunch. I have a show tonight and she has to contend with Boston traffic to get home. I've so enjoyed my day with her, though, I'm thinking of setting up dates with her other friends. Might as well know really well what I'm stepping into, right? Besides, from the way Maddie talks, these girls are going to be my family. And *family* is how I will treat them.

My phone pulls me from my thoughts. I answer, knowing it's my mother as I have one of those funny ringtones to tell me so. "Well?" is how she greets me.

"I bought the most perfect ring for her," I say with a smile that could possibly take up my whole face.

My mother screams with excitement. "What does it look like?" she finally asks. I give her all the details. "Did you ask about the history of the ring?"

"No. Why?"

"What if the marriage ended up in disaster? You don't want that ring to curse your marriage!"

"Oh for fuck's sake, Mum!"

"Don't you use that language with me!" she yells.

"I didn't ask. Here's the thing, Mum. I know you believe in all this hocus pocus shit, but what if something tragic did happen to the marriage that this ring was involved in? What if this ring was meant to go through that to end up on Maddie's finger for a good marriage? Honestly, you can't think like that!" I bark. I can't stand that crap.

"But what if it brings all it's bad stuff from its past?"

"What if I bring all the bad stuff from my past? Oh, that's right—already done that! It's rubbish, Mum—stop!" I yell.

"I haven't thought about it that way. I suppose you're right. I just want you to be happy, Dec. I don't want to see you go through anything remotely close to what you went through the last time," her voice quivers.

"I don't either, Mum. I'm telling you, I know for sure that this time is much better. I am happier than I have ever been. I'm more excited than I have ever been. It's different this time."

"I know it is, son. And, we just absolutely adore Maddie. She's perfect. We're proud of you. I just want the best for you. I worry. It's my job! I will worry about you beyond my last breath; you have to know that."

"I do, Mum. I love you, too."

We talk about a few other things, mostly Christmas, and then hang up. I wish I could just go home. Had I known a year ago that my life would pull a one-eighty, I would've taken this week off. Only two more days, though, and I'll be home.

"Show me!" Rosie exclaims when she gets me in Maddie's bedroom by myself. I quickly lock the door, eager to show her. "It's beautiful!"

"Rosie! Are those tears?" I ask half teasing, half in disbelief.

"Shut up! I'm allowed to be ridiculously happy for you!" She smacks me. I'm starting to notice a pattern with the women in my life being very aggressive like this. "When are you going to ask her?"

"After Christmas. I don't want the whole cliché Christmas proposal. I think it's rather lame."

"Good call. Too many people do that."

"Exactly! Oh, Rosie . . . I'm so happy. I'm just so in love. Who would've thought a year ago I would be experiencing all of this? I never thought this would be possible for me again. It's so much different this time, too."

"I'm so happy for both of you." She hugs me.

"Thank you. Now, let me hide it again before we head out there. By the way, where are your crutches?" I ask her in my most stern, parenting voice.

"Don't ruin the beautiful moment we just had, Dec." She pats my shoulder, turns away from me, and hobbles to the door.

"Wait!" I say in a hushed panic. I show her the box when she looks over at me.

"Well, hurry up! I can only stand so long, you know!"

I'm not even going dignify that with a reply. I just rush to my secret hiding spot behind one of her books on the very top shelf. Then, I jog over to Rosie as she opens the door. We head down the hallway, acting very giddy. I've been acting this way all week. It must be terribly annoying to anyone around me who is miserable in the current state of their life. Oh well. . .

Just as we approach the living room, Maddie charges through the front door with a ridiculous amount of bags from various places, mostly The Christmas Tree Shop (her favorite). She has the wild look in her eyes that she had when the girls had their weekend. I don't know whether I should offer to help or get the hell out of her way; either choice makes me question the safety of my life. "Are there any more bags in the car?" I ask, opting to be helpful and get the hell out of her way all in one shot. Told you I was intelligent.

"Yes. Babe, I'm so overwhelmed!" She drops the bags. "I just needed a few things. And then, I realized all of the fucking people I forgot to buy for! I can't believe how unorganized I am this year; it's Christmas Eve!" She looks as if she's about to be in tears.

"We have all night." I rub her upper arms. "All you have to do is tell me what you'd like for me to do, whether it be helping you wrap, or just getting out of the way. I am at your beck and call. It will be fine. And once you're done, I'll give you some Christmas Aussie kisses." I smile.

"What's an Aussie kiss?" Mum asks as she walks into the living room.

"They're like French kisses but down under," I recite Maddie's explanation.

Maddie closes her eyes like she's asking God for strength, let's out a big gush of air and looks over at my mother. "They're my favorite." She shrugs.

"I rather like those ones myself," Mum agrees.

"Oh, God—Mum!" I yell disgusted.

"Hey!" Maddie points her finger up at me, "You asked for that, buddy!"

"I'm going out the retrieve the rest of the bags before you two scar me anymore." I shake my head and go to leave, letting a chill escape my body. Their school girl giggles haunt me on my way out.

Hunter stopped believing in Santa Claus a long time ago. Maddie fussed about this, last night, with a passion that is just indescribable. She showed him all of her antique Christmas snow globes. Apparently, since she is a grown woman and not into toys anymore (well, not the type of toys Santa would bring), he brings her an antique snow globe every year. Later, she grabbed my son by the hand and dragged him up to the attic to climb onto the little balcony outside the window. They then proceeded to throw glitter (as best as they could) onto the roof. Nine carrots were placed on a separate plate next to Santa's cookies. *"These are for Santa to bring up to the reindeer."*

"Don't they eat oats?" Hunter asked.

"Usually, but it's Christmas, and they are working really hard; I like to give them something extra special," she answered. He nodded. I fell more in love with her. In one night—only a matter of hours—she brought the magic back to him.

In return, I brought *a lot* of magic to the bedroom last night. I also gave her the other private gift I wanted to give her. It was completely out of character for me, but I've been climbing out of my comfort zone more often than not with her. Maddie, about a month ago, introduced me to her Tumblr page where she mainly follows erotic blogs. That's what she called them. Between you and me—porn. Straight up, hardcore porn. Well, there's some soft porn, too. She's got a great mix on there. After a few times of watching together, I asked her what she thought of these jeweled anal plugs some of the women wore. The tempo of her breathing changed slightly and she just simply stated that they were pretty. I got her an amethyst one, and I nearly busted my nut sliding it inside of her. From then on, it was an uphill battle, trying to control myself to last as long as I could. But, I took her from behind and was hypnotized by the jewel, never mind the extra sensation of her being even tighter from it.

I have to admit; I'm a little horrified as some of the posts on that site. Maddie told me the more hardcore ones were from research she had to do on a client's fear. I told her that's what they all say, "research." I got a smack on the chest for that one.

This morning, though, hearing Hunter yell for us excitedly—it was like a movie. That, alone, was the best gift anyone could give me. We ran out to the living room, just as excited as he, I'm sure. He looked at us and started crying. *"Hunter? What's the matter?" Maddie went to him and pulled him into her arms, swaying him slightly and kissing the top of his head, "Are you ok?"*

He looked up at her. "I have two parents. I woke up on Christmas morning, and my wish finally came true. I know it might seem silly, but I have no memory of ever calling for her on Christmas morning; just Dad. I always wanted to call out 'Mom and Dad', wait, and have two happy parents come running out to me. That just happened and it was way better than I ever imagined it would be." He wiped his eyes with the back of his hands. I was doing the same only a few feet away from them.

"You did . . . you yelled out 'Mom and Dad," Maddie said as if in

disbelief. She looked over at me, her eyes welled up.

"You ran with me without the slightest bit of hesitation." I smiled as I approached them.

"I know," she said then looked back at Hunter. She palmed his face. "I love you, Hunter."

"Can I give you your gift first?" he asked.

"Right now?"

"Yes, please." And with that, he turned away from her and went over to her enclosures. He pulled out a black velvet jewelry box with a red bow on it from behind one of her books. Hmm . . . like father, like son. He walked back over to her and placed the box in her hand. Maddie gave him a curious smile, tilting her head, as usual, and slid the ribbon off. "I picked it out all by myself, and spent my own money." It was clear—he was very excited.

Maddie opened the box and covered her mouth when she gasped. This was immediately followed by sobs and her pulling him back in for a hug. Not able to stand the suspense anymore, I took the box out of her hand and looked at it. Inside was a silver necklace with one single charm, shaped like a heart. Inside, it said, "I love you, Mom."

"When? Who took you?" I asked as I took it out of the box and placed it around Maddie's neck.

"Brogan's mom," he answered and smiled once the necklace laid in place. "It's perfect. Now everyone will ask you about it, and you can tell them all your son gave it to you. You can tell everyone you're my mom."

"You really want me to be your mom, Hunter? You're sure?" she sniffled.

"Yes, so be on your best behavior, Dad!" He gave me a stern look.

"What? Why are you warning me?!" I laughed. They both gave me the stare down. "Great; I guess it's two against one from now on."

"From now on," Maddie repeated me and I pulled them both in for a group hug.

"Did a pet die or something?" My Dad asked from behind us.

"*The squirrel kicked the bucket, Gamps,*" Hunter said without missing a beat. *Maddie laughed herself straight into a snorting fit.*

So far—Best. Christmas. Ever!

"You ready?" Maddie asks, placing her hand on my forearm.

"Oh, yeah," I say quickly, snapping out of it. I didn't even realize that we were here already. I also didn't realize I had already cut off the engine. "Sorry." I smile over to her. "My mind went wandering." I waggle my eyebrows. She blushes slightly and leans over for a kiss before we get out and walk up the walkway.

"You're never late!" Ava comes outside to meet us.

"Well, Santa came for more than just me this year," Maddie reminds her.

"I'm just glad CiCi wasn't here to hear what you just said." Ava laughs and hugs her.

"Let's get inside so I can introduce everyone," Maddie suggests. We do have quite the line-up out here.

"Sorry! C'mon, c'mon!" Ava states excitedly and turns to go back in.

TWO HOURS IN and we're all ready for a Christmas nap. I have *never* seen so much food in my life. The herd moves on into the St. Claire living room to work up an appetite for dessert by opening presents. I take this time to grab Ken's attention and pull him away from the crowd. I'm pretty sure he has a new train he wants to show me, or . . . at least, that's what we'll tell everyone.

"Ken," I start quickly.

He holds up is right hand with a slight smile. "Do you love her more than anything in the world?" he asks.

"With the exception of my son, yes." I nod.

"Do you promise to always take care of her, look after her best interest, always make sure she feels loved and appreciated?"

"Yes."

"You have my permission, Declan." He holds out his hand for a shake.

"That was rather easy." I laugh nervously.

"I pay attention to my daughter. She, along with others, may not realize it, but I'm always watching, making sure she is happy. I've never seen her so happy in all of her life. And, I couldn't have asked for a better, more stand-up guy than you to be the one who finally swept her off her feet. I'm looking forward to finally having that dance with my Maddie." He pats my shoulder before releasing my hand.

"You and me both, Ken."

"Alright, let's get back to the party."

"Yes, sir." I turn and head back up the stairs we came down not two minutes ago.

I find my spot next to Maddie and instantly get an elbow to my ribs. I look down at her. "Look!" she says in an excited whisper. My eyes travel in the direction she's pointing to find Rosie and Kurt, Ava's dad, in a deep conversation with, what seems like, slight flirtation. "They are really taking to each other. Kurt has never looked at another woman since Ivy passed, let alone, *flirt!* I'm so excited," she squeals lightly.

"Don't get ahead of yourself, sweetness. And don't meddle or push!" I warn. "Let it happen naturally, if it's going to happen."

"Yeah, yeah. . ." she humors me.

Suddenly, we all hear the front door slam open. "Maddie! Ava!" a woman yells.

"Julie?" Maddie stands up just as Julie comes around the corner. Her face is tear-stricken, and she's visibly shaking. "What's the matter? What happened?!" Maddie works her way around the piles of gifts as quickly as she can. Ava is doing the same.

"We have to go," Julie sobs.

"Go where?" Maddie finally gets to her and places her hands on Julie's upper arms. "Parkland. We've all been trying to calling you guys for the past hour. Charley's water broke," she cries.

"*What?!* No! It's too soon!" Ava says in disbelief and instantly begins to cry.

"C'mon, baby!" Trent throws her coat over her shoulders.

"Dec?" Maddie turns around for me, but I'm already on her heels with her coat. "You have to drive."

"Yes." I turn to my parents.

"Go!" They both yell. "We've got Hunter and Rosie—just go!"

"Right!" I turn back and usher Maddie out of the house, following Trent and Ava. "You're not driving, mate!" I bark at Trent. "Either get in with us or with Blake and Julie, but you are not driving!" I grab his keys from him. He nods in agreement and jumps in my passenger seat. Maddie and Ava climb in the back, buckle in and hold onto each other. I do something I haven't done in a very long time. . .

I pray.

Chapter Twenty-One

Maddie

THE MINUTES SEEM LIKE HOURS. ALL I CAN DO IS PACE AND WORRY. How am I going to help my friends through this? I have no words. I have no guidance to give. I'm useless. Another wave of sobs hit me; Ava and I both became moms today. Both of us received that title in an unconventional way, when you think in biblical terms.

I will go home and hug my new son.

She may never be able to bring her daughter home.

Or hug her.

Or hear her say, "I love you, Mom."

"Sweetness. . ." I feel his hand on my shoulder.

"Out of all the people in the world, why them? Haven't they suffered enough?"

"Nobody should go through this uncertainty or pain,"

"I know that, Dec! But, Jesus Christ! Enough already! They've been through enough!" I bury my face into my hands. He swirls me around and wraps me in his arms.

"I don't care, Kyle!" CiCi yells as she comes barreling into the chapel. "She's two hours old, and she's already been through hell! She's not a god damn science project; they need to leave her the hell alone!" she continues as she makes her way up to the big wooden cross. "AND YOU!" She points at the cross. "You can go fuck. *Your. Self!*" With that comes a procession of "Fuck yous" and matching hand gestures.

"CiCi!" Kyle grabs her. "Stop! We're not the only people in here."

"I gave all my flying fucks to this asshole!" She points to the cross. "You know what I'm going to do, God?" She now looks up as she yells. "I'm gonna send my guardian angel up there to shit on your pillow while your head is resting on it and your mouth is open. You hear me? You can eat angel shit!"

"I don't believe God sleeps, dear," an elderly woman says.

"You're right," CiCi says calmly. If you know CiCi as well as I or the other girls, you know that a calm CiCi only means it's time for the straight jacket. "Who's got time to sleep when you're so busy fucking up people's lives? *You selfish motherfucker!*" She raises both barrels at the sky for her encore.

"Are you done now?" Kyle, ever-so-patient, asks. CiCi nods slowly then weeps with so much heart in it, you can feel your own break a little more.

CiCi is not really mad at God.

CiCi is mad at herself.

Okay . . . God, too.

I don't blame her, do you?

The door swings open and Julie, Blake, Jay, and Vic come walking in. "Your turn, Maddie," Julie says quietly.

"Thanks. Keep an eye on Ceese; she just went all *Lieutenant Dan* on God." I jerk my head in her direction.

"She just threatened to throat punch our niece's nurse, if she went at her with one more damn needle." Julie bites her smile back.

"Our niece. . ." I trail off into a hiccuppy gasp.

"C'mon, sweetness." Declan grabs my hand and leads me out, saving me from breaking down again.

It's all still touch and go. Hope arrived today because of complete placental abruption. One minute, Charley was garnishing the turkey platter, the next, she was standing in a puddle of amniotic fluid, mixed with blood. She screamed for Mitch as she doubled over in pain.

Charley is beside herself. She had been experiencing discomfort all week but just chalked it up to growing pains: ligaments stretching. She had no idea what was really happening. Nothing actually seemed out of the ordinary. By the time she got to the hospital, she was about ready to push. They tried to hold her off a little. They had given her steroids for Hope, to help her lungs. It was all deemed pointless once they saw what caused the early labor. They gave Hope a dose after, knowing she never received a drop of the first one. Now she's in an incubator in the NICU. As soon as she is stable enough, they will move her to another local hospital more equipped to handle preemies like her. I'm staying positive. I refuse to listen to the doctor's grim predictions. Her name is Hope, and hope is what we all have for her.

We step quietly into the NICU and find Ava and Trent at the incubator. Ava is reading softly to Hope, her hand inside one of the circular openings on the side, caressing Hope's skin with her finger. Declan walks around to Trent and pulls him in for a hug. I look in on my beautiful niece. She's so tiny at a little over a pound. "It looks like I'll be sharing my nickname with you," I say softly. "It's a good thing, too—it's lonely down here by everyone's kneecaps. I'm glad for the company." This comment brings a small laugh from my friend, and I am thankful. I went over a million different things to say, in my head. Everything sounded so cliché. I decided to just act normal, say whatever comes to me, not what I had rehearsed.

Ava grabs on to me with her free arm, still gripping the book, and she lays her head on mine. We both stare at Hope, watching her little chest rise every time the breathing tube pushes oxygen into her lungs. "I want this story to have a happy ending. I want to wake up, five years from now and tell Hope how she came into this world on Jesus's birthday without a wing and a prayer. I want to tell her how we all banded around her and lifted her up with our love, becoming her wings and her prayers. I want to tell her how strong she was, that she fought with us and that is why she made it through. I want her to know that she is my miracle baby and that God has wonderful plans for her. She will grow up into a kind, caring, and smart person full of purpose. He'll give me that little daydream, right, Maddie?" she asks through her tears. "He wouldn't really do this to us . . . to Hope. He wouldn't be so cruel, right?"

"I don't have the answers to this one, Ava. All I have is my heart, my shoulder, my ears, and my positive thoughts. I can't tell you everything will be alright. But, I can tell you that while you were mentioning this future conversation with Hope, I could see her, as clear as day, sitting on your lap while you put her light brown hair in a ponytail, smiling away and hugging your arms to her. As clear as day . . . That's what I'm going to focus on. She's already proved she's a fighter; let's hold on to that." I encircle my arms around her waist and hold her tightly.

One Hour Later

"Is she still sleeping?" I ask Mitch as I walk into Charley's room.

"Yeah," he sighs.

"Jesus, what the hell did they give her?" I sit across from him on the other side of her bed.

"I can't remember, but it worked pretty fast," he says. His face contorts slightly, and he takes in a deep breath like it will help him fight off whatever emotion he is feeling right now, only for it to burst through his lips. His shoulders begin to shake and, for the first time since I've known him, Mitch weeps. "You should've seen her, Maddie. I can't even describe the devastation. She lost it—she completely lost it. They had to sedate her; she went wild."

"What do you mean?" I knew they gave her something to calm her down, but nobody has told me what happened.

"She was screaming, started pulling IV's out, trying to get out of bed, knocking stuff over. It was like she was a completely different person. I don't even know where she got the energy from." He wipes at his tears.

"What was she saying?"

"That she should've paid more attention. She was supposed to protect her, keep her safe, and she failed. And then she kept calling out to Ava, saying she was so sorry over and over again. It about killed me to see her this way. She wouldn't even let me hold her. She didn't want anyone to touch her. Her blood pressure shot through the roof. She projectile vomited. Alarms were going off. It was a shit show. They had to hold her down. I felt like I was watching a movie; it was surreal. How is she going to survive this, Maddie? The guilt is too much for her to bear." He laces his fingers with hers and brings her hand to his lips for a kiss.

"She's got you; that's a real great start. Nobody will understand what she is feeling more than you. You know firsthand about that guilt, Mitch. You'll help her through. And the rest of us will help, too, in our own little ways. Besides, Hope may make it. All this worry may be for naught. Charley had no control over what had happened; the doctor told us that much. We just all need to stay as positive as we can." I hope what I'm saying really resonates with him. "Mitch?"

"Yeah?"

"What did Ava say when Charley said all of this?"

"They were already gone. They left with Hope a few minutes earlier. It started slowly. First, she was just crying and then suddenly, it escalated to the level I mentioned."

"Ok." I nod.

"Have you seen Hope, yet?" he asks.

"Yes. I just came from there." I shuffle through my purse for a mint. "Want one?" I offer.

"Yes. Thanks." He leans over Charley to get it. "I haven't gone."

"That's understandable." I jerk my head toward Charley for emphasis.

"CiCi offered to sit in with Charlotte while I go over. I can't." His chin quivers again.

"Because of Isabella?"

"Yes," he cries. "I can't go in. She would be the same size as Isabella. That's who I would see, even though I never got the chance to lay eyes on her. I just can't do it, Maddie." He let's go of Charley's hand and buries his face into both of his. I jump up and race around the bed to him, quickly wrapping my arms around him. It's a bit awkward since he's sitting and hunched over, but whatever. "I feel like such a selfish prick; I'm making this about me."

"Mitch, you're right. It's not about you—it's about all of us! This affects all of us personally. I want you to picture something. Sit up," I command. He straightens up and wipes at his eyes one more time. I look around the room and march over to the dry erase board. "This small circle here is little shortstack," I say as I draw it.

"Little shortstack?" he laughs lightly.

"Yeah, she's my understudy." I smile. "Now, pay attention."

"Go on."

"Her life, her circumstance affects us all in different ways." I draw the first line from the circle. "This is Ava and Trent. I think it's pretty obvious how this affects them, so we'll move on. Here's Charley." I draw her line. "Charley has had three successful biological pregnancies. Her best friend came to her for help, and even though it could've cost her relationship with you, she did it. She wanted to make Ava's dream come true. She didn't want to see her friend in pain anymore. In her eyes, she failed. Next, we have you. Not only were you against this in the beginning, you have to relive the trauma of what you went through losing your own daughter. If they lose her, and God, I hope not," I stop to clear my throat, "you will understand their pain the most. You may also feel the most guilt given the situation," I add. He nods slightly in agreement. "Next, we have CiCi. I don't know what you know about that."

"Kyle told me. I get it." He holds up his hand.

"Then you know how this affects Kyle. He may have to work at reclaiming a few steps with CiCi." I draw his line. "Julie. She's watching a mom practically bargaining with the devil to save her daughter. I'm sure she's wondering if there was any moment in her life that Cynthia would've done that for her. Blake . . . well, I'm not exactly sure how this would affect him personally, yet, besides the obvious layer we're all feeling. Declan had a child with somebody who should've never been a mom. Renee tried to choke the life out of Hunter and Ava is doing everything she can to continue breathing life into Hope. Why are moms, like Renee, always blessed with healthy kids or even the chance to get pregnant in the first place?" I shake my head and put the cap back on the marker.

"You forgot you, Maddie," he reminds me. "I think you do that too much."

"Shh! You're starting to sound like Declan." I uncap the marker and draw my line. "Today, I realized that Ava and I became moms on the same day."

"You're pregnant!" he practically shouts.

"No." I then explain to him about the conversation we had with Hunter this morning and I show him my necklace. "I'm glad it happened this morning, even though I can't really announce it. See?

We all have, what seems like, selfish thoughts. But, that is because we are all going through it . . . just at different angles. The point *is*—we are all connected to this little girl already; she's brought up a lot of different feelings from all of us. Feelings and experiences that we can all use to help somebody in this circle," I connect all of our names into a big circle around Hope's little one, "derive strength from to then send onto this little one." I trace over the lines down to her name. Satisfied, I recap the marker again.

"Kyle's going to be pissed he missed your diagram; he's never seen a pie chart or graph he didn't love." Mitch smiles. "Charlotte's right about you."

"Why's that?"

"She says that you always know just what to do and say to make things better."

"Alas, I am not that powerful." I laugh lightly. "I just place in front of people what they've avoided with their blinders. You can't fix a problem or even begin to know what to do with it if you don't look at it. It's that simple. Every once in a while, I'll throw in a 'how does that make you feel?' just so I remain legit in their eyes."

"Well, you don't have to do that—we all know you're legit."

"Too legit to quit," I add.

"If you announce 'Hammertime', I'm checking out," Charley says grumbly, then falls back into a deep sleep, equipped with snoring. Mitch and I both chuckle at her.

The Fourth Hour

Another person couldn't fit in this chapel if they wanted to. All of the parental units are here: the St. Claire's, the O'Brien's, Kurt (he's been here the entire time, though), and believe it or not—Cynthia.

Yeah, we're all in shock about that one. Charley's kids are with Gram, Maggie, and Kyle's parents. Hunter is obviously with Dec's.

We've all been taking turns going in to see Hope, as well as Charley. All of our parents brought food from our earlier celebrations. Jay and Vic went home. I don't know why for sure, but nobody's upset about it.

It's all been a waiting game. For the first twenty-four hours, that's all it can be. And then, we all collectively turn our heads to the sound of the door opening. It's Kailash, Hope's nurse. Her eyes are filled with tears. "I'm very sorry," she starts.

"No!" CiCi yells. "No! Just get out!" she screams.

"I'm so sorry," Kailash says again, though it's broken up.

"Oh God . . . oh God," I cry under my breath and look to Declan, shaking my head. He mouths that he's sorry and holds my hand to his heart. I look around the chapel at all of my friends . . . my family; shattered—all completely shattered.

"She doesn't deserve this," CiCi cries in Kyle's arms, beating on his chest. He just holds and rocks her, battling his own tears. Shannon and Happy rush over to her. Julie is quietly crying on Blake's shoulder. Cynthia is staring at her daughter, silently sobbing herself. Because I can't help myself, I find Cynthia's behavior very curious and unlike her. My mom and dad both place a hand on each of my shoulders and squeeze; they are behind me.

"We'll be moving Hope to a larger room so that you may all come in at once . . . get a chance to hold her," Kailash speaks up again.

"Is that what Ava and Trent want?" I know we're close, but I would completely understand if they wanted this time to themselves to say goodbye.

"They requested it. They want Hope to have her whole family around her." She gives me a slight smile. A sob escapes my throat. And here I thought I was all out of sobs. "I'll come back when they are ready for you," she says before she leaves.

"Who's going to tell Charley?" Happy asks.

"I think if it's anyone out of us, Jack, it should be you; she's going to need her daddy," Shannon chokes on her words.

And now, we wait . . . again.

Roughly an hour later, Kailash comes back in and has us follow her to the new room. As we walk, she apologizes for the delay but I cut her off at the explanation. We already learned from Happy that Charley was awake. They wheeled her in (since she was still a little groggy) to say goodbye to Hope first. Apparently, she held her for a very long time, crying and kissing her, apologizing for not being a very good Godmother. Her guilt will be alive and well for a long time, I imagine. Mitch didn't go in with her. I'm sure that was a tough decision for him, but his past won out.

We walk into a rather large room that seems to be wasted space, really. There are a few chairs in there for us and a lonely bassinet. Ava, God bless her, is rocking Hope in the rocking chair, singing to her. My heart just shattered a little more. She looks up at us and frowns deeply before starting to cry again. She stands up, keeping Hope cradled closely to her. "Who wants to say goodbye first?"

Slowly, we all begin to take our turn. Our parents will want to come in, too, but right now, they felt we should be in here first. They are still in the chapel. Before long, we've all had our time, CiCi being last. She's really had the toughest time out of the three of us (her, Julie, and myself). Just then, Mitch finally makes an appearance. He doesn't look at Hope, but he goes directly to Ava and Trent.

"I'm so sorry, man." Mitch reaches out, but before his hand can land on Trent's shoulder, Trent smacks it away.

"You're *sorry*?! You're not fucking sorry! You didn't even want Charley to do this!" Trent screams in Mitch's face. "I bet you're glad her part is over sooner rather than later. Only six more weeks and you can start making your own baby, Mitch! Happy now?!" Spit flies from Trent's lips, his anger rising, heating his face to a shade of red I don't believe I've ever seen on a human.

"I know you're angry, man. I know how you feel," Mitch says calmly, "You need someone to blame."

"You don't know how I feel!" He pushes Mitch. "I bet you prayed for this every night, didn't you?" Another push.

"Alright . . . let's do this!" Mitch pushes back. "You want to fight? You need to hit something?! Come on, Trent! Fucking hit me!" he taunts Trent, pushing him again. "C'mon!" he screams. Not another second goes by, and Trent gives him a right hook, causing Mitch to stumble, but God-almighty, Mitch comes back at him. "Come on! That's all you got! She only lived for four hours, and that's all you've got?!" Mitch is relentless.

"Trent! Oh God, Trent, stop!" Ava tries to rush past me, but I grab her and hold on.

"Don't. Just wait," I instruct her.

"He'll kill him, Maddie!" she says in a panic.

"No, he won't," Kyle coughs up as he, too, watches the scene unfold before us.

Only moments have passed and Trent has laid into Mitch so good, his left cheek may need stitches. The sound of his knuckles cracking into Mitch's face is unbearable. He grabs Mitch's shirt, pulling back his right fist to get another one in, but he hesitates. "C'mon, man. I'll be your punching bag; it's all I've got to take away some of your pain, even if for only this moment," Mitch says through gasping breaths.

The tension slowly dissipates from Trent's shoulders. "Ten years, Mitch. We've been dreaming about and waiting for our little Hope. Ten years," his voice trembles into a soft cry. "*Why?!*" Trent cries out. "Why did it have to be our little girl? Haven't we been through enough? Why . . . why . . . why?" Trent cries, lowering his fist and giving into his sobs. Mitch pulls him in and he just about collapses, letting his friend hold him. The very same friend who just took one hell of a beating for him.

"I don't have the answer for you, man. I wish to hell I did. It's almost unbearable—almost. But, you will bear it because you have Ava relying on you and your two other children, who will need you to be strong for them. Today? You let your heart break; there's no need to be strong today. You and Ava are surrounded by people who love you both, as well as Hope, more than anything in the world. We'll hold you guys up as best as we can," Mitch's voice shakes so much, it's obvious he's trying to keep it together.

The seven of us, who just bared witness to this, move toward them and slowly, we all latch on in a massive group hug, our bodies shaking with grief.

Hope Charlotte Carter is in the arms of her Grandmother.

I take so much comfort in that, and I know . . . someday, Ava and Trent will, too.

Chapter Twenty-Two

Declan

I'S BEEN TWO WEEKS SINCE HOPE PASSED AWAY. TODAY WAS HER memorial. It was unseasonably warm for this time of year, almost like spring. Ava felt it was a sign that Hope was with us today. Maddie incorporated that belief into her eulogy so beautifully. She said, *"Like most of us, I've been thinking real hard since Christmas day, trying to figure out why stuff like this happens to good, loving people, and I could only come up with one conclusion: maybe some guardian angels are born first so we can physically see who will be looking out for us on the other side. We can know them, love them, and trust them. Earlier, Ava said that she felt like Hope sent us this weather today to let us know that she is here. There's about twenty of us in this room that can actually picture Hope's sweet little face—we know who the angel in the room is. I can almost bet that she will be the guardian angel to her siblings. That's what big sisters do, right?"* She went on to talk about it a little more, but that part about guardian angels being born so you can know them, love and trust them to look after you, really stuck out to me. It actually makes a lot of sense.

Vic shut his restaurant down to host the reception afterwards—free of charge, of course. It was also a surprise. He and Jay announced it at the memorial for everyone to come, and handed out directions. Ava and Trent tried to give them some money as there was quite a crowd; the restaurant was full. Vic wouldn't hear of it, though. He told Maddie and me later that it was the only way they could make up for all of the times they would've spoiled her, had they had the chance.

That is where Blake and I performed a song that could've gone really bad. He approached me about the collaboration last week, us both being musicians. It's not like either of us could give a eulogy like the others; we're the newbies. The reason this could've gone really bad is because, after much thought, he wanted to perform "Coming Around Again" by Carly Simon, but the version with "Itsy Bitsy Spider" in it. He played it for me, and I told him he was fucking nuts and that I didn't want any part of it. Then, he explained it to me. I got his vision. But, I told him that he really needed to explain it before we performed it because if no one knew his thinking than they may find it a very cruel song to perform. He agreed, and he introduced it like this.

"Can I have everybody's attention?" He tapped on the mic. *"Seeing as we are men of music and not many words, I asked Declan to collaborate on a song with me today. Erm . . . I'd like to explain this song choice before we perform it and you possibly think me cruel. You see, I wanted to find a song that would not only represent Hope, but Ava, Trent, and their twins. We all have seen how life can change in a moment. How a perfect dream can be shattered and seem unreachable again. But, that's not the case. Carly Simon sings, 'nothing stays the same.' I agree. Nothing really does, because we're always evolving,*

we're always dreaming. It doesn't have to be a bad thing. Ava . . . Trent, think of all you have been through together in the past decade. Has everything stayed the same?" he asked. They shook their heads no. Blake gave them a warm smile. "This song is for all of you. It's to remember and honor Hope. It's to remember and honor the love that got her here and her siblings. It's to honor dreams that should never be given up on, no matter how painful it can be to hold on. It's to remind us that the sun always comes out to dry up the rain. Without further ado, this is 'Coming Around Again/Itsy Bitsy Spider' by Carly Simon." And with that, Chase, the drummer from Blake's band started the beginning of the song, and then I came in with the cello. Blake played the piano while he sang. It was nerve wracking and calming all at once.

Ava and Trent held onto each other and cried the whole performance.

They weren't the only ones.

At the end of the reception, Ava and Trent presented all of the girls with special silver heart pendants on silver chains. They have the words *Always in my heart* inscribed on the front and *Hope Charlotte Carter* on the back. Inside each of these hearts are some of her ashes. They are mini urns. Brilliant and bittersweet.

Needless to say, it has been a long emotional day. I kid you not, all six of us laid down for a nap when we got home. I'm the first one up and am desperately trying to figure out what to do with myself. We already took the Christmas decorations down a week ago after finally exchanging gifts with Maddie's family. I can't help but feel selfish when I think about how unfortunate the timing was; everyone's focus was on the loss of Hope (as it should've been) and not Christmas. But, at least everyone got to have their own private celebrations in the morning before tragedy struck, especially for the kids. I don't remember the last time I've seen Hunter look so happy on a Christmas morning.

I bought Maddie the usual boyfriend stuff: jewelry, pj's, slippers, perfume, gift cards for her hair, nails, and books. Then, I got her usual Declan stuff: Emoji Heart Eyes Chia Pet and a voucher (made by me) for a two-week antique trip next summer. I gave her a list of the top twenty-four places in America; she can pick where she wants to go, and I will make all of the arrangements. She was over the moon. My parents didn't understand the Chia Pet. Rosie threw a pillow at me for it, but Maddie thought it was hysterical.

Maddie got me a Viking ship in a bottle. Everyone but Hunter laughed at this, knowing the reason behind it. She also got me a new watch by Diesel made with gunmetal. It showcases three time zones, which she already had two set to US and Australia. The third, she said I can set it to whatever country I'm in when I'm on tour. She also pointed out that this watch was in the Mr. Daddy series, giving us all another chuckle. The rest of the stuff was the usual stuff you get from your girlfriend: cologne, underwear, clothes, et cetera, et cetera.

All in all, it really was a wonderful first Christmas.

I still haven't asked her. You know—the *big* question. A "right time" hasn't really presented itself since Christmas. I sort of wish I'd gone with the cliché proposal. So not us, though. Before everything happened, Charlotte suggested that I ask in private; Maddie would want this moment all to herself and be more thrilled to share the news with everyone. See why I can't find a right time? How is she supposed to share this news guilt free, what with everything that has happened? It's too soon. I don't want her to feel like she has to hide her good news.

"Is there anymore coffee?" Mum asks from behind me, placing her hands on my shoulders and kissing the top of my head.

"Yes. I only made it about twenty minutes ago. Dad still sleeping?" I smile up at her.

"Snoring like a banshee."

"Mum, you do realize that banshee is a spirit of a woman who wails to warn family members of impending death?" I turn in my chair slightly to watch her as she goes over to pour herself a cup.

She stops and looks up at the ceiling as if she's thinking real hard. "Yup . . . that's what he sounds like . . . a wailing woman." She nods in agreement with herself. I can't help but laugh. "Maddie still asleep?" she asks as she walks back over to me with her cup and takes a seat.

"Everyone is. Mum, can I ask you for some advice?"

"Of course! What's going on? Are you and Maddie having a hard time again?" She grabs my hand.

"No. We're good. I mean, this has really hit everyone hard. Maddie's on overload, checking in with everyone. I worry about that."

"That girl takes on the weight of the world like it's a feather. It's quite remarkable to watch."

"But it's not a feather; it drains her." I sit back and cross my arms.

"I'm sure it does, sweetheart. Is that what's troubling you?" She puts her cup down and lifts the lid of the pastry box that was left on the table. She swipes the last almond cookie. "I'll buy her more." She shrugs at me and takes a bite. It's Maddie's favorite cookie, but it's also my mother's. Last night, Mum left it there because she's a guest and, knowing it's Maddie's favorite, didn't want to be rude by taking the last one. I guess she's gone from having will power to reasoning with her actions. Knowing Maddie, she'll be more thrilled than upset about the missing cookie; she'll feel like she won this round of temptation.

"No. What's bothering me is that with everything that's happened, I haven't found the right time to ask Maddie to marry me. I don't want to seem selfish or uncaring. And, I don't want Maddie to feel like she has to hide her happiness from everyone," I point out.

"It's nice," Mum sighs.

"What's nice?" What an odd remark.

"It's nice to hear you have your confidence back. A few months ago, you would've never assumed she would be happy about you asking her. You didn't feel like you were good enough for her." She reaches forward and palms my left cheek. "I'm so glad you know now that you do make her very happy and that you are *very* good for her, as she is for you." She taps my cheek.

"That's lovely, Mum, but, can you help me figure out this little timing problem I'm having?" I smile a little, trying to hide my impatience.

"Declan, you can't always steer your ship in the same direction as everyone else even though you're relatively close to each other in the same ocean."

"I love you, Mum, but what the hell does that mean?" I throw my hands out.

"It means . . . the ocean's current doesn't hit every ship the same."

"Mum!" Okay, I'm a little impatient now.

"Life, Declan! Life is the ocean's current. You may all be traveling on this journey together, but life will hit you all differently. You have to steer your own ship and not worry about how everyone else is steering theirs; you can only be there to help when they need it and cheer them on when they're managing the waves well on their own. My point is, while it is good to respect what others are going through, you can only do that for so long. Don't lose sight of your own course. After getting to know Maddie's friends, seeing how *all of you* are with each other, I don't think you have to worry about them not being there to cheer you guys on. I don't think they will be upset about your happiness. I think it will take away from all of the sadness. Give everyone something to look forward to. I think you need to give them more credit than you are, Dec." And with that, she pops the last bite of cookie in her mouth.

"I know all of this. Truly, I do. I just don't know how long I should wait, for respect's sake." I let out a big gush of a breath.

"I think you know the answer. You just need to trust yourself . . . your instincts." She winks.

She's right.

"You always manage to help me get out of my own way, Mum—thank you." I stand up slightly to wrap my arms around her and plant a big kiss on her cheek.

"Yes, it's rather exhausting at times," she teases. "Speaking of exhausted," she says as I sit back down. "Dad and I are leaving in a week; we've stayed as long as we could. Jolie said the orders for certain pieces are getting behind; we don't have any in stock," she informs me. I want to protest, but I have no right to. They've stayed longer than what they had originally planned. I'm sure I could've twisted their arms for an even longer visit, but if my cousin Jolie is telling them orders are backed up, I can't keep them here. That's a really good sign that must not be ignored.

"I'd like to argue with you about this, but I know I can't. It's been so wonderful having you guys here; I'm going to miss you both." I frown.

"Bring your whole family to us! Maddie would love Australia."

"We will, Mum—I promise."

"What do you promise?" Maddie asks as she breezes in behind us.

"That we'll get out to Australia this year." I grab her arm, pulling her over to me.

"I need coffee. I really could've stayed in bed for the night." She pouts as she plops onto my lap. I kiss her shoulder.

"We're all going to have our sleep schedules off for the next day or so," Mum adds.

"I think you're right, Daisy." Maddie smiles. "Thanks for being there for me and my friends." She reaches and grabs my mum's hand. "It really meant a lot to me to have you there."

"I'm glad we were able to. I like your friends very much, and they seem to have adopted my son, which makes me like them even more."

"Yes . . . he's been sucked in; there's no escaping now." She gives me a cheeky smile.

"As if!" I guffaw. She presses her lips to mine, still smiling as she kisses me. My heart jumps all over the inside of my chest, beating out a happiness I have never known until I met her.

Yes . . . it's time.

"I feel like we're being rude," Maddie says again as I get situated in the driver's seat.

"I'm not going to say it again, sweetness." I start my SUV up. My parents are leaving tomorrow, and, unfortunately, this was the only evening I could do this. My parents are very understanding and more than on board with it. I'm sure Maddie will be too, once she sees why and what we are doing tonight.

"But we can go out any night, Declan."

"You've spent the entire day with them, Madelyn—now, stop," I'm more stern and throw the formal name card in, as well.

"Ok. I trust you." She takes in a deep breath and blows it up through her bangs.

"That's comforting." I laugh. "I think you'll love where I'm taking you," I add.

"I'm sure I will." She smiles over at me. "Alright, Mr. Viking, I'm going to give you my full attention for the rest of the night and will no longer dwell on the fact that we are not spending the evening with your parents . . . on their last night here . . . even though we're not sure when we'll see them again. Just saying. . ."

"Are you done?" I smirk.

"Yes."

"Promise?"

"Promise."

"Good. You forgot to put your seatbelt on, please do so."

"Aye, Aye, Captain." She pulls the belt over her shoulder.

"I thought you were the captain?" I joke.

"Shut it!" She whacks my leg. I bite back my smile and wink at her. She lets a giggle escape.

Within a half an hour, we arrive at our destination: Peabody Essex Museum.

"Wow. I haven't been here since a field trip in high school," Maddie says as we walk in hand-in-hand.

"I think you'll appreciate it much more, this go-around." I smile at her and squeeze her hand. I pray I am right about that assumption.

I flash our tickets as I received them ahead of time. Bill Thompson's (Woodwinds section) wife is one of the curators at this museum. She helped me to set everything up, right to our private dinner in the Copeland Gallery. That, of course, will be the last leg of our tour tonight.

For the next two hours, we take everything in. Well . . . Maddie does. I take *her* in. I knew this would make her happy between her love of history, art, and antiques, but this is like watching a kid in a candy store. "Wait!" I pull her back as she starts towards the American art exhibit.

"What?"

"I fear I should warn you before we go in there." I try to give her the most serious look I can muster up.

"Why? What's in there?" Her eyebrows knit together.

"There are all sorts of antiques besides furniture, art, and clothing—there are *shoes!*" I say with excitement.

"Shoes?!" she squeals.

"The largest shoe collection in the world," I answer matter-of-factly.

"Holy crap!" She bounces in her own heels. "Let's go!" She pulls on my arm, soliciting a laugh from me. I let her have her way and follow her. Seems only fair, since I'm pretty sure I'll have my way—with her—later tonight.

"This is amazing! Why didn't I know about this? I need to tell Cory!"

"Cory?"

"He was the guy my mom was trying to set me up with the night you were supposed to originally meet my folks," she says nonchalantly as she stares at the many different shoes.

"We've come a long way since that night, huh?"

She looks over her shoulder at me. "Yes, we have. I'm so glad too." She turns and slides her hands up my chest to my shoulders. I lean down and offer her a sweet, gentle kiss on her lips. "I love you." She breathes against my mouth.

"I love you, sweetness."

"Can I get back to my shoe porn now?"

"Will it get you all hot and bothered for tonight?" I slide my hands on her hips and squeeze.

"No, but I know you will." She smacks her lips against mine real quick then turns to get back to the shoes. I'd be a little upset, however, there is a lovely view on display; Maddie's skirt is hugging her arse rather nicely.

Down, boy, down!

Another forty-five minutes goes by, and that's from me rushing her. "I'm sorry, sweetness, but I have dinner reservations for us. We can come back another time; we'll bring Hunter," I add. Maddie loves doing anything and everything as a family. I'm really lucky, aren't I?

"Alright," she sighs in defeat, grabbing a hold of my extended hand.

"This way, my lovely lady." I shuffle my other hand out in a fancy manner, making her laugh lightly at me.

I guide her into the Copeland Gallery, filled with porcelain from China. There is a table set for two. She gasps lightly. I lead her over to a chair and push her in as soon as she's seated. I walk around and take mine. The waiter comes over and pours us a red wine. I'm not sure what it is; I asked for the best.

"What are those?" She points to three portrait-like items on easels.

"Oh, I've arranged for you to see a few new pieces before they are exhibited anywhere else," I make light of it before I thank the waiter for our salads. "I hope you don't mind that I pre-ordered our meals. I went with stuff I know you like."

"That's fine, baby. But," she furrows her brows again, "how did you do all of this?"

"I know people." I huff onto my fingernails then buff them on my suit jacket.

"I know people, too. That's how you get free drinks at Mick and Marley's."

"You definitely know more impressive people than me, sweetness." I reach for her hand and pull it up to my lips, kissing the back.

"Clearly," she says as she looks around the room. *God, I love her.*

Done with our salads, he brings out the soup—French onion; one of her favorites. I watch as she meticulously separates the cheese from the sides, pushing it all into the broth to get more melty (as she says), then she grabs some of it and with the help of her free finger, she wraps it around the spoon before dipping in for some broth and a piece of the bread. She lifts it up to those sweet, full, delicious lips, and blows before taking it in her mouth. And yes, I'm thinking "that's what he said," because these girls wear off on you something awful.

"Aren't you going to eat your soup?" she asks as she notices me noticing her.

"I'm rather enjoying watching you eat it." I lean my cheek on my fisted hand.

"Elbows," she says, looking at mine. I remove my elbow from the table. "Usually the guys I date complain about how I eat my soup," she adds quietly before looking down.

Whoa! Where'd that come from? "Test car dummies."

"What?" She jerks her head up.

"Ever see those commercials with the dummies they use to test car safety?"

"Yeah. . ."

"The guys you dated before me—same thing. They were all test dummies." Honestly, what the hell was wrong with these guys? Just how many were there anyway? *Shut-up, Dec! Don't you dare ask her that!* Right! I'm just glad they were too stupid to see how wonderful she is.

"They were pretty stupid," she surmises and gets back to the joy of eating her soup. I continue to be fascinated, slurps and all.

Onto the next course, she moans when she is presented with Filet Mignon wrapped in Rosemary Prosciutto on top of mashed potatoes. Sautéed Asparagus lie on the side. "God, this is going to be so worth the stinky pee," she says then gasps, covering her mouth. "I said that out loud, didn't I?"

"Yes, you did." I try to hold back my smile.

"Sorry."

"I'm so fond of the random things you say, Maddie; never apologize." I grab her hand again and squeeze. She tears up. "Hey . . . hey, what's this now?"

"It's just really nice to finally be with somebody I can be one hundred percent me around."

"Always. I find these little things about you so charming, even when you fart in the middle of the night like I'm not there."

"Shut-up! I don't do that!" She laughs, though she seems a little nervous about it.

"No, you don't." *She totally does.* She relaxes and grabs her glass of wine, stealing a sip before she digs into her steak. I follow suit.

"Are you nervous about your surgery?" she asks mid main course.

"Just that it won't work. What's with the random thought?"

"It's not that random; you're having it done in three days," she opposes. "Also, it came to me after I realized I'm about to have a food baby," she admits.

"It made you think of other babies you may be having soon— my babies?" I'm not even going to pretend that didn't make the Viking down below twitch and want to come up to the top deck. *He always finds a reason to raise the sails on his vessel.*

"Yes." She fidgets with her fork, pushing food around on her plate. This subject should thrill me, but I'm a little concerned; she hasn't bothered me about a proposal never mind mentioning marriage to me. Does she not want to get married? *No. I know that's not true.* Well, then, does she not want to marry me? *That can't be right.* Shut-up, Dec. She said "yes" to everything that comes with being the mother of my children. Maybe that's why she hasn't badgered me. *Don't forget Hope, arsehole!* Right.

"Finish your dinner, sweetness." I point with my fork. "I want to see these last pieces for tonight's exhibit, and then get you home." I lick my lips, thinking about tonight. Her breath quickens as she nods and gives her plate full concentration again.

After another ten minutes, the waiter takes our plates. "Would you like a break before dessert?" I ask her.

"I don't think I can do dessert," she groans, falling back in her chair.

I stand up and hold my hand out to her. "C'mon, let's get up and work the food baby off a little."

"I don't think it will help, but I'll try anything." She grabs my hand, and we begin a slow stroll around the gallery, looking at all the artifacts. "Declan?" she says after several minutes.

"Hmm?" I pull her closer to me as her back is up against my chest.

"I want to know what's under those drapes." She points to the three items on easels.

"Yes. Let's go and have a look." I kiss the top of her head, then lead her over. I give a nod to the museum employee who's stayed on tonight to assist us.

We stand in front of them. I give the lady another nod, and she reveals the first one. It's a silhouette of a man and woman kissing. "Oh wow! Oh my gosh! Are they going to start an exhibit on silhouette art?" she asks the lady. Sydney (the lady) only offers Maddie a slight knowing smile. Maddie walks up to it, studying it. Just as she's about to run her fingers over the piece, she stops herself. "Am I allowed to touch it?" she asks.

"Yes," Sydney says.

Maddie traces over it lightly with her fingers. "Declan? Am I seeing things or does this couple resemble us?" She looks over at me.

"I hope it does, or I'm asking for my money back."

"What?"

"That's us on Christmas morning. My mother took the picture," I slowly let her in on my grand surprise.

"This. . .?"

"Us—yes." I palm her face and kiss her forehead. "Next, please," I say to Sydney.

Maddie jerks her head quickly toward the easels as Sydney reveals the next one. Maddie gasps as she takes in the sight of the silhouette portrait of Hunter, she, and me. "I thought it would be nice to start a wall of our story." I nod to Sydney. "What do you think, Maddie?" I ask as the last one is revealed; a simple silhouette of the words *will you marry me?*"

She turns quickly to find me on one knee, holding up the box that has been burning a hole in my pocket for weeks. Her hands slap across her mouth, and a sob escapes. I'm half concerned until she practically tackles me, kissing all over my face, saying "Yes" a million and one times. I quickly put her ring on and try to explain the history behind it but am cut off by her lips attacking mine.

I shall not complain about that at all.

Chapter Twenty-Three

Maddie

Months later. . .

"THIS IS RIDICULOUS!" I ANNOUNCE ON THE PHONE. I'VE conferenced called the girls. "I don't give a rat's ass what you all are doing tonight; we're going to Mick and Marley's—the five of us!" I put my foot down.

Look, I know we've all been busy. Three of us are now engaged, and Ava is in her last trimester. Julie is up to her knees in love. It's really fucked up that we all haven't been together since Hope's memorial. It's downright bullshit, and I'm tired of it. Life fucking happens, but there is some shit you can't let slip away for too long.

"I'm in, shortstack," CiCi caves first.

"Next!" I verbally tap my foot. Shut-up; that too makes sense!

"I'll be a miserable bitch, but I think Trent would like to pass that torch onto you guys for the night," Ava admits.

"And?" I ask.

"Ok," Charley gives in too.

"Julie?"

"Duh, my boyfriend owns the place; of course I'll be there."

"Ok. It's settled. I'll see you bitches at eight." I slam the phone down. Well, if it was the nineties, I would've slammed it. I hit "end." I miss old school shit, like slamming a phone in someone's ear to really get a point across. Technology is a bitch, if you ask me.

I call my fiancé. Yes, I say that shit all of time; I'm one of *those* girls. I'll own it—whatever! It took me a long god damn time to acquire one of those, and he's a Viking, so suck it.

"Hey, sweetness," he practically coos into the phone.

"I'm going out with the girls tonight; don't wait up," is how I answer.

"Negative?" he asks.

"Yes." I try to hold back my tears.

"You don't want it to happen till after we're married anyway, remember?" his voice is soft and gentle.

"Yes. I'm still disappointed, though."

"Are you going to work out wedding dates with Charley and CiCi tonight?"

"I don't know . . . maybe."

"Maddie!"

"I know. I will. I promise," I urge.

"I'm not waiting much longer. If you don't come home with some sort of idea tonight, I will pick the date myself and make your friends work around us," he practically yells. I don't blame him; he's been very patient about this.

"Ok. I will work on it. I want this too, you know."

"I'm beginning to find that hard to believe," he states.

"C'mon, baby," I groan. "Baby?" I question when I hear silence.

I pull away and look at my phone. The call has ended. See?! This is what I'm talking about! His hanging up on me would've had a lot more thunder if I heard him slam the phone. This new way, you don't even know someone's hung up on you till five minutes pass of them not saying anything!

Yes, I'm wound up tightly today. I sort of want to crawl out of my skin. I should've known not to take the pregnancy test. My fire breathing is quite the indication that Mother Nature will be laughing at me as I pop *Midol* like it's candy in the next day or two. On the plus side, I'm off tomorrow and am free to drink tonight.

I could really use a drink.

There has been so much going on lately that requires more thinking than doing. For example, Rosie's leg has healed up very nicely, and she is no longer a prisoner to a walking boot. The problem is, we've been trying to figure out our living arrangements. After living together for two months, it's hard to separate our lives again. We both own our own homes, and while I'm more attached to mine than Declan is to his, Rosie has her own apartment over there. So far, what we've decided to try out is to have Rosie go home at night and come back early in the morning. My concern is that it's a big house, and she's all by herself. She's been with Declan and Hunter for several years now; I'm sure these arrangements feel awkward to her. I wouldn't doubt she's thinking we're pushing her out the door, but that is so *not* the case. Her workload may not be as heavy, per se, put she's added my life into the mix. She's got all three of our schedules down pat and keeps us on our toes.

I did have an interesting idea to solve this issue. Ava loves the home she grew up in. Kurt lives there all by himself, and the place is huge. He does it because Ava begs him not to sell off her childhood memories. Sounds selfish, but I know it's her way of holding on to her mom. I may or may not stand next to her begging, as well. My thinking is, maybe Kurt can move into Declan's place. He and Rosie have become quite the item since Christmas, though they won't fully disclose the nature of their friendship. He could live there rent free. Ava and Trent could sell their townhome and give it to Kurt as a down payment on her family home. They could move in there since it's what Ava actually wants and it's bigger for the twins to grow into, and they can give Kurt monthly payments until they reach the amount he would've acquired in a sale to someone else. It's a win-win! Nobody loses money. Nobody is without a home. *Nobody* is alone, and all guilt is gone. I think it's a brilliant plan. Now, I just have to sell them all on it. I don't think Declan will be upset about not receiving any payment as he wouldn't sell with Rosie there anyhow. Hmm . . . okay, I'm not actually sure about that. We'll see. . .

Obviously, there's the wedding date issue. CiCi got engaged around the holidays too. And, like me, kept it under wraps for a little while. And by that, I mean about a week after the memorial. She couldn't help it; there was a whole "dipshit" portion of the proposal she needed to tell us about. We all responded appropriately; we laughed our asses off. I don't know if they've worked out a date. I think they are still waiting on Charley and Mitch, who got engaged first. It's pretty understandable why she (Charley) hasn't been in a rush. She's still beside herself. At this point, it's just going to take time.

Then there's the biggest issue—Renee. We were recently informed that she had checked herself out of rehab a month ago. Declan hasn't been able to find her, though, I know he's not looking too hard. He has vowed that he will no longer let her actions dictate the course of his life or Hunter's. I'm so proud of how far he's come along in the past year. However, I'm not going to act like I'm not a little nervous about her M.I.A status.

My cell alarm goes off, indicating that my next client should be here. She's new. Her name is Sonya Plech. I'm not even sure what her concerns are; she danced around my questions. I slip my feet back into my heels and walk over to the door. Just as I open it, I find Cynthia on the other side, about to knock.

"Cynthia?" I jerk my head back.

"I'm here for my appointment." She breezes past me.

"Erm . . . I don't have you on my books. I actually have a client for this slot." I watch as she sits in the armchair.

"Yes—Sonya Plech—that's me." She crosses her left leg over her right.

"You made up an alias to come and speak with me?" I close the door.

"I had to. I need your help and I couldn't risk you trying to push me off on someone else." She fidgets with her skirt.

I sit across from her. "You know it would be unethical for me to take you on as a client."

"How so, Maddie? You're not breaking any rules. I need to talk with someone close to the situation. I don't want to lose my daughter. I don't want to lose any more years with her. I believe I made a terrible mistake, years ago, and I need to work out how to correct it. Please help me, Maddie." Her eyes fill up.

I'm utterly speechless. I've never seen Cynthia look so desperate. I can feel myself cave in, but then I remember that this is how Julie gets sucked in constantly. I need to put my strong suit on. "I will try to help you, but I have rules," I say as sternly as I can. She nods in agreement. "If at any moment I feel that this is a ploy to help me get Julie to talk to you, again, I will pull out of this agreement and never give you another chance. You will not fool me like you do Julie. Do you understand me?"

"Yes."

"Ok. Where do you want to start?" I reach over to my desk, grabbing my notepad.

"I wasn't always the way I am now," she starts. "Ask Shannon."

"Shannon, who?"

"I believe you call her 'Ma.'"

"O'Brien? How would she know how you were?" I jot down Shannon's name.

"Because she was my best friend, once upon a time," she informs me. I look up from my notebook—shocked. "Ahh . . . something you didn't know."

"No. But, I suppose it makes sense. She's very patient with you even though you knock CiCi down every chance you get."

"I'm jealous of CiCi."

"You're admitting that?"

"Yes. She has the relationship with Julie that I will never have." She uncrosses her legs. "Look, I don't know where to begin, really. The best I can do is dump everything on your lap and work with you to sort it all out." She reaches down into her purse and grabs an envelope inside of a Ziploc bag. She passes it to me. "I need you to read this. I know you won't say anything to anyone about it."

"Right now?"

"Yes, please." She sits back and brings her fingers up to her mouth where she starts biting on the tip of her index one. I look at the bag and unzip it, retrieving the letter from it. Opening it, I begin to read.

"Wait—what?!" I jump out of my seat.

"It was all a lie; he was no goddamn hero," she says angrily.

"Where is he?" I look up from the letter.

"Dead. That wasn't a lie."

"I don't understand."

"Here." She hands me another envelope. Inside is a paper clipping of what happened.

"I'm not the bad guy. I never should've been. That was my fault, and I need to correct it. I need your help, Maddie. I need Julie to know the truth . . . to understand why I've always had a wall up. It was never meant to be up to prevent her from coming in; it was supposed to be a teaching tool for her. I messed everything up and with each passing year, I only made it worse," her voice quivers and tears slowly fall from her eyes.

"This isn't right, Cynthia. I shouldn't know this before Julie

285

does!" I'm actually pissed right now.

"I need your help. She may need *your* help through this." She stands up.

"Cynthia, you should have gone to somebody else—not one of her best friends!" I pace.

"You are the keeper of all of their secrets, aren't you?"

"Secrets *they* tell me! Not secrets about their lives that I keep from them! Why didn't you eventually tell her the truth?" I hold the letter out.

"I didn't want her to feel like I did . . . like something was wrong with her . . . that she wasn't good enough."

"You made her feel that way *anyhow!*" I yell.

"Oh God, I know," she breaks down into heaving sobs.

"I need to end this session now. I need to think. I need to figure out the best course of action." I fold up the letter and slip it back into the envelope before giving it back to her.

"Ok. Just call me when you're ready to see me again. Maddie?"

"What," I ask as I walk back over to my desk.

"I was a really good mother once. She has always been my world; I just stopped showing it."

"You stopped *showing up* all together, Cynthia." I'm so friggin' mad right now.

"I'd like to show up now. I refuse to believe it's too late." She slides the strap of her purse up her shoulder.

"You know this is going to take a long time. It's not going to be a one night, rip the Band-Aid off quickly, thing, right?"

"Yes. I'm willing to do the work."

"Ok." I nod. She gives one more good wipe under her eyes and leaves my office.

I am officially fucking done with this day.

The downside to being so short is that when all five of us girls ride together, we take Charley's Highlander because it has third row seating. Guess who ends up in the third row? I'm glad for it tonight, though. I don't want to sit next to Julie, knowing what I know. And no, I'm not telling you, either. That's her story to tell. It's bad enough that I know! *Fucking Cynthia. . .*

"Sorry, Maddie, but the preggers gets shotgun and CiCi and I are too tall," Julie apologizes.

"You're tall, high-tower; I'm slightly above average. Only in height, though . . . in bed—I'm a rockstar," Ceese quips.

"It's fine, really. I've had a sucky day, and I just want to decompose back here, so I can be a little more fun when we get inside." *Ain't that the truth!*

"Do you want to talk about it?" Julie offers. Why the hell is it that the person you are trying to avoid speaking to always has all the damn questions? It's Murphy's law.

"Not really, Jules. Thanks for asking; I love you."

"I love you, too. Are you sure you're ok?"

"Yes. Honestly." And by the grace of God, Charley turns on the music, causing a wonderful distraction. "Brass Monkey" by the Beastie Boys is on. Need I say more? We may be making Charley's SUV look as if it has hydraulics. *Ohh . . . that funky monkey. . .*

Within moments, we pull into the parking lot of Blake's prestigious establishment. This is *our Cheers!* It's much cooler, if I do say so myself. Fixing the strap on my heel once I climb out (it got stuck on something, and I almost face-planted on my way out of the vehicle; wouldn't that have been the cherry?), we make our way inside. The girls halt abruptly, leaving me to bounce up and down, trying to see what the hell has stopped them dead in their tracks. Having enough (I mean, embarrassing much? I hate being short), I push Julie to the side so I can squeeze in.

Oh. . .

Sitting at *our* table are four very blonde, very pale women. Their eyes (some blue, some green) practically glow. How bizarre that I can even see them when it's so dimly lit in here. We all just stare, gaining the attention of two of them. If it wasn't so loud in here, you could hear a pin drop—that's how intense the stare down is.

"I see you all lost your battle with the fucking peroxide," CiCi starts, "so how about you all get up from our table and maybe sit over there," she points to a smaller one across the room, "and we'll let this shit slide."

The one who was talking to the other stops and looks our way. *Move over, Elizabeth Taylor! Those have to be contacts! No way do purple eyes like that really exist!* She looks around the table at her friends, then back at CiCi. "Survey saaaaaays—fuck off," she states, then immediately dismisses us and gets back to her conversation.

"Damn it; that was a good comeback. If they weren't totally pissing me off by sitting at our fucking table, I would totally like that chick," Ceese says quietly.

"Yeah, I think you two got your lady balls from the same shop," Charley quips.

"Right?! I mean, who knew that shop even had another customer." CiCi's eyes go wide.

"Look, girls," Ava speaks up (it's more of a whine), "I'm fucking preggers with twins. I'm uncomfortable and cranky as fucking hell. Either sit your asses some-fucking-where-else or make some fucking room at our Goddamn table for us before I breathe the same fire on you I just hit my husband with."

Bette Taylor's Eyes jerks her head back in horror at this announcement. I mean, I'm ready for her to go all Jamie Lee Curtis on our ass in a minute as she looks down at Ava's belly. "Pregnant? This shit is spreading like a fucking epidemic, so you better take that shit somewhere else before I catch it," she bellows.

"Just keep your mitt closed and you won't catch *shit*," CiCi snaps. "Blake!" she calls out over to the bar at him. Blake rolls his eyes up to the heavens. I'm pretty sure he's asking God to give him a fucking break. He throws the bar towel over his shoulder and lifts the hinged section up before heading over to us.

"Baby, can you please let them know this table is reserved?" Julie purrs and makes promises to him with her eyes. And, damn it, I just got the visual. *Maybe Dec should wait up for me tonight. . .* Oh—sorry! Back to the here and now. Blake, of course, is melting in her palm but gives her a look that makes my friend blush and her breath quicken. I suddenly notice my own breath picking up pace. *Jesus, get a hold of yourself, Maddie!*

"Well, now, Stuart," Purple eyes says to Blake before he answers Julie. He raises an eyebrow. "I imagine you are man enough to please more than one woman at a time." She looks him up and down with hooded eyes, lingering over his peace pipe (that's what Julie calls it because it magically makes all well in her world). "I think it's important to show you that I can be generous and flexible." A smile that would have the Cheshire cat tuck his tail between his legs, spreads across her mouth.

"Physically flexible," the chick in the black peasant blouse says, wiggling her eyebrows. "Like a twisty tie," she quickly adds.

Purple Nurple (that's what I'm calling her now since she's being a real tit!) winks at her friend before bringing her attention back to Blake. "So, how about I let Red, here, take this seat, and you and I can go somewhere and explore safewords." She pauses, looking thoughtful, "I recently fired my fuck buddy, and his are big . . ." she trails off, letting her eyes fall to the provider of the money shot in all of Julie's sexcapades (Ok . . . I watched Tumblr porn with Dec last night; cut me some slack!). " . . . shoes to fill. But, I'm confident you'll work . . . hard." And with that, they all start laughing.

Oh, I'm about to throat punch this bitch!

I think the girl wearing the funny unicorn t-shirt can sense that I'm about to lose my shit because she stops laughing and turns to Purple Nurple, "Fate, stop being such a whore. Can't you see this guy is head over heels for The Little Mermaid? Don't get him into trouble." She gives him an apologetic glance after stifling her final giggle.

"Little Mermaid? Pfft—more like Jessica Rabbit! Get your hot redheads straight!" I bark. I still want to bite, but at least I barked.

"He's not getting in any trouble," Julie says from next to me. I look up at her. "She has nothing over me." She smirks.

"I'm fucking sitting!" Ava announces and grabs a seat.

"You're in my spot, Barbie," CiCi snarks at Fate (I guess that's her name).

Fate narrows her eyes at Ceese but a slow, condescending smirk pulls at the corner of her mouth. "I don't see your name on it, Birki-ta."

What. In. The. Actual. Fuck?

Can this day get any weirder?

"How the? Who told you to call me that? Do you know Kyle?" CiCi is in full-on panic mode. I don't blame her, and I'm really not that far behind. Nobody calls CiCi that but Kyle. It's what she named her dragon tattoo a long time ago.

I'll settle this! "Her name is right here." I stab at the area of the table CiCi always does her artwork. Others may call it carving or defacing property. I freeze as I find the usual "CiCi is the shiznits" gone and replaced with "No, Fate is. #FuckOff."

Yes, it can.

The answer to my earlier question.

"Kyle? The fucking smirker?" Fate asks, using CiCi's nickname for him. "Nope. Never met him. I just thought it was a fitting name for you and your strong, stubborn ass." After a moment, Fate winces like she just experienced a twinge of pain.

"Wait!" Charley interjects. "You called Kyle the fucking smirk-er. Are you a medium?"

"Nah—she's a small!" the girl in the turquoise shirt answers for her, causing us all to laugh. I snort, as usual.

"That was so good," Ava tells her and lets out a big sigh.

"Blake!" Julie grabs his attention. You can note the level of pissed off frustration in her tone.

"Right!" his British accent booms as he claps his hands together. "First of all," he points to CiCi and introduces her, then Charley, Ava, me, and Julie. He adds a little pat on the ass for her. He folds his arms across his chest and gives Fate a nod, indicating that it's her turn. Obviously, we learned Fate's name already, but the peasant blouse is Hayleigh, turquoise is Laila, and the unicorn shirt is Shaylee. Incidentally, it says, *When I look in the mirror, I see a unicorn. A badass unicorn.* I need that shirt in my life! "Let's settle this argument the right way," Blake speaks up again once Fate is done with her introductions. "I want all of you girls up on the stage for a Karaoke battle." He points to the stage. "C'mon, now—get up. Move your pretty little arses!" he encourages us. Well . . . mostly them. Hayleigh looks a little panic stricken. Us? Half of us have already made a bee-line for the stage. But, I didn't have to tell you that.

Climbing up on the stage, I give all of Blake's bandmates a hug, then help CiCi, Charley, and Julie with the mics. CiCi turns hers on, "Testing . . . one . . . two . . . three," she says into the mic. "Attention, everyone, there will be a five-minute delay due to the waddling wonder, making her way up here." She points to Ava. Ava shoots her a double salute, soliciting a laugh from all of us. "Come on, you big, adorable heffer."

Shaylee gives Ava a look of sympathy from behind as they all make their way up to the stage. Fate goes to the guys in the band like she's got a magnetic pussy she can't keep under wraps.

"Wait until it's your turn," Ava says in a huff as she grabs Julie's hand to help her up onto the stage.

Just then, Blake grabs a mic. "All right, everyone! We need help over a little dispute. And you know how we settle disputes at Mick and Marley's!" he grabs everyone's attention. "These lovely ladies have taken up residence at the GEG table." The crowd "oohs."

"That's right, people! It's time for an impromptu Karaoke battle for the GEGs to get their table back. What shall be the fighting song?" he asks the crowd.

"We Will Rock You!" someone shouts.

"Beat it!" another patron calls out. Several more titles are shouted out.

"Let's start with 'We Will Rock You!'" He hands Julie the mic and gives her a wink. She practically gushes. I'm so glad she has Blake and that she's finally given in to her feelings for him. She's going to need him once the shit hits the fan. I wish I were over-exaggerating, but I know that I'm not. My friend is going to hurt a helluva lot more than she has in the past. It's going to bring a lot of things up that she's tried to bury, as far as feelings go toward her mother. I shake my head, trying to push these thoughts away . . . stay in the here and now.

I grab my mic, as well as the others. Suddenly, I feel a little breeze coming from Hayleigh as she steps up. She and Fate seem to be having some words with each other, and they don't look too pretty. The words that is. *They* are both drop dead gorgeous, even though they are freakishly pale and give platinum blonde a whole new meaning.

Blake starts banging at the drums behind me. It vibrates the stage. The whole crowd starts stomping their feet and clapping their hands to the famous beat of this kickass song. CiCi starts the first stanza, traveling across the stage like she does this for a living (I told you; we're still holding onto the dream). The whole bar joins in for the chorus. I've never seen it so alive in here. The energy is amazing and for the first time today, I feel a smile take over my lips. *This is exactly what I needed.* Fate's up next, and she's got Freddie Mercury cheering her on from the grave. Well, he would if he could hear this shit (the good kind of shit). Charlotte and I run up dead center, pumping our fists for our verse. Mike then hits us up with the guitar solo—killing it—as usual. The guitar fades, allowing Blake to switch tempo with the drums, then comes back strong for "Hit Me With Your Best Shot" by Pat Benatar. Shaylee comes forward, bringing her inner Pat with her and rockin' the stage like it's 1982 and we're in the middle of a new video for MTV. Ahh . . . remember when MTV played videos? Do people even make videos anymore? I wouldn't know what to tune into.

Julie breezes past me, bringing me back to our performance. Only she turns and sings the verse to Blake, eye fucking him so hard, I may climax. *Jesus, I'm going to need the Viking tonight, for sure.* Of course, we GEGs are handling the attention of the crowd. Us and Julie's ass, that's nicely on display for them.

Fate yanks Hayleigh forward and says something to her. When the next verse comes, Hayleigh floors us all. Even her friends are standing behind her, jaws dropped. It takes them a moment to shake the shock of her voice off.

Ava finishes the song off. I don't care how pregnant she is—girlfriend's got moves! We all join in on the last leg of the chorus, dancing our asses off. As soon as the band starts in on "Beat It" by Michael Jackson, we all try to get serious again and square off on the stage. The blonde bombshells start off first, then us. By the chorus we're all in on it, doing the moves from the video. It's hard work being this awesome, but all nine of us are making it look easy. And, I'm saying this sober as hell.

The music tapers off, and we are all out of breath and laughing together like we've known these chicks our whole lives. I no longer want to throat punch Fate. As I take in this moment, the piano starts up behind us and brings a smile to all of our faces. Each of us loop an arm over the shoulder of the person on our left, our free hand holding our mics. We begin to sway and sing "We Are The Champions" by Queen.

It's like the end of a movie. Every single person in the bar is singing along with us. Cell phones are being held up with their flashlight screens on, swaying with us. When the song ends, there is a calm before the storm of clapping, whistling, and catcalling. We take a dramatic bow as a group then each of us run up for our solo applause, eating that shit up.

Needless to say, four more chairs were added to our table, and most of us drank and laughed ourselves into a stupor over the last few hours. Blake has now informed us that we are all cut off. Except for Ava—she can have all the non-alcoholic beverages she wants. *Bitch.* Ok, I know that's no fun, but he should've kept things fair. Her ass is driving, though.

After giving our new friends a hug goodbye, I grab Fate by the arm, dragging her to a more secluded area. She seems to be the designated driver, and I'm concerned.

"I'm not drunk," she states off the bat.

"How did you know I was going to ask that?"

"I could see it all over your face. Relax, shortstack, don't get your panties in a bunch. I've been drinking water the past hour." She smirks and ruffles my hair like a kid.

"Dude!" I protest knocking her hand away.

"Sorry. You're just so little and cute." Her eyes widen, and she makes a gagging sound. "Sorry, sugary bullshit makes me sick. Especially when it comes out of my mouth."

"Yeah, yeah. That wasn't water, Bette Taylor! Unless they changed the name to vodka!" I argue.

"Bette Taylor?" She laughs then hums the song. "I like that. And it was water. I told Blake to only give me water when I asked for Vodka."

"Why?" I jerk my head back. I slightly feel some spinning action happen that I wasn't quite prepared for. Better not do that again. No. Sudden. Movements.

"Haven't we covered this? Because I'm the shiznits. Only smarter." She winks.

"I should take a page from your book." I wince, waiting for the spinning to stop.

"I have a page for you, but I expect you to burn it after you read it. Because if you don't, it will self-destruct and take you down with it. Got it, shortstack?"

I go to give her the look I usually give my friends when they say something like that because they know I would never.

She gives me a half smile like she already knew that. "Listen up, Maddie." Her face sobers, and her eyes turn serious. "I need you to hear me, so listen carefully. There is going to be a moment, in the near future, where you will absolutely not be sure what you should do. It is critical that you remain calm and very still, and know that, if you do this, *everything* will work out as it should." She holds onto my upper arms. "Do you hear me, Maddie?"

"Yes. But, I don't understand." She's freaking me out a little.

"You won't until it happens. Remember what I said to you and everything will be fine." Her look goes from serious to playful in a millisecond. "If I tell you any more, I'll kill you. Also, you should consider yourself lucky; I don't often give advice to those who think about throat punching me." She raises a brow.

I'll say it again.

What. In. The. Actual. Fuck?

"I feel like I'm on an episode of *Unsolved Mysteries*. You're freaking me out."

"I don't know what show that is, but I get that compliment just about every day of my life," she quips. "I'm off like a prom dress. Keep it real, shortstack." And with that, she turns and leaves.

I CLOSE AND LOCK the door behind me, trying not to wake the boys up. The whole ride home I was in a daze, and not because of the alcohol. I can't stop thinking about what Fate had said. And no matter how much thought I put into it, I still can't come up with something that would warrant that advice. We all agreed in the car, though—that chick is definitely psychic or a medium. Both, perhaps? I should ask Gina Mahoney if she knows her. She's the medium/psychic that the girls and I go to down in Revere. Now *she* is the shiznits!

"Sweetness?" Declan mumbles sleepily as I pad into our room.

"Mm-hmm," I answer as I strip down to my panties and grab one of his undershirts out of the drawer for a nightgown. I saunter over to him (it sounds much sexier than admitting I'm trying not to have an impromptu date with the floor).

"What's the verdict?" he breathes.

I ignore his questions, opting for a chorus of "Oh shits and Oh fucks" in my head. He holds up the covers for me, and I slip in, immediately painting his chest with kisses. Praying to keep him distracted, I travel down at a more hastened pace than usual. I pull at his boxers. "I want to taste you, baby," I lick and nip at his v-line as I get a better grasp of his shorts. He lifts his hips up for me.

"This better be one epic blowjob, sweetness, because my guess is that you have no answer for me about a wedding date."

One epic blowjob—coming up!

Chapter Twenty-Four

Declan

Maddie came up with an idea a month or so ago about everyone's living arrangements. Oddly, we all agreed on it. But, she was wrong about the guilt part. I feel terrible leaving Rosie here while we're all at Maddie's. It just doesn't feel right at all. What if I need advice when I don't think I need it? Who's going to call me out on being an arse? Ok . . . I have no shortage in that department. I feel like I'm going off to college . . . leaving the nest. Sounds silly because she has her own sons, but, they're not here; I am. She's like another mum to me. I don't want her to feel abandoned, especially after knowing what she's been through.

Speaking of, while the investigator I hired hasn't been able to find Renee yet, he has found Rosie's sister. That's what I've come home to talk to her about. I need to know if she wants to follow through with seeing her.

Just then, my phone rings. Seeing it's Rosie, I answer, "Hi."

"Hi there. You gonna come in and tell me what's on your mind or are you going to stay idle in the driveway like a creepy stalker?" she asks. I laugh.

"I was just getting ready to cut the engine and come in because I realized it's Tuesday and I only stalk on Wednesdays. See what happens when you have a Monday off? It messes you up all week," I tease.

"Get in here, smartass," she says, and my screen lights up, indicating she's ended the call. I cut my engine off and do as I am told, remembering to grab the manila envelope from the passenger seat. It isn't unusual for me to stop here first, on my way home, a few nights a week. Because of my schedule, I don't get to see her when I come home; she's already gone. So, I know my news will really catch her off guard.

I get to the front door and breeze past her. "Whoa! What's the matter?" she asks right away as she closes the door behind us.

"I found your sister Pamela," I blurt out. You just don't get any smoother than me. *Christ, Almighty!*

"I . . . I think I need to sit, Dec," she barely gets the words out, and her face pales as if she's seen a ghost.

"Yes, of course!" I walk back over to assist her. "I'm sorry, Rosie, I didn't mean to blurt that out like that." I'm such an arse!

"I don't understand," she says as she sits on the sofa. "I didn't know you were looking for her."

"I wanted to put your mind at ease. I wanted to do something. I haven't contacted her. I thought I'd leave that ball in your court," I stop mid-ramble but decide to continue as she is just sitting here, staring at me. I place the large envelope in her lap, and I sit next to her. "In here is everything you need to know. She's in Vermont, Rosie, about four or five hours away from here. There are pictures inside; she looks a lot like you, just not as hip." I try to solicit a laugh from her, but all she has are tears that are building up in her eyes. *I think I may have made a mistake.*

"Children? Husband?" she asks. I want to say no, just she and her thirty cats, but this isn't my usual Rosie; I can't joke around with her to make this easy.

"Four children. Her husband had a terrible stroke a few years back; he's in a wheelchair. She's his sole caregiver."

"Where are her kids? Don't they help her?"

"They are pretty spread out, and there were no Aussies in the area for her to adopt." I tried not to joke, but at least this little one is making her smile a bit.

"Lucky her." She nudges me. "They have a habit of putting their nose in where it doesn't belong, even though the person they do that to is very thankful for it." Her chin quivers.

"Did I do good, Rosie?"

"You did real good, Dec," she cries and throws her arms around me. "Wait!" She pushes back. "What if she doesn't want to see me?"

"I think she will. Why don't you write her a letter? See what she says."

"I need to show you something. I'll be right back." She gets up and leaves the room. No more than ten minutes go by, and she walks back in with a file box in her hands. She sits back down and places the box on the floor between us. "When we were little girls, we loved to play post office. We would each sit in our own rooms, write letters to each other, and then run out in the hall to place them in our makeshift mailboxes. Pamela and I loved getting letters so much, it didn't matter what they said." She laughs. "Like most little girls, we thought about how things would be when we grew up. As you know, I was older than her, so we surmised that I'd be the first one gone and married. We worried that our husbands would whisk us far away from each other, so we made a pact." She opens the lid on the box. "We promised that we would take time to write each other every week, so we always knew what was going on and that we were thinking of each other. I started doing it the day I pretended not to know her." She picks up the top envelope. "It's the thickest one, telling her everything, and . . . how much I love her. How sorry I am," she chokes on her words.

"The others?" I ask, looking down.

"I started off weekly, then monthly, quarterly, till finally, I went yearly. There's well over two hundred letters in here. I've numbered them all as I've gone along. Can you do me a favor?" she asks as she slides the center drawer open on the coffee table and pulls out a notepad.

"Of course," I say as I watch her scribble out a note.

"I can't do it, Dec—I'll chicken out. Can you send her these letters? I want them all in a box, so she has every one. I know you may not be able to use this box, but they should all be together, so she can read them in order if she chooses to." She hands me the note. I lift it slightly, asking permission to read it. She nods.

Dear Pamela,

I kept our promise—mostly. I just never knew where to send them.

I hope that you can find it in your heart to forgive me enough to read them. I never stopped thinking about you. I will always love you.

Your sister,

Rosie

"This is lovely, Rosie. I'm sure this will bring her great joy to have all of these from you. I will do it tomorrow—first thing." I pull her into my arms for a hug.

"Ok, now go. I've cried in front of you enough tonight. And, I want to read up on my sister." She smiles and hugs the envelope to her chest.

"As you wish." I kiss her forehead. "I'll see you in the morning?"

"Yes. Lock the door on your way out."

"Ok. Goodnight, Rosie." I stand up.

"Yes . . . it is," she answers. I watch as the fingers of her shaky hand slide under the flap to open the envelope. I leave her to it, locking up as I was told to do.

"Who's that?" I quietly inquire as I take off my shoes. Maddie is sitting on the bed with her legs crossed, talking on the phone.

She holds the receiver and still only mouths "Preston." I nod and signal that I'm going to go in for a shower. She blows me a kiss. Now that's the most action I've gotten all week. I'd get mad but half the time, it's my fault. My schedule has been all over the place. I've been sucking it up because we're taking the whole month of September off. Maddie and I, that is. Yes, we've settled on a September wedding. It's a beautiful time of the year here, and my parents will be just coming off of winter; they'll be glad for the warm weather.

I'm not religious enough to have sought out a church here, so we're getting married at the one Maddie grew up going to, and still does. She's been working with Bill's wife on reception plans at the museum. She's so happy we were able to obtain one of the galleries there. I am too. That place holds one of my most important memories.

It's not just the wedding plans, though. Maddie is bogged down by a client. Usually, she's so excited about helping her clients, like the girl who thought she had different parents. It turns out she did. She is actually her mother's niece. Her parents witnessed a crime down in Boston that involved the mob. They went into the witness protection program, asking the government to wipe out all records of her giving birth and change them as if her sister did. What makes the story even wilder is that her birth mother and mother who raised her had only known each other for under a year. They were both adopted and didn't find one another till they met in college and became friends. They noticed they looked similar and had a similar history. They decided to get a DNA test for fun. By then, her client was already one-year-old. So, by the time she was two, when all of this went down, she had already grown familiar with her adopted mum. It made the transition much easier. Unfortunately, her parents didn't make it. They saved her life. Crazy, huh? Maddie had mixed emotions about this outcome. She was glad that her client had valid memories but sad that she never got to know her parents. It was very lucky for her that she had her aunt, whom never treated her as if she wasn't her own. Maddie mentioned that too and what should've been a happy note, made her sad. She won't talk about this client at all. Just that it's really difficult and it's making her constantly question her ability to handle it. I told her to ask someone else to take this person on. For some reason, she can't.

I rinse out my hair before turning the shower off and stepping out. I shake a towel through my hair then wrap it around my waist before rejoining Maddie in the bedroom. As soon as I turn the corner, I see her sprawled out on the bed, wiping her eyes. "What's the matter, sweetness?" I rush over to her.

"I need a break." She sits up. "I *really* need a break. I can't listen to another person's problems right now. I need some sort of sabbatical, and it can't wait till September; I'm going to snap, babe," she confesses through her tears.

I snatch my phone up and begin texting several replacements for this weekend. "Done," I say. "I'm working on it, but consider it done. Let's go away."

"Yeah?"

"Absolutely. I've never seen you like this, and it's been going on for a while." I set my phone back down.

"We'll bring Hunter. Just a family getaway, okay?" She climbs up on her knees.

"Sounds wonderful, sweetness." I lean in and sweep her lips.

"Are you too tired?" She looks up at me with the most innocent look in her eyes; it causes movement under my towel . . . ahem.

"I don't want to fuck, Maddie. I want to take my time savoring every inch of you." I run my finger down her cheek.

"It's after midnight; can I get the combo platter?" She smiles coyly.

"As long as it's not the drive-thru."

"Deal. Except, now I'm hungry," she pouts.

"Don't worry, sweetness, I've got something to fill that sexy mouth of yours with." I grab the back of her thighs and toss her onto the bed. She screeches and tries to get away (not very hard, mind you) but submits once I catch her nipple with my mouth, over my t-shirt. She's gotten into a habit of wearing my undershirts to bed. "When are you going to wear some of the sexy lingerie I've bought for you?" I slowly guide the shirt up her stomach and over her chest.

"I don't feel sexy in them."

"You feel sexy in this frumpy thing?" I pull on the shirt.

"You think I look frumpy?" she asks as she pushes the shirt back down.

One year later . . . still complete shit at this.

If sex was a sport, the ref would be throwing a flag down on this play, and he'd announce:

COCKBLOCK!

"Are you due for your. . .?" *Dear God, what is the matter with me?!*

"Wow, you must *really* not want to get laid tonight!" she snaps.

"I am pretty sure my mum dropped me on my head a few times when I was a baby. I'm still waiting on confirmation from her, but I think tonight is certainly solid proof." I keep my eyes shut tightly so that hers don't burn into me. She nudges me and turns over, giving me the cold shoulder. This does nothing but turn the fire inside of me into an inferno because now I have her lovely arse in my face. I groan before bite her left cheek gently. She gasps and tries to move away, but I kneel up and grasp her hips, pulling her back before I tear her panties off. "Dec!"

I smack her right cheek before gripping both of them and squeezing till she yelps. "I haven't been doing my job well, again. Otherwise, you'd know you're sexy as fuck in anything you put on." I slap her left cheek and grip them again, spreading them wide so I can feast my eyes on all that is mine.

"Please," she whimpers.

"You know you're sexy. I know you know. It was all over your face when you looked up at me before, asking me if I was too tired for this." I slide my cock up and down her slick center. She pushes towards me. "Not until you tell me." I pull back.

"Tell you what?" She rests her forehead on her arms.

"That you know how beautiful you are to me. That you know you're all I ever think about. That I crave the softness of your skin, feeling my hands glide over your curves. That I love the sounds that escape your mouth when I'm making you feel good." I take in a deep slow breath, trying to steady myself.

"I know, baby. It's all me tonight. I'm sorry." She looks over her shoulder at me.

I lean back and tap her right hip for her to flip onto her back. When she does, I hover over her, lining myself up. I kiss her nose, both of her eyelids, and then her lips. "I don't like when you feel bad about yourself. It makes me feel like I'm not giving you enough attention. Do you need more from me, sweetness?" I nudge her nose with mine before resting my forehead to hers.

"God, no, baby!" She palms my face. "I'm letting work and everything else affect me. I'll work harder at keeping it all separate." She brushes my lips seductively.

"If you need to talk, I'm always here to listen," I remind her.

"I know. And, I do. But, we both know there are certain things I can't discuss. Some of it's just been weighing me down. It'll get better soon, I promise." Maddie tightens the grip on my face as if to emphasize. When I nod in agreement, she rolls her hips, allowing my cock to slide up and down her center. "Do you still want to make love?" she practically coos.

I answer her by entering her with one deep thrust. Her head arches back violently at my intrusion. "Hold onto me, sweetness," I command softly. She wraps her legs and arms around me, and I take her slowly.

Chapter Twenty-Five

Maddie

"Hunter, are you coming in with us?" I look over my shoulder to the backseat.

"Is it ok if I just stay out here and play on my tablet?"

"Yeah, we won't be long." I roll the windows all the way down and turn off my car.

"I can come back out once I'm done peeing," Ava offers before opening her door and trying to climb out.

"Wait! Let me help you! I told you, *no going into labor on my watch*!" I remind her.

"How about peeing myself because that's going to happen in a minute if you don't hurry up!" She huffs and rocks, trying to get up.

"Gross, Aunt Ava," Hunter mumbles from the back. Ava and I make an "aww" face at each other because he called her aunt. He's done it before, but it's still all so new.

"Hurry!" She slaps me.

"Ah! Sorry!" I race out of the car and around to her, helping her, on three, to get up. "Not much longer, kiddo." I offer her a sympathetic look. She's been carrying these twins like a champ. Everything has gone wonderfully with her pregnancy. I thank God every day. We just need these babies to come into this world safely and healthy.

I follow her up the stairs. At eight months pregnant, I can pretty much confirm that Ava's Spirit animal is the sloth. "Go around! I can hear you mentally huffing and puffing behind me." She waves for me to go. I don't hesitate.

I unlock the front door and leave Ava in my dust while I go and search for the pocket watch Declan wanted me to find. It was a gift he'd received from his grandfather. It's been in his family for generations. He wants to get it repaired and pass it down to Hunter on our wedding day as a gift for being his best man (well, one of them). The grown up version of that role is going to Blake. He and Declan have really bonded over the past year. It's probably due to their mutual interest in music, their accents, and because they're hot. Julie and I added the last two idea—they're legit ones.

I rummage through all of the drawers he told me it might be in. I asked Rosie, but she didn't even know he had this watch. I search in his closet, pulling out the drawers in there. Man, he has a lot of shit! "Finally!" I cheer as I find it in a box that was way in the back of the bottom drawer. I quickly grab the cufflinks he wanted, as well and head down the hall. "Found it!" I call out to Ava as I step into the living room.

I freeze.

"You're her," she says matter-of-factly. "The woman who stole my life. It's a comfortable one, isn't it?" Renee waves her gun around.

"I didn't steal your life, Renee," I say as calmly as I can. She doesn't seem to be high. Actually, she looks well. I'd almost say she looks as if she's stayed clean, but, obviously, I couldn't be a hundred percent sure.

"You know my name?" she asks with childlike excitement.

"Of course I do. You're Hunter's mother."

She immediately bursts into tears. "That's right! *I'm* his mother—not you!" Spit flies in the air as she points her finger at me dramatically. Oh my God. Did she see him outside? Did she do something with him? I fight the urge to ask her. If she didn't see him, I certainly don't want to bring any attention to his presence. Jesus—where's Ava?!

I need to keep her busy. I don't know what her intentions are. "He knows that, Renee. He even has a picture of you both, framed on his wall."

Her face contorts. "He does?"

"Yes. And, he has a book with all of his family history from your side." I leave out the fact that we did this together. I don't want to do or say anything that may trigger her to use that gun. If I keep me out of it, I'm hoping that my importance in his life, however grand she has made it, will start to seem insignificant.

"He doesn't know me now. He only knows you and the lies that you and Dec have told him about me!" she yells that last part.

"I don't know you, Renee. What lies could I come up with? Hunter knows I don't know you. Besides, Declan never says a negative thing about you to him; I can assure you."

"You can *assure* me?" she seethes. "Oh, that's right—you're a shrink. You know just what to say and do, don't you?" her tone is condescending. "You people think you know how to fix people like me? Nobody can fix me!" she screams through her tears, pointing her gun at me.

"Did you say something, Maddie?" Ava calls from behind. Renee jerks the gun in Ava's direction.

"No!" I gasp.

"Oh God. . ." Ava whimpers under her breath from behind me. "*Who are you?!*"

"Please, Renee, she has nothing to do with this. Let her go, please," I beg calmly.

"Come forward," she instructs Ava, and my heart leaps into my throat. Ava sniffles as she gets next to me. "I was pregnant once," Renee says, smiling at Ava's belly. "I was so excited. I was so in love with my husband, and I couldn't believe that we were going to be a mommy and daddy. He even gave me a white picket fence," her voice begins to shake again. "I fought the voices off for a year. Then . . . they . . . they just got so loud," she cries. "I couldn't get them to shut up."

"Are they talking to you now, Renee?" My eyes flicker from hers to the gun and back.

"They. Always. Talk!" She grits her teeth.

"That's why you turned to drugs? To quiet them?"

She sniffs and runs the side of her free hand up her nose. "Yes."

"Did they help?"

"Better than any of those stupid prescriptions I was given." A disgusted look comes across her face. "I wanted to be a good mom. I was a good mom," she cries again. "He loved me, my little bear." She gives into her sobs. "I have nothing now. I'm clean. I did this for them, and they abandoned me, leaving me with these voices." She touches her forehead then starts smacking it over it over. "They won't shut up! Shut up! Shut up, shut uppppp! I don't want to hear you anymore!" She suddenly stops and looks me straight in the eyes. "I can't. No—I won't! She's all he has. Stop it! Stop it!" She begins smacking her head again and pacing.

Oh God, I'm going to throw up.

I don't know what to do.

What do I do?

I glance over at Ava; I've never seen her so frightened. Not even in the hospital with Hope. Tears are streaming down her face, and she's visibly shaking.

"Renee? What are the voices telling you to do?" I keep my voice steady.

"Put a bullet in her head. Put a bullet in her head," she says over and over again so fast. Ava lets out a yelp. I slowly grab her hand and squeeze.

"Is your gun loaded, Renee?" I am praying with everything that I've got, that this a toy gun. She holds it above her head and lets off a round, hitting the ceiling. Ava and I jump. Ava is now hysterically crying.

"Shut up! Shut up!" Renee yells, pacing again. Ava and I remain still, our hands squeezing each other so tight. "I never wanted this," she begins crying again. "You took them away from me. I was getting better. You just stole my family. He was waiting for me. And, Hunter wants to dance with me—his real mother—at his wedding. I was learning how to knit, so I could make things for his babies. You took them all away from me!" she starts yelling and pointing her gun at me again. She's talking as if Hunter is grown. She's back and forth; there's no definitive line of reality for her. *I don't know what to do. God, please help us!*

"Mom, are you okay?" Hunter asks as he opens the front door. *No! No! No! No! No!!*

"Hunter bear?" Renee smiles and turns to him. His eyes widen in panic. "I'm okay . . . now that you're here! That's so sweet of you to check on Mommy." She opens her arms to him. Hunter's chin starts quivering and he slowly shakes his head. I want to run to him so badly. "Do you know why I named you Hunter?" she asks cheerfully. "It was after my grandpa. He loved to hunt. I was his buddy. He taught me all about guns and how to shoot," she carries on, reminiscing as if nothing is out of the ordinary here. "Why are you crying, Hunter bear?" She pouts.

"You're scaring me. Why do you have a gun?" he chokes through his words. "Please don't hurt her."

"I'm not going to hurt you." She steps towards him, but he backs up and lets out a soft whimper. I instinctively rush forward to protect him, but I don't get too far before she has the gun pushing against the center of my forehead.

I close my eyes and listen to the sound of my deep breaths.

There are so many things I didn't get to do.

But, I have loved hard.

That was the most important thing of all.

"Do you remember the first time you held Hunter in your arms, Renee?" Ava pipes up. The pressure of the gun lightens up. "You swore you would always keep him safe? Give him everything he needs?" she continues.

"I never knew my heart could feel that much love," she answers quietly.

"You need to get past what the voices are telling you, Renee. He loves Maddie very much, and she's good to him; she loves him. If you hurt her, you will be hurting him."

"Please don't hurt her, Mom. I'll do anything. I'll come with you," Hunter pleads.

"You can't come with me, baby." She starts crying again. "I love you, Hunter bear. I need you to go outside now. Just remember I love you. Shhh . . . shh," she chants quietly, closing her eyes tightly.

"No! Please don't hurt her," he begs again.

"I promise I won't hurt her, baby, but I need you to go outside."

I open my eyes and look over at him. I give him my nod of approval. "Promise?" he asks, looking back to her.

"Cross my heart," she says and crosses her heart. "I love you. Always remember that."

"Go, Hunter," Ava says. He finally turns and goes out the door. I bring my focus back to Renee, who is silently battling the voices again.

"Look in Hunter's top drawer," she says as if she's got a migraine, wincing and rubbing her temple. She backs away from me, still holding the gun toward me. She takes in a shaky breath. "Take care of them," she says then quickly turns the gun and pushes it into her mouth. Before I can move a muscle, another round sounds off, and a few warm specks of liquid hit me. The rest of it is splattered on the wall and furniture behind her body that has fallen to the ground. Ava screams from behind me, but all I can hear clearly and feel are my lungs trying to draw in a breath.

"Nooo!" I yell as Hunter runs back in. "Don't come in here!"

But . . . it's too late.

Hunter stands frozen, staring at his mother on the ground. I rush to him, trying to shield him from this God awful sight. "Please go outside," I plead as I hug him tightly. Shell-shocked, he nods and turns to go out the door. I grab the phone off the side table and dial 911.

"We're going to need two ambulances," Ava says. "I know you asked me not to go into labor on your watch, but given the circumstance, I don't think you can get pissed off at me," she breathes through a contraction.

"Oh, Ava," I start to cry and walk over to her. She leans over, holding on to the arm of the couch. I rub her back as the operator picks up. I tell them that we'll need two ambulances. I explain what happened, and I stay on the line with them until someone arrives and I can start calling everyone else. Most important, at the moment, is to get Ava and Hunter out of here.

I glance over at Renee's lifeless body, and an uncontrollable sob comes over me. Such a young and promising life wasted. Why is it so much harder to get mentally ill people to stay on their meds than people with conditions like high blood pressure, diabetes, or heart disease? There are still so many stigmas around mental illness. I can't think of another reason why they neglect themselves like this. Mentally ill people are not weak. They are not freaks. They are people, just like you and me, who want to live ordinary lives. Unfortunately, to most of them, that means medication free. They think they can do without it . . . prove that they are not weak . . . that they *are* mentally sound. That's the moment that they truly choose to lose everything and everyone that matters in their life because they become blind to their own actions. They hurt the ones they love, accusing them of being the villains. Accusing them of never giving them the validation they feel they deserve. Most, like Renee, develop their own form of reality. It's exhausting to the family members and friends involved. Even the therapist, if there is one. I give a lot of credit to my colleagues who handle cases like this every day. I couldn't.

Of course, there are different degrees of mental illness, many different facets. I don't mean to generalize. There are wonderful coping mechanisms that actually do work well for people, but they are usually the ones who aren't severe cases, even then, they may need meds to help. It's all very complicated, and I always knew that would never be the area of concentration in my practice. That's why I specialize in phobias, because once my clients graduate from the chair in my office, I know they will be ok; I have given them the skills they can use on their own in the future.

"Maddie," the operator grabs my attention.

"Yes?"

"Do you see or hear the ambulance and firetrucks, yet. They should be coming up to your house any moment.

"I hear them." I nod even though she can't see me. I walk over to the front door just as a police officer arrives on the stoop. I let him in and tell the operator, allowing her to disconnect with me. I quickly explain everything that happened as we allow the EMTs to get to Ava. "Please, officer, I need to call her husband, and my son is outside. Can I go to him?"

"Yes, Miss St. Claire, we have all the info we need right now. We'll be in touch if we have any more questions." He closes his notepad.

"Absolutely," I say before heading off to Hunter. He's with a female police officer. They are leaning with their backs up against my car. As soon as he sees me, he bolts. I run, as well, and we practically tackle each other. "I'm so sorry you saw that. I'm so sorry you were here. What are you thinking? What do you need?" I pull back, grasping his face.

"I just need to hug you. Are you okay?" he cries. "I was so scared. I thought she was going to hurt you. I don't want anything to ever happen to you. I. Don't. Want. To. Lose. You," he says as if he's hyperventilating. I pull him back in, crushing him to me.

"I'm here. I will always be here. I love you, Hunter. I love you so much." I cry into his hair. And then I cry even harder for the mom who missed out on this incredible boy. I hope she's at peace . . . finally.

It's like déjà vu, except we're all waiting on Ava to give birth. Declan joined Mitch, Kyle, and Trent on the company jet to get up here from Boston. If you don't live in this area, you'd probably think that's ridiculous, but a twenty minute (if that) flight, in an emergency situation, is much quicker than two hours of sitting in Boston traffic. Mitch has had his captain on stand-by in case Ava went into labor while Trent was at work. Nobody, of course, planned for the events of today.

About an hour ago, Declan had to formally identify Renee's body. When he came out of the morgue, he slid down the wall, falling apart, crippled with grief. "I failed," he sobbed.

"You did everything you could for her, baby." I knelt down next to him.

"It wasn't enough. I could've done more—I should've!" He gritted his teeth.

"No, Declan, you couldn't. Nothing you did would've ever been enough or been the right thing to do; not in her eyes."

"I should've given her another chance . . . something. I gave up on her."

"You gave her many chances. It was time for you to give yourself a chance. Please stop, baby. Nothing . . . no amount of guilt will bring her back or change things. I am sorry for your loss, but the woman you lost has been all but gone for almost ten years." I took his hand in mine.

"I told her I hated her."

"You hated her illness and the decisions she made about it. That's perfectly ok and natural. Don't go looking for things, Dec." I stood up, and he followed me.

"How am I going to help Hunter through this, through what he witnessed?"

"You won't; we will." I wrapped my arms around his waist and hugged him.

"How am I going to help you?"

"We will help each other." I smiled up at him.

We walked back up here, hand-in-hand, and have been waiting since. So far, everything is going well. Ava, the champ that she is, is doing a vaginal delivery, though it is becoming more common for women with multiples to opt for a c-section.

Parkland Medical Center's Labor and Delivery floor is tiny with only five rooms that ever get used. Because Ava is the only one on the labor side today, and the nurses remember us all from when Hope was born, they have allowed us to stand outside the delivery room instead of sitting in the waiting room.

We all silently cheer as somebody in the room yells about the head crowning. You know how people start doing the wave at sporting events? All of us girls just did that . . . except our waves were burst of tears. After ten long, excruciatingly painful years, our best friend's dream is finally coming true. I don't mean to take anything away from Hope; she made Ava a mom first. But knowing that our friend actually gets to be a mom this time—there are no words.

The first cry.

"It's a boy! I have a boy!" Trent yells. We all respond like the Patriots got a touchdown. Trent runs out to us. "I have a son! He's so perfect."

"You're not done, yet—get back in there!" Mitch laughs.

"Right!" he says and goes to turn.

"Wait!" I stop him. "How big is he?"

He holds his hands up a little, looking down at them. "About . . . this big." He pulls them apart and shows me a measurement. I snort and push at his arm to get back in there.

Three minutes pass by, and we hear the other baby testing out it's lungs. "It's a girl! We have another little girl." Trent starts off strong with the announcement but you can hear the mixture of happiness and sadness in his last sentence. The girls and I go into a huddle shaped hug.

Finally pulling away, I notice that not only is Mitch missing, but Declan, too. "Mitch followed after him. He looked like he was having a tough time," Charley informs me.

"I didn't even notice that he left." This makes me feel like shit. I didn't even think about how this may be affecting him. I'm sure hearing the first baby cry and the announcement of it being a boy, the excitement in Trent's voice . . . it must have stirred up a lot of memories.

"I know what he's going through must be very hard, shortstack, but there are too many things that could've gone wrong today. We could've lost you or Ava. I'm sorry that chick felt like that was her only answer, but I didn't know her. You had a very traumatic experience today. You deserve every minute of sharing in Ava and Trent's happiness. Just stay focused on what you need right now. The Viking will respect that," CiCi finally finishes, and I stare at her in disbelief.

"It's official; I'm rubbing off on all of you. You've all got a little captain in ya," I imitate the commercial.

"You're so compact, Maddie, we can stick you anywhere." Julie waggles her eyebrows at me.

"You've been trying to rub one off on us for years," Charley adds.

Well, I walked into that with my eyes wide open.

"Girls," Kyle interjects, "You want to pay attention? They just told us to come in."

"That's what they said?" CiCi teases.

"Let's go." He smirks and holds out his hand.

"Wait for us!"

We all turn to find Jay and Vic jogging down the hall. "Tell Daddy Warbucks to wait for all of the orphans next time!" Jay says to Charley.

"What are you talking about, Jaitlin?" That's her new nickname for him.

"We were in Boston," Vic explains. "We got the bat signal too late. We also didn't know Mitch had one of his planes on standby."

"What the hell, guys? Don't you want to meet our kids?" Trent pops his head out the door.

"Coming!" we all chime at once and head in like a freight train.

Ava looks up from her baby girl and smiles at us, her eyes full of tears. "What do you think, Maddie?" she asks as I make it over to her first.

"Oh, Ava," my voice shakes as I begin to cry again. "She's so beautiful. Good job, Mom." I lean down and kiss Ava's head before the baby's. "What are you naming her?" They've kept names a secret from us and the genders a secret from everybody, including themselves.

"Ivy Madelyn Carter," she states clearly.

"What? Really?" I may actually die of emotional overdose today.

"I was more scared for you today than myself," she ignores my question.

"Why?"

"Because all best friends swear they'd take a bullet for each other. I can imagine that very few have the opportunity to prove it. Today, I knew, without a doubt, that you would've jumped in front of a bullet aimed at me. I saw it all over your face, in the way you handled the situation. And then Hunter walked in. The panic that struck your face was almost unbearable to watch."

"And then you saved my life after I did something very stupid," I add.

"You weren't being stupid; you were being instinctual. And of course I saved your ass—somebody has to be Ivy's Godmother. I knew right then that you were the right choice, that you'd always look out for my child, even with death staring you in the face." She lifts Ivy up to me and tries to imitate the opening tribal call in *The Lion King*. I'd say she must have something sweet pumping through that IV, but I wouldn't be fooling any one of you. You all know we don't need anything in our *Kool Aid*; it's *au naturale*.

I hold her close to me and kiss her little nose. "It is an honor for me to be your Godmother," I say softly. The rest of the girls come over to take a peek, and I finally pass her over to go see little Grady Johnson Carter.

"While I love Grady's name," CiCi calls over to Trent and me. "You have to know that he will be teased about it. Everyone will call him Greedy Johnson."

"Everyone, including his aunt CiCi," Trent answers.

"Well, that shit's gotta get started somehow. Might as well be me!"

"Don't curse around the babies, Ceese," Ava groans lightly.

"Dude, if they didn't come out your snatch yelling *what the fuck?* I don't think you'll have to worry about cuss words around them until they are two."

I snort and turn back to Grady, just as I feel two hands slide around my waist from behind. "I'm sorry," he breathes in my ear. "I just needed a moment."

I crank my neck to look back and up at him. "It's ok. I completely understand." I pucker up for him to kiss me. We both look back down at Grady and collectively sigh.

"We'll be next," he states.

"I hope so. But, if not, it will happen when it's supposed to." I look around the room at all of these amazing, albeit slightly crazy (in a good way), people in our lives, taking in all the love, shining through.

"Thank you." He squeezes me to him. I crank my neck again to look up, not understanding why he's thanking me. But then I see it; he's looking around the room, too. His eyes are filled with warmth and respect as he watches *our* friends. He looks as if he's come home after being away for so long. I nudge a little and nod toward them when I grab his attention. He lets go of my waist but keeps his hand on my back as we walk Grady over. Ava looks completely wiped out and content at the same time as she watches us all laughing and cooing at the babies, and laughing and teasing each other. And, in true Ava style, she lets her eyes fill up, holding this memory in place. I join her. Because this is what happiness and love is about—holding onto the joy of the little moments inside the big ones; they're the glue that keeps it all together. When you lose sight of these little moments, that's when you can no longer see the big picture. Ava has always been the keeper of our little moments. *She's* the glue—not me.

Then again, I guess maybe we all are, in our own little way.

Epilogue

Maddie

Two years later. . .

"THERE'S A REASON WHY YOU CONNECT THE BORDER OF A PUZZLE first before you start messing with the center pieces; it's a guide to the finished goal, helping you stay organized. People will say that life is a puzzle, yet many do not treat it as such. You have to set goals first, then fit the pieces in to obtain it. Sometimes pieces don't fit where you think they should. You don't throw the puzzle back in the box, complaining about that one piece that messed up everything. You find the piece that fits. There will *always* be a piece that fits. Don't ever give up. Don't lose yourself amongst the pieces you think are missing."

That's how I opened up my very first LCG meeting last night

at Two Steps Forward. LCG stands for Life Coaching Group. It was an idea that Mitch came to me about several months ago. He and Charley have opened up a foundation called Two Steps Forward. It's for people who just don't know where to turn to get help for what they are going through. I know from a lot of my clients' experiences that you can end up being directed to ten different places for assistance (whatever kind that you may need) and never come across one that really helps, or you end up on a waiting list. The main goal is to get people back on track mentally, physically, and financially while only having to go to one place to set those goals up. Anyways, my diagram stuck with him and he broached me about doing a group like that, where all the participants add their input or help. I loved the idea and jumped on board to volunteer my time. When they had the opening ceremony, Charley spoke about sometimes needing a second pair of eyes to find the right pieces to your puzzle. I loved that metaphor, so I "borrowed" it in a sense but put my own twist on it.

The nice part about volunteering there is that we do it as a family when Hunter is off from school. The other nice part is that Declan and I drive into the city two days a week. We treat the commute like it's a date. Every once in a while things get carried away and a horn will honk at us to move.

So much has happened in the past two years. I've had to work through what transpired that day with the help of my colleague, Lana. I still have nightmares every once in a while. I worry about Hunter. He has talked about that day very openly. However, he doesn't seem traumatized by it . . . by losing his mother. I fear that one day, he will snap; it will just come out of nowhere. Thankfully, the angle he saw her from didn't reveal all of the gory details; all he saw was his mother lying there, dead, with the gun and a lot of blood around her. Lana thinks that, while the event was traumatic, it may never be the level I'm thinking it should be at, simply because whatever bond he may have had with her (if any), it was either gone or barely there. Besides that, Declan has always been honest with Hunter about his mother's illness to a point, given his age. That, in the long run, has seemed to help Hunter in knowing that there wasn't anything anyone could do. That what she did couldn't be measured by whether or not she loved him. It simply was a battle with her own demons that she didn't win. However, given his history of nightmares from other traumatic events with her, I will keep a close eye on him . . . just in case.

Declan has had his up and down moments. He realized that his biggest guilt was that he felt free. He had loved her with his whole heart, once upon a time. The girl he loved is the one he feels crippled with guilt over. It took some time for him to know that it's perfectly okay for him to feel free because he is. He's free from hospitals, rehabs, private investigators, lawyers . . . all of the things he became burdened with. He's also free to love her again, remembering fond times . . . the little moments. She no longer has to be that woman who made him feel hatred. He's free to share these memories with their son, so Hunter can learn about and love the girl with the infectious laugh. The woman who fell so in love with her son the moment he was placed in her arms. Actually, she helped him with that. . .

It was almost a month later when I remembered that she instructed me to look in Hunter's drawer. What we found took our breath away. She had made her son a scrapbook, telling him the story of her love for him in her own words. Declan was shocked; he had given her these pictures upon her request, over the years, but never believed she hung on to them. Each page held a special memory whether in picture or words. She did a beautiful job; you could tell she'd really put her heart into it. The very last page broke both of us. It was a picture of her holding Hunter in her arms and kissing his forehead. Centered underneath was a handwritten note from her.

Mommy is with Jesus now.
He has made her all better.
Now she can be there for me.
All I have to do, when I'm
sad, scared, or happy is close
my eyes. Stay very still. And
then, I will feel her arms
wrap around me. I will smile
to let her know I feel her
love.
I love you, Hunter bear.
                    Love,
                    Mommy

Though she battled greatly with herself, that day, it had never been her intention to harm me; she was there to say goodbye.

We gave him the book, later that night. Both of us sat across from him in the living room while he took his time with each page. When he got to the last one, I squeezed Declan's hand so hard; I was on the verge of tears for Hunter. We watched as he closed the book, then his eyes. A moment later, a soft smile graced his lips, and he whispered, "Thank you." I don't know if he actually felt her hugging him, but if believing so brought him some sort of comfort, neither one of us were going to say different.

Declan didn't bother having a memorial for her. There wasn't anybody, but us, to come. So he had her cremated and shipped her ashes out to her parents in Oregon. She'd been estranged from them for several years. They were going to fly out here, but for what? To see their daughter in the state she was in, missing a chunk of her skull and brains. No, they didn't need that to be the last time they saw her. They did, however, schedule (tentatively) when they would come out to see Hunter. It's been years for that, too.

After the cremation, we all went to Mick and Marley's that night just to give Declan some support. Blake dedicated a song in the memory of Renee and, quite frankly, it brought us all to tears. It was "Heal" by Tom Odell.

Declan and Blake have ventured into recording an album together. Some of the songs are covers, and some are originals. They came up with this idea after Declan had recorded the symphony he wrote for me. The very same one he had several mates from the orchestra perform during our wedding ceremony. It's so beautiful and moving. It's called "My Journey To You."

We are now embarking on a new journey; one that has ten tiny fingers and toes. She'll be here in September. Charley and I are excited because that will put our girls in the same grade! Bernadette (Charley and Mitch's girl) and Piper (ours) . . . I can't wait to watch them grow. Of course, CiCi had to bring up the fact that Piper's initials will be P.P. When I told her Piper's middle name would be Amelia, after my grandmother, there was no bringing her back from her laughing fit until I told her I would buy Patrick a journal so he can write all of his captain logs down (because they named their son Patrick Stewart). "But where will you write all yours down?" she quipped. Yes, they still call me "captain" but now it's "Captain Shortstack."

Ava, Trent, and the kids have been living in her childhood home for over a year now; it's bittersweet. It's so different (in an amazing way) to watch them as parents now, instead of the couple weighed down by the struggles of infertility. They're a great team, and I never see them take one single moment with their kids for granted. I wish Cynthia could take a page out of their book and then travel back in time to utilize it.

Oddly, even with all of the bullshit Cynthia has put Julie

through, she can always separate things—always had that ability. So, maybe Cynthia wasn't too off in her thinking. It was just her delivery that sucked.

It's bewildering when I reflect back and think of how many significant changes we went through in a span of a year: finding love, suffering a great loss, learning to trust . . . to forgive, and be reminded that life is short. But, what I think we learned the most is that our friendship can pass any test thrown at it. We have proved it over the years, but never like this. It made me think back to that Christmas sleepover when CiCi and I were discussing that I should put "Make love epic" on the wall behind my bed. I did end up stenciling that on my wall but in my living room. Around it, in a circular formation, are framed pictures of *all* the people we love fiercely. When you allow yourself to be surrounded by people who are there one hundred percent, make you laugh, cry, build you up, and still wrap you in their arms when you are a complete shit—that's how you make love epic. It isn't just boy meets girl (though that shit has been pretty epic, if I do say so myself) . . . or boy meets boy (Jay would call me out on this!) . . . or girl meets girl. There's a love story between you and every important person in your life. Remember to always add more chapters because you never know how quickly that story will come to an end.

Shannon O'Brien had turned me onto the advice of a rather brilliant lady, if you ask me: Eleanor Roosevelt. I refer to her a lot, these days. I'll leave you with this. . .

"In the long run, we shape our lives, and we shape ourselves.
The process never ends until we die.
And the choices we make are ultimately our own responsibility."
~ Eleanor Roosevelt

The End

SHOWING UP
GEG SERIES #4

BY
JACQUELYN AYRES

CHAPTER ONE

Julie

RED'S GOT THE BEAT
BLOG POST:
Love isn't always about finding the right person and building a life around that discovery. We all know that there are many different levels to such a big emotion. But we're all different when it comes to this word, aren't we? Why? What makes our tickers tic differently?

Sometimes you have to go back to the beginning . . . to the first person you loved. And you may realize you didn't love that person exactly the way you should have. But, it's not because you made the choice not to, it's because you were never given the choice. Not only that, but the very person, you were supposed to feel this amazing bond to, ends up being the culprit. You are left to ask the question *why*? And no matter how many answers you get, it never quite fills the hole.

My mother has this amazing ability to constantly make me feel like that five-year-old little girl on stage, in a school play, searching the crowd frantically as far as her eyes can see, thinking *maybe this time, she'll show up!*

I'm thirty-five now and . . . I'm still waiting for her to "show up."

She was my "first love." And I'm pretty convinced that she is the reason I have been so cynical, when it comes to that emotion, for so long.

Until I met *him* (Insert dreamy sigh).

And strung him along. . .

And hurt him. . .

And acted like I didn't care. . .

Then, I looked into the mirror (figuratively because if I'm looking into a mirror I don't have "deep" thoughts, I have concerns about "deep" wrinkles. . . which I don't have even though I smoked a cigarette once. You never know when shit will spring up, out of the blue, and you're all like "It was ONE time!" right? Shit—sorry!) I saw her instead of myself. Nothing puts your ass in check quicker than realizing you're turning into your mother!

Acknowledgments

I want to thank all of my readers for the patience you have displayed (read: lighting many a fire under my ass) over the past year and a half. I am sorry that you waited so long for Maddie's book, but I really hope you found it to be worth the wait. You have no idea how much you inspire me to keep marching forward with this dream. Or how much it made my year to meet so many of you at the different book events I was able to attend. And, it makes my day any time I get a message whether on FB, Twitter, or email from any of you. That's the best part—getting to connect with you. Thank you all so much! Don't be a stranger, but always say more than just "Hi" because it's too subtle and sort of freaks me out. It's a lot of pressure because then I have to come up with something more clever, like "Hello." And then, what? Then, we both have Adele's song stuck in our head, and once that song is in there, we both know it's not coming out. Better to start off with a random comment like "I just pissed myself." And I'll be like, "Dude, what chapter? Lol." See? Much more natural. No pressure.

I am beyond blessed to have my own GEGs. Sadly, we don't all live in the same town, but that's the beauty of fiction; I get to put us all in the same one. Instead of each of these women having one specific character modeled after them, they all are. Every single GEG has a little bit of my best friends and me in them. There were a lot of scenes in this book that really portrayed the heart of this friendship. I would've never been able to write anything like that if I didn't have moments like those (heartbreaking and joyful) with my own friends. It is one thing to be blessed with this kind of friendship; it's another to be completely aware of it. Jennifer Bedet, Holly Dirato, Lorin Falana, Nicole Gibson, Amanda LaVita, and Bernadette Titterington—thank you for filling my life with laughter, my heart with love, and my mind with amazing memories. I love you all so much. #JuliePosse

Wendy Shatwell and Claire Allmendinger, someday I will send you both your pink capes. What is there left to say except that I cherish our friendship beyond words? You both have given me just as much (if not more) emotional support this year as you have professionally. I love you both to the moon and back.

I have an amazing group of girls on my street team! You girls rock! I've been so bad at popping in everyday to say hello, but when I do, you all virtually wave like I haven't missed a beat. I love you all so much and am so blessed to call you my friends!

Beta Readers: LeeAnn Wright, Wendy Shatwell, Elle Christensen, and Mel Samples, I can't thank you ladies enough! You did an awesome job!

Stephanie Krulewitz, thank you for not only being one hell of an awesome friend, but for guiding me and keeping me in check on a lot of the psychology in this book. You are a blessing to not only me, but all of your patients!

Elle Christensen, I had such a blast writing that crossover scene with you! Thank you for helping me with the extra part on my end! Our characters kick ass, that's all I can say about that!

Stacey Blake, you patient soul, you! I can't thank you enough for always putting up with me running behind on deadline! I know the pages to this book will be as gorgeous as the others, so thank you in advance!

Robin Harper! This cover—holy crap! You took my vision and nailed it beyond anything I could've imagined. I'm so proud of it, and so proud to tell everyone who designed it for me! You are amazing at what you do!

Claire Allmendinger, you're a saint! Thank you for editing this for me on the fly! You rock!

Bloggers: There are so many of you that always give me such great support—like spanx. You hug me like spanx and help me show off my goods to the world! Thank you so much! I am so grateful for all that you do!

A big shout out to Gina Mahoney! Maddie mentions her in this book, and I swear by her! If you are ever looking for spiritual guidance; she's your girl! Also, she'll totally have you laughing your ass off! www.ginasreadings.com

Lastly, I would like to thank my family for all of their love and support, especially my mom, who has really stepped up to the plate this past year. I love you!

Aunt Madelyn, I hope you love Maddie as much as I do!

About the Author

I am a domestic engineer (born and raised in New Jersey) whose sole responsibility is guiding three young, impressionable kids into becoming phenomenal adults. This challenging yet rewarding work requires a lot of love (coffee), patience (wine), and determination (periodic exorcisms). I work all of this magic from the beautiful state of North Carolina.

Before becoming a domestic goddess (not really), I spent over a decade working in the medical field, where I wore more hats than the queen.

I have loved the written word and the great escape it provides since I was a little girl. When I wasn't reading about people and the places they lived, I created my own characters and adventures.

Finding myself again through my writing in The Lost & Found Series, The One, and The GEG Series has been nothing short of a dream come true. Also, it makes people feel better when I laugh randomly or talk to myself, knowing it's my characters and not "the voices" . . . that would be creepy.

www.authorjacquelynayres.com
Spotify playlist: spoti.fi/1QTGdcb
Facebook: www.facebook.com/JacquelynAyresAuthor
Twitter: twitter.com/JacquelynAyres
Goodreads: www.goodreads.com/author/dashboard?page=1
Google+: plus.google.com/u/0/+JacquelynAyres/posts

Chasing Hayleigh

The Fae Guard, book three
By
Elle Christensen

"Sometimes the person who tries to keep everyone else happy, is the most lonely person."
-*Unknown*

About the Fae

It is common among humans to see things not as they are, but as what their imaginations perceive them to be. Experiences are romanticized, and folklore is created. However, some of these tall tales are not as far-fetched as you might think. For within a lie, there is always a kernel of truth. Among these legends are those of otherworldly creatures and people. Nevertheless, the truth is often so wildly distorted that you may not recognize them for what they are. So, let me enlighten you.

There is a world beyond the human realm. One of creatures whose nature is between human and angel. In fact, they are said to be descended from fallen angels. They are a species who crave the sun, for without it, they will lose their pure magic and wither away. They can see beyond the human eye and hear beyond the human ear. They possess white-blond hair and bright blue or green eyes that shine like jewels. Their natural bodies are light, though not see through, but with an astral glow. Yet, the Fae are changeable and when they venture into the human world, their skin loses some of its luster, taking on a matte sheen that blends them in with the humans.

They are a people of magic. Magic that is protective in nature, used for the care of innocents, the healing of wounds, and to fight the evil forces that would threaten the vulnerable. Though they can confuse you with their words, they cannot lie. For if they do, they will become a part of a darker world, an evil existence. Their glow will dim, their lustrous blond hair will bleed into black and their eyes will become the shade of the mud that has colored their soul. They will endeavor to bring more light over to the dark.

Children that are a mix of this people and humans are targeted because they are easier to turn. They must spend their early years in the human world until they are marked at the age of twenty-one. Then their mixed nature will be detectable and the magic will flow through their veins, allowing them to enter both realms. But, there are those who can seek the dormant magic lying in wait to be released. They are protected because knowledge of their true people is built upon the folklore of the humans. They cannot fully comprehend what they will become and the importance of keeping the existence of this people a secret. They are more susceptible to be courted by the darkness, and in the dark, they are as their ancestors are, one of the fallen.

They are the Fae.

Read 'About the Fae' before beginning the prologue

Brannon

They say when you meet the one you're fated with, there is a rush of power, a feeling of strength and endurance which disappears the moment you are no longer in their presence. They say you can feel your souls fuse together, a connection that is almost unbreakable.

The first time I met Hayleigh, I didn't experience any of those feelings. The first time I met Hayleigh—I fell in love. An eternal love that had seeded itself so deep in my heart, I knew no one else(fated or not) would ever erase what I felt for her.

It would be ideal to find the one the universe has created to complete your soul. However, being fated has nothing to do with the heart. Accepting this fate is a choice and if you aren't in love, what is the point? Increased power is no substitute for an eternity without the person you love with your whole heart.

Even without the fated connection, Hayleigh owns me—body and soul.

Chapter One

Hayleigh

"I'm pregnant." Laila's face is glowing with complete happiness and I feel a little pang of envy, but I drop kick it back to the back of my head, where it belongs.

The sun is shining through the wall to wall windows in Laila's and Ean's apartment. It surrounds them, and I swear I can see the bubble of love and joy enveloping them. Laila is sitting on Ean's lap and he's staring at her like she's hung the moon . . . or rather, the sun.

Brannon and Kendrix walk over from the doorway, where they'd been leaning, to give Ean a backslapping hug, and squeeze Laila, before Ean frowns and pulls her back into his arms. Aden and Shaylee are cuddled up on the loveseat across from my chair, watching the scene with knowing grins.

I smile genuinely, and stand up from the couch, crossing over to them to pull Laila up into a hug. She's a tiny thing, so I lean down a little and whisper in her ear, "Congratulations, girl. That's incredible." When I let her go, she's smiling so wide I'm afraid it will split her face, and it makes me laugh.

Ean jumps up and opens his arms, "Hey, I made it. Don't I get a congratulations?" Laila doesn't even look at him when her hand flies back and hits him in the gut.

"Yeah, you really did the hard part, Ean." She rolls her eyes and laughs when he grabs the offending hand and pulls her back into his side, smacking a kiss on her forehead. He again holds out his arms to me. I hesitate, but then force myself to step into his embrace and return his hug stiffly.

I step back quickly, but give his hand a squeeze before dropping it. I love my friends. They are the first people I've allowed myself to get close to in a long, long time. However, after so many years without much social interaction and even less physical contact, I'm still adjusting to the dynamics of this group I've become a part of. Everyone is affectionate, comfortable in their own skin, accepting, and for the most part, pretty outgoing.

I moved to Mivo around three years ago. And when I met with the head of the Fae Guard here, he asked me if I'd spend some time helping in the training program. He felt the level of my skills (particularly in hand to hand) would be an asset to the training of young fae and halfs. He steered me to Laila and right away, she treated me as though we'd known each other all of our lives. *It's hard not to love Laila.*

She took me out to the local bar, Rock Falls, run by a half fae who had been raised in Canada. We met a large group of people, but spent most of our time with her brother Aden and his best friends, Ean, Brannon, and Kendrix, the latter two being twins. I'd taken one look at Brannon and something passed through me . . . something that almost had me taking off to another city. The attraction that zinged was not unwelcome, but the emotional connection was.

After having my family—my whole world—shattered to pieces when I was young, I was cut off from everything familiar. I lost everyone I loved, was ostracized and punished for the sins of another, and was left with only one option—to leave. I struck out on my own and tried to find somewhere else to fit. Instead, I was treated similarly any time I let down my guard enough to share my background. I learned a valuable lesson: letting anyone in on my secrets only led to heartache, and I was better off alone.

After over one hundred years of staying on the fringes of society and isolated, I'd finally given in to my desperation, my need to be around other people. I decided I could start over, become someone else. As long as I kept my past to myself and didn't let anyone too close, I could have friends, a home; a life.

Brannon walked up to me with a bright smile showing off two deep dimples, sparkling sapphire eyes surrounded by laugh lines, a strong, cut jaw, softened by his shortish, messy looking (as though he constantly runs his fingers through it) blond hair. To make matters worse, his body was sexy (capitol S-E-X-Y) as hell. He was tall (as least six and a half feet), dwarfing my five foot, ten inches, and making me feel dainty. His muscles strained against the sleeves and across the chest of his black t-shirt, but without looking bulky. I'd never thought of myself as an ass woman, but when Laila had called his name, he'd been facing the pool table across the room and I'd clocked his ass right away. The man had a little more in the trunk than most men, however, it was tight and perfectly shaped. I'm pretty sure I drooled a little bit. I wanted to pinch it and see if all that perfection was as hard as it looked.

Then, he turned around, and after I got a shot of lust right to my core, I immediately noticed the personality practically effervescing from him. He was clearly outgoing, full of fun and laughter, and so magnetically charismatic. The last thing I needed was to be sucked into a false sense of safety, feeling as though I could spill my guts to this guy.

My suspicions were confirmed when, instead of taking my outstretched hand and shaking it, he grabbed it and pulled me into a big bear hug. I'd stiffened like a board and practically jumped out of his embrace. Not only because of the unfamiliar sensation of touch from another person, but because a sense of safety and security had started to creep over me the moment his arms were around me.

He'd let me go, but he'd continued to study me, his blues filled with curiosity, and a dimpled grin. "We'll have to work on that hug, doll," he teased. I'd kept my face straight and managed to stay upright on the weakened knees his smile was causing.

I'd shaken the hands of everyone else, and was proud of myself for my steady grip. I wasn't able to stay long; the crowd was overwhelming me and I needed to return to the familiarity of my solitude. Brannon had instantly offered to drive me home. Laila must have sensed my hesitance because she announced she was ready to go too and would be leaving with me. She'd stopped after the first drink and had been nursing ice waters all night, so she grabbed her keys and we headed out.

Laila drove us home, walked with me inside. We took the elevator up and before hopping off on her floor, she told me she looked forward to getting know me and hoped we'd become great friends. Not once did she ask about my aversion to physical contact, my awkwardness in the crowded bar, or my need to escape it so early. It was at that moment I realized Laila was far more perceptive than I'd thought; she knew I wasn't ready, but she'd left the door open. I desperately wanted to develop a friendship with her, so I smiled and agreed.

Over the following months, Laila and I grew close, though I still kept my past to myself. Laila never asked, never pushed. I was amazed to have stumbled into a friend who made me feel so accepted and as if there was nothing unusual about my habits. She began to make me believe I could grasp onto the life I'd dreamed about.

Unfortunately, the same couldn't be said of Brannon. He took every opportunity to ask me out, to be near me, and to touch me in anyway, even if it was only a brush of our fingers. What shocked and worried me the most was my reaction to his touch. I didn't feel a physical urge to sever the connection; my body seemed to crave the feel of him. In fact, my body ached for him, for his presence. The very fucking thought of him brought an onslaught of desire so strong, it sometimes threatened to knock me over. However, my brain was keeping me in line, being far more sensible, wary of what giving in to him could lead to. Besides, what was the point? It was clear he wanted to see where a relationship between us would go. I already knew the answer—nowhere.

For almost four years now, he has steadily tried to convince me to take a chance on him. And for four years, I've succeeded in keeping our relationship firmly in the friend zone. *Have you? Have you really?* Ok, so it's possible I've let him seep past those friendship barriers in my mind and heart, but I've been able to keep that little tidbit from Brannon.

As I stand here congratulating my best friend and her fiancé, I can't help but admit that my resolve is starting to weaken. I'm so happy for Laila and Ean; they fought through a lot to find their way to each other. Ean had run away from her to deal with his demons, despite the fated linking of their souls, until he finally realized she was the answer to finding peace and balance. Now, they are engaged and having a baby. I don't want to pay attention to the envy surfacing inside me, making me want things I shouldn't, with someone I shouldn't want.

"Um. . ." My thoughts are interrupted by the other couple in our group. Laila's brother, Aden, had fallen in love with one of the leath leanbh—a half human, half fae child—he was protecting as a member of the Mie'Lorvor, The Fae Guard. A couple of years ago, Shaylee had turned twenty-one, the age half children are marked. With the mark of Fae, a tattoo of wings (yes, this contributed to the spectacularly stupid human belief that faeries can fly), their magic is unlocked and they take on the characteristics of the Fae: the ability to control the elements (air, water, earth, and fire), to cross realms, to be fated, and the need for the sun to survive.

He'd brought her to Rien and while she was training, he made her recognize the love between them, adding to the fact that they were fated. Now, they are married and have twin girls, and a baby boy. Amidst the small yearning I felt for what they had, there still remained a mountain of doubt. I believed in the love these couples had between them and I hoped it would last, because being fated is no guarantee you'll be happy and faithful forever.

I look closer at Shaylee and Aden when she speaks. Aden looks—well, his seriously muscular chest is practically puffed in pride. Shaylee looks sheepish and keeps throwing Aden dirty looks. Oh no. . . I know what's coming. "I'm pregnant too," she announces.

I can't keep it in. I swear I'm trying, but laughter bursts from me and I double over, holding my stomach. I can't see them since I'm bent over, but I hear Brannon and Kendrix laughing right along with me. Shaylee has been pregnant for the majority of the time I've known her. After the twins were born, they had an "oops" within a few months (unplanned on the Shaylee's part anyway. I'm not so sure it wasn't Aden's plan). Now, Puck, their youngest, is barely three months and here she is—knocked up again.

"Anybody ever tell you you're too easy, doll?" Brannon pipes up, and when Shaylee pouts, I laugh harder. Ean and Laila are sniggering, Kendrix and Brannon are smiling hugely, and Aden is glaring at all of us, clearly unhappy we are pissing Shaylee off.

She's mad at Aden for not being careful, but I know Shaylee; she adores being a mom. Under the irritation, she is excited. Aden's arm slips around her waist and tugs her into his lap where he promptly sticks his face in her neck and nuzzles her.

"Congratulations to you two, too." I shake my head, still amused. Another pang of longing hits me and I glance away. *Bad idea.* My eyes meet Brannon's knowing ones. How does he see through me? It's unnerving. I school my features quickly, and his normally smiling lips pinch a little, making my eyes drop guiltily. He doesn't understand why I'm fighting him so hard. But, the truth is, I'm not cut out for the life my friends have.

And yet. . .for the first time, I wonder if I could, at least, have a piece of it. Would Brannon settle for what little I can give him? Now that the thought has entered my mind, it starts to grow and becomes tremendously hard to ignore.

Other Books

THE LOST & FOUND SERIES
Goodbye Caution, Book 1
Goodbye Secrets, Book 2
Goodbye Uncertainty, Book 3
Goodbye Reservations, Book 4

The One

THE GEG SERIES
Under Contract, Book 1
In the Mix, Book 2

www.ingramcontent.com/pod-product-compliance
Lightning Source LLC
Chambersburg PA
CBHW050544260626
47157CB00002B/429